"Commander Kang, you are holding one of my people . . .

and certain materials belonging to the Federation. I formally demand immediate return."

Kang smiled openly. "Surely you jest, Captain. Lieutenant Czerny is bond to me. She is a very valuable pawn to me for the moment. I have no intention of releasing her yet."

"Kang, when your ship was destroyed and I took your crew survivors aboard my ship they were well-treated. I expect the same for Czerny. I will hold you personally responsible for her treatment." Kirk rubbed his right cheek with an unconscious gesture as he recalled the image of Kang standing over Chekov's writhing form with the Klingon Agonizer pressed to his face. . . .

Look for *Star Trek* fiction from Pocket Books

PAWNS AND SYMBOLS

MAJLISS LARSON

A STAR TREK® NOVEL

PUBLISHED BY POCKET BOOKS NEW YORK

Distributed in Canada by PaperJacks Ltd., a Licensee
of the trademarks of Simon & Schuster, Inc.

Another *Original* publication of POCKET BOOKS

POCKET BOOKS, a division of Simon & Schuster, Inc.
1230 Avenue of the Americas, New York, N.Y. 10020
In Canada distributed by PaperJacks Ltd.,
330 Steelcase Road, Markham, Ontario

ISBN: 0-671-55425-5

First Pocket Books Science Fiction printing November, 1985

10 9 8 7 6 5 4 3 2 1

Printed in Canada

to
Al, Cheryl, Chris, Julie, and especially Rhonda
who were my first editors and critics

Pawns and Symbols

One

HER CHEEK FLAT against the lab table, Jean Czerny watched the slow drip of water from her improvised charcoal column. Barely two centimeters of water in the beaker since morning. Hunger no longer bothered her but she was very thirsty. She had to depend on ground water that seeped through the wreckage and dripped from the beam above her column. Drop by crystal drop it emerged from the column. She poured out half and drank it. Not enough. Listlessly, she picked up her lab log and looked at the last few entries.

Quake yesterday. Alone in my lab wh— it started. Tried to get door open. Must have been hit by so— thing. Came to. Dark. Been calling for help all day. No answer. Can't move debris to get out.

Headache bad today. No food, little water. No sign of anyone. Must have more water. Can't think well. Must rest.

10/5/06?? Better today. Found ration bar in my lab drawer. Rigged a filter to catch ground water. Recovered my new strain *quadrotriticale* seed undamaged and

1

stored it in the drivault. No sign of anyone. Can I hold out until the *Enterprise* arrives next week?

The entries went on. On the sixth day she had written a long summary on her new *quadrotriticale* strain. The eighth day she had forgotten to write an entry. Yesterday she simply wrote:

Very weak and thirsty.

She picked up her pen and meticulously lettered:

10/11/06 Ditto.

She giggled, then began to cry. She added:

Dear God, please don't let the *Enterprise* be late.
. . . so tired . . . get a little sleep . . . a big drink of water . . . everything will be fine. . . .

A resounding crash brought her struggling back to consciousness. Through a thick pall of dust she foggily made out two uniformed figures pushing into the lab. Everything was confused and indistinct.

"Thank God, you made it," she mumbled and fainted again.

Some things never change and one of them is the antiseptic smell of a sick bay. Before she even opened her eyes Jean knew she was in sick bay. She shifted slightly. The bed was very hard. She raised her head and opened her eyes. They wouldn't focus; "Dr. McCoy? Someone? Help, I can't see! What's wrong?"

A dark face floated into view and hands pushed her back down firmly. "Doctor, she's coming around now."

Not a voice she recognized—something funny about her hearing too—it didn't sound right. Another strange voice— "Lie still. You had a bad drug reaction but your vision will clear in a few minutes. Hand me that second dose now and the stim shot."

Jean winced slightly at the sudden grip on her arm and the sharp stabbing sensation that followed. It didn't feel like the usual hypospray. And what was a stim shot? Whatever it was, it worked. Her head cleared, her shakiness disappeared, and her eyes began to focus. She stared up at the black canvas webbing of the bunk above her for several seconds before she realized that this couldn't be the *Enterprise* sick bay. She looked at the green-smocked figure standing beside her. "Where am I? Who are you?"

At that moment three black- and gold-clad figures approached. "Commander, just in time. She has regained consciousness—wants to know where she is." Turning to Jean, the man added, "Since he is here, perhaps Commander Kang will enlighten you himself."

The central of the three newcomers approached the foot of her bunk and smiled perfunctorily. Tall even by Klingon standards, muscular, with fine black hair, piercing eyes, and an expressive mouth, this commander wore his arrogance easily—as birthright. "Ah, Miss Czerny, you are feeling better I see. Dr. Eknaar has done well. You were in rather poor shape when I brought you aboard yesterday. As you see, you have the honor to be aboard a Klingon imperial battle cruiser—mine." He bowed slightly. "Commander Kang of the Imperial Fleet. We picked up your distress call from Sherman's planet but reconnoitered a day before responding because we've had false distress calls involving the Federation before. However, this one seemed to be genuine, so we rescued you."

Klingons! Jean's mind raced past a dozen questions. Klingon attack? Sabotage? Their intentions? Other survivors? Her pulse must have raced too, for she saw both Kang and Eknaar glance at her bedside monitor. She would have to proceed very carefully. She picked a peripheral question. "Kang? I thought Commander Koloth was assigned to this sector."

"We're here on special assignment." His eyes narrowed. "Is it usual for an agricultural specialist to be briefed on our military deployment or do you serve an additional function on Sherman's planet?"

Jean tensed. "Given the situation, all of us at the Sherman's planet station are carefully briefed on Klingon movements. You can confirm that with any of my colleagues."

"Unfortunately, I cannot. It seems you are the only survivor of the earthquake."

Now the monitor was undoubtedly reflecting her rising blood pressure. She didn't believe him. "Someone must have survived to send out the distress signal. I certainly didn't," she snapped.

"Yes, we did find a man in the communications room, but he expired shortly after our arrival. Before he died, I understand he said something about the *Enterprise* being due soon."

Although she distrusted Kang, unfounded accusations were unlikely to be productive, Jean decided. Even if the Klingons were responsible for all or part of this disaster, honey would gain her more than vitriol at this point.

Maybe. Swallowing her suspicions, she replied coolly, "Yes, the *Enterprise* is due any day now for a routine check. If I'm in fact the last survivor, let me express my gratitude for your response and aid. However, it won't be necessary to trouble you any further. If you'll return me to the station, I can wait for the *Enterprise* there."

"Impossible." Kang smiled faintly. "I'm sure you understand the delicacy of the situation if our ship were found by the *Enterprise* at the scene of such an unfortunate tragedy to one of your research stations. We've already left that star system. You'll have ample opportunity to show your gratitude for my hospitality before it comes to an end."

Maybe not. As she had feared, there was a barb in the bait of Klingon altruism. Might as well expose it now—they surely had her hooked and netted. "Never let it be suggested that a Klingon would be guilty of so soft an emotion as compassion for a human. Why did you really rescue me, Kang? What do you want?"

"Although I don't expect you to believe it, in fact, we rescued you without any prior expectations. However, we now find there are two simple things you can do: open this box of yours containing the new *quadrotriticale* seed and decipher these notes." He waved to one of the other

4

Klingons who produced a notebook. Jean recognized her lab log.

Her determination to remain cool suddenly vanished. "My new strain! You had no right to steal that from our station!" She sat bolt upright on the edge of the bunk, almost striking her head on the tier above in her haste. Amber lights blinked frantically on her monitor. Angrily, she brushed the connecting wires from her arm and temple. "Kidnapping and piracy! That's what it is!"

"On the contrary, I rescued you and saved your life. Therefore, I have every right to you and your possessions. I don't intend to spend time arguing with you. Will you open the drivault and decipher your notes?"

"I'll see you in the ninth ring of hell first."

Kang shrugged. "It will be yours, my dear, not mine. We have ways of persuading one to see our point of view. Dr. Eknaar, start with the truth serum."

The Klingon doctor had been trying ineffectually to ease Jean back into her bunk and monitor. He glanced worriedly at Kang. "Commander, we already tried that as soon as Aernath translated her notes. She had a severe allergic reaction to the lourkain—that's why it took her so long to come around."

Kang looked annoyed. "Then use the agonizer. But get the information." He turned to leave.

"That won't work either," Jean quickly interjected.

Kang paused and looked back. "You are allergic to the agonizer too, I suppose? No matter. It will accomplish the task nonetheless."

Jean was glad the monitor was disconnected and could not betray her. "Not exactly, Commander Kang. I told you we were carefully briefed on Klingon affairs. Our current station personnel were also carefully selected and conditioned. Since you have already discovered the allergic reaction, I may as well tell you that torturing me with the agonizer will only produce my instant demise, *not* get you the information you seek."

Two full strides covered the space between them. Brushing aside the murmuring medic, Kang seized Jean's shoul-

5

ders and pulled her upright until her toes barely reached the deck. "Is this another of your Kirk's devious plots?" he snarled. Jean met his scowl steadily. "No, you're lying. Kirk always has a surprising trick or two in hand but he is congenitally incapable of sacrificing his troops even when good tactics demand it. You're bluffing."

"You know Captain Kirk fairly well," Jean replied quietly. "He also knows quite well what to expect from you. The intent was not to sacrifice us but to spare us unnecessary suffering given your known propensity for 'tactical sacrifices.' "

She caught her breath as Kang's grip on her shoulders tightened painfully. He stared darkly at her face for a long moment. "I still think you're bluffing. Lieutenant, your agonizer."

"But, Commander," protested Eknaar, "if she isn't bluffing and you use that, you'll never get the seed. Aernath says blasting it open will incinerate the stuff. You need her alive to get it."

Kang suddenly dropped Jean's left shoulder and whirled, sending the doctor stumbling back to avoid him. "Stick to your needles and nostrums, Eknaar, and don't presume to instruct me on the obvious. Tell me, what is her current physical status?"

Eknaar hunched his shoulders worriedly. "Oh . . . with the stim shot and all, I'd say normal human female by now. At fifty kilos she's a little undernourished but I have her back in basic balance."

Kang returned his attention to Jean. "Well, Czerny? Do you want to reconsider before we turn—courtesy of Captain Kirk and his machinations—to older and less efficient methods? A simple gesture of gratitude would make it easier for all of us."

Jean caught a momentary flicker of some strange emotion in his eyes. She decided to try another appeal. "I can't give you that grain, but Captain Kirk would have the authority. If it's that important to you, go back to Sherman's planet and ask for some of the seed in return for my release. He would honor that request, I'm sure."

Kang laughed. "Ask? Ask Kirk for something I already rightfully possess? You have a poor sense of a Klingon commander, my dear."

The ship's intercom interrupted, "Bridge to Commander, it is twenty-six fifty. Bridge report, and course changes are due soon."

Kang released Jean's other shoulder so abruptly that she staggered against the tiered bunks. "Acknowledged. I'll take it in the Council room." He turned. "Bring her up there."

As Kang left, Jean found herself brusquely hoisted up by his two lieutenants, propelled out the door and along a series of narrow corridors. She cooperated just enough to keep her feet under her and keep the pressure on her arms bearable. She wanted time to collect her thoughts and assess the situation. By a stroke of luck and a bit of bluff she had won a brief reprieve from the agonizer but she wasn't sure Kang was convinced. Even if he was, what would happen then? They mustn't get the new grain! Why had the Klingon ship been there in the first place? Why Kang—not Koloth? It couldn't be the seed strain—that was too new. No one else knew about it beyond the station personnel. Personnel: had there been any other survivors? Had the *Enterprise* picked up their distress signal, too? So many questions. It didn't look as if she was likely to get any answers soon. Jean fought down a rising flush of panic. Survive and succeed: the Klingon credo. Well, that would have to be it for now. Simple basics. One challenge at a time. The first thing was to stall Kang as long as possible—give the *Enterprise* a chance.

The Klingons shoved her unceremoniously into a small wood-paneled room. Kang occupied the chair behind the single desk. Other chairs were ranged in front of it. He was addressing the desktop intercom: "—and hold to that course until further notice. Anything else to report?"

"No, sir. End of bridge report, Commander."

"Very well. I'm not to be disturbed unless it's urgent. Kang, out." He flipped a lever on the console and turned to the trio in front of him. He gestured to the opposite wall. "Proceed."

Jean was shoved against the wall facing Kang. Suddenly

one of the guards brought his boot heel down heavily on her foot. She gasped and curled involuntarily only to be met with a blow which snapped her head back against the wall. Cold fury sifted through her. "Filthy Klingon cowards! You call yourselves Imperial officers. You're not fit to do my wash."*

This brought a brief laugh from Kang. "You see, Tirax?"

The lieutenant who had hit her flushed. "With your permission, Commander?"

Kang smiled thinly. "Just don't kill her, Lieutenant." He opened a drawer in the desk and took out a dagger. "Catch, Czerny." He lodged it in the wall next to her shoulder. Tirax had drawn his dagger. The other guard released his grip and stepped aside grinning.

Jean pulled the knife from the wall and hefted it experimentally. She was no duelist, but on Aldebaran Colony as a girl she had been amateur stiletto champion. Then, she could hit a five-centimeter target at ten meters. That was a long time ago.

She and Tirax circled slowly. If she could move away from the guard at her back before Tirax made his move. . . . Tirax lunged and Jean threw. He missed her and came up against the wall gazing with astonishment at the haft of Kang's dagger in his right upper chest. Dropping his own dagger, he pulled hers out and then collapsed as the inrushing air compressed his lung. Jean snatched up the free dagger and backed away.

Kang smiled appreciatively. "Not exactly standard Klingon dueling form but nicely done—for a human female. Lieutenant, take your comrade to sick bay, then report back."

"Yes, sir." No longer grinning, the other officer helped the gasping Tirax to his feet.

Kang stood and deliberately removed his blaster, placing it in the drawer and thumbing the lock. Keeping his eyes on Jean he circled the desk, smoothly retrieved his dagger from the floor and faced her. "Now . . ."

Jean fell back a pace and raised her free hand in protest. "Kang, please, I don't want to fight you. For God's sake,

---

* Vile Klingon insult. Laundry is a menial task traditionally done only by low-caste servant women—hence demeaning, especially to a male.

listen to me. You can't get away with this madness. Stop before it's too late. Take me back now and we'll forget about all this. Don't violate the treaty any further!"

Kang wiped his dagger meticulously on his thigh. "I haven't broken any treaties yet and I don't intend to." He looked at Jean appraisingly. "Guard!"

Again, Jean protested, "Kang, please! I . . . I don't want to hurt you."

"Hurt me? Kill me would be more like it. Now that would be a pretty stroke, wouldn't it?"

"No," persisted Jean stubbornly, "if I fight you, I lose either way. You know that."

"Then meet my demands."

"I can't."

"All right. Defend yourself."

They circled each other warily, waiting. There was a door opposite—the one by which they had entered. When Jean had her back to that, she threw her dagger—momentarily pinning Kang to the paneling through his left shoulder.

Desperately, she dove for the door praying it would be open. It was, but Kang caught her as she reached it. They went down in a tangled heap, and shortly, Kang had her pinioned beneath him.

Jean glared up at him. The shoulder wound was more superficial than she had intended. With a slight shake of his head, Kang remarked conversationally, "Never turn and run from a superior force. That's always a tactical error, my dear."

"Like you're running from Kirk?" Jean challenged.

Kang grinned broadly. "*This* time, Miss Czerny, I am not the inferior force as Kirk will discover if he chooses to pursue me."

Jean held her breath as his dagger slowly descended to her stomach. He slit her tunic from navel to jugular notch with just enough pressure to scratch but not break the skin. She could feel her throat pulse against the point. Kang's face bent a scant ten centimeters above hers. He moved the dagger point to her chin turning her face to his with it. "And you promise to be an important pawn in the game. Rescuing you was a fortunate stroke of serendipity."

"Pirate!" The dagger did not allow much room for speech.

"Plucky pawn. You just keep coming, don't you? I like a good fighter. Don't worry, you'll survive but it will be my success. I like that very much." His mouth came down hard on hers, and Jean felt his dagger hand on her skin. She winced as a whistle shrill to the point of pain assaulted her ears.

With a muttered oath Kang got to his feet pulling her with him. He snapped the lever on the desk console. "By Durgath, what is it?"

"Federation starship closing on us, sir. We've kept hailing frequencies down as ordered. They fired a signal shot across our bow. Shall we open fire on them now, Commander?"

"Do you have a positive identification yet?"

"It is the *Enterprise*, Commander."

"Excellent." A look of grim satisfaction settled on Kang's face. "Status Amber—full battle readiness. Open hailing frequencies sequentially. I'm on my way to the bridge."

The outer door opened to admit the returning officer. "Orders, Commander?"

"Keep her here until further orders." Kang turned to Jean. "It seems your Captain Kirk has decided to cross swords with me again after all. Listen to the intercom. You should find it most instructive." He left.

The Klingon took in her deshabille with a leer, then turned to the console. Jean sat down in one of the facing chairs. The *Enterprise* had arrived! If only there was some way to signal them. At least she could hear the interchange. That was something. She heard Kang arrive on the bridge and order the channel opened to the *Enterprise*.

"So, Captain Kirk, we meet once again! I trust you have good reason for invading Klingon territory and firing on an imperial battle cruiser." Kang's voice was cool and dry.

"Commander Kang. You know full well why we are pursuing you. This time the evidence is unequivocal. I charge you with violation of the Organian peace treaty." It was the familiar voice of Captain Kirk.

"Violation of the treaty? Unequivocal evidence? Come now, Captain Kirk, state your case precisely."

"Kang, we know you have just left Sherman's planet. We

found your newly established outpost there. Do you deny it?" Kirk sounded impatient.

"Outpost? Captain Kirk, that's a scientific mission. Under the terms of the treaty, Sherman's planet belongs to whomever can most efficiently develop it. The Federation's efforts to date have not been spectacularly successful. Now, with your most recent disaster, it seemed that we were justified in applying to the Organians for equal status on Sherman's planet. We have so notified them. We have honored the treaty to the letter. Now, may I suggest that unless you wish to provoke an incident, you leave Klingon territory at once. If you do, I am prepared to overlook your aggressive behavior."

"Just one minute, Kang. I'm not through yet. I further charge you with assault, murder, and destruction of Federation property on Sherman's planet. I want an accounting—"

"Surely, Kirk, you're not accusing us of creating an earthquake just to destroy your station?" Kang sounded amused.

"No, the station tapes document that was a natural event. However, there were survivors and you were there after the quake. You murdered Jones, the communications officer, plundered the agricultural lab, and abducted or murdered Agricultural Specialist Czerny. *Those are* acts of war and I demand an accounting as well as custody of those responsible."

"Those are grave charges, Captain. On what do you base them? What is your so-called evidence for these alleged acts?"

"We found fragments torn from a Klingon uniform in the debris where you forced entry into Czerny's lab. She is missing and so are items from her lab. Dr. McCoy has established that Jones died following administration of lourkain and a sedative, neither of which are stock Federation medical supplies. Now, do you deny responsibility for this?"

For the first time, Kang sounded slightly annoyed. "Your men have certainly been efficient. My particular compliments to Dr. McCoy for his thoroughness. However, I can establish beyond any doubt that we took no hostile action.

11

You misinterpret the facts. Allow me to set the record straight." Jean heard a click, then Kang's voice continued. "Dr. Eknaar to the bridge." Another click. "Lieutenant, bring your charge to the bridge."

"Yes, Commander." The man grasped Jean by an elbow and steered her out the door. Once again threading narrow corridors, she marshaled her thoughts. Kang was going to acknowledge her presence on his ship. Would she have any chance to communicate directly? What was most important to say? Could Kirk force Kang to hand her back? What kind of trap was Kang trying to set for the *Enterprise?* There was so much data she didn't have!

The addition of Jean, her escort, and Dr. Eknaar made the Klingon bridge very crowded. Ignoring the banked displays of the weapons officer to her left, Jean looked past the high back of Kang's seat to the viewscreen. There was the familiar bridge of the *Enterprise* with Captain Kirk in his command chair. Behind him, she could see Lieutenant Uhura bent over her communications console. Ensign Chekov, the navigator, and Helmsman Sulu sat at their posts. Her throat ached to call out. Though she had served only briefly in the science section aboard the *Enterprise* prior to the Sherman's planet assignment, those familiar faces felt like home. She noted Kirk's jaw tighten and his fist clench momentarily as he caught sight of her. She became acutely aware of her own appearance.

Kirk addressed Kang again. "It seems you merely confirm my charges. I insist you return—"

Kang interrupted with preemptive gesture of his head. "Dr. Eknaar, describe the condition of Specialist Czerny when we found her."

"Certainly, Commander. She was semicomatose, suffering from acute nutritional deprivation, marked electrolyte imbalance, critical dehydration, evidence of concussion—probably of eight to ten—"

"In your estimation, how much longer would she have survived in that condition without treatment?"

"Mmm . . . probably less than thirty hours, sir."

Kang turned to the viewscreen. "We picked up a distress

12

call from Sherman's planet. Reconnaissance showed no Federation ship in the area. There were two survivors. We found the communications officer in a terminal state and made him comfortable. Czerny, we were able to revive. As you would phrase it, a simple humanitarian act, Captain Kirk."

"And how did you come by that, Specialist Czerny?" Kirk gestured to her tunic.

"I . . ." Jean began, momentarily confused by his question.

Kang intercepted smoothly. "Ah . . . Captain . . . Miss Czerny took umbrage at one of my men and challenged him to a duel." He turned his head and raised his hand to conceal a fleeting smile. "She won. As a result, one of my best lieutenants will be spending some time in sick bay. Naturally, I was annoyed. . . ." He shrugged expressively.

"Czerny?" Kirk queried.

This time, Jean was ready. "Captain Kirk, among the items removed from my lab was the drivault containing the new resistant strain of *quadrotriticale*. In seeking information from me about it they have discovered my allergy to lourkain so I told them about my conditioned fatal response to the agonizer. Under the circumstances, I didn't see any point in concealing that."

Kirk didn't even blink. "Of course, Lieutenant Czerny. On status X you have that latitude." Jean did blink at her sudden rise in rank. What in space was status X? Lieutenant/ status/latitude . . . Was there something she had forgotten? Kirk continued. "Commander Kang, you are holding one of my people and certain materials belonging to the Federation. I formally demand immediate return and also detention of those responsible until judgement is rendered by the Organians in this matter."

Kang smiled openly this time. "Surely you jest, Captain. . . . Czerny is *bond* to me."

Kirk looked puzzled. *"Bond?"*

"By Klingon custom, and I remind you Captain Kirk, you are in Klingon territory. By our custom, if a person's life is saved by another, then he—or she in this case—becomes

13

bond-person to the rescuer until he sees fit to release that bond. Your lieutenant is a valuable pawn to me for the moment. I have no intention of releasing her yet."

Kirk's face took on a stubborn set. "Czerny is an Aldebaranian citizen and a member of the Federation. As representative of the Federation, I demand her immediate release."

"Do I take it then, that you do not recognize Klingon custom and practice in this instance, Captain?" Kang demanded in a steely voice.

"Correct," Kirk snapped.

"Then neither do I recognize Federation jurisdiction here, Captain Kirk. I suggest you take it up with the Organians. We'll transmit our tape of this encounter to them. Now, unless your orders cover starting a war, I suggest you leave Klingon territory immediately. Let me point out that you are at the moment flanked by two additional cruisers. We don't take kindly to invaders, Captain Kirk."

On the viewscreen, Spock, the Vulcan first officer, straightened from his computer console to meet Kirk's querying gaze. "Confirmed, Captain. Sensors show three Klingon cruisers."

Kirk chewed his lip in frustration. "Kang, when your ship was destroyed and I took your crew survivors aboard my ship they were well-treated. I expect the same for Czerny. I will hold you personally responsible for her treatment."

Kang's face darkened momentarily. "I shall keep that in mind, Captain, in detail." Then he added mockingly, "Until we meet again, Kirk." Abruptly he snapped off the communication lever and stood, his face suddenly dark with fury. "Now, who is the tatterdemalion galley scum who left his uniform all over that lab?"

"Here, sir." A sturdy young Klingon was pushed forward by another Klingon guard.

"Well?" Kang demanded sharply.

"No excuse, Commander." the Klingon replied stiffly.

"Eknaar, stand by." Kang nodded to the guard. "Quarter-strength, standard duration, then confine to quarters for sixty hours."

Jean watched in horror as the guard applied the agonizer

to the hapless Klingon. She had never seen it in action before. Intense nausea assailed her as the man collapsed screaming. His screams ended abruptly as he stiffened in convulsions. The guard replaced his agonizer while Eknaar checked the unconscious man. Jean gagged, then leaned against her escort for support. Eknaar stood up. "He's stable. Take him to quarters."

Jean saw Kang glance at her curiously. She straightened herself with some effort. Kang turned to Eknaar. "And what about that communications officer? I said I wanted no traces left."

Eknaar's shoulders assumed their worried hunch. "With the higher human metabolism, they should have been eliminated. Maybe he didn't live as long as I predicted. I told you it was—"

"I know, I know. You warned me it was risky. What I want from you is results, not risks." He started for the door. "Lieutenant, bring the human. Eknaar, after we finish with her, confine yourself to quarters for thirty hours."

Thoroughly unnerved by what she had witnessed, Jean let herself be virtually carried by the guard. At sick bay entrance Kang instructed Eknaar curtly, "Baseline readings, then send her to detention." He disappeared down the corridor.

Numbly, Jean lay on the diagnostic table and submitted to various scans and probes. She had stalled successfully awaiting the *Enterprise*. Now it had come and gone. Rescue suddenly became remote. Though she regained her physical equilibrium, her mind refused to compute anything but the image of the convulsing Klingon.

At length Eknaar dismissed her with a casual slap on her thigh. "Off you go, my girl. A final piece of advice. Don't count on your Captain or the Organians. Even if they should come through, it may be too late to do you any good. If you cooperate with Kang, he'll give you a fair shake—even now. Just don't push him too far."

Jean simply stared at the stocky, gray-haired Klingon medic. She couldn't think of any response.

Somehow she managed to navigate the corridors again and ended up in a small cubicle furnished with a cot, a table, and a three-legged stool. On the table sat her drivault. Kang was waiting with another Klingon whom she had not seen before. Kang eyed her carefully and again she caught a flicker of an unnamed emotion that crossed his face. He indicated the slender Klingon at his side.

"This is Aernath, our agricultural liaison. He is working on your notes and has clearance to see you at will. It would be in your best interests to cooperate with him. Now, open the vault."

Stolidly, Jean kept her eyes fixed on Kang's shoulder. He'd done nothing about the dagger wound as if it were of no import, but she saw that he moved the arm a bit stiffly. She clung to that bit of knowledge for the small comfort it yielded. She did not dare to meet his gaze or speak, knowing that if she did her control would break. Mutely she shook her head.

Kang stepped forward, grabbed her hair at the nape of her neck and tilted her face up to his. He spoke softly. "Don't try to wait for Kirk or the Organians. I don't —*you* don't have that much time." The ice in his tone sent chills down her back.

She shut her eyes and focused her entire will into a final effort. "No."

Kang released her with a jerk that sent her tumbling back onto the cot. "Very well. We'll restore you to the condition in which we found you—with one minor variation. Dr. Eknaar will give you glucose injections to keep your ketones below the point that they kill your hunger pangs. You can eat when we get the wheat." He indicated the drivault. "It's wired. All you have to do is touch it to activate the signal. Someone will come at once."

The three Klingons left. Through the transparent top half of the cell door Jean could see the guard posted outside. He, in turn, could see her entire cubicle from outside, except the lavatory offset in the same wall. The lavatory contained a sonic toilet and a sink. The sink was dry. No water. Carefully avoiding the table, she returned to her cot and lay face down. The tension was finally too much, and she began to sob silently until her whole body shook. Eventually she fell asleep.

Two

ON THE BRIDGE of the *Enterprise* Captain Kirk stared at the blank viewscreen. "Retrace course to Sherman's planet, Mr. Sulu, and put up the exterior view of those three cruisers as we go." The bridge crew watched as two cruisers disappeared rapidly. The third trailed them slowly as they turned and headed back out of Klingon space. Finally, satisfied that it was merely surveillance, Kirk said, "Cancel Red Alert, Mr. Sulu. Yellow Alert until that cruiser turns back. Mr. Scott, you have the con." He stood up giving a brisk tug on his shirt and glanced at Dr. McCoy standing near the turbo lift. "Bones, Mr. Spock."

The two science officers followed him into the turbo lift. "Conference Room," he directed the turbo. Mr. Spock, his Vulcan first officer, stood at easy parade rest, his face impassive from black bangs and pointed ears to his angular chin. To his left, Dr. McCoy, senior medical officer, stood with one hand under the other elbow while he chewed thoughtfully on a knuckle. His slim figure conveyed a sense of worried concentration. "Well," Kirk said, "we know she's alive and headed into Klingon territory. Beyond that—"

The turbo lift door opened and the trio moved into the

conference room. McCoy and Kirk picked up coffee and the three sat down at one end of the large conference table. Kirk's voice was sober. "You both saw the whole thing, including Czerny's appearance and the Klingon's report of her condition. What do you think? Bones?"

McCoy shook his head. "It's hard to say. If the Klingons are telling the truth about the condition they found her in, and it's plausible based on what we found on Sherman's planet, then probably she's suffered a moderate to severe concussion. There's no predicting how that will affect her memories or her actions, or for how long. Without a chance to examine her that's about all I can say."

"Well, she's obviously alert and functioning now. What about her comment on Iourkain? Any mention of that in her medical history?" Kirk asked.

"As you know, Jim, Starfleet doesn't make a habit of interrogating people with that stuff, but she does have minor allergies to some related compounds. My hunch is they used it on her and found she really is allergic." McCoy grimaced. "It's a nasty reaction to handle from what I read, but their M.O.'s must have a lot of experience with it."

"So that might not indicate anything about her memory. Do you think she's amnesic? If so, how much and how long?" Kirk pressed his medical officer.

"She certainly could be. Concussions almost always produce amnesia for the immediate injury event and can produce more widespread memory loss. It's totally unpredictable. In this case I'd say it's quite likely. I saw no response the whole time she was on the bridge. Did either of you?"

Both Spock and Kirk shook their heads. "Not even to the code." Kirk ran his fingers through his hair. "And where in blazes did Kang come from? We expected the raid but Starfleet Intelligence was sure it would be Koloth!"

"Actually, Captain, it was estimated that there was an eighteen percent chance that it could be Commander Kang and a seven percent chance of some other Klingon cruiser based on analysis of past deployment of Klingon forces," Spock pointed out.

"That's still three-to-one odds on Koloth, Mr. Spock. All right, what do we have on Kang's cruiser?"

Spock called up a Starfleet Intelligence report on the viewscreen, and the three men regarded it glumly. "We have no current information on that, Captain," Spock finally observed.

"Great. So she's amnesic, on the wrong ship, and from what she said she has some new strain that Kang wants information about." Kirk rubbed his right cheek with an unconscious gesture as he recalled the image of Kang standing over Chekov's writhing form with the Klingon agonizer pressed to his face. "He'll kill her if need be to get what he wants." He drew the hand down across his chin in a gesture of frustration, then slapped it flat on the table. "And I can't prevent it."

Spock displayed another report on the viewscreen. "Jean Ly-Kieu Czerny. Eurasian. Science Section, agricultural specialist. Her psychometric profile was reviewed before she was considered: xenophobic index remarkably low, less than average paranoid tendencies, generally flexible and resilient in stress situations. Her Sherman's planet assignment was voluntary. You have no reason to berate yourself for a logical command decision," Spock pointed out.

"Spock, I swear that green blood of yours is pure computer coolant!" McCoy exploded. "Dammit man, that's a living, breathing, feeling woman he's talking about. Kang is probably slowly torturing her to death this very minute. It's only human that Jim should be upset about it."

"I'm well aware, Doctor, of human characteristics," Spock responded frostily. "I merely—"

"Gentlemen, please." Kirk raised a hand at each. "You're both right, but that's my problem and your arguments will help neither me nor Czerny. Let's take up the problem of the Klingon outpost on Sherman's planet. That's another contingency that we didn't foresee."

Three

ON THE THIRD day the vault began to sing to her. She ignored it except twice during the thirty-hour Klingon day when the guard set her water ration next to it. Now it hummed mockingly, *You can eat when we get the wheat*, over and over. Her stomach cramped viciously. The water didn't help. Earlier that day Eknaar had come with his needles and sugar water. Now the cramps were worse. Jean stared at the dark duralloy container. It would be so easy. Just a few seconds . . . it would be open . . . *you can eat, give up the wheat—*

"Oh shut up!" she said to it angrily, "Shut up!"

The door lock whirred and broke her hypnotic concentration on the drivault. With relief, she got up to meet the diversion. It was Aernath with a sheaf of notes in one hand and a piece of fruit in the other.

"Hi! Mind if I come in?"

She shook her head dumbly. He pulled up the stool and sat down next to cot spreading out his notes on one end of it. Jean looked at him curiously. Delicate, slender, he topped her by about fifteen centimeters and weighed perhaps sixty-four to sixty-five kilos. Fine, black hair, long mustache, no beard, and startling eyes: deep blue, almost purple. Primarily, her attention was drawn to the fruit he was holding. It was about the size of a grapefruit with a firm peach-colored flesh and a frantically enticing aroma. He nibbled on it absentmindedly as he spread the papers out. He was talking in between bites. Even white teeth took a bite. The morsel disappeared. Another bite. Gone. Jean watched fascinated as a large drop of juice ran extravagantly unheeded down his thumb. Another bite. The amethyst eyes were looking at her now.

"Have you heard a word I've said?"

"Excuse me, what?" She could barely take her eyes off the fruit to meet his question. He followed her gaze to the fruit.

"Oh. Of course." He pulled a smaller dagger out of his boot. Every Klingon seemed to carry one of these, Jean thought. He neatly sliced the fruit in two and handed her half. She hesitated, glancing at the door. "Forget it," he said. "He's on break. Won't be back for a while." He watched her eat with obvious enjoyment. "Like it?"

"Yes. What is it?"

"Not standard cruiser rations, I assure you. Grew it myself in the lab. It's from one of our outpost worlds on the other side of the Empire. Got an unpronounceable name. I call it glory fruit. Bears year round but only one fruit at a time. I'll show it to you sometime. By the way, how does your head feel?"

"My head? Okay, I guess. Why?"

Aernath handed her a sheet of paper. "Take a look at this." It was one of the last pages from her lab log, the one with the long entry about the *quadrotriticale strain*. He watched her scan it. "Pretty scrambled, isn't it? Drove me crazy trying to make sense of it. Finally I went back to the beginning and tried deciphering your lab notes. At least they're not incoherent. But there's water damage in some places. Can't make it all out. Say, did you really get that high a protein content over all those moisture ranges?" He picked up another page and handed it to her. It was one of her data runs. "Those are moisture ranges, aren't they?"

She nodded reluctantly. It seemed a small thing to confirm, what he had already figured out, but it made her uncomfortable. Aernath whistled through his teeth. "*Siee*. That's a phenomenal protein content—and through the whole range at that. I only know of one other that comes close and it drops off more in the higher ranges."

Now Jean was interested. "Really? You have a grain that yields more than twenty-five percent protein? What?"

"*Klibicule*. But it bears only in the second year, so its not very practical as a food grain." Aernath launched into an exposition of the plant and its cycle.

They talked animatedly for some time. Aernath asked a couple more confirmatory questions about her notes and then left. He said nothing about coming back. The cubicle was very quiet. Jean found herself staring at the drivault again. Her *quadrotriticale* strain. It held so much potential for the Federation. A hardy, high-protein grain, it could be priceless to settlers opening up new worlds. New worlds. That was what had drawn her into Starfleet: the chance to use her skills for people opening up new worlds, the challenge, the adventure. She grimaced. This was a little too much adventure. She'd been sincere in her offer to share with the Klingons but to be expropriated grain, data, and scientist, tout ensemble; that she would not accept. Nor would Starfleet.

However, here and now she was all there was of Starfleet. Should she let the Klingons have it and hope to find an eventual escape back to Federation space with some of the seed or should she hold out for possible rescue? If Mr. Spock were here how would he state the odds? Of course, if he were here the odds would be different. "I need some more leverage," she said aloud. The drivault faced her silently. At least it wasn't singing to her anymore.

The hunger cramps woke her early the next morning. She marked passage of time by the guard changes: three shifts a day. She called the shifts with water rations day and the other one night. Not that it really mattered. Time becomes very distorted when there's nothing to do. She felt guilty and annoyed at the inordinate pleasure she felt when Aernath appeared at the door.

"Hullo. It's me again." He sat down with his papers and

22

handed her a small paper-wrapped packet. "Saved you something from lunch."

Jean looked at him warily. The amethyst eyes gazed back clear and steady. In a low whisper she asked, "Isn't this room bugged?"

"What?"

She gestured, "You know, wired for sound?"

Suddenly he nodded. "Oh. No, they had to disconnect that to wire your little box there. You can say anything you like and I'll be the only one to hear it."

"Why are you doing this?" Jean demanded.

"So you'll talk to me and tell me the truth. You will, won't you?" He paused. She nodded reluctantly again. "Besides," he continued, "you'd do the same for me if it was the other way around, wouldn't you?"

"It wouldn't be necessary," she replied stiffly. "The Federation doesn't treat prisoners like this."

Aernath smiled indulgently, as if humoring a small child. "Sure. Well, help yourself."

Jean didn't press the argument. She opened the packet. It was a sticky bread about the consistency of cold corn mush and had a slightly sour taste. Aernath was thumbing through the notes. "This stuff is really impressive if it will perform in the field like you say it did in the lab. You haven't plot tested it yet, have you?"

She shook her head.

"How'd you develop it anyhow? I haven't found anything about that here yet."

She folded the paper packet into a small rectangle and handed it back to him. "And you won't either. That's my secret."

"But it is a variant strain of *quadrotriticale?*"

"Yes. Tell me, why is Kang so interested in this? Is this going to be the Klingon development project on Sherman's planet?"

"Sherman's?" Aernath looked startled, then uncertain. "Well, uh . . . sure, guess there's no harm in saying that."

Jean was puzzled and irritated. "Look, I know you've left a landing party there. That's no secret. But why is it so important to Kang? This isn't even his quadrant."

Aernath waved at the table. "Well, why don't you give him the stuff and ask him why it's so important?"

Her mouth set in a stubborn line. "Because it doesn't belong to him. You can't—" She stopped as her stomach spasmed again.

"He saved your life," observed Aernath reasonably.

"And that gives him total rights to me and my 'possessions'?" snapped Jean peevishly. "Do you really practice that custom? Or is it just a cover story for Kang's maneuvering?"

The Klingon sat quietly a moment, then slowly gathered his notes. Jean shifted restlessly, massaging her stomach. Finally he said, "The custom is real, though not often invoked."

She leaned toward him. "Do you mean to tell me that if I saved your life, you would consider yourself . . . uh . . . *bond* to me for the rest of your life?"

He looked at her quizzically. "A Klingon seldom spares the life of an enemy nor does he expect it in return, but yes, that's the way it works. Or until I save your life in return. Then we're even."

Jean looked at the vault very thoughtfully for a long time after he left.

Aernath didn't come the next day and time dragged interminably. The following day Eknaar came and she was almost glad to see even him.

"How do you feel today?" he inquired.

"Not as bad as I will when you're finished," she said.

"My girl, you're a fool." That was all he had to say.

The hunger was worse after he left. She spent most of the day on her cot dozing when she could. The vault was mocking her again. She kept her eyes shut and floated in limbo as much as possible. Aernath came late in the second shift.

"Hi! Back again. Uh, oh. Doc was here today, wasn't he? You look terrible."

Jean mustered a faint smile. "You have a terrible bedside manner. You'd better stick to plants." Nonetheless, she was glad to see him.

"Yes. Well, I did spend most of the day with my plants but I spent some time on your notes—your early sampling reports just after you arrived. Some interesting variations. You know what I think? I think you developed your strain from a sport you found in those early samples. Right?"

She shrugged. He was very close to the truth. When she made no comment, he changed the subject to regular *quadrotriticale*. He was doing some work on samples of those too. He reached into the pocket of his lab coat—and produced a vial. "This is the *klibicule* I was telling you about. Funny looking stuff, isn't it?" From his other pocket he produced a food packet.

She took it gratefully. "Thanks, Aernath. I appreciate that." They went over more notes discussing various details before Aernath left.

This pattern went on for several days. Jean found herself eagerly awaiting the visits and talking more about her work, or anything, just to prolong them. On two further occasions she refused Aernath's casual suggestions that she relent and open the vault. However, it was increasingly difficult to be vehement about it.

One day, during the second shift, Eknaar appeared with Kang. She watched nervously as Eknaar did his tests. The doctor drew a blood sample, ran it, then turned to Kang. "You see. There's no question." The Commander nodded but said nothing.

Jean felt the old fear rising again. What was going on? She could gather no clue from their faces. Aernath was due shortly. What if he came while they were here? Her apprehension grew. Eknaar gathered and packed his things. The guard outside the door looked in and tapped. Eknaar slid his things under the cot and both men stepped back into the lavatory alcove. The door lock whirred and Aernath entered.

"Helloo . . . hey, what's the matter?" Then he stopped as he saw Kang and Eknaar. He moved aside as the guard joined them in the room.

"Search him," Kang ordered curtly.

Jean stifled a gasp.

25

"My dagger is in my right boot loop. I'm carrying no other weapons." Aernath's voice was steady but his face was pale.

"We are not looking for weapons," Kang replied coldly.

"Then what's the matter?" Aernath asked.

"Eknaar's tests show someone is feeding her," Kang said. The guard produced a packet from Aernath's pocket. Aernath's face grew whiter still. "My orders were explicit: no food for the human. You knew that, of course."

"Yes, Commander."

"Do you have anything further you wish to say for yourself?"

"No, sir."

Kang motioned to the guard. "Your agonizer. Full strength, lethal duration."

"No!" Jean screamed. The four men turned to look at her but all she could see was a vision of Aernath's form convulsing on the floor while those amethyst eyes stared lifeless at the ceiling. "Wait!" she said hoarsely. "You're not going to kill him just because he gave me a little food, are you?"

Kang was looking at Aernath. "He disobeyed a direct order. Repeatedly. That's a capital offense."

She was standing between them now. "But he only did it to try and persuade me to cooperate with you. That's not disloyal."

"But he did not succeed and he disobeyed orders," Kang pointed out inexorably. The guard had the agonizer in his hand.

Jean moved toward Aernath flinging one arm out to fend off the guard. "Stop. Oh, please wait," she implored. She faced Kang again. "Listen. If I agree to open the drivault now will you spare him?"

Kang scrutinized her closely. "After refusing all this time you would do that now to spare one Klingon? Why?"

"Because he was kind to me," Jean blurted. "Because he doesn't deserve to die."

"You just said he did it to gain your cooperation. Now you claim he did it out of sympathy for you. You're not making sense," Kang pursued.

She shook her head weakly. "Oh, I know I'm confused. I

wish I could think straight . . . but I'm right . . . it's all a question of approach . . . he can be both." She tried desperately to get hold of the panic, to banish the image on the floor. There was the one main point. "My question. You haven't answered my question! If I open the drivault will you spare him? Let him live?"

"I will."

Jean looked at Aernath uncertainly. "Will he? Can you trust him?"

Aernath looked stunned. "The commander has given his word. Of course he'll keep it."

Kang's voice came softly from behind her. "Will you open the drivault now?" She turned in time to catch that strange look again.

"I'll do it." Hastily she moved to the table and unlocked the vault. Aernath fingered the samples carefully.

"Well?" Kang demanded.

"They're *quadrotriticale* all right. Beyond that I can't say without further tests. I can tell you some things by tomorrow."

"Fine. Do that."

Jean looked at the Klingons with sudden suspicion. "Did you set this all up? Was this all just an elaborate charade to get the vault open?"

Kang regarded her speculatively. "If I was prepared to execute him in either case, then it really doesn't matter does it?"

"You really intended to kill him?"

"Of course."

"But now he is free—without reprisals?" Jean persisted.

Kang gestured impatiently. "Obviously."

"Well," Jean said determinedly, "if that's truly the situation, then I saved his life. He is *bond* to me. Right?"

There was a charged silence. Aernath paled again. Then Kang threw back his head and roared with laughter. "Sturdy pawn. You do keep coming, don't you? If we were bluffing, you've called it nicely. Well done." He bowed slightly toward her. "He's yours," adding intently, "I wish you better of yours than I've yet had of mine."

Jean touched Kang's arm lightly. "Sometimes learning

27

new customs comes hard. Perhaps I'll go more gently than some."

"Gently, my dear? I doubt it. You've the instincts of a fighter. But I like that." He lifted her chin with one hand. " 'Tis a pity you're not a Klingon."

" 'Tis a pity you're not human," she reciprocated.

Kang chuckled. "I'll leave him to you now. There will still be a guard posted but you are free to come and go as long as you are escorted. Join me for dinner tomorrow. Until then."

The door closed behind them leaving Aernath looking acutely uncertain. Finally he met Jean's scrutiny.

"Well, did Kang set this up with you?"

He shook his head. "My orders were to enlist your cooperation by any means I saw fit. I had no further conversation with the commander on the matter."

"That's all? And you knowingly ignored his other order because if you succeeded it would be overlooked? Survive and succeed—it really works that way with you, doesn't it?"

"Right," acceded Aernath sullenly, "except that I *didn't* succeed and now . . ."

"But you did succeed!" she insisted. "It was because of your kindness that I . . . did what I did."

"No," insisted Aernath stubbornly, "it was because of the commander's threat that you acted."

She decided not to tell him how close she had been to simply opening it on his request. Instead she merely said, "The point is you made me care enough about you that I was willing to open it to save you."

"And now what do you require from me?" His voice was bitter.

"Your lab coat," she replied promptly.

Startled, Aernath complied. She seamed it closed with a finger and relaxed. It felt good to have her slit tunic covered. She pulled out the packet of food and sat down cross-legged on her cot. Aernath remained standing where he was.

"Please, sit down." He complied. Jean looked at the stiff figure perched in front of her, then said gently, "You're humiliated and angry. Look, don't forget I'm in the same position as you are and I haven't grown up with these crazy customs. All I really want from you is something I think you were prepared to give anyway—friendship. I need someone I can trust and depend on, someone to keep me out of trouble for as long as I'm stuck in your Klingon Empire. Will you do that for me?" The blue eyes met hers. God, she thought, the effect was startling—that limpid blue against the dark complexion. She had the feeling that if she ever touched them, she'd get a electric shock.

"If you command it. Does that include keeping *me* out of trouble so I can keep you out of trouble?"

She laughed. Some of her tension drained away but the Klingon did not relax. Sobered, she replied, "Right. I expect you to keep your skin whole. If Kang or someone else does you in, I'm right back where I started." She brushed a few crumbs onto the paper packet, crumpled it, and stood up. "What I want right now, in the following order, is something to drink, a shower, and some clean clothes."

Aernath escaped from the human's presence as soon as possible and headed forward to his quarters, one thought beating a bitter refrain in his mind: *Bond. And to an alien female!* He was Cymele-crossed for sure. His normal healthy sense of Klingon superiority had always been flawed by this strange fascination with xenobiology: alien plants, alien animals, and now a Federation alien—a human. He'd made a bad miscalculation as a result. He should have listened to older, wiser warriors. *"Sssts"* they called them: soft skin, sharp teeth. "The only good *Ssst* is at the other end of a blaster: *Ssst!*" He'd heard that often. But he'd let his fascination make him overconfident and he'd failed. Well, past is past. Survive and succeed. There was still his vow and his mission: Since he was *bond-obligated* to keep this human alive, perhaps. . . . Taking his foil from his room, Aernath went down to the gym and set the fencing master at level three. He drilled until his mind and body were too exhausted to harbor troubling thoughts.

Jean spent the entire next day familiarizing herself with Aernath's lab which was small but well equipped. Finally, she settled down to reviewing tapes of Klingon empire flora while Aernath ran analyses on her seed. She chatted casually with him across the lab until he unbent a bit. She elicited information about him, Kang, and the ship. Slightly younger than she, this was Aernath's first deep-space duty assignment. Most of the crew were from Kang's home planet. Aernath was not.

"You say you're from Mara's planet? You mean Kang's wife?" He nodded. "They're not from the same planet?"

"No, same star system but she's from the outer of the two habitable planets. Kang's is the inner one."

"Being so close to Klingon space on Sherman's planet, we had briefings on your fleet but not much about your planets. However, one hears a lot of stories. Is it true, the rumors we've heard—that she left him?" Jean asked curiously.

Aernath bent over his table concentrating on readout. "Uh huh. Shortly after their encounter with the *Enterprise* when Kang lost his ship."

"Why did she leave him?"

Aernath straightened up and leaned against the table. His voice hardened derisively, "She went soft on the Federation—left the fleet, went home, even went underground. The commander holds Kirk responsible for it. He'll never forgive him for that."

"If Kang has a personal vendetta going against Captain Kirk, why didn't he try to kill him when he had him in Klingon territory?"

Aernath hesitated, then said, "I think he wants to discredit and ruin him, not just destroy him. Besides . . ."

Jean waited, but he did not finish. "Besides what?" she prompted.

"Nothing. I don't know," Aernath said curtly. "Guess you'll have to find out from Kang himself."

She saw Aernath wouldn't pursue that subject any further. "And you, how do you feel about us, about the Federation?"

He shrugged noncommittally. "How should I know? You're the first human I've met. Are you typical?"

She didn't know how to answer that question so she tried another. "Well, what about me? How do I fit into Kang's plans? He keeps talking as if I'm some kind of a chesspiece in a game he's playing."

Aernath was clearly uncomfortable. "Well, it's obvious that Kang's holding you angers Kirk. Beyond that . . ." He hesitated, then said, "Look, you said I should protect myself. I've said enough. You'll have to get any further information from the commander when he wants you to have it."

Four

Captain's log: Stardate 5960.2 We have ascertained that there was indeed one survivor of the earthquake on Sherman's planet: Agricultural Specialist Czerny, and that she was captured by Klingon Commander Kang. We have returned to Sherman's planet to reestablish the agricultural work and monitor the Klingon outpost there while awaiting a response from the Organians.

CAPTAIN KIRK FINISHED recording the log and turned to Lt. Uhura. "Any results yet, Lieutenant?"

"None, sir. If they have any communication capability at all they must have received us by now. They are maintaining complete communication silence."

Kirk swung his command chair to face Spock's position. "Sensor scan, Mr. Spock? Are they still where we first spotted them?"

"Affirmative, Captain. They have entrenched themselves at Mousse Rock, two-point-six kilometers upriver from our agricultural station."

"Moose Rock, Mr. Spock?"

"Mousse, Captain, as in the Terran French dessert. I understand Lieutenant Le Clerc of the initial survey team

32

fancied it resembled that confection. It would appear they are developing it as a natural fortification."

"Any better reading on how many there are there?"

"Only a rough approximation on life-form readings—thirty-five to fifty is as close as we can estimate."

"Lieutenant Uhura, any report from our landing party we left at the station when we went after Kang?"

"Yes, sir. Lieutenant DeCastro reports all is quiet and cleanup work is progressing nicely. No sign of the Klingons there."

"Fine. I want that station functional as soon as possible. First priority is to get systems going, especially communications. Notify transporter room that first relief team will consist of Chief Engineer Scott, Lieutenant Kevin Riley, Lieutenant Johnson and Ensign Tamura from Security, and yourself, Lieutenant Uhura." Kirk noted Sulu's sudden glance at the mention of Riley, a good friend of his. Sulu hadn't been off-ship for some time . . . "And Mr. Sulu, also," he finished.

The helmsman flashed him a grin of startled pleasure. "Thank you, Captain."

Kirk nodded. "Both of you get your reliefs up here and report to transporter room in thirty minutes."

Sulu looked around curiously. They had beamed down near a building that had been undamaged by the earthquake. It was a single-story, flagstone house set in a rather extensive garden. A short distance beyond, the flat land gave way to a series of craggy outcroppings of dark rock and low rolling hills. Sulu's hobby was botany, not geology, so he had paid scant attention to the discussions on the earthquake. He was satisfied to know that it was due to a singular concatenation of events unlikely to recur for a century or more. The garden, and most particularly that part of it devoted to local flora, was what interested him. Despite the slight autumn nip in the air, he was looking forward to the next several days here.

Off to his left, Lieutenant DeCastro, of the first landing party, was briefing Lieutenant Johnson while the second of his three units slowly dissolved in the transporter beam.

This house had its own generator which had been restored to working order. The communications room of the central administrative complex some distance away was the only part of that building not totally destroyed. The main power supply for the colony was gone. Restoring those two items was the top priority now.

Soon, Sulu and Riley were helping move and catalog equipment near the administration complex while Scott monitored its arrival from the *Enterprise*'s cargo transporter. The five remaining members of DeCastro's detail were working with them while Uhura meticulously checked relays and circuits in the communications room. It was a hot, tired group that gathered at the house late that afternoon. DeCastro ordered the last of his detail into position for beam up. Uhura and Riley headed for the two available showers. Sulu sat down on the front steps, his eyes fixed on the spot where the relief detail would materialize. They didn't appear.

A short distance away Scott muttered impatiently to himself, then snapped open his communicator. "Scott to transporter room. Kyle, what's keepin you, mon? Let's get them down here."

The answer was prompt but not reassuring. Instead of the soft British accents of the transporter room officer, they heard a melee of muttered oaths and directions. Lieutenant Kyle's voice came through briefly. "A moment, sir. We've a problem here." More confusion, then Kyle's voice again. "There's the last one. Move, man—get him out of there." A sharp report. "That tears it!" Kyle's voice carried as much disgusted frustration as Sulu had ever heard from the man.

Scott could contain himself no longer. "Will somebody up there tell me what in the name of little green gremlins is going on?"

"Sorry, Mr. Scott, we ran into a transporter malfunction on that last transfer. We almost lost them. I pulled them in all right, but I had to augment so much that we blew the main circuit. At least. I suspect a couple of secondaries are gone, too. I'm afraid you'll have to wait awhile for the relief detail unless you want me to send them by shuttlecraft?"

Scott swore softly. In his lexicon of disasters, there was

34

only one thing worse than having something go wrong with his ship, and that was having something go wrong with his ship when he wasn't in a position to do anything about it personally. He turned to Lieutenant Johnson. "Lieutenant?"

The hefty, brown-haired Security man shook his head. "We can manage until tomorrow, sir, if we need to. DeCastro reported no activity outside of the Klingon compound since they arrived—not even recon patrols. We've got trip alarms around this compound."

Scotty addressed his communicator. "No, Lieutenant Kyle, no need for the shuttle yet. Just get a maintenance crew on that transporter and see if you can get it operational by tomorrow. Scott, out."

Johnson promptly assigned Ensign Tamura first watch and put himself on mess detail. As Johnson disappeared in the direction of the kitchen, Scott, mopping his brow, sank down on the steps of the porch beside Sulu. Together they watched the petite Japanese woman disappear around the corner of the house. "What are the chances they can have it fixed by morning?" Sulu asked.

Scotty shook his head. "I canna say without seeing it. But even if it's just the main circuit it's not likely to be ready for a good eighteen hours."

Sulu shook his head sympathetically but he wasn't unduly worried. There were still the *Enterprise*'s firepower to back them up in the event of trouble with the Klingons. Otherwise there was no problem—just maybe a couple extra days planetside. He certainly wasn't going to object to that.

A damp but enthusiastic Riley stuck his head out the door. "Next. My shower's free. Hey! Where is everybody?" Sulu explained the transporter mishap. "Uh, oh. My first planet assignment since I'm back on the *Enterprise* and this happens. Doesn't say much for the luck o' the Irish, does it?"

Dinner was a pleasant surprise. Rusty Johnson was a gruff, taciturn man of generally solitary pursuits but it turned out that gourmet cooking was one of his seldom indulged hobbies. As they polished off the crepes suzette, Scotty happily threatened to put him on permanent mess duty as soon as reinforcements arrived. The engineer was so pleased he even volunteered to help Uhura with K.P.

As they worked on kitchen clean-up, Uhura finished filling Scott in on the results of her afternoon's work. The Scotsman was as thoroughgoing and meticulous in the kitchen as he was in the engine room, she observed. One of the more important satisfactions of being a Starfleet officer was the satisfaction of working side by side with extremely versatile as well as talented colleagues. Continued surprises.

Kevin Riley wandered into the kitchen humming "My Wild Irish Rose." "Uhura," he said gleefully, "you'll never guess what I found in the den closet!"

Uhura straightened from putting a pan back in its place. "Well, with that cat-ate-the-cream lilt in your voice, Kevin, I'd say it had to be either a pair of Irish colleens or a leprechaun with a pot of gold."

"Nope!" he declaimed triumphantly. "One genuine, intact guitar. How about a concert tonight?"

Uhura bestowed a warm, motherly smile on the eager young engineer. "Well . . ." she glanced at Scott who was putting a final polishing touch on the counter top as if it were one of his Jeffries tubes.

"Och, and why not, Uhura? As long as there's no sign of trouble, I kin scarce think of a better way to spend an evening."

She gave him a teasing smile in return as she agreed. "All right. At least it will keep your mind off the transporter room which is where you'd be spending your off-duty evening if you were aboard ship." The wry grimace he gave her in reply merely confirmed what they both knew.

They gathered in the den. Rusty Johnson, seated in the doorway where he could watch the front door and security console, tilted his chair back against the door frame and discreetly lit his pipe. Uhura tuned the guitar then treated them in succession to an east African lullaby, a Scottish air, a Welsh ballad and an Irish sea chanty. Then she played a nonvocal Vulcan piece followed by "Beyond Antares."

Kevin said quietly, "It's been a long time since I first heard you sing that."

Unwilling to let them slip into a somber mood, Uhura

strummed a few brisk chords. "Here's one that none of us wanted to hear again for a very long time." She broke into "I'll Take You Home Again, Kathleen" to the accompaniment of mock groans and grimaces from the sofa. Even Rusty managed an oblique smile. Kevin turned a delicate shade of red. A lighter mood restored, Uhura relaxed into a series of improvisations.

"That has the sound of a new song. Am I right?" Scotty observed from the sofa.

Uhura nodded. "It's something that's been running through my head for a couple of years. I guess being back near Sherman's planet brought it up."

"Try it out. Let's hear it." Sulu urged.

"All right," she laughed. "I call it 'Uhura's Lament.' "

I'll sing you a song of Cyrano Jones
    Redoubtable space trader he,
Scourge of the Klingons and bane of James Kirk,
    Blithely he wanders the galaxy
Trading *tribbles* and flame-gems and gleaming
   glow-water
    To poor hapless tourists like me.

Oh . . . The trouble with *tribbles,* the trouble with
  tribbles
    They don't come in dribbles . . . or dabs,
    But in boxes and barrels
    And soon the world narrows
    To nothing but *tribbles* . . . and you.

I'll sing you a song of Cyrano Jones
    Irrepressible entrepreneur.
Mandates and warrants and angry fleet captains
    Just come in the line of his work:
Marketing treasures and making a living
    From poor hapless tourists like me. Oh . . .

The others joined her as she launched into the chorus for the second time, finishing with hearty laughs from the sofa and doorway. Kevin looked puzzled. "It's a nice song but what's so funny? And what's a *tribble?*"

"Och, lad, if ye dinna know, dinna ask and thank yir lucky shamrock for yir blissful ignorance," Scotty answered emphatically.

But Sulu came to his friend's rescue and explained how Cyrano Jones had given Uhura a warm, furry little creature on Space Station K-7 some time earlier and had thus precipitated a plague of the creatures on the *Enterprise* as well as in the space station itself. He went on to relate how this had ultimately served to uncover a Klingon plot to poison grain destined for Sherman's planet, so Jones ended up something of a hero as well as a scoundrel. As Sulu finished his tale, Rusty observed laconically that it was eight o'clock. Kevin Riley was slated for next watch.

"Thanks, Uhura, for this much. I hope we can look forward to more," Kevin said as he headed out the door.

As Riley left, Sulu remarked, "You know, there's another of your compositions I haven't heard in some time, Uhura. You know, the Canopian love sonnet you set to music."

"Yes. 'The Nightingale Woman' by Tarbolde." Uhura nodded and began the introduction. Keiko Tamura came into the room mid-sonnet and settled on the hassock Kevin had vacated. Uhura elided into a Balinese temple song and then finished with another African lullaby.

Sulu stretched with a yawn. "Since I have dawn patrol I think I'll hit the sack. But don't let me stop the rest of you. And thanks, Uhura." He retired to his quarters and drifted off to the faint sounds of guitar music.

It was midafternoon and the transporter was still not close to functional. Kirk sat on the bridge pondering the situation. Scotty had just been on the communicator asking about progress for the fourth time. Perhaps it was time to send the shuttle down. . . .

"We're receiving a distress call, Captain." It was Lieutenant Alden at the communication console.

"From the planet?" Kirk swung around to face the communications officer.

"No sir. Deep space. Six-zero-three mark seven."

"Any details?"

"The distress call is urgent. They have sustained damage

38

to their life-support systems—estimate total shutdown in less than twenty hours."

Kirk muttered a choice expletive. "What kind of a ship is it?"

"A freighter, sir—the U.S.S. *Dierdre* under Captain Naranjit Singh."

"Randy Singh?" Kirk responded.

"You know him?"

"Yes, quite well. His freighter was the first to arrive with emergency food for Tarsus Four after the massacre there. But what's he doing in this sec . . . never mind. Mr. Spock, ETA for those coordinates. Are there any other Federation ships in this sector who can answer that call?" Kirk looked at his first officer.

"No, Captain, there are none closer than the *Enterprise* and it will take us approximately seventeen-point-two hours to reach those coordinates. However, I should point out that a false distress call using the name of the U.S.S. *Deirdre* has been used by the Klingons when we were on Capella Four."

"Are you suggesting that this is a decoy, Mr. Spock?"

"It is a possibility that must be considered," the Vulcan replied.

"But if it's genuine, we don't have much margin . . ." Kirk weighed another difficult command decision. "Mr. Spock, assemble the relief crew in shuttlecraft bay. Instruct them to brief Mr. Scott on the situation. If the Klingons are monitoring our ship-to-planet communications we won't give them any confirmation of our plans. Mr. Chekov, plot a course for that distress call." Kirk punched an arm console button. "Kirk to Scott."

The answer was prompt. "Scott here, Captain."

"Scotty, since it's going to be a while before the transporter is fixed, I'm sending you an additional relief crew by shuttlecraft."

"Aye, sir. Would ye like me to come up by return shuttle?" the chief engineer suggested hopefully.

"Thanks, Scotty, but that's not necessary yet. Hang on to the shuttle for a while. Kirk, out." When the word came from shuttlecraft bay that the shuttle was well away he nodded to the helmsman. "Take her out of orbit, Lieutenant

Hadley. Ahead Warp two." As he did so, he wondered if he had made the right decision or if he had just condemned his landing party to a Klingon countermove.

Lieutenant Willinck eased the shuttlecraft into a gentle orbital descent that would carry them fairly close to the Klingon outpost on their final approach to the Federation station. "Ensign, see what your scanners register as we go by. This may be our best chance to get a reading on how many of them there are."

Deep within the Klingon fortress by the dim yellow glow of the Command room lights, the duty officer watched the blip that was the *Enterprise* shuttle as it settled into its final approach pattern. "That trajectory will bring them within a half-kilometer of us, Commander."

"Get me Ordnance and Weapons."

"Yes, sir." The duty officer opened the intercom to the Ordnance and Weapons station.

"Status Amber. Hold and monitor." Lieutenant Klen, the squat, slightly balding commander of the outpost paced tightly from one rocky wall to the other.

"We're being scanned, Commander!" The Klingon's voice rose a fraction as he exclaimed, "She's hit! Off course, going down rapidly."

Klen uttered an explosive epithet and headed for Weapons. He burst in on the exultant crewman. "You unexpurgated idiot! I gave no order to fire!" He laid the crewman flat on the floor with an angry blow and took over the firing console.

"But they were scanning us, Commander!" the crewman protested.

"I know that," Klen shouted. "Ordinarily sufficient, but our orders are explicit. We must wait for them to fire first. You're on report. Confine yourself to quarters for thirty hours." Then, seeing his subordinate's crestfallen demeanor he added gruffly, "Your hit will be registered nonetheless. And you will have another chance to fight and earn a warrior's death—no fear of that. It goes against the grain, this waiting, but our orders are quite clear: they must come to us and they will pay dearly for every meter they attempt to gain. Dismissed." He suppressed a twinge of guilt as the man left. It was an unforgivable breach of discipline not to punish such a blatant disregard for orders, but this woman-ish waiting was getting to all of them.

Scott saw the attack and watched helplessly as the craft bucked and yawed unevenly down to impact slightly under two kilometers away. Obviously someone was still fighting to control its flight. "Scott to Kirk. Scott to Kirk. The Klingons have fired on the shuttle!" There was no answer. A swift check of his communicator assured him it was in working condition. Where was the *Enterprise?* He turned to Johnson who had come out with him to meet the shuttle-craft. "See if you can raise the shuttle." Then he charged into the communications room where Uhura and Sulu were at work. "The Klingons shot down the shuttle and I can't raise the *Enterprise* on my communicator. You got anything here in operating condition yet?"

Two startled faces looked up from a disemboweled panel. "Not quite, sir," Uhura replied. Another hour, maybe. Here, try my communicator."

He tried. "Scott to *Enterprise*. Come in please." Silence. "Sulu, you and Johnson round up Tamura and Riley. Recon the shuttle and see what can be done there while we try to get this communication console going. Something tells me the *Enterprise* has been diverted somehow, tho' I canna see why the captain dinna notify us, unless . . ." he left the grim thought unfinished as he joined Uhura at the console.

Sulu scooped up his tricorder and departed at a trot, checking his phaser as he went. Riley and Tamura were already approaching rapidly from the direction of the house when he reached Johnson.

"No response from the shuttle," Johnson said.

"What happened to the shuttle?" Riley demanded as they came into earshot.

"Klingons shot her down," Johnson replied. "And we can't raise the *Enterprise* with our communicators."

"Uh, oh," Riley whistled. "Trou . . . ble." His dawning concern was reflected in Tamura's face also.

Johnson turned to Sulu. "Instructions from Commander Scott?"

"Recon the shuttle. He and Uhura are trying to get the console up—probably be about an hour," Sulu replied. The Security man looked at him expectantly. Sulu realized that he was ranking officer. He waved a deferential hand. "Security. Take charge, Johnson."

The Security man beckoned for them to follow and set off at a lope in the direction of the downed shuttlecraft. It had come down nearly one-and-a-half kilometers from the communications building on the far edge of a thick copse of trees. As he ran, Sulu glanced at the Security woman beside him. He wondered briefly if Johnson should have left her on guard with Scotty and Uhura. Might be less risky.

They entered the copse and took advantage of its cover to approach the shuttle. Though quieter, theirs was not the only approach. From the direction of the Klingon outpost less than a kilometer away came the clear chug of a vehicle. As it came into sight, Riley muttered, "Bloody thievin' crows! That's a Federation tractor. They must have stolen it from our station."

But there was no time for discussion. From the shuttlecraft came the distinctive whine of phaser fire. A return volley came from the wagon behind the tractor. Apparently several Klingons were concealed in it. The tractor and wagon dipped abruptly into a gully, and soon it was clear that the Klingons had dispersed to other cover. Scant meters away, the shuttlecraft faced them, nose embedded in the ground, the primary exit jammed partway open facing the open field beyond the copse of trees.

Johnson swore softly under his breath. "Bastards have them pinned. Emergency exit's useless in that position and they can't get out the main door under that fire. We're going to have to take out that Klingon patrol. Riley, you come with me to the left. Sulu and Tamura you cover the right flank. I think there's five of them. Let's try to get one for interrogation; otherwise shoot to kill." He and Riley moved off to the left through the underbrush.

As Sulu turned to follow Tamura, he noted movement at the front of the shuttlecraft. A Security ensign emerged from the shattered forward window, dropped to the ground and started to move toward the trees. He got about two meters. To Sulu's right, a Klingon rose from behind a hillock and fired. It was his last kill. Twin phaser blasts from inside the shuttle and from Tamura dropped him, too.

"That's one," said Tamura matter-of-factly. She moved off to the right.

Sulu followed. Even in the heat of battle he watched her movement with appreciation of the artistry. Moves like a ninja, he thought; if it weren't for the red uniform, no one could spot her. As it was, she would be rather a visible target . . . hastily he rubbed handsful of dirt on his own yellow tunic. The whine of phaser fire droned behind him from the left of the shuttle. No more figures emerged from the windows.

He inched his way forward, constantly checking the terrain ahead and to his left. A movement near the back of the shuttle caught his eye—Another Klingon working his way toward the main door, out of the line of fire from whomever was inside. Sulu took careful aim. . . . "That's two," he said softly. Now, where was Tamura?

There was a flash of red ahead. He froze. What was she doing breaking cover like that? He saw the Klingon edging toward her but couldn't get a clear shot at him. Suddenly Tamura dropped, just an instant before the Klingon fired. She gave a sharp cry then began to crawl rather clumsily back in Sulu's general direction. What the devil was she doing? Sulu was virtually certain she hadn't been hit. A moment ago she had been moving as silently as an assassin's shadow. Now her progress was clearly audible. The Klingon was following her.

Then Sulu understood. He reset his phaser on *stun* and made himself part of a shadow.

Tamura's timing was hair-trigger fine. Her trail intersected the Klingon's a mere two meters from Sulu. She rose to one knee, the Klingon leapt and Sulu fired. The man dropped like a ton of neutronium. Tamura fell sideways, firing at the same time. An incoming blast caught the Klingon's shoulder and grazed Sulu's arm. The Klingon responsible for that shot evaporated in a crossfire from Tamura, the shuttle, and

43

someone off behind the shuttle. "That's four, I believe," she said.

"Possibly five, I hope," Sulu said faintly. Nausea swept over him as the pain from his arm hit him. He lay flat on his back.

Tamura rolled the Klingon on his side making a bit more of a barrier and wormed her way over to Sulu. "You hit bad?"

"No, I don't think so. Just grazed my right elbow a bit."

"Here, slide back down here and let me see it." She urged him back down a slight slope, then deftly tore back the sleeve of his shirt. "You're right. Just a surface burn. Hurts like blazes tho', doesn't it?"

Sulu nodded tightly. "You said it."

Tamura reached down and detached the tiny first-aid kit from her boot. "Some spray-plast and a dose of delta-endorph ought to hold you until we get back to the station. Hold still."

Sulu watched her work, devoutly thankful that he had voiced no reservations about her presence on this patrol. Security people were always well trained but this one could go far in Security. "That was well done," he said, indicating the Klingon. "I think you're due a commendation for this assignment."

She flashed him a quick smile. "Thank you, sir." Brushing dirt from her knees, she got up. "That's all I can do for your arm at the moment. I guess we better look after our prisoner here before he wakes up and gets nasty."

Sulu retrieved the Klingon's weapon and covered him while Tamura tied his hands securely with strips from his own uniform. From the direction of the shuttle they heard Johnson shout. "Ahoy, shuttle. Hang in there. We're mopping up out here. Lieutenant Sulu! Tamura! Are you there?"

"Over here!" Sulu responded.

A few moments later Johnson cautiously emerged from the underbrush, glancing at the Klingon." You got one. Good." He took in Sulu's arm. "Bad?"

"No, just grazed. Where's Kevin?" Sulu asked.

"I sent him into the shuttle," Johnson replied. "If you'll keep an eye on this one, Tamura and I will check out the tractor."

Soon Sulu heard the chug of the tractor heading toward the shuttle. The Klingon at his feet had just started to stir when Tamura and Johnson reappeared. Tamura knelt and massaged the Klingon's chest with her knuckles. "Come on, you, wake up!" The man opened his eyes and glared at her. She pulled out her first-aid hypospray and gave him a shot.

"You only got four doses in there. Why waste one on him, Tamura?" Johnson asked.

"So he can walk," Tamura said. "No point in crowding the wagon."

"Fair enough," Johnson agreed. He gave the Klingon a nudge with his toe. "On your feet, Klingon. Sulu, if you'll get everybody loaded on and drive the tractor, we'll start out with this fellow. When you catch up with us let Ensign Ahmad relieve me. I'll want to talk to Willinck."

Sulu was met at the shuttle door by a grim-faced Riley. "Three dead, another fellow in there with a bad head injury, Lieutenant Banerjee's got a cracked shoulder and some cuts. And Sulu—"

"Yes?"

"The *Enterprise* has left orbit to answer a distress call. That's why we couldn't raise her. Captain Kirk sent the message with the shuttle so the Klingons wouldn't intercept a broadcast."

Sulu grimaced. "So we're on our own in this one. How long?"

"Lieutenant Willinck said Spock estimated forty standard hours, minimum—if it's a genuine distress call and not a Klingon trick."

It was a sober little group that gathered in the house that evening. Four fresh graves lay on the hillside behind the station. The ensign with the head injury had died en route to the station. Uhura and Scott thought they had the main communications console operative but did not want to test it until the *Enterprise* was back. No point in alerting the Klingons unnecessarily. Double sentries were posted.

After supper, Johnson, Tamura and Sulu took a tray and some questions to their prisoner who was tied up in the laundry room. He was not in an accommodating mood.

45

After a drink of water, he used his one freed hand to hurl the plate of food at Tamura along with a string of Klingon epithets.

Johnson was equally unaccommodating. He seized the Klingon by his injured shoulder and shook him vigorously. "Listen, Klingon, listen well. You've had your first and last free medicine and food. From now on you *earn* it—with answers and a little civility. Is that clear?"

The Klingon answered him with a sullen growl.

"If you cooperate, you'll be transferred to the *Enterprise* brig as an official prisoner of war until this thing is sorted out. If you don't . . ." Johnson shrugged expressively. "Now—identity?"

"*Tormin*,* first rank, Klingon Imperial Fleet, assigned to Klolode Two."

"That's it? No name? No number?"

"Not for you, human!"

"Suit yourself, *Tormin*." Johnson responded. "Your mission? What's your objective here on Sherman's planet?"

"To annihilate you humans!"

"That goes without saying. I'm interested more in specifics. What's your garrison strength?"

"More than enough to wipe you out."

"Unlikely, *Tormin*." He seized the Klingon's hair and pulled his head back. "Numbers. I want numbers. What's your garrison strength?"

The Klingon glared at him defiantly. "If you want to know—go count'em!"

"Who's your commander there?" The Klingon sat in stony silence. When Johnson repeated the question, the man spat contemptuously at him. Johnson flushed, then struck the Klingon with a resounding backhand that snapped his head against the plumbing. Still no reply. Johnson sighed. "All right. Tamura, tie him up. We'll let him think about things overnight."

Captain Kirk looked at the freighter hanging motionless in front of them on the viewscreen. It was the U.S.S. *Deirdre*

* *Tormin.* A rank in Klingon Security Forces roughly analogous to sergeant.

46

all right. The *Enterprise* had been traveling on Yellow Alert since they had left Sherman's planet but there had been no sign of Klingons. "Red alert, Lieutenant Hadley. Lieutenant Alden, see if you can raise anyone aboard. Life readings, Mr. Spock?"

The turbolift whooshed open to admit Dr. McCoy to the bridge. "Emergency medical team is standing by in the transporter room in case this is the real thing, Jim."

"Thanks, Bones. Spock?" The two men looked at the Vulcan.

"I pick up five life readings—Captain. Three of them are weak."

Lieutenant Aldren broke in. "I'm receiving a signal from the ship now, sir."

"Fine. Put it on visual, Lieutenant Hadley. Chekov, anything else in the vicinity?" Kirk queried.

"Negative, Captain."

The viewscreen image changed to the dim cabin of the freighter. Center screen was filled with the stocky weather-beaten frame of a man in a Freighter Service uniform and a white turban.

"Captain Kirk to the U.S.S. *Deirdre*. Come in please."

"Jimmy, boy! Is that really you? Now, there's a drink of cold water for a man in the desert. We seem to be in a spot of trouble. Can you lend us a hand?"

McCoy looked at Kirk. *"Jimmy boy?"*

Kirk grimaced. "I *was* a *very young* midshipman when we met on Tarsus Four." He punched a console button. "Randy, you old buzzard. You haven't changed a bit. Stand by to come aboard. How many of you are there?"

"Just four crewmen and myself, Captain."

"I'll see you shortly after you're aboard. And, Randy—your story better be good. You've got some explaining to do."

"My pleasure, Jimmy. Darndest yarn you ever want to hear. Singh out."

The viewscreen reverted to the external view of the freighter. Kirk turned to McCoy. "Notify me just as soon as you've cleared Singh. If he's able, I'll see him in the conference room. Lieutenant Alden, confirm these coordinates with Space Station K-Seven so they can arrange pickup of the freighter. Lieutenant Hadley—any signs of activity out there?"

"Negative, sir."

"Fine. Yellow Alert. Lay in a return course to Sherman's planet. Ahead Warp Six. You have the helm."

"Aye, Captain."

Kirk stood up and looked at his first officer. "Mr. Spock?" The two of them entered the turbolift and headed for the conference room. Captain Naranjit Singh joined them a few moments later, already looking and sounding more robust.

"Thanks, Jimmy. A couple more hours and we'd have been goners."

"What happened, Randy? This isn't your sector."

"Don't I know it! We were two sectors away on a routine run—carrying *ryetalyn* and some other ordinary medical supplies—nothing strategic, when we caught a fair-sized micro-meteorite amidships. Played hob with our life support system. We put out a general distress signal and were all working on the system when—Boom!—out of nowhere— here's this Klingon battlecruiser."

"Which one?" Kirk asked sharply.

"Blamed if I know. I never even saw a boarding party much less the commander. They radioed us that at the first sign of resistance they'd blow us out of space. Then they took us in tow. Looked like they were just going to tow us plumb into the Klingon Empire while we slowly asphyxiated. Then they dropped us where you found us—after they disabled our main drive to make sure we stayed put. Those Klingons are as looney as space monkeys come, but why this?"

"A decoy, Randy. You were bait. One they knew I wouldn't ignore. The question is who and why. Mr. Spock, show him what we've got on Klingon battlecruisers. See if he can identify which one it was."

Captain Singh identified the *Devisor*, Captain Koloth's ship as the one that had diverted him. Kirk thanked him and let him go back to his crew. Then he turned thoughtfully to his first officer.

"Well, that explains where Koloth was. Obviously, he and Kang acted in concert. What do you make of it, Mr. Spock?"

"It would appear that the Klingons intend to keep us busy. If they are unsure of the extent of our intelligence data, this may all be an elaborate ploy to divert us."

"You mean the Sherman's planet garrison as well?" Kirk mused.

"It would be a logical maneuver," Spock replied.

"Mmmm. Yes, I see what you mean. If that's the case, then we could expect them to hole up and hold out as long as possible. It also means we may have a whole rash of Klingon instigated incidents to deal with. If that's the case, the best way to handle Sherman's planet is to send down a fairly hefty contingent to the station and then ignore the Klingon outpost—just let them simmer away under their rock."

"That would also be a logical move," Spock concurred.

"Meanwhile, the original problem remains—*and* we don't know Czerny's whereabouts or status. If that's not resolved, the instability in this quadrant will increase phenomenally. We need to know about Czerny!"

"Starfleet Intelligence is not that fast. It will be some weeks before we can expect any further news," Spock pointed out.

Kirk punched the communication console button with a sigh. "I know, Spock. You're right. For now, the only thing I can speed up is the *Enterprise*. Kirk to Bridge. Lieutenant Hadley, have engineering take us up to Warp six-point-five. I'm on my way to the bridge. Kirk, out."

Five

ALONE IN HER cubicle, Jean surveyed herself critically. The black undergarments of the Klingon uniform gave a leotard effect. She slipped on the tunic and tied it with a length of botanical twine at her waist. Maybe tomorrow she could find a way to mend her own clothes as an alternative. She took a long look at her room before calling the guard to take her to Kang. With rescue now more remote, this cubicle was at least a place of retreat where she was left alone. She was reluctant to leave it for whatever awaited her with the commander.

She was taken to the same wood-paneled council room where she had been before. Kang sat at the desk finishing some dispatches which he then handed to a waiting crewman. As the man left, Kang rose and crossed to Jean, taking in her new attire with an amused smile. Indicating the opposite door, he took her arm saying, "This time, let's walk through, shall we?" His smile broadened as she stepped through the door and realized that this was the Commander's personal quarters. "Yes, my dear, you were headed out of the frying pan into the fire."

Jean made no reply. In spite of her apprehension she looked about curiously. A small spartan room by *Enterprise* standards, it contained a bed, a small table, two chairs, and a low hassock. The opposite wall contained a clothes locker and a door apparently leading to the head. Above the bed was a mounted case containing a collection of dueling swords. The third wall contained a built-in bookshelf and a niche which held a small stylized image of a ferocious, fanged beast. Below the niche the table was set for two. The fourth wall, opposite the bed, was a huge viewscreen. Kang locked his blaster in a small cubicle above the clothes locker, then sprawled across the bed and slid back a wall section below the display case. Behind it was an elaborate control panel. He touched two buttons. The viewscreen beside Jean suddenly lit up with a view of space.

"That's the view dead ahead," Kang informed her. "I like to keep track of things when I'm in here."

She had remained standing where she came in. "Where are we headed?"

"The heart of the Klingon Empire." A tap on the door behind her caused Jean to jump. Her nerves were taut to the snapping point. "Come," Kang ordered. The door opened to admit a young crewman pushing a small servocart with covered dishes. He positioned it beside the table and started to transfer the dishes to the table. "She can do that. Dismissed."

Jean considered a protest and thought the better of it. It gave her something to do besides stand there and try to keep from screaming. Kang watched her from the bed.

"How long had you been stationed on Sherman's planet?" The question was quiet but Jean jumped as if he had shouted.

"About two planetary years."

"And before that?"

"I served a short time on the *Enterprise* prior to assignment to Sherman's planet."

"And before that?"

"I . . . I was born and raised on Aldebaran Colony. After university I worked a while at Aldebaran Three research outpost."

"Where'd you learn to throw like that?"

"Excuse me?"

"Where did you learn to fight, to throw a dagger like that?"

"Oh, that. It's not fighting really. I mean I didn't learn it as a combat form. It's a game I used to play as a child. The stiletto is smaller than your dagger, and thinner. We threw them at targets." Jean glanced at him briefly, wondering if her nervousness showed or if he saw it and was playing on it. He stretched and came off the bed in one smooth roll.

"It's an interesting style. I've never seen anything exactly like it. You will teach me how to do it after we eat." He sat down at the table. Jean followed suit, grateful for the knowledge that after-dinner entertainment would be target practice and not her.

Her days settled into a routine: breakfast in her room, the entire day including lunch with Aernath in the lab, and dinner with Kang. After dinner was devoted to dagger throwing or trying to master the intricacies of a Klingon game, *tsungu,* that reminded her of the Chinese chess that her grandfather used to play. During the day she kept her mind occupied with the work on the *quadrotriticale* and her "Czerny strain"—as Aernath called it. Although stiff and withdrawn if anything happened to remind him of his bond-status, Aernath seemed comfortable enough working with her. Many of the experimental conditions he set up seemed to bear no relationship to conditions on Sherman's planet but she could get no explanation from him.

One question she did get answered. "What's the heart of the Klingon Empire?"

"Our star system, of course."

However, each evening as she prepared to join Kang the sense of apprehension returned. She was walking in a fog, knowing neither destination nor terrain. Kang's behavior remained bland and innocuous as if, having obtained her initial cooperation, he had declared a truce. A brief truce she was convinced as she watched him warily. These evening tête-à-têtes were not merely for his amusement. He seemed to be observing her, measuring her, though for what purpose she could not fathom. His occasional questions and even more occasional comments yielded few clues. So she waited, afraid to disturb the calm.

Tonight she entered the council room just as Kang finished perusing the last dispatch. He sent the crewman off with orders for immediate transmission and hardly seemed aware of Jean as he got up and strode into his quarters. Stowing his gun, he pulled off his tunic and boots and sprawled on his bed. Tonight he called up section after section of the ship on the viewscreen snapping an occasional order to a startled crewman. Finally he put up the forward view and lay there staring morosely at the starscape.

After some moments she broke the silence. "Which star is our destination?"

Kang roused himself and rose in a single fluid movement. For a big man he was surprisingly quick and graceful. He padded over to the viewscreen. "That's it."

"When will we reach your planet?"

"Sometime tomorrow ni—" He whirled, demanding fiercely, "Who said it was my planet?"

"You did," said Jean, suddenly frightened. "You told me we were going to the heart of the Klingon Empire."

"And you deduced that was my planet?" Kang asked sharply.

"Isn't it?" Jean responded, determined not to reveal any further knowledge. Kang did not reply. Striving for a lighter tone she asked, "Shall I ring for dinner?" At Kang's nod she leaned across the bed to push the call button. She straightened and turned to find Kang directly in front of her. Her stomach turned to ice and her legs to water. He seized her hair in both hands, pulled her around and sat down on the bed forcing her to her knees in front of him.

" 'Lieutenant' Czerny, is it? I've checked your story by all the sources we have. It all tallies—but that. The unknown in the equation is the *Enterprise*. Why did Kirk call you that? What's your game? Is your story straight or is this another of Kirk's tricks? Because so help me, if it is, I'll kill you with my own hands—slowly—by inches. You have my word on that."

Warm, red terror washed over Jean. She didn't know what Kirk meant either—it was as if she'd forgotten something . . . "Please believe me, Kang. I'm telling the truth. No games. My problem is that I don't undersand what's going

53

on. Why have you brought me here? What do you expect me to do? What are you going to do?"

"What am I going to do?" Kang repeated softly. "Play some pawns and preserve an empire. I hope. And you, my dear, will do exactly as I tell you to do with no tricks. You're the unknown symbol in the equation all right and I don't like nasty surprises. If you do exactly as you're told, and we succeed, then afterwards you can name your price. You have my word on that, too." He released his grip abruptly and Jean collapsed forward until her forehead rested against the edge of the bed between his knees.

She struggled for calm, fought to make her body still, her thoughts rational. She had seen the Klingon commander angry before but this was different. He was like coiled steel ready to snap at any instant, wound taut by some urgency, some crisis she still didn't grasp. Gradually her breathing slowed, her trembling diminished. Still she knelt, staring at her knees, not daring to move. She felt Kang's hand on her back, lifting a lock of her hair, coiling it in his fingers. She glanced up. He was staring abstractedly at the viewscreen oblivious to her presence.

The tap on the door broke his reverie. "Come." The crewman entered, positioned the cart and left. With a sigh Kang rose, pulled her up and went to the table. They ate in silence. Finally he spoke. "We should attain orbital position around Tahrn sometime tomorrow night. We will beam down the following morning. There will be a ceremonial procession and an audience with the emperor. That will be conducted in ancient Court Klingonese. No translation will be necessary—simply follow my direction. After the audience you'll be assigned to the Royal Agricultural Station near the capital where you will work. If asked, you will declare your vow of unserving loyalty to me. You will not mention or discuss the Federation with anyone."

He seemed at an end. "And Aernath?" Jean ventured.

"He will work with you, of course. Also I've detailed Tirax to accompany you as my personal envoy. He will ensure that things go according to plan."

Jean shivered. She had only encountered Tirax once since

the duel and she did not relish the thought of extended contact with him.

When they finished eating, Kang dismissed her. On her way back to her room, she considered asking the guard to take her to Aernath's quarters instead. She needed the reassurance of talking things over with him. However, it could wait until morning, she decided. She valued the free and open working relationship Aernath had established with her, but it was still fragile. He became stiff and distant whenever anything reminded him of his bond status. Intruding on him now might precipitate that again.

She spent a restless night going over and over Kang's words trying to see how she and Sherman's planet fit into the picture. At last she fell asleep.

The next morning, still apprehensive, she ate little breakfast. Summoning the guard, she said, "I'll carry the dishes. We can drop them off on the way to the lab."

"No lab today, Czerny. You're confined to quarters."

"What!" Jean fairly shrieked in dismay. "But, why?"

"Kang's orders." He picked up her tray to go.

She seized his arm. "No, wait. Please go get Aernath then. I have to talk to him."

The Klingon looked annoyed. "My orders are to stand guard not run errands. I can tell you I'm not about to get decked just before planetfall. Now let go of me." He left, locking the door behind him. Jean went to the lavatory, buried her face in a towel and screamed. Then she cursed the guard and Kang, methodically consigning them to the nine consecutive rings of Aldebaranian hell. She settled down to wait. Perhaps Aernath would come on his own. Lunch appeared, then dinner, but not Aernath. She spent another sleepless night.

She did have a caller the following morning: a young woman carrying several bundles. The two women stared at each other curiously. "Who are you?" Jean asked.

"I'm from Court Protocol and I've been assigned to help you get ready for the audience." She proceeded to unpack her bundles on the table while stealing sidelong glances at Jean. Suddenly she blurted, "Are you really a human?"

"Yes," Jean answered. "Why?"

"Well, I . . . I've never met a human before."

"I suspect none ever got this close to Tahrn before," Jean commented drily.

"I wouldn't know about that," the woman answered hastily. She walked nervously around Jean, surveying her from various angles. "I'll do your hair first."

Jean sat quietly feeling strangely calm. Perhaps two sleepless nights and little food had something to do with it but the proceedings took on an unreal dreamlike quality. The woman fussed over her hair for a long while, combing, parting, braiding and pinning. "Do all humans have such pasty white skin?" she asked as she finished.

Being Eurasian, Jean had never considered her skin as pasty white. "Oh, no," she assured the woman solemnly. "We come in all colors—black, white, red, yellow, green and orange as well as your usual brown." The woman looked suitably impressed.

Her dress was of scratchy silver material which clung from shoulder to ankle. The short sleeves and cowled neck stood out stiffly. Jean insisted on retaining her leotards but the top undergarment had to go. With a flash of foresight, she gathered up her meager belongings into a bundle and took them along.

Though she had undoubtedly been transported aboard, Jean had no memory of the transporter room. She looked about curiously. Her attention was drawn to a pile of objects in one corner. She recognized Aernath's equipment, apparently awaiting transhipment. This confirmation of Kang's promise lifted her spirits. Aernath was going planetside, too. She stuffed her bundle in among the data sheets. At a slight sound she turned to meet the insolent appraisal of Kang. He had exchanged the somber uniform of the Imperial Fleet for an elaborate costume replete with jeweled dagger, dress sword, and shoulder cape.

"Excellent. You'll make a passable Klingon, yet," he said.

Although his tone was light and bantering, she read grim warning in his eyes. Their performance had begun and she was expected to play her role well. With just the merest hint

56

of defiance in the lift of her chin she replied evenly, "At your service, Commander."

He was flanked by Tirax and three other officers wearing black and silver uniforms, also new to Jean. In addition to swords they wore their phasers. Kang took the foremost transporter position and motioned the others into position behind him.

They materialized in what proved to be the Imperial Capital Spaceport. After reception formalities they moved by glide-car to the periphery of the port. The considerable traffic between Tahrn and her sister planet occupied much of the central spaceport. In addition, loading docks for interstellar freighters, berths for the occasional itinerant space trader, and various shuttlecraft from interstellar cruisers were scattered throughout other sections of the port.

The black and scarlet uniforms of Imperial Security were conspicuous among the ground personnel. Catching their arrogant stance and hostile glances, Jean began to see Tirax's presence in a new light. If she was important to Kang, he would protect her, and well she might need that protection in this hostile world! She shrank lower in the seat to be as inconspicuous as possible.

At Port Control they left the glide-car and walked a gauntlet of Imperial Security Guards. While Kang acknowledged their salutes casually, Jean kept her eyes on his heels, thankful for the flanking escort that surrounded her.

Awaiting them outside was a high-wheeled, canopied conveyance drawn by two beasts that at first glance she took to be the reality of the symbolic beast she had seen in Kang's quarters. A second glance revealed that they were not but produced the firm conviction that she desired no closer acquaintance. Kang entered the carriage and motioned. Awkwardly, she clambered up. He took a seat and indicated a small pillow at the heel of his left foot. "Kneel there and keep your head bowed." The four lieutenants stood on a platform at the back of the carriage.

The air was chill and the canopy blocked the faint sunshine. There seemed to be nothing warm about this world for Jean. Even with her head down she could see the crowds thronging the roadway, dressed mainly in browns, blacks, and maroons. Everywhere there was the scarlet flash of the grim-faced Security. Nonetheless, there was an air of festivity, of anticipation, and an enthusiastic reception of Kang. Whatever she might think of him, clearly he was popular here.

As she watched the passing crowds, something subliminal tugged at her awareness. Something wrong. Beneath her personal foreboding and the cheers of the Klingons there was something else. She redoubled her attention, searching the faces as they went by. What was she missing? Then she saw a woman holding a small child:—pot belly, stick legs, pinched listless face. Her memory supplied the high-pitched cry—*Marasmus!* Now she scanned the crowd intently, picking it out everywhere: thin arms, pinched faces, clothes too voluminous for their wasted occupants. Widespread evidence of malnutrition and near starvation! Forgetting her instructions, Jean looked up at Kang. His face was grim. "Kang!" she whispered. "Your people! What's wrong?"

"Famine!" One word through clenched teeth.

"Famine! But how? Why?"

"Blight. The fools! I told them that viral warfare was foolhardy. They wouldn't listen. Some escaped, mutated. Now both our major grains are affected. You see the results."

Suddenly Jean held the missing pieces of the puzzle. "The *quadrotriticale*—"

"Is resistant. Especially your strain."

"Why in the name of space didn't you tell me all this in the first place?"

He turned full face to her and demanded fiercely, "Would you have believed me?"

Her intended affirmation died under his glare. "I . . . no, I probably wouldn't have." Then she exclaimed, "Sherman's planet! That was just a feint to divert the *Enterprise,* wasn't it? Oh, Kang! Why didn't you just ask for the help?" Then she saw that strange look of his once again. This time she understood it for what it was: urgent need, pain, and indomitable pride.

Kang turned his face away. His voice was low and harsh. "A Klingon commander does not beg!"

Jean bowed her head, rested her cheek against his knee and shut out the faces of famine. "Kang," she said softly, "you don't need to worry. Given the situation I am truly at your service." This would be no disloyalty to the Federation.

The only reply was a single finger coursing down the back of her neck.

As they entered the city, she began to look about again. Massive was perhaps the most appropriate word for Klingon architecture. Buildings were almost all of stone or orange-colored bricks. Roofs were flat or dome-shaped. Not much precipitation here, she deduced. The city was laid out along broad avenues with heavy muscular statues of military heroes at intersections. She caught glimpses of crowded alleyways which formed a network of busy commerce between the broad avenues. Grand transport consisted mainly of small three-wheeled rigs pedaled by their occupants. She also saw large two-wheeled carts drawn by goatlike creatures. The ony powered vehicles in evidence were the sleek black glide-cars of I.S.G. patrol.

The procession ended in front of an imposing building whose dusky pink facade was decorated with silver and white tiles. Above the massive wooden doors was the same image Jean had seen in the niche of Kang's quarters. They left the carriage and climbed the steps between two rows of honor guards in the same black and silver uniforms as Kang's lieutenants. Music piped thinly as they walked the hall to the audience room. Spaced along the corridor were more members of the I.S.G. at stiff attention, their faces as hard as the stone at their backs. The audience room was filled with Klingons—the men in uniform, the women in more elaborate versions of the dress she wore. The far wall was a huge tile mosaic depicting the now familiar fanged beast rampant against a field of stars. In front of this was a raised dais with a single seat.

Jean gave an involunary start as she caught sight of its spare-framed occupant. Also wearing silver and white, this gray-haired Klingon bore a startling resemblance to Kang! Kang halted and raised his arm in formal Klingon salute. The emperor acknowledged his greeting. Unclasping his sword, Kang advanced to the dais, placed it across the emperor's knees and knelt, head bowed. The emperor extended his right hand for a ritual kiss. There was a brief exchange, then Kang rose and received his sword back. Another formal interchange and Jean caught a sharp glance in her direction from the dais. Further exchange. Then Kang beckoned her forward. She repeated Kang's obeisance. The emperor's hand was cold on her lips. She returned to her place as the ceremonial exchanges continued. At length the emperor rose and all the Klingons responded with a formal salute. After his exit the others followed, Kang in the lead.

In the hallway, Tirax pulled her to one side and took her along a side corridor accompanied by an armed member of the I.S.G. After several turns and a descent of steep narrow steps, they emerged outside. The waiting glide-car was gunmetal gray. The three of them got in. Jean had a brief glimpse of the driver's black and scarlet uniform before their escort opaqued the rear compartment windows.

Being wedged between the two Klingons in the small compartment gave Jean a claustrophobic feeling. The two men carried on a desultory conversation in that strange dialect she could not understand. She fought the sense of entrapment and isolation by reviewing her impressions of the Klingon capital. Most intriguing was the question of Kang's resemblance to the emperor. Were they related? She would have to ask Aernath. Aernath! How she longed to see a friendly face. She desperately needed to talk to him—the one person she could trust and rely on in this nightmare. She would never survive without the anchor of that relationship.

The ride stretched interminably. When the vehicle finally slowed, the guardsman cleared the windows. They were stopped at a checkpoint. On either side of the road as far as the eye could see stretched a four-meter metalmesh fence topped with flash rods. Any contact with that would be instant electrocution. The I.S.G. sentry checked their papers, scanned the occupants, and waved them through. A few meters down the road they were passed through a second barrier. The glide-car moved more leisurely now and Jean watched the countryside. This must be the agricultural station Kang had spoken of. Neat plots on both sides of the road contained dozens of kinds of plants. A few she recognized as species that she had seen in Aernath's collection. When she made it back to Federation territory she would have a wealth of new information to add to the botanical archives. But when would that be? She firmly refused to admit the "if" that hovered darkly in the back of her mind. Somehow, she promised herself grimly, she *would* get back.

The soil was sandy yellow. The experiment station blended neatly into the background as they approached. Only the bamboo-like windows surrounding the building made it noticeable. She had seen no true trees on this planet, only a scrubby growth reminiscent of the Aldebaranian *lesquit* bush. The glide-car stopped at one of the sand-colored one-story buildings. The ubiquitous I.S.G. sentry appeared and saluted stiffly as they emerged from the vehicle. *Space! They're everywhere,* Jean thought. Nowhere in the Federation had she been so oppressively aware of military structure as on this Klingon planet, not even at Starfleet Command!

The station administrator was a nervous little man in a brown uniform. He greeted Tirax effusively and eyed Jean apprehensively. "Is this the human who is going to work with Ag Tech Aernath?"

"That's her," Tirax affirmed.

"She has all the proper clearances?"

"For this project she does," Tirax growled.

"I see. Uh . . . is she clean?"

"She's housebroken." Tirax sneered, then added maliciously, "But don't let her scratch you. She might give you *aitchnit* fever."

The administrator looked flustered. "No, no, Lieutenant. I mean, are you sure she's not carrying any *Tseni* virus?"

Jean had suspected that Tirax nursed a grudge against her but he seemed equally bent on affronting this man. "Don't know how in space she could unless she's . . ." He made a crude reference to her anatomy. "Ask Aernath."

And may the Aldebaranian snilfpox *consume your genitals,* Jean thought viciously. She detested this Klingon as much as he seemed to despise her.

"Yes, of course, Lieutenant. I'll have you shown to your

quarters now." The administrator, eager to be rid of them, turned them over to an aide and rabbited back into his office.

Tirax held her elbow all the way to her room. It would be bruised for a week. He insisted on inspecting her room in maddening detail before he finally left—simply to harass her, she was convinced. Tirax gone, she went to the bathroom. As she was washing her face she heard her door open. Thinking Tirax had returned, she emerged braced for a confrontation.

Aernath stood in the doorway holding her bundle. "Hullo. Welcome to you . . ." He stopped short at the sight of her. "By the teeth and claws of Durgath! For a moment there I thought you were a Klingon!"

That blow breached her shield; Jean's defenses shattered. Aernath shut the door and dropped the bundle as she threw herself into his embrace. "Oh, Aernath!" The rest was incoherent sobs. She had not cried since that first night in detention on Kang's cruiser. All the accumulated terror, confusion, loneliness and need came pouring forth.

Aernath held her for a moment, then awkwardly patted her on the shoulder. "*Siee* . . . what happened? Did I insult you? Cheerny! Jean! Are you hurt?" He tried to disengage himself.

She clung to him even more tightly. "No, hold me."

Aernath's confusion turned to alarm. "What in space has happened to you? Cymele help me, is this normal human behavior? Are you all right?"

Jean nodded, then shook her head, then simply continued sobbing. Finally Aernath stood still, woodenly enduring her sodden embrace. Eventually, her tension spent, she became aware of his stance and released him. She smiled wanly. "Really, Aernath, it wasn't anything you did. Calling me a Klingon was just the final blow. I reached my breaking point. From now on—don't ever go a day without checking with me as long as I'm stuck in this damned Klingon Empire! I've been frantic the last two days to talk to someone I could trust."

"Understood. I shall do so," he said stolidly.

She looked at him. Damn! She'd pushed that button again. There he was: "No-excuse-Commander-Sir" bondperson.

What had done it this time? "Blast it, Aernath. I need a friend, not a puppet. You've gone all rigid and distant again. Of all the times—please, not now. What did I do wrong?"

He relaxed a trifle. "Well . . . first, let me ask. Is this . . . uh . . . typical human female behavior?"

"Women who make it to Starfleet aren't given to hysterics, but under the circumstances . . . yes, I would call it a normal response."

"Check. And what would a human male, a colleague of yours, do and feel under the circumstances?"

Jean wasn't sure what he was driving at so she chose her words carefully. "Pretty much the way you did at first. He'd try to comfort her, find out what was wrong, apologize if it was something he did. Some would feel awkward, some protective. Why do you ask?"

"No offense to you but a Klingon woman would never cry before a man. To do so implies either she is crazy, or he has humiliated her beyond endurance, or . . . she considers him less than a man. You're obviously not crazy. You knew I meant no insult when I called you a Klingon. That leaves—"

"Omigawd!" Jean groaned, "Aernath, look—"

He ploughed determinedly ahead. "You have that right. But you requested an explanation and I'm trying to give it. I told you once that *bond-right* is seldom invoked with an enemy. Klingons usually kill. This situation is especially bizarre. You're a human and a female . . . well, it's hard to know where one stands."

"Aernath," she said quietly, "I consider you as a man who is my friend and . . ." This was getting sticky. Aernath was the most compassionate, non-aggressive Klingon she had met. The last thing in all space she wanted to do was insult him. Yet how could she handle this without triggering in him some need to prove his Klingon masculine dominance? It was corny but she tried the old cliche, ". . . and like a brother to me."

The effect was astonishing. "Well, why didn't you just say so in the first place?" The embarrassed stiffness disappeared.

Obviously she had said just the right thing but she didn't

know why. "I didn't know that would mean so much to you."

Aernath chuckled. "Only one problem—you're older than I am."

"What's that got to do with it?"

"These days Klingons don't usually have more than two children," he replied as if that explained it all.

Jean was puzzled. "I don't see what that has to do with your being my brother."

Now Aernath was puzzled. "To be your brother, I'd have to be the third born."

She gasped, "Do you mean to tell me the first-born is always male?"

"Of course. First-born male, second-born female. Isn't it that way with humans?"

Jean giggled. "No, by and large we take potluck—at least the first time around. Say, speaking of families, is the emperor Kang's father?"

Aernath looked startled. "No, his uncle. What made you think he was his father? Succession is always through the sister's son."

"Well, he looks so much like Kang that . . . what did you say?"

But Aernath exclaimed simultaneously, "You *saw* him?"

"Yes," she said matter-of-factly. "I accompanied Kang for an audience today. Now what did you say about succession?"

He whistled softly. "The emperor is Kang's maternal uncle. In the normal course of events, Kang will be the next Klingon emperor. I thought you knew that."

They stared at each other soberly for a long moment. Then she said slowly, "Let me fill you in on what's happened to me in the past two days and then I think it's time you gave me a crash course in Klingon sociology and politics."

"Agreed. But we can't do it sitting here. Why don't you change into work clothes and I'll give you a tour of the place."

While Aernath waited outside, Jean retrieved the black pullover and her own now mended tunic. Hastily she undid

Protocol's two hours of work on the hair and tied it loosely at the nape of her neck. Then she joined Aernath.

He looked at her curiously. "That was a drastic change. Does it really bother you to look like a Klingon?"

"If all Klingons were like you, Aernath, it wouldn't bother me a bit. Unfortunately, you seem to be the exception that proves the rule."

"I guess you couldn't have a balanced and objective view of us growing up under Federation propaganda. Anyway, tell me what has happened to you for the past two days while I've been getting us transferred here."

Aernath gave her an extensive tour of the rolling fields around the experiment station. Ostensibly they were seeking suitable sites for growing *quadrotriticale*. As they walked, she retold her experiences beginning with dinner in Kang's quarters two nights earlier and finishing with Tirax's behavior on arrival at the station. "Now you can see why I was so upset by the time I saw you today. In spite of my bluffing with Kang, I know very little about your Empire. I was frantic to talk to you—get some information. And Tirax terrifies me. Is there any way we can keep him away from me?"

"Siee. You have had a full sixty hours, haven't you? Forget about Tirax. He can be handled. What about Kang? How do you feel about him after today?"

The question seemed casual but it touched the Gordian knot at the center of Jean's tangled emotions—a knot she was reluctant to cut open and examine. Hence, she avoided those penetrating blue eyes and did not notice the intense scrutiny Aernath gave her as she struggled with her answer.

"I honestly don't know, Aernath. Until today I would have called him a ruthless, unprincipled, but forthright scoundrel. But that was before I knew he was emperor-elect of the Klingon Empire. Space! You'd have to be tough as duralloy rivets to run this show!" She did not note his quick nod of assent. "The other thing I didn't see . . . that he didn't *let* me see until today . . . is how much he really cares about his own people. He talks of pawns and tactical sacrifices and he doesn't hesitate to use them, but underneath he feels the pain. Your culture has made the individual more expendable than ours. Kang accepts that, but in an odd way I think he cares, even about me. He showed restraint. Eknaar tried to tell me that, but I couldn't hear it. From what I've seen, that kind of restraint is a rare commodity among Klingons." She touched his arm lightly. "Don't be offended. I find him fascinating, but I don't share your loyalty."

"Nonetheless, you assess him accurately. The Commander and his crew are different from the average battle cruiser's. Kang can be a diplomat as well as a battle commander and he carries the soul of his people in his heart. He has the potential to make a great emperor."

"What makes it so tragic is that indomitable pride of his. He guards so carefully against any appearance of weakness that he can't even acknowledge his feelings. Does he ever unbend to anyone?"

"He used to—to one."

"Mara?"

Aernath nodded. "Yes. That first crew of his was even more remarkable than this one. It was a terrible tragedy when he lost that ship. I don't think he'll ever fully recover from that blow. And then, when Mara left him—"

"Yes, Mara. There's another piece of the puzzle I don't have. How does she fit into the picture?"

"The Klingon emperor doesn't really rule the entire empire autarchically. He is the chief Prince among equals. The second in rank is the regent of my planet, Peneli. Mara's brother occupies that throne at the moment—"

"Her brother!" Jean exclaimed. "Then that means—"

"That *if* Mara had a son by Kang he would occupy the throne of Peneli. Such a close alliance of the two premier planets of the Empire has not existed for generations. As you might imagine, there are some who would welcome this and some who would not."

"Well, that's all theoretical now. With Mara in exile there's no chance—"

"She's not in exile; she's underground. Her brother has never theld-barred her. As long as he doesn't, nobody dares touch her personally. And I don't think he will. After all, that would kick off a tremendous struggle over succession.

As it is now, things may change and then it would be convenient to return Mara—"

"You mean her brother would turn her over to Kang, force her to bear his child?"

"Of course."

"That's barbaric! If Mara is pro-Federation and Kang is determined to destroy us, then—why, he'd kill her!"

Aernath looked at her curiously. "Whatever gave you the idea that Kang wants to destroy the Federation? I never said that."

"You don't have to," Jean sputtered. "Just listen to him talk. He hates Kirk's guts for a start. Of course, he won't start anything right now because of this crisis with the grain but after that—"

"That's a strange thing for you to say if you're going to work to solve that crisis."

"Aernath! I can't stand by and let people die, even Klingons. Besides, the Federation is strong. It can take care of itself."

"*That* is just Kang's point," he answered. "He never said he wanted to destroy the Federation. He just doesn't trust you. We must negotiate from a position of strength, but he was willing to negotiate—eventually. His mission with that first ship was to assess the Federation's strength. He and Mara came away from that *Enterprise* encounter holding very different positions. Kang was badly shaken by the experience of losing his ship and most of his crew, being outwitted by Kirk, then having to accept Kirk's magnanimity in delivering him to a safe port of transfer. Now he's doubly sure he can negotiate only from a position of overwhelming strength. Mara, on the other hand, felt immediate negotiation was the best approach."

Jean shook her head. "It's so incredibly complicated. And now the food crisis. How bad is that? Kang didn't tell me much. Is it only on Tahrn?"

"No, it's worst here but it has spread to Peneli also and at least one other planet that I know of. Kang would know if there are more."

"How about you, Aernath? Where do you stand in all this?"

"Where do you think I ought to stand?" he countered.

"Well, obviously I think Mara is right but I guess that would be a dangerous position to hold as a crew member on Kang's ship."

He grinned. "Obviously. Each crew member must tender and pass Vow to his commander. He may never be my emperor but he is my commander. Besides, you've ordered me to keep my skin whole too."

Tahrn was a hot planet with a slightly higher gravity than Aldebaran Colony. Jean soon adjusted to her surroundings, but the obverse was not true. Meals were served in the station mess hall. Hostile silence would descend with her entry and persist until she left. Klingons avoided her table or any near it—all except for Aernath who did join her until she insisted he stop. It was clear that he enjoyed the camaraderie of his colleagues and she feared if he persisted it would jeopardize his acceptance by them. "After all, we work together all day," she pointed out. "I can stand an hour of isolation." Nonetheless, she found she preferred to take her tray out to the shade of the *seyilt*, the bamboo-like plants, in the courtyard. That was how she met Tsuyen.

Tsuyen's family was one of several who lived on the station and served as laborers.. She worked as a general kitchen maid and also helped in one of the livestock barns. She customarily ate in the courtyard and after a few days her curiosity overcame her cultural reservations. Through her Jean began to gain insight into some of the more mundane aspects of Klingon life that Aernath neglected in his complicated disquisitions on interplanetary politics and intrigue. In return, Jean provided an endless source of fascination and amusement to Tsuyen.

This evening after third mess Jean lingered in the courtyard. Tsuyen had promised to demonstrate the use of a Klingon lap loom to her. The women of this region were apparently famous for their weaving and on several occasions Jean had noticed them at work by their doorsteps. Her kitchen duties done, Tsuyen appeared with her loom. Settling her back against the low stone wall of the courtyard, she bunched her skirt above her knees. With one sturdy foot planted in the dirt, she held the loom taut between toes and waist. With the other foot she worked the two wands attached to the warp. Jean watched as she worked rhythmically. "Let me try it," she coaxed, as she pulled off her boots and sat on the ground beside the Klingon woman. Tsuyen helped her attach the loom to her waist and showed her how to hold it. Jean worked with clumsy concentration until suddenly her toes slipped.

With a peal of laughter, Tsuyen pushed her over into the basket of weft threads. The loom was a tangled mess. "You're as clumsy as a boy-child with that. Here, give it to me." She retrieved the loom and skillfully untangled it. Then she set to work again. "Is it true Commander Kang captured you and spared your life?"

"He pulled me out of the wreckage of my lab after an earthquake. I'd have died if someone hadn't come along about then," Jean replied.

"So to repay your *bond-debt* you're working on a new food grain to feed his people. That's good." She nodded her vigorous approval. "It's a fitting tribute to that commander. You're fortunate it was Kang. From him it may even win you your freedom if you succeed."

"It better," Jean said drily. Then she asked, "What would you say if I told you it was a gesture of goodwill from the Federation, that they would have given help anyway if you had asked?"

Tsuyen spat derisively at her feet. "That's a very bad joke. Just the sort of sneaky trick your Federation would try though, to spot our weak points. But you're not like that. You'll work out your *bond-debt* like a true Klingon." As far as the woman was concerned that settled the issue.

Jean glanced at the lengthening *seyilt* shadows across the courtyard and realized with a start that Tirax was lounging in a doorway watching her. She wondered if he had caught any of their conversation. Kang had been explicit about not discussing the Federation and she felt sure Tirax would delight in reporting anything that would compromise her position. Seeing he was noticed, Tirax sauntered past the two women and left the courtyard. Jean suppressed a shiver. At Tsuyen's glance, she explained, "I think that man really hates me."

69

"Then stay clear of him," Tsuyen responded promptly. "He's about as safe as a cornered *slean*." The *slean* was a furred predator of the Tahrnian grasslands. Jean had seen one that had been bagged on the station perimeter by Security. She found the comparison apt.

They had arrived in early spring. In addition to regular test plots, she and Aernath were testing both kinds of *quadrotriticale* under various special conditions. The work was going well. Spending her days in the fields or lab with Aernath and the field hands, Jean could almost forget she was deep in hostile territory, half a galaxy away from her own planet.

This morning the illusion was almost complete. She had risen early and left the compound before first mess. Now, seated in the grove Tsuyen had showed her a few days before, she reveled in the tranquil scene below her. The sun had just risen. A light dawn breeze rippled the surface of the pond in the hollow. The normal sounds of birds and insects rose around her. A graceful orange-furred animal was feeding at the edge of the pond. It fished here and there in the shallows with quick movements of its forepaws. Suddenly it reared, alert, and faced in her direction. Could the breeze have carried her scent? Jean wondered. The sudden crack of a branch behind her brought her to her feet.

Tirax stood a short distance away holding the snapped stick in his hands. He continued his ominous appraisal of her. At length, in a tone of quiet menace he demanded, "Do you have a dagger with you, human?"

Jean's heart was pounding and her throat went paper dry. She tried to keep her voice steady. "Why should I need one here?"

He tossed aside the sticks. "You are a fool. Do you know what I can do to you?" Panic rooted Jean to the spot. Tirax watched her, somehow cognizant of her terror, deliberately savoring it. Then he sprang, seizing her wrist and twisting it cruelly behind her. He pulled her roughly against him, glaring pure venom. "Any—thing—I—want—to . . . So could anyone else on these grounds. If anything happens to you, Kang will personally claim my life by slow torture. Now you get back to the compound and don't go wandering off by yourself." He released her abruptly and turned on his heel without a backward glance.

Frightened, Jean started to follow automatically. Then she rebelled. Running forward, she confronted the startled Klingon. "No!" she screamed furiously, "I'm not going to let you take away what little bit of peace and beauty I can find here. Kang ordered me to work on this station. He ordered *you* to protect me. I'm doing my job. Now you do yours!" With her last bit of fury she added viciously, "And stay out of my sight while you're doing it. You proved this morning you can do that!"

Tirax stared at her in astonishment. The hatred in his eyes was joined by a grudging respect. *"Siee!* Kang is right. You'd defy Durgath himself in his lair. Fortunately for you, human, I follow orders. But someday your usefulness to Kang will be at an end. Then we shall see how tough you are." He strode off in the direction of the station.

Amazed at her own audacity now that the fury had passed, Jean contemplated the receding back of her foe, knowing that nothing but Kang's word stood as shield between her and that implacable hatred. She had best take what precautions she could. That afternoon she persuaded Aernath to give her a dagger. Although she persisted in her solitary walks she never again ventured out without it in her boot, Klingon-style. Whether Tirax trailed her, she never knew. If he did, he took her advice and stayed out of sight.

Carefully worded questioning of Aernath yielded the information that Tirax also was not of Tahrn but from Tsorn, one of the rim planets of the Klingon Empire. While apparently completely loyal to Kang as his commander, he made no attempt to conceal his hostility to humans and the Federation. He was of the faction most opposed to any negotiation. "And therefore, he would also be opposed to any reconciliation of Mara with Kang," Aernath concluded. "Though, of course, he would never say that openly."

Jean drew her cloak tightly around her shoulders, shivering slightly in the early morning chill as she and Aernath watched the ploughman. Both the Czerny strain and the regular one had done well. Some of the early stands were near maturity. The Klingon laborer was preparing a fall-planting test plot, using the traditional animal drawn plough still in common use in much of the countryside. They watched the ancient double plough lay down neat dead-furrows. The moist smell of fresh turned soil permeated the air. She filled her lungs appreciatively.

"Let's go check plot K-Thirty-six and see if any heads look ready yet," Aernath suggested.

Jean toed a clod of dirt pensively. "Aernath, how long will we be left here? Do you know?"

He shot her a quick penetrating glance. "Hard to say. My orders were 'detachment for temporary duty assignment'. That is usually less than a year, but it could be longer."

"How will you know? What will happen next? And what about me?"

"I'll get my orders sent from Kang. The next step—for you or me—that's up to him. We'll just have to wait." He put a cloaked arm around her shoulder drawing her closer to his side. "Meanwhile, you couldn't ask for a better place to work than here. Let's look at K-Thirty-six."

"You mean *you* couldn't ask for a better place," Jean said. "I could—any place in Federation space would do."

Aernath stopped and drew her into a gentle embrace. "Heeey! You're really upset this morning. Has Tirax been after you again?"

She shook her head, then simply stood a moment savoring the physical pleasure of cloak and body warmth and the mental comfort of a friendly touch. Such a fragile thing against the weight of hostility and the vast stretches of space that separated her from home. She tried to put her despair into words. "No, but Tirax symbolizes the whole Klingon Empire that stands between me and home. You make it possible for me to endure it but there's no way you can change the outcome. That leaves Kang. He frightens me, but he is my only line back to the Federation. What if he simply leaves me here—abandons me—to Tirax? There's nothing I can do to stop it."

"We are all prey for Durgath's palate," Aernath responded soberly. "But don't go looking for his lair. His claws haven't closed on you yet. Tell you what, after we get

72

this plot planted let's take the rest of the day off and hike up to your pond. Maybe we'll even see your mystery animal."

Obviously he meant to cheer her up. She smiled and changed the subject. "I keep hearing references to Durgath. Who or what is he anyway?"

"The giver and taker of life, also the Klingon god of war. You must have seen his image in the emperor's reception hall?"

"The beast on the mural?"

"Yes."

"Oh! And the image in Kang's quarters on the cruiser."

"Right. All cruisers are dedicated to Durgath. On most worlds the ruler is accepted as his temporal representative. He also plays a prominent role in the m—*Siee!* Look at that! I told you this plot would be ready today."

In the cool morning sunlight the heads of grain gleamed coppery gold. Other things forgotten for the moment, Jean watched as Aernath plucked and threshed one on the palm of his hand. Blowing away the chaff, he held out his palm to her. She took a few kernels and chewed them experimentally. Aernath popped the rest in his mouth. "Yeah. It's ready. Let's get some samples for analysis. They can cut the rest this afternoon."

This first plot had been planted under standard conditions. Some of the later experimental-condition plots were nearly ready, too. They completed their tour of the plots with satisfaction. Aernath handed her the harvested samples. "Here, take these back to the lab and thresh them out. They'll be dry enough for analysis tomorrow. Then why don't you see if you can talk Tsuyen out of a food parcel for this afternoon? I'll go supervise the fall planting."

Back in the lab she spread the newly harvested kernels carefully on a shallow rack, then gave some brief instructions to Kuri, the young ag-tech apprentice who had been working with them for the past few weeks. She found Tsuyen in the kitchen and wheedled a promise of a food basket out of her. Then she rejoined Aernath.

The point of this planting was to duplicate conditions as they existed in much of the planet's rural areas. Thus, much of the work was being done by hand. After ploughing, the land was worked with a heavy double-headed implement, a sort of cross between a mattock and a rake. She tried her hand at it but that caused so much general merriment and distraction among the field hands that she gave it up. One old farmer patted her arm consolingly. "Don't be discouraged, daughter. It takes long years of practice to swing it smoothly. You'll get it in time."

Jean was both warmed and saddened by this. She encountered little personal hostility among the farm laborers though their prejudices against humans in general were intact and vigorous. But was she in fact condemned to spend the rest of her life here?

By mid-afternoon, the planting nearly done, they directed their attention to crews cutting plots K-36 and K-43. Aernath had decided the second one was ready as well. The autumn sun was at its warmest. Satisfied that all was going according to schedule, Aernath turned to Jean. "Well, shall we pick up the basket and head for the pond?"

They had a pleasant hike to the pond. Seated on a flat rock at the water's edge watching small pond creatures skim below the surface, Aernath returned to her gloomy forboding of the morning. "There's no love lost between Klingons and humans as you well know. Your Federation now lies athwart our natural path of expansion. The hostility is natural. So are your fears I guess, but I don't think you understand the importance of what you and I are doing here. It's vital. Because of that no one is going to harm you. We have the finest resources of the Empire at our disposal. Surely that says something to you."

"Weighed against that is what Tirax says," she replied grimly. "That when my usefulness to Kang is at an end then he will be waiting to get me. I don't flatter myself that I'll get a chance to defend myself then. By our success it would seem I am signing my own death warrant. What's to stop him?"

Perhaps she had cut close indeed. Aernath's response was angry. "Kang's word and mine, that you are indispensable to the project. After all these months you still really don't give Klingons any credit for honor or integrity, do you? The Commander has given you his word! Or does that count for nothing among your Starfleet officers?" His blue eyes flashed.

Jean swallowed an angry retort. "Aernath, I'm sorry. It's just that I feel so vulnerable when Tirax—"

"Tirax!" Disgustedly he flung the straw he had been chewing into the pond creating a microcosm of watery pandemonium. "Yes! He *would* cheerfully cut your throat and sometimes I think I understand why. By the claws of Durgath, he is a Klingon Imperial Fleet officer! He lives by his vow. He will not contravene his commander's orders."

In his agitation he stood and strode to the bank. "Jean, your 'Czerny strain' is the more promising of the two. You're the originator of that grain. If we encounter any problems, your knowledge and experience with it will be irreplaceable. Kang understands that—I've told him more than once. Controlling access to you as well as seed supplies gives him tremendous power in the cultivation and use of this grain. And, Cymele help us, we *need* that grain!" He dropped to her side again with a groan. "The death rate on Tahrn this year is approaching two percent. Infant mortality is soaring. The harvest is very poor this year and the emperor has just announced more stringent rationing for the winter. There have been riots, including a small one in the capital itself. And I heard this morning that the virus has spread even more rapidly on Peneli and Klairos than here."

This was news to Jean. With a jolt she realized how isolated they were in the cocoon of the experiment station. Here, there was no evidence of famine and starvation. Hearing no news from beyond the gate, she had gradually banished the images of suffering from her mind. Now she saw them again in Aernath's face. "Aernath, forgive me. I didn't know." Impulsively she reached out to cradle his head against her shoulder. It was the wrong move. She felt him stiffen and withdraw.

"I shouldn't have spoken of it. However, you can take comfort in knowing there are that many fewer Klingons waiting to cut your throat."

"Now that's really not fair! I didn't ask to be brought here. But I *would* have volunteered to come and help stave off this famine if you could have swallowed that damned Klingon pride long enough to admit the disaster and ask for help. I want to save those lives as much as you do. But for God's sake, don't ask me to pretend the hostility isn't there or that some days it doesn't half terrify me to death." She was shaking with indignation.

Aernath took this in with some consternation. "All right. All right. Truce. *Siee!* I intended this afternoon to cheer you up and now I'm only making it worse. I hope I have at least convinced you that we are not about to toss you bound into the teeth of Durgath?"

She was not entirely convinced that her position was so secure as he painted. Despite what he chose to tell Kang— for whatever reasons of his own—she knew Aernath now knew almost as much as she did about her grain. Nonetheless she managed a smile. "Well, you have convinced me that you won't and that you firmly believe Kang won't either. For the moment, I'll have to be content with that."

"Let's eat." He opened the basket, poured and handed her a cup of Tahrnian ale, "To our success and survival."

"I'll drink to that!" she responded fervently.

Their picnic was cut short by dark masses of clouds rolling in from the northwest. It had also grown markedly colder. The storm struck before they reached the station compound and both of them were soaked to the skin by the time they reached their quarters.

The storm lasted much of the night and in the morning Jean found a light dusting of snow on the ground as she stepped outside. She immediately turned in the direction of their test plots. Aernath had beat her there. They stared in dismay at the wind and snow damage. A couple of plots were completely ruined. The others would recover or could be salvaged by immediate harvest.

"At least it didn't lodge badly. We can save most of it."

"Yes. I'll get the hands on it right after breakfast. It's good we got the first two plots done yesterday. We can run those analyses this morning. Come on, let's go eat." He set off for

76

the mess hall. They ate together and shortly were joined by Kuri who had also been out to survey the damage. Aernath gave him the responsibility of supervising the salvage harvesting.

Heads together, Jean and Aernath bent over the analyzer watching the results emerge with mounting elation. "And protein . . . twenty-six point nine percent!" *Cheerny!* We did it!" In his exultation he seized her in a hug and swung her around. "Now *that* will feed an empire . . ." Abruptly his voice trailed off and he stiffened, looking over her shoulder toward the lab door. Jean turned in his grasp to see what had startled him.

An eminence grise, Kang stood in the doorway regarding them somberly. One could not tell whether he had just arrived or had been observing them for some time.

"Commander Kang! I . . . uh . . . we . . . were not expecting you," Aernath stammered.

"So it would appear," Kang responded drily. "You seem inordinately exuberant this morning. I trust you have results to report that are commensurate with your emotional display?"

Jean moved quietly to one side of the lab as Kang took a seat and Aernath launched into an enthusiastic and detailed report of their summer's work. Kang's appearance had produced a strange melange of feelings and Jean welcomed a few moments to sort them out. Much as she had wanted him to appear, now that he was here the old fear was back—and the fascination—in the sense that Spock would use the word. The Klingon commander was a complex and intriguing person and it was fascinating to watch him in action. Fascinating, that is, as long as she was the observer and not the recipient of his actions. She also felt relief and even genuine pleasure, which surprised her.

They had done a good job and she knew it. Aernath was giving her due credit in his report. Kang had promised her her own price if they succeeded. In her optimistic moments she convinced herself that he would indeed keep his word and release her. His presence now seemed to confirm this. That could certainly account for the pleasure at seeing him she decided.

Kang interrupted Aernath's report. "Czerny, report to the administration building."

On her way, she stopped in her room. She was not surprised to find it empty of her belongings. The only items remaining were two weavings on the wall. She retrieved them quickly. One was her own and the other a gift from Tsuyen. She made a detour to the kitchen and left hers as a parting gift to Tsuyen. The woman seemed geniunely sorry to see her go. "Good-bye, *Cheerny*. Clear space and good landings."

Six

THEY DROVE DIRECTLY to the spaceport and beamed aboard Kang's cruiser. A crewman took her to a room forward in the officer's section. She explored her new surroundings curiously. A bed with attached small sofa occupied one corner. At the foot of the bed was a small desk. A table and two chairs completed the furnishings. Recessed over the bed was an aquarium with a number of small brightly colored fish. The niche over the table held not the familiar image of Durgath but an exquisitely wrought statue of a lithe female form: Cymele, the goddess of the fields and forests. Tsuyen had told her that Cymele was also the protectress of women. Thoughtfully, Jean turned it over in her hands. It was made of some unknown ivory-colored substance, warm and satiny to the touch. Replacing it she turned to unpack her belongings. Inside the clothes locker were several standard female Klingon uniforms. Startled, she momentarily wondered if she had been assigned to bunk with a female crewmember. She had seen none on board. Moreover, there was no other evidence that the room was occupied. The clothing must be for her. It fit. Emboldened by her apparent change in status, she opened her door and checked the corridor. The guard was there.

"Do you require something?"

Nonplussed, she gave the first command that popped into her head. "Accompany me to Aernath's lab."

If he was surprised to see her he didn't show it. "Hi. You're just in time to help me unpack."

As usual she was impatient for news. "Aernath! What did he say to you? What is going to happen now?"

He shook his head briskly. "Here, help me with this, will you?" He carefully positioned a large potted plant, then turned to her with a wicked grin. "Now all they'll pick up is static if they're monitoring. It drives Security crazy. They must check that 'bird' a dozen times a year, but it only 'malfunctions' erratically. That," he indicated the plant, "produces electromagnetic impulses that jam the pickup. An obscure botanical fact I've never bothered to publish."

Though chagrined at forgetting Security for a moment, Jean giggled. Sometimes Aernath seemed almost human. "O.K. Give. What did Kang say? Where are we going now?"

"Klairos. I was hoping for Peneli but seasons are wrong and besides, the blight is worse on Klairos I gather. So that's where we go. Kang is very pleased—whatever his grand plan is, he says things are going accordingly." He frowned. "I wish I had a better idea what he was thinking."

"What can you tell me about Klairos? And did Kang say anything about me?"

"It's a fairly recently settled rim world. Primitive culturally. Most of the inhabited areas are mountainous. The lowlands are largely marsh I gather—not reclaimed yet. I'll get the tape for us to review tomorrow if you like. As for you, no, Kang didn't say anything specific. But I told you he was pleased. I expect he'll let you know himself."

"I guess he already has, in a way. I've been put in officer's quarters."

He grinned. "See, what did I tell you? Hope he put you next to Tirax. It would serve you right after all your suspicions."

She smiled wryly, not bothering to belabor the point that a gilded cage is still a cage. So far Aernath had been right in his predictions but she still harbored that cold 'if' whenever

80

she thought of home. Kang held the key, but did he ever intend to use it?

The lab shipshape once more, Aernath invited her to eat with him in science mess as Kang and his lieutenants were winding up a couple of days of meetings planetside. "And I'd give my glory fruit bush to know what they're talking about. There's a full hand of cruisers in orbit here right now, and a Romulan ship, too. I sure hope the *Tseni* virus hasn't hit any new planets."

Eager to exploit her new status, Jean readily accepted Aernath's invitation. The mess room was largely empty. Most of the crew, being from Tahrn, were apparently taking shore leave. Not surprisingly the xenozoologist who joined them was from Peneli. She listened as he and Aernath exchanged snippets of rumor and speculation about Peneli. The conversation turned to their stay on Tahrn. Aernath reported not only their success but also the latest inroads of the famine and the populace's response to more stringent rationing.

"It's a grim time," the zoologist agreed. He gestured at the half-empty room. "Those who've taken shore leave come back with similar reports." He shook his head. "I've no desire to revisit Tahrn at a time like this." The two Klingons lapsed into a gloomy silence.

Jean changed the subject. "Then you've been on Tahrn before?"

"Yes, I did field work here for some time."

"Perhaps you can identify an animal for me. No one at the station recognized it from my description." She described her orange furred fisher.

"Sounds like a *boryx*—not too common. Nasty little beast."

"Why do you say that?"

"There are two varieties: barred and plain. Won't share a territory. Vicious fighters—the males castrate each other frequently. So they aren't too common. But that's nothing to what you'll face on Klairos. Now there's a planetful of nasty creatures."

"You've been there, too?" she asked.

"Nope. Wouldn't mind spending some time there collect-

ing specimens—if I had a healthy supply of photon torpedoes and a reliable scanner alarm. They come at you from
air, land and marsh."

"Sounds like a great place for a quiet little agricultural
experiment." She grimaced. "I'm not sure I want to know,
but what can we look forward to?"

Among the zoological delights that awaited them according to him were the dagger-tooth: a 120 kilo, furred predator
of the mountains; the greater snowbird with a three-meter
wingspread and talons that could carry off a full-grown
Klingon; plus a host of uncatalogued amphibians that made
the marshes acutely inhospitable. Dr. Eknaar joined them as
the zoologist completed his description of one amphibian
that sounded to Jean very much like the mythical Terran
dragon she had heard of from her grandfather's fairy tales.

"Some of their microscopic creatures aren't too pleasant
either," the doctor added. "At least for Klingons. My guess
is they'd work about the same on human physiology. You
better come by with Aernath tomorrow and start your
immunizations."

"Thanks, I will."

As they recycled their trays Aernath remarked, "Well, I
think I'll go play a little tsungu down in Security and see
what I can pick up about the conclave. Want me to see you
to quarters first?"

She shook her head decisively. "No thanks. I can get
myself there." It wasn't exactly home territory, but the
cruiser had a familiar feel to her now. She was prepared to
use her new freedom of movement aboard to the hilt. She
passed through the corridors unchallenged and the guard at
her door merely nodded as she approached. At the door she
touched the interior thumb lock. It worked. Casually she
asked, "Will you be here all night?"

"If you wish."

"I do not," she replied firmly. "You may go. Good night."
When she checked a moment later he was gone.

She thumbed the lock and cheerfully made for the head.
Inside she looked with sudden dismay at the opposite wall.
There was another door obviously connecting to adjoining
quarters. The door leading to her quarters had a thumblock

but this one had none. Whoever occupied the other room could lock her out but she could not reciprocate. Her new sense of security and confidence evaporated as she recalled Aernath's joking comment. Had Kang put her next to Tirax? There was no sound audible from the other room but she knew Tirax was with Kang. Well, no shower tonight she decided. Quickly completing her toilet, she went back to survey her room thoughtfully.

Pulling off her boots she slipped out her dagger, then installed herself with pillow and blanket on the floor of her clothes locker, leaving one door slightly ajar. Not especially comfortable but it afforded a measure of cover in case of an uninvited visitor. She spent a cramped but otherwise uneventful night.

The cruiser had left orbit by morning. After a call at sick bay for immunizations, they spent the day viewing tapes on Klairos. Jean learned that among the customs Aernath had characterized as odd and primitive were the practice of having several children, an extremely low status for women even by Klingon standards, and direct patrilineal inheritance. Of the latter he said, "Barbaric custom. Very antisocial. You can't maintain a decent social structure with an ingrown system like that."

Apparently, the bewildering system of inheritance through the maternal uncle fostered a set of interrelationships and loyalties that were of great value in Klingon society. Someday she must explore this in more detail. At the moment their task was to make plans for introducing the new grains here. They would be arriving at the end of winter and would need to get underway at once as the growing season in the mountain highlands was very short for their purposes.

"It would be extremely helpful if we could field-test it in the lowlands as well," he fretted. "I hope we can requisition at least one small section of polderland while we're there."

"That would mean a full twenty day gain in growing season but a lot more moisture. May drop the protein a bit. It'll be interesting to see what happens." Given the choice, she would have preferred to be working in Federation territory. Nonetheless, Jean was caught up in the rising excitement of another chance to test her strain's performance under diverse conditions. And, she hoped, halt a famine in the process.

She returned to her quarters at the end of the day to find the guard had a message. "The commander sent a package for you and expects you for dinner."

The package was a dress of some soft shimmering material. Kang must be pleased indeed, she reflected as she dressed for dinner. Perhaps she should approach him not only about security from her adjoining crewmember but also with the question of her release. They had heard no reports of any virus spread beyond the three original planets. If work went as well on Klairos as it had on Tahrn, surely Aernath could tackle the problem on his own planet without her aid. If she could get Kang to give his word now, she could face the months on Klairos with equanimity. If . . . if . . . if . . . finally there was that last cold "if" still sitting on the threshold of her consciousness. In spite of Aernath's assurances, could she really trust a Klingon commander to deal fairly with someone from the Federation? Especially this one? But tonight she felt optimistic. She greeted the guard almost gaily. "Commander's quarters please and then you may go for the night."

She was surprised to find Kang's quarters were close, in fact, around the corner on the next corridor. He seemed geniunely pleased to see her. "You're very formal this evening, my dear."

She smoothed her skirt with unaccustomed diffidence. "Well, it is a beautiful gown and it seemed appropriate to wear."

"Of course. What I meant is I expected you to come through from your quarters." As they entered his room, he gestured to the opposite door.

Suddenly the geometry clicked and Jean realized her quarters adjoined his. She laughed in instant relief at being delivered from Tirax. Seeing his questioning look, she explained, "I was afraid you had put me next to Tirax. Aernath said it would serve me right for being so suspicious."

"Yes, both Aernath and Tirax have reported your . . . um . . . antipathy." He smiled. "It's a pity. He is one of my top lieutenants. Do you realize what a formidable enemy you have made?"

"It's his choice not mine. I bear no enmity toward anyone unless they mean to destroy the Federation." She stared pointedly at Kang.

The Klingon nodded. "Tirax feels the Federation is soft and can be easily defeated. I do not share that view but it is important that I hear it—that Tirax sit on my council. It has not interfered with his loyalty to me nor my ability to meet situations flexibly. Can you live with that?"

Jean returned his gaze. "It looks as though I'll have to. But you know my feelings on the matter."

He sighed. "I wonder . . ." He stowed his gun and brought out a bottle and a small wine glass which he set on the table.

"Speaking of my feelings: the work has gone well. It promises to be a success. You once said that if we succeeded I could name my price. I'd like to name it now."

He glanced up from filling the glass. "What is offered is not enough?" He seemed surprised.

A gilded cage . . . thought Jean tiredly. "No."

"Very well. Name your price."

"Release me. I want my freedom."

He smiled again. "Appropriate. Consider it done." He took the wine glass and solemnly spilled a single drop before the image in the niche. Facing her he asked, "Will you share my cup?" She nodded. He raised it in formal salute. "For survival and success—yours and mine." He took a sip and handed the glass to her.

Intent on his long awaited promise, she took the glass and repeated the toast, "For survival and success—yours and mine." As he seemed to expect it, she drained the glass and handed it back to him. He set it carefully before the image, then turned back to her. "Will you arrange to return me to the Federation after the tour on Klairos?"

Again he looked surprised. "Return you after Klairos? That would be decidedly premature. For one, you know entirely too much to be released so soon to say nothing of other considerations . . ."

"Well, if not then . . . then when?" Jean demanded in dismay. The icy "if" plunged full across the threshold.

"In good time, my dear, in good time. But as for now . . ." She suddenly found herself in Kang's grip. It happened when she least expected it. Fearing that ultimate tribute exacted of women by triumphant adversaries from time unrecorded, she struggled desperately, but he held her as easily as an Aldebaranian *jequard* holds her kit. He pulled her to him forcing her lips against his. That same cold fury with which she twice had fronted Tirax rose again. Wrenching her lips free she hissed, "Let go of me! Don't touch me." To her peripheral astonishment he released her. Trembling with fury, she faced him. "All right. You've got your pawn and symbol! I'm powerless to do anything about that. But so help me, if you try to lay a hand on me I'll kill myself and take you along in the process if I can!"

Kang seemed stunned for an instant, then his face contorted with anger. His voice was low and menacing. "Get out of here before I save you the trouble of killing yourself. Get out!" With the last words he seized the wine glass and hurled it at her. She fled to the sound of shattering glass; through to her room, out her door, and down empty corridors to the lab. There she locked the door and proceeded to barricade it with miscellaneous moveable lab equipment.

Alone with the icy conviction that she now had no hope of seeing Federation territory again, she waited for the inevitable assault on the door. Methodically she went through the lab collecting her seed. It made a considerable pile. As she worked she attempted to marshal her thoughts. Damn! She'd been such a fool to think one could trust a Klingon. Obviously Kang had never had any intention of releasing her. But Aernath was the worst. Sometimes he seemed so human that she'd let herself be persuaded by his apparent conviction and had relaxed her vigilance. No more. She paused with her hand on the handle of the disintegrator chute.

Stick-limbed children with pinched faces marched in front of her eyes. She brushed her hand angrily across her forehead as if this would physically dispel them. She would not let that hold her hostage any more. She tried to banish it with images of home, her friends, Starfleet, the *Enterprise*. That was where her loyalty lay. What she got was an image of the *Enterprise* officers as she had last seen them from Kang's bridge. Strangely it didn't help. That vague unease she had felt at Captain Kirk's last words returned again. Something she felt she ought to remember but it just eluded her grasp . . . something Spock had said . . . 'there are always choices'? . . . no, something else . . . 'considerable latitude'? . . . it wouldn't come . . .

She smiled bitterly to herself. What choices would the Vulcan find in her situation now? She saw precious few. Dump the seed in the disintegrator and try to destroy as much else as she could before she was stopped. Or . . . wait. She waited.

She must have fallen asleep. Noises at the door awakened her. It must be Aernath; no one else could unlock it from outside if she had locked it properly. Slipping out her dagger she waited by the disintegrator as the door slid open. She heard his angry muttering as he pushed through the tangle of equipment she had piled in front. Then he caught sight of her. "Jean! What in the name of space is going on here?"

"So they sent you, did they? What do they think you're going to do—talk to me again, 'explain' everything? More lies, more promises? Or are you just a diversion while they break in from another direction?"

"Jean! What are you talking about? What happened? They, who?" He closed the door and started toward her but stopped at her gesture of the dagger. "Put that thing away and tell me what's happened. There's no one here but me." His perplexity seemed genuine.

"Klingons!" The word was bitter in her mouth. "You're the worst. You convinced me I could trust at least some of you. Including your generous, diplomatic commander! Ha! Kang tried to rape me."

"What!" Disbelief and confusion were mingled on his face. Then he demanded, "What do you mean 'tried'?"

"I told him to let me go. That I'd kill myself if he tried to lay a hand on me."

"I don't believe it. The commander has no reason to do

that, and besides, if he intended to, he would have done it—not 'tried.' "

"I don't give a tinker's dam what you think. I know what happened and all I . . ."

He interrupted her. "Jean, where did you get that dress?"

She looked at the dress with distaste. "Kang sent it to my room along with the invitation to dinner last night."

"And where is your room—exactly?"

"It adjoins his quarters. Why?"

"Mara's room." Aernath let out a long breath. He skirted her, carefully positioned his plant, and sat down. "I think you'd better start at the beginning and tell me precisely what happened last night."

Something in his tone and manner sobered her. In spite of her suspicions, she found she wanted to talk to him—needed to discuss it with someone. Setting aside her anger she tried to give a calm account of the previous evening. Several times he interrupted her, probing for details, words. He grew increasingly agitated. As she recounted her final defiance of Kang, he jumped up and seized her by the shoulders. "You fool! Don't you see what you've done?"

"What *I've* done! Well I like that! Dammit. It was Kang who attacked me—not the other way around."

He shook her. "He let you go! A lesser man would have killed you on the spot. I would have." Alarmed, Jean raised her dagger. He brushed it aside. "Oh, forget it. I'm not going to do anything." He let go of her and began to pace nervously. "But why? And why now? I can't see what he expects to accomplish . . . There's Tirax of course. And Mara will be . . . By Cymele! I wish I knew more about how things stand on Peneli!" He seemed to have forgotten Jean entirely.

"If it's not too much trouble, would you mind giving me your version of what in space is going on? Or are you still thinking up a plausible story?" she inquired acidly.

He turned angrily. "Idiot! . . . No, you really don't understand, do you?" He paused, searching his memory. "I'm sure I told you about Durgath and the . . . no, we were interrupted. What you've just described is the *consort-rite*.

Oh, admittedly the simple military version but it's adequate and binding. You went right through it—accepted his cup and then . . ." He gestured expressively, obviously still angry with her.

"Marriage! Don't be ridiculous! Obviously I didn't know what he was doing. How could you . . . anyone . . . possibly think I—"

"Doesn't matter. What's done is done. Blast it. Jean will you try for just one minute to think like a Klingon? Kang's an Imperial Fleet commander and someday emperor. He offers you *consort-right*. You seem to accept it and then reject him. What do you expect?"

She did try. "Oh . . ." Then she protested, "But he's still married to Mara. You told me that yourself."

"That doesn't matter either. He can have six if he wants them. But a human?" Aernath seemed more preoccupied with Kang's motives than Jean's predicament. "What we do next depends so much on what he's planning."

"We?" Jean squeaked. "What makes you think I'm going to do anything you say? I don't even know if you're telling me the truth. Maybe this is just another elaborate Klingon ruse. How do I know I can trust you?"

He gave her a peculiar look. "You don't," he said flatly. "If you persist in believing that we are all scoundrels with no sense of honor then there's no basis for trust. Where does that leave you?" When Jean made no reply he continued in a softer tone. "On the other hand, if you are willing to grant us our own kind of integrity, then . . . I am still . . . bond to you. I didn't manage to keep you out of this particular dilemma, but I will try to help."

Jean sat down wearily. "I don't know what to think, Aernath. I want to believe you but . . ."

As she moved, Aernath caught sight of the grain sitting on the disintegrator hopper. "Jean! The grain—what in space did you think you were doing?"

She watched as he hastily removed it from danger. "I was going to destroy it, of course, and anything else I could before I was stopped."

He regarded her narrowly. "But you didn't. Why?"

"I . . . I couldn't." She felt a little ludicrous trying to explain it. "A friend of mine is fond of saying there are always choices. I guess I was trying to figure out if I had any other choices."

"You do have a couple—if you want to take the risks." He looked at her curiously. "Tell me, if you had understood Kang's offer, what would you have done?"

Jean pondered the hypothetical question a moment. "I'd still have asked to be sent home, but . . . I guess I'd want to know why he made the offer."

"I doubt he would have told you. Would you have accepted?"

She answered slowly, "I don't know. My feelings are so muddled by now because of what did happen. I can't say."

"All right. Suppose he were willing to give you another chance. Could you accept it now?"

"Give *me* another chance!" Jean bridled.

"Dammit, Jean, don't be so touchy! Okay, okay. Let me rephrase it. If Kang is willing to overlook the misunderstanding, can you?"

"Look, if he can do it he can undo it, too, can't he?" she parried.

"Dissolution? That's another possibility but I think that's even more risky. That would mean he would have to abandon whatever plans he has in mind. Kang doesn't take kindly to being thwarted."

"I don't take kindly to being treated like a piece of chattel. Pretty wretched set of choices, if you ask me."

"Do you have any other suggestions?" he asked curtly.

"No." She realized he was waiting for her decision. Could she accept Kang's offer? If she had understood the situation yesterday, had had time to think it over—possibly. But now . . . she shook her head. "I . . . I can't."

He nodded. "I thought you'd say that."

"So what do we do now?"

"Wait for Kang to make the next move. But, by Cymele's cloak, stay out of his sight! If you're not prepared to apologize and ask for clemency, don't let him set eyes on you. It could be fatal."

90

"And if I were, what then?"

Carefully Aernath outlined the procedure for her. "He still might kill you. Who knows? But there's a good chance he wouldn't."

"Hobson's choice. It's his move either way. I'll stay out of sight."

They tried to maintain the semblance of a normal day's work but Jean was jumpy as a cat. She accomplished very little and finally gave it up. A cold shower, a light supper, and bed were in order she decided as she entered her quarters.

She set the shower dial, pushed it and turned for the soap. The stream of water that hit her back was scalding hot. Screaming in agony she reached through the spray to pull the dial off, then fumbled for the door. Suddenly it was yanked open and she collapsed in a pink haze of pain. Kang scooped her up and dumped her on his bed. "Imbeciles installed the hookup backwards. I should have had maintenance fix it long ago. Here, lie still." From his first aid kit he produced a small cylinder. It hissed softly as he sprayed her neck, shoulder, back and arm in rapid succession. He leaned over and pushed the intercom button. "Kang. Eknaar to my quarters immediately. Out." With one finger he touched her shoulder experimentally. "Still hurt?"

She grimaced. "It's a little better, I think, except my face."

He sprayed some foam into his hand. "Shut your eyes." Deftly he applied the medication with gentle strokes from forehead to earlobe. He paused, then disappeared and returned with her bath towel which he draped over her.

Eknaar arrived and took in the scene. "What happened?"

"Blasted shower is hooked up in reverse. She scalded herself." He watched as Eknaar completed a swift evaluation. "Well?"

"Not too serious. First degree most of it. May blister a bit on the shoulder here but getting the spray on it right away will minimize that. She'll be all right."

Kang seemed visibly relieved. "Fine. Then get her out of here." He left abruptly.

Eknaar looked up quizzically. "Funny. It's not like him to get queasy over a little burn."

"I don't think that's it," said Jean faintly. "He's mad at me."

Eknaar snorted. "Nonsense. He's upset all right, but that's not the way he acts when he's angry. Come on, let's sit you up." He got her into her own room, gave her a sedative, and promised to see her in the morning. She was groggily perplexed when he wakened her in the middle of the night. After another injection she promptly went back to sleep, and did not notice that the Klingon medic exited into Kang's room rather than the corridor.

She was feeling much better when Eknaar and her breakfast tray arrived simultaneously the next morning. "Good morning. I wasn't sure I'd see you this morning after that late night visit."

The doctor made a face. "Not my idea I assure you. Orders! If you were that bad, I'd have put you in sick bay. How do you feel this morning?"

"Stiff and sore, that's all."

"Of course. Let's see the shoulder . . . couple of small blisters, not as bad as I thought. Spray really did the trick." After another application of spray and a plastiderm dressing over the blisters he admonished, "Stay in bed for the day. Leave the dressing until it comes off by itself. And stay away from hot showers."

She did. From the sounds next door she gathered that the shower was being fixed. By evening she was feeling nearly normal and somewhat restless. When Aernath arrived with dinner for two she was geniunely delighted. "Just following orders, ma'am." He mimicked her voice: "Don't ever go a day without checking with me as long as I'm stuck in this damned Klingon Empire. How are things in the DKE today?"

"Aernath, I think you'd joke at your grandmother's funeral. But thanks for coming. Sit down and let's eat."

"I hear Kang dragged you out of the shower and has been badgering the daylights out of Eknaar ever since. Is that true?"

"More or less," she admitted. "Tell me, Aernath, would you say he's made his move? Eknaar doesn't know the story, of course, but he swears Kang is more upset than angry."

"It's possible. You were there. What do you think?"

"Well, if he intended to do me in that would have been a good opportunity."

"So, what are you going to do now?"

"Make the next move."

He gave her an odd look. "Are you really sure you want to do that? Don't try it unless you're sure."

She responded soberly, "It isn't really a question of what I want when it comes right down to it, is it?"

"Probably not. All right—*can* you do it?"

"I think so." She had no intention of telling him how she planned to do it.

It had been a long thirty hours. She intercepted and dismissed the crewman at the council room door, adding her dish to the rest on the servocart. According to Aernath, custom dictated she prepare it herself and she had raided his fruit collection to do it. Kang's back was turned as she entered. He gave a start of surprise when he saw her. "I didn't send for you. Who let you in here?"

Eyes appropriately lowered, she offered the bowl. "Will you take some fruit, Milord?" She held her breath through the interminable pause that followed.

Finally Kang reached out and took a single *pomfrit*. "I will hear you."

Jean took a deep breath and launched on her own course. "I do not intend to apologize. I have nothing to apologize for. But I do have an explanation. I was ignorant of your ritual. I took it for an older and more primitive one, and it was that I rejected." She met his gaze steadily. "I had no desire to insult you."

His eyes narrowed. "Do you understand what you are doing now?"

"This time I do."

His eyes held a glint of grim amusement. "But still you will do it your own way, won't you? Why?"

She lifted her chin defiantly. "Because I think you already realize what happened and if it wasn't for your damned Klingon pride you'd have apologized to me!"

He chuckled as he took her upturned chin in one hand. "Still coming, aren't you? If the truth be known I think you nearly match me when it comes to pride. Can you match me in other things as well?"

"I think so," she replied evenly.

"We shall see." His other arm encircled her and pulled her to him. She felt his mouth again, hard and demanding on hers. His hand moved across her left breast and paused below it. Abruptly he pulled her head back searching her face carefully. "You're still afraid. You've chosen this as the best of bad choices, haven't you?" Jean kept her eyes fixed on his belt buckle scant centimeters away from the bottom of her ribcage. Kang's left hand moved slightly but insistently at the nape of her neck. "Look at me." She raised her eyes to meet his. "You're right to fear me. Given my position you can't escape being a pawn. If I'm forced to it, you're expendable." A vein in his temple throbbed and his jaw tightened. "Mara understood this and she took the risk with me until your Kirk seduced her with his hypocritical human sentimentality!" The bitterness lingered in his eyes a moment as he returned to the present. "But I want more from you than fear. By giving you *consort-right* I have placed my political as well as my personal power around you. That's a formidable barrier. It's also as much freedom as I can give you at the moment."

His dark eyes watched her somberly; around her, his hands waited. She regarded the belt buckle in front of her ribcage for a long moment. Then raising a finger to Kang's cheek, she asked gently, "Is that how a Klingon commander says 'I love you'?"

His face softened in a brief smile. "Human sentimentality! My dear, I have just handed you a far more dangerous weapon than my knife. Use it very carefully or you may destroy us both."

"That," she responded warmly, "I have no desire to do." She pulled Kang's mouth down to her own. It was hungry but gentle to her now. Her belly shifted softly against the belt buckle. Arguments, she decided, could wait.

Much later, Jean lay and watched the blue green flicker of her aquarium light ripple across their skin. "Why did you offer me your cup?"

With one finger, Kang idly traced circles on her shoulder. "You don't believe it was for mere sentiment?"

She shook her head. "No."

"There were several reasons, of course. Let me see if I can find one you will believe. Maybe . . . because of my bet with Tirax?"

Jean tensed. "Bet with Tirax?"

"He was with me when we found you on Sherman's planet. When we decided you would have to open the vault for us his comment was 'no problem, she'll break easily.' I wagered you wouldn't. I was right. You bend like a Blinghat rapier but never quite snap—just spring back unexpectedly." He smiled. "I won. But I didn't wager I'd nearly lose my lieutenant in the process."

"I can't honestly say that I'm thrilled with his survival; or that reason," she responded drily.

His hand moved to the angle of her jaw. With his thumb he traced the outline of her mouth. "You may not like it. But you believe it, don't you? Try this one: because you stand outside the Empire. And, I know where you stand. There is no one that can be held hostage for you—be used against me."

That gave Jean pause for a moment. After some reflection she said with some reluctance, "I do have a brother."

"My dear, you can have a planetful of relatives in the Federation. That doesn't worry me a bit."

"No," she corrected, "I was referring to Aernath."

His hand tightened fractionally on her chin. "I see. I shall remember that." Then he asked carefully. "Is there any other in the Empire who could be?"

She understood his question and answered it honestly. "No. Besides, if there ever were another, I think he's the sort who would never let himself be held so."

"There are some luxuries even the emperor cannot command," he acknowledged.

Turning her head slightly in the cradle of his elbow she fingered the new scar on his arm. "Does that ever bother you?"

"On the contrary, it's a valuable reminder." To her cocked eyebrow he explained, "Whenever my advisors wax enthusiastic about attacking the Federation it will be there as one more reminder that although you humans appear soft you have sharp teeth."

Jean sighed. "I don't suppose there is any hope of convincing you that we are not so predatory as that. Remember, too, that I tried to avoid it. It doesn't have to stop with an uneasy truce enforced by the Organians. We could pool our efforts, help each other. If you would just trust us—"

Kang snorted. "Trust? You suggest I trust the likes of Kirk? Do you trust Tirax? Or me, for that matter? Don't lecture me about trust!"

She made a wry face. "Touché. But it has to start somewhere. And we haven't attacked you or invaded your territory."

"Elementary strategy. Any commander worth his ship wouldn't attack without reconnoitering, assessing the enemy's strength. No, Starfleet is just waiting for the right opening, a weak spot—"

"Like the *Tseni* virus blight?"

"Precisely. Which is one of the reasons I can't allow you to return to the Federation until the crisis is over. In the meantime, it is instructive to me to have you here."

"And after the crisis?"

"You have my word. Trust me?"

She acknowledged the irony. "It's not easy, I know. But I do trust Aernath—most of the time—and he's convinced you'll keep your word. I guess that's where I start."

Casually Kang ran a fingertip down from throat to navel recalling to Jean the course of his dagger. Her involuntary shiver caught his attention. He brushed it aside with a faint smile. "And one might say I start with you . . . but you humans . . . I wonder—"

"Humans aren't all cut from the same mold—no more than Klingons. But I think I'm a fair representative of what you would have to deal with."

"I said it was instructive to have you here," Kang replied drily.

Instructive for me, too, thought Jean ruefully, *though I don't have the option to drop the course. Then again, perhaps Kang doesn't either.* She wondered how much insight she really had gained into his motives and plans. "Why did you let me go the other night?"

He shrugged. "I could have taken you by force anytime, if that's what I'd wanted. But I told you I wanted more from you than fear."

"And that is?"

"*Aetheln,*" he said softly.

"What?"

"It doesn't translate directly. I'm not sure I could explain it to you. Anyway, it means I wanted you to come to me of your own choice."

She took a shot in the dark. "Because of Mara?"

His laugh was short and bitter. "Actually your captain gave me that idea: 'Your people were well-treated on my ship. I expect the same for Czerny. I will hold you personally responsible for her.' " His pain was almost palpable. Gently Jean reached out to touch him. His eyes searched her face carefully. "But it's not the same for you, is it?"

"I don't know," she replied slowly. "Perhaps in a way it is. I'm still loyal to my Federation. Where does Mara stand?"

"Against her own empire," he said grimly. Then he added musingly, "But she said a peculiar thing before she left: 'You already have the strength but you won't see it until you use it.' " He looked at her curiously. "Why did you come back this evening?"

She thought a moment. "Best of bad choices," she admitted. "Possibly more. Tell me, if you were to become convinced that the Federation was not out to destroy you, would you be willing to negotiate cooperation?"

"That's a very large 'if' my dear, but yes, if I were convinced, I would."

She grinned up at him impishly. "All right. Match me."

Kang stared at her for a moment, then roared with laughter. "You do play for high stakes, don't you?"

The highest, Jean thought. Then he pulled her to him exchanging one mode of communication for another.

Seven

Captain's Log: Stardate 6100.0 Reports of Romulan
activity in a sector of Federation space tangential to the
Romulan neutral zone led Starfleet Command to assign
the *Enterprise* to that area. Reconnaissance has not
confirmed these sightings. However, petty incidents
and "accidents" have continued to occur along the
interface of Klingon and Federation space. Starfleet
Intelligence reports indicate the situation within the
Klingon Empire has not changed substantially. We have
been recalled to Starbase 10 to take aboard additional
personnel for Sherman's planet. We are now enroute to
that planet which has been quiet since the initial hostile
incident with our shuttlecraft.

IT STARTED AS a very quiet Sunday morning. Kirk and
Spock were finishing a game of chess in the rec room. Or
rather, Kirk was finishing it. If a Vulcan face could look
glum, this one could be called positively morose.

"Your move, Mr. Spock." Kirk could not suppress a hint
of glee in his voice. He didn't beat Spock very often. Spock
made his move. Then Kirk. "Checkmate, Mr. Spock."

Spock tipped his king in acknowledgement of defeat. "An

interesting variation on the Vlaskov maneuver, Captain. I commend you. However, I must point out that your move of the king's knight was highly illogical. You didn't need to save your queen to complete the game."

Kirk grinned, "Spock, I just can't resist a lady in distress." He glanced at the transparent cube sitting on the table beside them. "Speaking of ladies, I wonder where Maevlynin is. I'm eager to see how this *xuan nam* cube you have built works." Maevlynin, an Estryllian, had recently joined the crew of the *Enterprise* and now was assigned to the medical section. She divided her time between sick bay and her botany lab. Lovers of games and puzzles, Estryllians had devised many intricate ones. *Xuan nam* was an example. A race of telepaths with powers of telekinesis, they played the game with balls simply suspended in mid air. Dr. McCoy had discovered that Maevlynin was passionately fond of this particular game. Unfortunately, no one else aboard the *Enterprise* had telekinetic powers sufficient to hold the balls in space and move them. McCoy had approached Spock with the idea of building a cube that would accomplish the same thing with colored lights and keyboards. Today they planned to surprise Maevlynin with it.

Kirk turned from the game-cube back to Spock. "Heading back to Sherman's planet reminds me—did anything come in on dispatches this morning about Czerny?"

"No, the only mention of her was the report several weeks ago that she was no longer aboard the Klolode Two. There was a briefing on Sherman's planet. The Klingon outpost weathered the winter well. They have steadfastly ignored all communication attempts from the Federation and the Organians. No apparent contact with the Empire either. They have not engaged the Federation forces since that incident with our shuttlecraft. The only activity our personnel have noted outside their fortress has been an occasional hunting party."

"Well, they seem to be busy enough elsewhere. Maybe that post has been overlooked, for the moment. Still, it's just one more thing we have to sort out with the Klingons eventually." Kirk fingered the *xuan nam* keyboard, experimentally producing a cascade of lighted dots from one corner to its diagonal opposite. "I'm glad this assignment on the Romulan neutral zone was a dry run. With the Klingon border so uneasy, all we need is trouble with the Romulans to boot . . ." He snapped the cube console off and stood up. "Can I get you a cup of anything, Spock?"

"No, thank you, Captain." The Vulcan was making some minor adjustments to the cube.

Kirk smiled as he crossed to the beverage automat and punched for another cup of coffee. His thoughts returned to Maevlynin. Like Vulcans, Estryllians were adept telepaths. Unlike Vulcans, they emphasized emotional development, but had a violent aversion to machines—especially complex ones. In their distant past, Estryllians had possessed an advanced technology and had almost destroyed their planet with it. In reaction, they had forbidden any use of complex machines or weapons, devoting themselves instead to the development and peaceful use of their mental powers and emotional range. However, Maevlynin had shown a capacity to adjust to a starship that, of necessity, depended heavily on complex technology.

At the moment, Maevlynin and Dr. McCoy were absorbed in another problem in sick bay. One of the men in the engineering section had slipped and fallen while working in the Jeffries tube. Although no bones were broken, he had painfully wrenched his back. While McCoy could resolve the problems with a few days sonic treatments and injections, he was rapidly developing a profound respect for the Estryllian approach to such injuries. He watched now as Maevlynin, a trained Estryllian healer, had the man sit bending this way and that. Her slender fingers probed gently along the spine. "The primary problem is here, with extension to L-two and L-three," she said.

McCoy beamed. "Exactly what my scanner showed."

Maevlynin wrinkled her nose. "Doctor, you really ought to dispense with those diabolical gadgets. They are unnecessary. Shall I proceed with treatment?"

"Those diabolical gadgets as you call them are extremely useful and they don't get absorbed in the botany lab," McCoy rejoined. "Yes, go ahead."

Again her fingers moved along the spine. One hand

grasped the man's shoulder from the front, turning him slightly while the palm of her other hand worked over the affected area. Her slightly pointed ears were hidden by her blond hair, but with her peaked eyebrows and pointed chin she still looked very much like a pixie. As McCoy watched, his feelings toward her were an amalgam of respect for a talented colleague and a . . . well, not exactly brotherly . . . feeling of affection. Sensing his feelings, Maevlynin glanced up at him and smiled her acknowledgement of them. McCoy felt his face flush. *Damn,* he thought, would he ever get used to this utter transparency of emotions that working and living with Estryllians brought? He turned and dropped a tape card into the reader on his desk, giving his attention to an emotionally neutral subject: review of this week's routine crew physicals.

Chekov saw it first. He was on bridge duty that morning at Spock's customary position. Scott was in the command chair. "Mr. Scott, sir, the sensors are showing traces of a matter-antimatter explosion and small pieces of debris compatible with a Romulan ship dead ahead of us."

Immediately Scott ordered the helmsman to reduce speed and notified Captain Kirk on the intercom.

"Yellow Alert, Scotty. Spock and I are on our way."

When Kirk and Spock arrived on the bridge moments later, the shattered shell of the Romulan vessel hung in the center of the main viewscreen. Moving to the command chair, Kirk snapped, "Report, Mr. Chekov."

"The ship is totally disabled, sir. There seems to have been some sort of explosion in their engines. No sign of life on the vessel. However, one small launch craft is missing so there may have been survivors."

"Any nearby planets capable of supporting humanoid life?"

"Yes sir. The nearest star has a class M planet, Persephone Two, that has been previously explored. It is capable of supporting humanoid life though none has emerged there."

Kirk weighed the possibilities: a chance to explore the disabled vessel and gaining important military information versus a possible wild-goose chase looking for survivors. The ship would wait, survivors might need immediate help. "Navigator, set a course for Persephone Two."

In orbit around Persephone Two, sensors showed that there was indeed a Romulan small craft on the surface with two survivors. Kirk, Spock, McCoy and Chekov beamed down near the vessel. It was empty. The party fanned out in four directions to look for the survivors.

Reena worked awkwardly with the knife in her left hand. Even to hold the carcass with her right hand was painful because of her arm and hand injuries. Her head wound, though not serious, was throbbing painfully too from all the exertion. But Lucius was in far worse shape than she and someone had to get food. He had seemed so much weaker this morning. She refused to think about that possibility. Could she survive alone on this planet until a Romulan vessel might come in response to their distress signal? She knew this was unlikely. The ship had been destroyed on the edge of Federation territory. Her mind turned away from that thought, too. She had enough horrors to contemplate without thinking of Federation stormtroopers! A slight sound behind her drew her attention. As if to give substance to her nightmare, there stood a figure in the dreaded blue and black uniform of a Federation starship. Dropping her knife, she lunged for her weapon lying on an adjacent rock. The phaser fire caught her just as she reached it.

McCoy knelt by the unconscious Romulan swearing under his breath. He had taken her for a youth when he first came over the rise. Now he had discovered she was a woman and injured as well. He should have aimed for her weapon instead of stunning her. "Maevlynin's right. Give a man a weapon and he just creates more trouble for himself," he grumbled as he worked over the inert Romulan. Satisfied that her condition would allow it, he scooped her up to return to the Romulan craft. As an afterthought, he hung the second carcass she had been skinning next to the one already on her belt.

Kirk's search had ended differently. The Romulan he found was already dead. He and Spock were in the process of burying him when McCoy returned bearing his limp burden. Chekov was scrutinizing the Romulan craft.

"Did you find the other Romulan yet?" McCoy queried.

Chekov nodded. "Captain Kirk did. He's dead."

McCoy thought for a moment that the woman he was carrying had regained consciousness. He could swear he'd felt her tense. He eased her down alongside the craft. No, no response yet. "Well, this one will come around any time now. She'll make it."

Kirk and Spock appeared around the front of the craft. "Ah, Bones. I see you found the other one. Good. The one I found—"

"You killed him!" The Romulan woman, obviously conscious, sprang at Kirk.

Unprepared for her attack, Kirk fell backwards but managed to grab her wrists as he went. Rolling to his feet, he pulled her up. McCoy saw her look over Kirk's shoulder at Spock. She shook her head in sudden disbelief, then looked back at Kirk.

"Spock! *Enterprise!* No." She wrenched free of Kirk's grasp and backed away, straight into McCoy's waiting hypo.

Spock's eyebrow went up. "It would appear that we have a most unfortunate reputation among the Romulan fleet."

Kirk looked at the unconscious Romulan and gave a low whistle. "Bones, it looks like you got yourself a handful this time. When she wakes up, tell her that her comrade was already dead and try to reassure her. Come on, Spock, let's see if we can recover the launch's log and computer tapes."

The woman was just regaining consciousness a short while later, as Kirk and Spock were preparing to beam up. Kirk turned to the doctor. "Well, how's your patient now?"

"I'd like to see her stabilize a little before I beam her up. Probably a few more minutes."

"We have the tapes. Mr. Spock and I will beam up and get a security team down here to work with Chekov. You bring her when you're ready. Scotty, two to beam up."

Reena sat up groggily. Her captor momentarily had his eyes on the two who were shimmering out. The other one was bending over the console, his back to her. If she could just reach the firing button. . . .

Chekov caught the motion out of the corner of his eye. His communicator lay in front of him. He flipped it on. "Deflectors! Scotty, quickly!"

A short pause. "Deflectors on. Mr. Chekov—what is happening down there?"

What was happening was pandemonium. McCoy got to Reena first. Chekov took a look at the panel: missile firing button depressed, one launch cradle registering empty. In a white-hot fury he lunged for the Romulan. "She fired on the ship! I'll kill her!"

"Chekov, stop it. Let me handle this." Jumping between them, McCoy shoved Chekov into a chair. He wondered wearily how many people he was going to have to knock out how many times today. It had started as such a nice quiet Sunday. He handed Chekov his communicator. Now Kirk was on the other end of it.

"Bones, Chekov. What on earth is going on down there?"

Chekov explained while McCoy none too gently placed the woman in a second chair and tied her there. "It's about time we reached an understanding. I'd like to have time to treat you instead of knocking you out all the time. Now sit still and behave yourself."

Reena watched the two Federation men with a certain grim satisfaction. For the moment she had put the entire starship on the defensive. Here, both men were preoccupied with determining exactly what had happened to their ship. The torture would come soon for information or revenge or both but with any luck it would be mercifully quick. Certainly if the younger one had his way it would be short. Her captor on the other hand struck her as sadistic. He might be capable of keeping her alive a long time. She shivered.

Slowly they pieced together the situation: Spock on the ship with the launch tapes and Chekov here at the console. The launch was armed with two probe missiles—a new device that would stay with the deflector shields until they were lowered, then home in on the targeted ship, activate and explode. They even determined that the timer had not been set; the device would take the maximum delay after attachment to detonate: two hours.

"Chekov, is there any way that device can be disarmed after launch?" Kirk asked via communicator. "The tapes don't have that information. I don't care what you have to tear apart. We've got to have that information."

"Yes sir. We'll do our best."

"Fine, let me know as soon as you have something. Kirk, out."

McCoy and Chekov looked at each other. Chekov picked up his tricorder and went out to have a fresh look at the remaining device.

McCoy considered his patient speculatively. Physical condition: weak but stable. The two Romulans had apparently been on limited rations for some time. Her physical reserves were depleted. Head wound—looked bad but minor really. Right arm and hand injury—now there was a nasty problem: a lot of tissue damage and infected too. Must hurt like the devil. It needed surgery but that would have to wait for sick bay. Mental condition: problematical. The woman was obviously frightened and angry—angry enough to attack Kirk and then later to fire the missile in spite of her weakness, a phaser stun, and a hypo. Panic triggered by the sight of Kirk and Spock . . . she must have heard terrible stories about the *Enterprise*. He had to get her calmed down. No telling how long they would be stuck here before Spock and Chekov figured out how to disarm that bomb. Too bad he didn't have some really powerful tranquilizer along but that wasn't standard medikit equipment.

McCoy pulled up a box that Spock had extracted from the console to get at the tapes and sat down beside the woman. "What's your name?"

She looked startled, as if that wasn't what she expected. She glanced at her uniform, then at the stripes on his sleeve. "Navigator R. Tertullian . . . Lieutenant Commander, sir," she hazarded.

It was McCoy's turn to be startled. "Yes, that's my rank but there's no need to be so formal. I'm Leonard McCoy, chief medical officer of the U.S.S. *Enterprise*. We found your ship and came looking for survivors. Unfortunately your friend was already dead when we found him."

Navigator Tertullian said nothing.

McCoy tried again. "How long have you been here?"

"I'm sure First Officer Spock has recovered that information from our tapes already," she replied icily.

"What happened to your ship?"

Her voice dripped with scorn. "As if you don't know already. Surely, Lieutenant Commander, you don't expect me to divulge military information to enemies of the Empire."

"All right. What about your comrade here? What was his name?"

The anger blazed. "If he died without telling you, you can be sure I won't tell you!"

Right back to square one, McCoy thought wryly. You sure aren't much of a psychiatrist. He shrugged. "Nice weather we're having. Do you think it will rain?" And he went out to see how Chekov was doing.

Chekov was doing well . . . and he was not. As McCoy came over, Chekov looked up from his tricorder. "I don't think the captain will be happy with my news. This device can be disarmed . . . but only by a Romulan. It contains sensors programmed to Romulan neural patterns. If anyone else tries to disarm it, it detonates immediately.

Suddenly, McCoy thought he knew how a lobster must feel when it tries to back out of a lobster pot. It wasn't a pleasant sensation.

Chekov whirled and sprinted for the inside of the launch. He seized the woman's hair and wrenched her head back. "Do you know how to disarm the device?" he hissed.

The woman seemed bent on suicide. "Of course I do, you slimy spineless stormtrooper, but it won't do your starship any good," she spat. "Sooner or later you have to lower your deflectors and then that mine will blow your ship into the next solar system. So much for your precious Captain Kirk and Spock!"

If McCoy had not been two steps behind Chekov, the

Romulan might have succeeded in her suicidal quest. As it was, McCoy found himself prying them apart for the second time. Once again, Chekov found himself in a chair addressing the captain via communicator. There was a long pause on the other end. "Only by a Romulan? Are you sure, Chekov?"

"Yes, sir. And the prisoner has confirmed it."

Another long pause. "Stand by, Mr. Chekov. I'll be back with instructions shortly. Kirk, out."

On the bridge of the *Enterprise* Kirk stared at Spock with dismay. "Spock, comment?"

"We would appear to have two alternatives, Captain. Persuade the Romulan woman to disarm it or have someone else make the attempt."

"Someone else. . . ?" Kirk's face lit up. "Vulcans and Romulans apparently spring from a common ancestry. Would your neural patterns be close to foil the sensor?"

Spock was already bent over his viewer consulting the ship's computer. He straightened. "Based on what scant data we possess of Romulan neurophysiology, there is approximately a fifty-eight percent chance I could succeed. The biggest uncertainty is how much that sensor is programmed to read Romulan emotions. Any significant degree of that would substantially diminish my chance of success."

Kirk's face clouded again. "Not good enough. We can't chance it. What are the chances of persuading the Romulan to do it?"

This time Spock did not consult the computer. Between them, he and Kirk probably knew as much about Romulan psychology as any starship computer. "I am not sanguine about that possibility either, Captain. Romulans seldom allow themselves to be captured let alone 'persuaded' to aid an enemy. I can't give you the probability but it is certainly low."

"Well, if she can't be persuaded, she'll have to be forced. Spock, what about mind-meld? Could you mind-meld with her and force her to disarm it? You've done it before—the Eminian guard for example."

Spock pondered the problem for a moment before answering. "This is a much more difficult undertaking. That required only a brief contact and a simple act—open a door or unlock a cell—an act frequently performed by the subject with little emotional investment. This would involve prolonged contact, performance of intricate maneuvers against considerable emotional resistance. She might go psychotic. That would be disastrous for all of us."

To say nothing, thought Kirk, *of your Vulcan aversion to the mind-meld itself let alone coercion.* Aloud he only said gently, "Spock, I won't ask you to do that unless we can't find any other way." Kirk prowled restlessly around his command chair.

"I know that, Captain." Spock reflected once again that it was a cage as much as a command post.

"Meanwhile, we have as much time as we want to take. The thing won't activate until it attaches to the hull. McCoy is a pretty savvy doctor. Maybe he can come up with some way to persuade her. Let's give him a chance at it. What have we got to lose?" The question was rhetorical.

"Nothing, Captain."

Kirk smiled. Literal Vulcan. "This is Kirk to Chekov. Are you there? Can you all hear me?"

"Yes sir, Captain."

As Chekov and McCoy listened, the captain's voice became unaccustomedly harsh—"Then hear this: the Romulan prisoner must be made to cooperate with us. I'm giving you six hours. I don't care how you do it, but she must be brought around. That is an order. Don't signal until you have results to report. And if you haven't succeeded in six hours, I'm going to turn Spock loose on her and Lt. Uhura loose on you, too. Do I make myself clear?"

Chekov goggled. Quickly McCoy picked up the communicator, "My God, Captain Kirk, sir . . . we're only human. I'll face Spock any day but please not Lt. Uhura!"

Chekov was beginning to catch on. "Captain Kirk, you know we will do our best, but please . . . not Uhura!" He sounded as if he were strangling.

"My orders stand. Kirk, out."

McCoy pulled Chekov out of the launch. "It's time for a little walk." What he really needed was time to think. The

109

same possibilities had run through his mind as Captain Kirk's. "Pavel, the chances of Spock disarming that thing by himself must be too low for the captain to risk it. Otherwise he wouldn't be playing this game. I would guess his trump card is a mind-meld with Spock. But that's risky, too; she's terrified of Spock. Did you see her face when the Captain said he'd turn Spock loose on her? She might crack completely. So it's up to us to try—we've nothing to lose."

"What are you going to do, Doctor?"

"I'm not quite sure myself but just follow my lead, Pavel. Follow my lead."

When they reentered the launch, it appeared that McCoy was going to do nothing at all. Chekov set to work under one console, proceeding with the original plan to collect all the information possible about the Romulan launch. McCoy sat on the floor beside him, holding lights, handing tools, and just making conversation. "Pavel, how did you come to join the Starfleet anyway?"

"Well, sir, since I was a small boy growing up in Novy Riga, I've been fascinated by stars. I got my first telescope when I was six. Could you shine the light here, please? My father helped me build it." The talk drifted on: Chekov's boyhood in Russia, McCoy's in southern Georgia. School, boyhood pranks and dreams, swimming, fishing.

Without appearing to, McCoy carefully watched the Romulan's reactions. She went from open-mouthed incredulity to suspicion to puzzled curiosity. Finally she relaxed, apparently having decided that, for whatever obscure reasons, they were ignoring her for the moment. He waited until she seemed to be lost in her own thoughts.

"How do you catch fish on your planet, Miss Tertullian?"

She snapped back to startled attention at her name. "What?"

"I asked, how do you catch fish on your planet?"

She looked wary, then apparently decided there was no harm in answering that question. "For sport, with a hand net or a spear."

"My grandfather used to talk about spearing suckers as a boy," McCoy mused, "but I never did it myself. Is it difficult?'

"I usually used the net, but with a little practice the spear is equally simple," she answered slowly.

McCoy stood and stretched. "Pavel, would you like a drink?"

"Sure, I'll be done here in a moment."

The Romulans had improvised a cistern near the shuttle. McCoy took back a dipperful and offered it first to Chekov then the Romulan. She started to refuse then thought better of it. Clearly she was thirsty; probably hungry too. From the looks of the campsite she'd not eaten at all today, McCoy thought.

"Why are you bothering to put it all back together?" the woman asked, indicating the console.

McCoy set down the water dipper and unslung his medical tricorder again. "After we get you put all back together you may want to fly it back to one of your ships." he said.

"Don't mock me, Human. You dishonor us both. Death on the battlefield or even quick death to a defeated enemy is noble. I accept that. Why can't you?" She drew back slightly from his medical scanner.

"My business is saving lives not dispatching them." McCoy replied. "Your head feeling better?" She nodded. He put away his instruments. "I don't know about you, Pavel, but I'm hungry. Let's see what we can do about some lunch."

Chekov was more the camper. McCoy set him to work skinning the second animal the Romulan woman had killed. Through the open doorway of the launch he saw her watching them, though she feigned indifference. He picked up a handful of tubers he'd found in the cook area and went over to the door. "What are these? Did you find them edible?"

She nodded. "Yes. They taste rather like *sashkas*, a common vegetable of ours."

Chekov had the fire going and the first animal spitted. McCoy couldn't find any cookpot. He went back to the door. "Do you have any kind of cooking pot here?"

She told him where to find it. "There's some salt, too, if you want it."

McCoy smiled. "Thanks." He found the pot but nothing that looked like a container of salt. "Chekov," he said, putting some exasperation in his voice, "bring her out here. I can't find that damn salt anywhere."

Chekov untied her. "Come on," he said curtly. She pushed away his proffered hand, stood up and started for the door when her knees buckled.

Chekov caught her halfway to the floor. "What happened?" he asked anxiously.

"Nothing. Just a little dizzy, that's all."

But he saw the white line of pain around her lips and felt the involuntary muscle guarding. He had jarred her injured arm badly when he caught her. She was so stubborn! After all, she could disarm the device and have it all over with. They had rescued her, treated her well. Surely she could see they had meant her no harm. But the ship has to be defended. It was her own fault. Her grip on his arm tightened, knuckles white as she fought the pain and weakness. For a fraction of a second, Pavel Chekov's universe blinked. When it refocused, he saw not an adversary but a fellow mortal being in agony. "Look, I'm sorry I bumped your arm like that. Here, let me help you."

He lowered her in the doorway of the launch and she leaned weakly against the doorframe. McCoy was there immediately. "What happened?"

"I think she stood up too quickly, Doctor, and got dizzy. I . . . I bumped her arm rather badly when I caught her."

"Get my medikit." He cupped her face in his hands and projected concern. "Take it easy now. You'll be okay." Chekov handed him the kit. He ran his scanner over the arm, her head, then nodded, apparently satisfied. "I can give you another hypo for the pain."

"No. I want no more of your serums or hypnotics. That won't work either," she responded.

"Nonsense. I've got nothing like that here. Just a painkiller." He held out the hypospray. "I'll give you that if you want it." She shook her head. He closed his kit and went back to looking for the salt.

She watched him for a minute, then got up slowly, came over and put her finger on an oil-paper packet. "The salt."

McCoy stared. "That's the damndest looking salt shaker I've ever seen."

"Unfamiliar things are not always what they seem, Doctor."

He gave her a searching look. "No, they often aren't, are they?"

He went back to his cooking and she resumed her seat in the doorway, cradling her arm in her lap. McCoy watched the stew while Chekov turned the spit, and talked about his last camping trip with Sulu. Absentmindedly, McCoy grasped the handle to shift the pot on the fire. He let go very quickly and swore softly as he examined his fingers. No serious damage—a couple of small blisters. He was not cut out to be a camper.

He glanced up to catch a fleeting smile cross the woman's face before she settled it back into an impassive mask. A bit later, he also saw her surprise when Chekov handed her a bowl of food. She ate a couple of bites, then sat and watched them.

Chekov glanced at her bowl. "What's wrong? Go ahead and eat."

"Nothing, but . . . might I have the other packet over there?" She indicated the spot where the salt had been.

Pavel got it, then watched as she added some to her stew. "What is it?"

"Ground *cumidin* seed. We actually use it more than salt."

"What does it taste like? May I try a bit?" Gingerly, he dipped a finger in the powder and tasted it. "Say, that's good."

"The seeds come from trees that grow high on mountain slopes near my home. The seedpods are bright orange and the leaves brilliant yellow. It's a beautiful sight at harvest time," she said.

"I saw golden trees like that once on Earth," McCoy mused, "in the high Uintas of the West—one of our last wilderness areas. Aspens, ours are called, and in late August they turn from green to pure gold. That was the year before Joanna was born." He turned to her. "What does the 'R' stand for?"

"What?" she asked, startled.

"Your name. What does the 'R' stand for?"

"Reena."

"I've already told you my name. This is Pavel Chekov, our navigator."

Her eyes widened in surprise. "A navigator? So am I. I thought you must be in engineering from the way you were working on that console."

Pavel looked pleased. He was beginning to like this Romulan woman in spite of her initial hostile action.

McCoy idly toyed with a bone but his mind was working furiously. So far so good. She was now willing to talk to them. But where to go from here? Clearly, one didn't sidle up to a Romulan officer and say, "There now be a decent chap, uh . . . lass, and put this nasty bomb you've launched out of commission for us." As well ask Spock to dance flamenco. Not much time left. McCoy sighed. "Come on, Pavel, let's clean things up."

As it turned out, Reena took the next step herself. Chekov had gone to get more water. McCoy was washing the dishes. Reena sat in the doorway watching him, her hand on her chin. "Dr. McCoy, you were serving under Captain Kirk at the time of . . . of the . . . *Enterprise* incident, weren't you?"

The spoon hung in midair. McCoy carefully kept looking straight ahead, not at Reena. "Yes, why do you ask?" He hoped it sounded casual.

"Why did Captain Kirk release our commander?"

"Reena, it is Federation policy to treat all prisoners kindly and humanely, to repatriate them whenever that does not pose a threat to our security. We had what we wanted from her flagship. And she was no threat to us. There was no point in holding her." *Please, dear God, don't let Chekov come clanking back with the water right now*, he thought desperately. Carefully he turned to look at her. "It could be the same for you, Reena. If you disarm the device you will not be harmed. We will return you to your own people."

She smiled sardonically but her eyes misted. "You overlook one vital difference between my situation and hers."

"And that is . . . ?"

"You require my cooperation. We are sworn to die rather than reveal information to our enemies let alone aid them. If you don't kill me, my own officers will. That is our oath."

114

McCoy was feeling his way. "Reena, are you saying you want to . . . to stay?"

Her eyes flashed angrily. "Don't be ridiculous. I am a Romulan. That is my home, my people."

"Yet if you cooperated with us and we released you, your own code would condemn you. How can they hold you liable? You've been through a terrible disaster, sole survivor, weak, badly injured. You're in no position to resist us."

"Merely the exigencies of battle, Doctor. That doesn't release me from my oath."

McCoy squatted in front of her and took her face in his hands again. "Reena, you *will* disarm that device. You know that. If necessary Spock will mind-meld with you in order to accomplish that. I don't think you will find that very pleasant. If you would disarm the device voluntarily, I promise you we will find a way to return you to your people safely. Can you trust me for that?"

She pushed his hands away and shut her eyes for a moment. When she looked at him her eyes were clear but distant. "Perhaps. But Doctor, I am Romulan, you know. I must do what is required of me."

And that, thought McCoy grimly, *could be interpreted in more than one way.* He stood up abruptly, "Well, it would seem the task at hand is to satisfy your Romulan code of honor, isn't it?" Reena looked at him levelly. Chekov came clanking back. "Lunch is over and time's short. Tie her up, Chekov."

Chekov looked puzzled but complied. "Yes, sir."

Wearily, McCoy finished putting things away. It certainly had not turned out to be a quiet day and it promised to get worse. Reluctantly, he went into the launch. Reena sat erect in her chair. Chekov leaned against the console. "Ensign Chekov, Navigator Tertullian and I had a little talk while you were gone. In spite of our patience and thoughtfulness she is not inclined to be cooperative. Time is short. We know the consequences if we fail. Hit her, Mr. Chekov."

Chekov nearly fell on the floor. He stared at McCoy as if he had gone mad. "Sir. . . ?"

"You heard me."

"Me? Now? Sir?"

"Now, Mr. Chekov."

Gingerly, Chekov slapped Reena on the cheek. She laughed. Chekov flushed. McCoy felt slightly nauseated. "I said hit her, Chekov." And he stepped forward and landed a second solid blow. Reena sat there stolidly. Chekov's hands were shaking and McCoy was definitely nauseated. He really hadn't the stomach for this. He flipped open his communicator, "McCoy to *Enterprise*."

Kirk's voice was still harsh, "Captain Kirk here. What progress do you have to report?"

"Captain, I think our prisoner is ready to come on board. Alert an emergency medical team. We can continue interrogation in sick bay."

Kirk's voice instantly dropped all pretense, "Bones! What on earth have you—"

"Just beam us up, Jim. I'll explain when I get there."

Kirk, Spock, and the medical team were waiting when they materialized. Chekov lifted Reena and placed her gingerly on the cart. McCoy gave a few directions, ". . . and take Chekov with you. I'll be right down."

Kirk's face was grim. "All right, Bones, what in the devil is going on? Is she ready to disarm the device? What did you do to her? I expected you to intimidate her, scare her, but . . . physical abuse? That's not like you, Bones. Surely you knew we could use Spock's mind-meld if we had to—"

"I know, Jim, I know. I also know it might kill her. I think I've found a way around it."

"You mean she's agreed to do it on her own?"

"Not yet, but I think she will. You know, it's funny. A few weeks ago I was reviewing some journal tapes on the psychology of old POW camps. You know back on Earth they used to . . ."

"Dr. McCoy, we have exactly one hour and forty-seven minutes before detonation," Spock interspersed. "May I suggest you be brief?"

McCoy decided Spock was not looking forward to the mind-meld either. He was positively edgy. "She's a well-disciplined Romulan officer, committed to her culture and her people. A direct attack wouldn't work. She'd die or go psychotic first. However, she's also young, bright, and open-minded . . . and she wants to go home. What they discovered with POWs was that sometimes meaningful interaction between prisoners and captors produced attitude changes. The key seemed to be series of events that slipped by the mutual defenses and projections that each side has set up. One meets the enemy on common ground. That's what I tried with her. The problem is—if she cooperates with us they'll kill her. It's their code of honor—sort of 'come back with your shield or on it.' Her injuries and isolation are not mitigating circumstances. She'll be questioned, maybe mind-scanned. We have to create the impression that she was pushed beyond Romulan endurance before she yielded to us or it's all up with her when she gets back. Spock, could you place a block in her mind as if something had been wiped out—erased?"

The Vulcan considered it. "There is such a technique, though I have never employed it. It would, however, be simpler than controlling her through the prolonged process of disarming that device."

"She will have to be quite terrified up to the block but unfortunately I don't see any way around that," McCoy said.

The trio entered sick bay. The Romulan was lying quietly in bed, with Dr. Chapel and Chekov at the bedside. "Her signs are stable, Dr. McCoy."

"Thank you, Dr. Chapel. You might start setting us up for surgery then—we'll be working on her arm a little later." He glanced at Chekov. "Captain, maybe you'd like Chekov to get a couple of life support units ready? She'll be ready to go out soon."

Kirk sent Chekov on his way. "Spock, let's get on with it."

Reena's eyes widened as she struggled to sit up. "No, not Spock! Doctor, you said . . . I thought you understood—"

McCoy cut in. "I know perfectly well what you thought. We have very little time. Now let's get this over with." He held her down on one side, Kirk on the other. She screamed.

Spock touched her face with the characteristic mind-meld position. The Romulan mind is in some respects like the Vulcan. That made it worse for him. Sheer terror. He couldn't even tell what exactly she feared—everything was blotted out by it. He almost broke the link. Then slowly, steadily he began to gather that fear, to pull it together, contain it. Finally there stood a firm barrier. He began to withdraw. The woman waited warily. "I have done what I came to do. Madam, I sincerely regret the necessity. Perhaps you will find consolation in the fact that it was equally distasteful to me."

"Understood," she acceded. He left. Reena looked up at the faces around her. Concern was written all over McCoy's. Kirk looked relieved and Spock—was Spock.

McCoy touched her chin lightly. "Reena, are you all right?"

"That is all?" she whispered.

"Yes, it's over," he said with relief. "Now that we've blocked out those horrible tortures we've put you through, let's substitute some pleasant memories. It would never do for your Romulan officers to get hold of our interrogation techniques. They might find a way to stop us."

The woman relaxed visibly. McCoy was no telepath but he could almost read her thoughts. He'd meant it. She would go home.

McCoy watched as Reena and Pavel worked their way slowly along the secondary hull toward the device. They had nineteen minutes to detonation. The doctor had worked steadily over the Romulan woman for some time to get her ready for this foray. She really was in precarious shape. Normally he wouldn't let someone in that condition out of bed. As soon as she got back, he wouldn't, he promised silently. Now he watched the viewscreen alongside Kirk, Spock, and Scotty while the two figures approached the device. They were nearly there. Reena withdrew her hand from Pavel's and motioned him back. She knelt beside it and her fingers moved over it, touching here, pressing there. Pavel watched anxiously—five minutes . . . four . . . She stood with one fluid movement, the device in her hands, turned and pushed it away from the *Enterprise* toward the atmosphere of the planet. It burned on entry.

"Reena, why did you do that?"

The look she gave him was unfathomable. "I was required to disarm it, not to turn it over to you. Let's go." She took his hand.

McCoy whisked them both off to sick bay again. This time he let Chekov stay with Reena. Maevlynin sat at Reena's head, one finger lightly on the woman's left temple. With her other hand she occasionally adjusted one of the silver needles inserted in Reena's skin. Pavel sat beside her, his dark head bent over Reena's. They spoke of navigation, ships, and stars. Not yet, Maevlynin thought with gentle amusement, did they talk of the emotions that flowed between them. Clearly this effect of McCoy's worked both ways.

Behind the surgical screen, Drs. McCoy and Chapel worked steadily on Reena's hand and arm. Once again McCoy was grateful for Maevlynin's anesthetic technique. Resembling a hybrid of telepathic touch and ancient Terran acupuncture, it was perfect for this kind of surgery. Although slower to produce an effect than conventional anesthesia, it was exquisitely precise. Dr. Chapel was working on the thumb while McCoy painstakingly reanastomosed the Romulan equivalent of the ulnar artery just above the wrist. "Reena, would you move your thumb now please? Fine. Now, Maevlynin, let's open up circulation in this artery again and see how it looks. Great." He leaned over the screen. "We're almost done now. I think you'll recover almost perfect function of this hand eventually." Reena acknowledged this report with a brief smile.

Dr. Chapel was fussing over Reena's bed while Maevlynin and Pavel cleared away the instruments. McCoy was talking to Kirk and Spock who had come to see how his latest patient was doing. "It's going to be strict bed rest for a few days but I think she'll be fine. It will be over two weeks though before she's likely to be ready for discharge. She's been through a lot." McCoy wanted to be sure that this patient was returned in mint condition.

Kirk acquiesced. "Scotty's bringing her launch up by tractor beam. Then we'll return to the Romulan ship and complete our survey of it. When you feel she's ready, we will arrange her release through the Organians."

"Dr. McCoy, I am particularly intrigued by your cultiva-

119

tion of this empathetic effect with Miss Tertullian. Could you describe your technique?" Spock inquired.

McCoy was rebandaging his own blisters. "Oh, it's really quite straightforward, Mr. Spock. I simply analyzed the situation logically and then let my intuition tell me what to do." And hoped that the Romulan would read, and believe his emotions telepathically, he thought, but he wasn't about to tell Spock that.

Spock's eyebrow went up a fraction. "Did your intuition 'tell' you to do that, too?" He indicated the blisters.

McCoy replied airily, "Simply one of the hazards of the assignment, Mr. Spock." He really had done a superb job and he wasn't going to let Spock needle him . . . Maevlynin's tinkling laugh alerted him. Kirk and Spock were gazing at something about a meter above his head: a basin of soapy water.

Spock regarded Maevlynin gravely. "Pride goeth before destruction, and a haughty spirit before a fall."

Maevlynin nodded and replied merrily, " 'Tis pride, rank pride, and haughtiness of soul. I think the Romans call it stoicism."

McCoy yelped, "Maevlynin! You wouldn't dare!" and made a frantic but unsuccessful grab for the basin. Inexorably, the basin tipped. McCoy spluttered helplessly.

Four days later, McCoy sat at his desk and ruefully surveyed sick bay. The place had become a zoo. Reena was a popular patient, a unique phenomenon: a Romulan willing to talk, to listen, to learn, to share about anything—except Romulan Space Service—and half the crew seemed to want to talk to her. Finally, he had put Chekov in charge of policing the traffic. He was spending all his free time with her anyway. It had been an excellent move. By limiting other visitors, Chekov had more time with Reena to himself, and McCoy had more of his sick bay to himself. Pavel certainly seemed good for her. She was recovering rapidly. Yesterday he had let her out of bed and now this afternoon Pavel had taken her for a walk.

His reverie was interrupted by the arrival of Captain Kirk. He glanced at Reena's bed. "Bones, where's Reena now? I see you've let her out of bed."

"Oh, she's in Sulu's quarters, Jim."

Kirk did a double take. "She's where?! Bones, are you out of your mind? We're going to return that woman. And you let her go—"

"She'll be all right, Jim. Chekov's with her. She just wanted to see Sulu's weapon collection, that's all."

But Kirk was not worrying about Reena in the clutches of his crew. He was thinking of his ship. "Worse yet. She'll probably talk the two of them into a full tour of the ship." He whirled, "Bones, now that she's out of bed I want her confined to sick bay and the nearest rec room. Nowhere else. That's your responsibility and if you can't enforce it she goes to the brig. I'm not going to release a Romulan with a mental blueprint of our ship."

Reena accepted the restriction quite calmly, saying she really hadn't expected that much. It would have been only logical to have put her in the brig once she was out of bed. The captain was most generous. She and Pavel were sitting on her bed in sick bay watching a portable viewscreen. It was tied into the crew assigned to explore the Romulan vessel. Pavel was helping her go through the exercises to restore hand function. They watched a crew woman on the screen as she walked down a corridor and entered a room. "Yes, that's it. She found my room." Reena was delighted that Pavel had arranged the recovery of her belongings. The crew woman left. Idly, Chekov switched scenes: crew's quarters, mess hall, engineering (a shambles), main computer, the bridge. Something made him glance at Reena. She was looking at her hands.

"What is it? What's wrong, Reena?"

"Please turn it off, Pavel. How would you feel if it were the *Enterprise?* If you had to sit and watch Romulans take apart the remains of your ship?"

Chekov was instantly contrite. "I *am* sorry, Reena. Sometimes I forget. You seem so comfortable here . . . with us . . . that I don't think of you as Romulan."

Reena smiled tiredly, "I know you mean that as a compliment, Pavel." She leaned back on her bed. "I'm tired. Please go and let me rest." He kissed her gently and left. Alone, Reena wept quietly into her pillow. It was so painful

121

and exhausting to live in two worlds. She was coming to appreciate this one. These humans were generous, well-intentioned. With the bomb incident past, their present cruelty was innocent. They had accepted her as a friend and forgot that she was more, or less, or different. Whatever—but it hurt. She saw more clearly the flaws in her own society and culture. But also its strengths. There was much that was good and vigorous and noble about it, much to build on. The same seemed true of this one. But they seemed so implacably irreconcilable. Yet she and Pavel had come together and now she felt as though they would be crushed by this collision of the Empire and the Federation. Pavel—this fascinating human. She cherished his similarities and delighted in his differences—long since she had admitted this attraction to herself. Where would it all end?

She felt a warm touch on her shoulder. It was Maevlynin. She sat up as she felt Maevlynin's mind brush hers lightly: *May I come in?* Wordlessly she accepted the contact. As Maevlynin rocked her gently, she felt the sorrow flowing out from her to the Estryllian. It was like standing on the ridge after the rain had stopped, the storm was spent . . . wet hair plastered to her cheeks and the world fresh and sparkling.

I know, my child, came Maevlynin's thought, *it is always painful when the soul is stretched. But we can do it. We are doing it, and sharing it makes it easier.*

Pavel, too, was distraught. Soon they would be finished with Romulan ship. Reena was gaining strength rapidly. Inevitably the day of her release was coming closer. He couldn't ignore it. And he wouldn't let her go! He had conjured up a dozen mad schemes to prevent her departure. She loved him. He knew that. She was well-liked by the crew. There was ample evidence of that. No one was forcing her to be repatriated. She could stay. Why wouldn't she? Why did she have to be so stubborn? And what would she face on her return? There was no guarantee the Romulans would accept her story in spite of Spock's mind block. They might kill her. He would be powerless to help her. He wouldn't even know!

McCoy was mildly surprised at the knock. If bridge or sick bay needed him they would use the intercom. Usually he was not disturbed by crew when off-duty. If he wanted company, it was easy enough to find . . . "Who is it?"

"Chekov, sir. I'm sorry to bother you but may I come in for a moment, please?"

Uh, oh. It had to come sooner or later. He snapped off his viewer. "Sure. Come on in, Pavel. What's on your mind?" As if he needed to ask.

Chekov poured out his story. McCoy had been with him from the start so there was much he didn't have to say explicitly. He sat on the edge of McCoy's bed, his hands moving restlessly. As McCoy watched him talk, his heart ached. Pavel could be his own son if he'd had one. And he had been responsible for getting Pavel involved with Reena in the first place. He hadn't given him any more choice than they had given Reena. Pavel finished with, "Doctor, what am I going to do?"

"Do, Pavel? What are your alternatives? You can't go home with her. She won't stay here. Suppose she would. What then? Even if Captain Kirk would allow it, Starfleet Command would never permit a Romulan on a starship. Sure the crew like her now—but Pavel, she's confined to quarters. She's not a threat. Think how much trouble Spock has with crew members sometimes and there's no question about his planet's loyalty to the Federation. Would you ask her to face that? Spock handles it, but he's a Vulcan. You can't turn a Romulan loose on the *Enterprise*. That's madness. If you resign your commission and take her off to some frontier planet that never heard of the Romulan Empire, what would either of you do there? The stars are in your blood—both of you. Pavel, you've wanted to be on a starship since you were six! You're a fine navigator. You may be a first officer or even captain of a starship someday. Can you give all that up for Reena? Would she let you?"

McCoy stopped. Maybe he'd said too much. Pavel's shoulders drooped, but his hands were still. For a moment McCoy's eyes mirrored Chekov's pain: another time, another place, another man and woman a long time ago . . . He sat down beside Pavel and put his arm over his shoulder. His voice was gentler now. "Pavel, it never works to force someone into the mold of your needs and wishes. It may seem to for a time but it ultimately fails. And you can't force yourself into someone else's mold. Let her go. Anything else will destroy someone."

"Thank you, doctor. It hurts, but I think I needed to hear that. I'll think about it. Good night."

Not far away the captain also had a caller in his quarters: Spock. "Two items, Captain, that I believe merit your attention this evening."

Kirk laid aside his book. Although his first officer frequently worked beyond his assigned duty hours, he rigorously respected the off-duty status of his human colleagues. This must be urgent. "Yes, Spock. What is it?"

"The Romulan ship's malfunction was not an intrinsic failure. It was sabotaged."

"Sabotaged! How?" Kirk was fully alert.

"By a very efficient Klingon device placed in the main engine room." Spock replied.

"Klingon! Are you sure?" Kirk demanded.

"I have the salvage team's report and complete analysis here. There is no doubt as to the origin of the device."

"Very conveniently having it occur in Federation space. Our Klingon friends seem determined to keep us busy, don't they? Has Starfleet Command been notified?"

"The report is ready for transmission. I thought it would be best to discuss it with you first," Spock replied.

Kirk smiled at the Vulcan. "All right, Spock. Analysis? Recommendations? What's on your mind?"

"It's only a matter of time before the Romulans locate their ship. They will discover precisely what we did and no doubt also ascertain that we have already been aboard her. Their conclusion, however, will be that the Federation arranged it to look like the Klingons. The ship *is* in a sector that the Klingons do not frequent."

"Mmm. You're undoubtedly right, Spock," Kirk mused. "But suppose we notify the Romulans first, give them a complete report. We might make it backfire on the Klingons."

"Precisely my thought, Captain," Spock replied. "Since we are diverting to Organia to return Navigator Tertullian, it would be a simple matter for me to accompany her and give the Romulan ambassador there a full account."

"That's right. The Romulans are due to open their diplomatic mission on Organia any day now, aren't they?"

"Reports are that the imperial flagship was to bring the ambassador and his staff to Organia some days ago," Spock replied.

Kirk's eyes twinkled. "Would our old friend still happen to be in command of the flagship, Mr. Spock?"

"She is still the commander of record," Spock said stiffly. Kirk smiled. Despite the circumstances surrounding their original encounter with the Romulan commander, Spock had as much as admitted his attraction to the woman. I think it would be most appropriate for my first officer to brief the Romulan ambassador." Spock's face remained impassive as Kirk expected, so he continued. "You said there were two items?"

"Yes, Captain. A coded order from Starfleet Command—for your eyes only." Spock handed him the orders.

From his wall safe Captain Kirk took out his personal code key and quickly worked out the message. Then he gave a low whistle. "Well, Spock, it looks as though you will be going to Organia in any event. Here." He handed the decoded message to his First Officer.

DETACH FIRST OFFICER SPOCK FOR TDY AT ORGANIA *ENTERPRISE* PROCEED TO SHERMAN'S PLANET AWAIT FURTHER ORDERS CZERNY LOCATED PENELI CONNECTION IMMINENT STARFLEET COMMAND

"I hope it will be a short assignment, Spock. I don't like being without my First Officer for long," Kirk said.

"Nor do I, Captain," Spock replied.

Reena and Spock would be leaving in the morning. Uhura and McCoy had organized a farewell party. Kirk stood musing at the scene in front of him: eight heads bent together over the cube. Maevlynin was trying to teach them how to

125

play the game. A Vulcan, an Estryllian, Terrans from four continents, and a Romulan. How long would it be before Romulans would participate in the diversity that was the Federation? Kirk wondered. In his lifetime? For Pavel and Reena's sake he fervently hoped so but it didn't seem likely.

The others had said their good-byes and left. McCoy, Maevlynin, Pavel, and Reena walked slowly toward sick bay. They paused at the door. Carefully not looking at them, Chekov said, "Good night, Maevlynin, Doctor," and deliberately set off with Reena in the direction of his quarters. McCoy looked at Maevlynin. Conspiratorily she raised an eyebrow in delightful caricature of Spock. They both grinned.

"Hell," grumbled McCoy, "Jim said it was my responsibility so I'm going to exercise my discretion. If he finds out . . ." He shrugged. Maevlynin headed into sick bay. "Where do you think you're going?"

Indicating Reena's bed, she said, "I think someone ought to sleep there in case you-know-who's famous intuition about his ship gives him insomnia tonight."

"Maevlynin, you're a gem." He kissed her soundly. Might as well—she knew how he felt anyway.

Maevlynin laughed delightedly. "Len, you're learning. Good night."

Reena, Pavel, and McCoy stood in the shuttlecraft bay next to Reena's launch. Spock was already aboard. The Organians had agreed to receive her and get her safely home.

"Well, good-bye, Reena, and good luck. Don't forget us."

"I won't, Dr. McCoy. You may be sure of that . . . and my gratitude."

McCoy suddenly remembered he had something very important to do in sick bay and left them alone.

She leaned her forehead against Pavel's shoulder. "Oh, Pavel. I wish we had another choice," she sighed. "We will do what we have to, but nothing says I have to like it. And I'm frightened."

His arms tightened around her. "That they'll kill you? But you said—"

She made an impatient gesture. "No, they won't. My story and Spock's mind block will take care of that. You have no concept of the diabolical image your *Enterprise* has in the minds of our High Command. They'll believe me. What I fear is losing you. Pavel, promise me you will stay with the *Enterprise*. I'll arrange to be assigned as far away from her as possible." Her voice was low. "I don't ever want to face an engagement with her knowing you're on board."

"I promise," Pavel's voice was bitter. "At least you'll know where I am. And me? How will I know where you are? I'll face that question anytime we meet a Romulan ship. Can't you arrange to stay planet-side?"

"Pavel . . . could you?"

He shook his head. "Let's not argue about it again. Here, I want you to have this. It's been in my mother's family for several generations." He dropped a gold locket into her hand. Reena stripped the silver ring from her finger—the one piece of jewelry she wore. It had the shape of a delicate flower.

"It's a *gilphin,* the native flower of my home, worn only by those from my village. Good-bye, my love."

"Good-bye, Reena."

She stepped into the launch. The door slid closed. Blindly, Pavel made his way across the hangar and into the airlock. Behind him the shuttlecraft bay doors now opened and the Romulan craft slipped into space.

Eight

JEAN STOOD IN the transporter room checking out the assembled materials a final time. They had achieved orbit around Klairos yesterday. Kang had spent the afternoon and early evening in conferences planetside. She and Aernath were expecting the order to beam down as soon as he emerged from this morning's session. Since the night she had accepted Kang's offer she had learned very little more about his thinking. If indeed he had been in the habit of confiding in Mara, he showed little inclination to do so with her. However, the arrangement did appear to satisfy him. At first, he had seemed quite relaxed, sometimes almost cheerful, but as they approached Klairos his manner became taut and moody, never, however, to the point of tension that Jean had observed the night before they orbited Tahrn. He had said nothing further by way of instructions to her and when she had asked him last night he had merely smiled and said, "Remember your position, try to think like a Klingon, and if you have any questions, ask Aernath. He seems to have advised you competently so far." For some reason she did not understand this seemed to amuse him.

Aernath was not amused. Since they had left Tahrn his manner had been distant and distracted. Although they continued to work together he frequently seemed preoccupied. He seldom manifested that almost boyish irreverence which provided her with such a refreshing counterpoint to the generally oppressive military atmosphere of a Klingon battle cruiser. On several occasions, she had become aware that he was scrutinizing her with the same odd speculative look she had noted that night over dinner in her room. Once she had wondered, wistfully, if it might be jealousy. "A half-credit for your thoughts," she had ventured.

"Peneli," he had said shortly and offered no elaboration.

So much for that theory, thought Jean ruefully, thankful that she had not voiced her thoughts more directly. Aernath was disappointed not to be going to Peneli and had every reason to be worried about his own people. Except for a couple of brief instances of tenderness, his actions toward her had never gone beyond those of a cordial colleague which, she admonished herself sternly, was more than one might reasonably expect of any Klingon under the circumstances.

Her reverie was broken by the arrival of Aernath and Tirax, who was again accompanying them on assignment. The clearance to beam down had come through, so Aernath went down to supervise the transfer there while Jean monitored their dispatch from the cruiser. Finally, she and Tirax beamed down to Klairos spaceport. They emerged in a large warehouse where she spotted Aernath and another Klingon overseeing the loading of a glide-car with their equipment. As Jean joined them, the Klairosian suddenly stopped his work and greeted her with an unbelieving stare. "Is this the human?"

"That's her," Aernath affirmed.

The man's hostility was evident. "A woman!" he spat contemptuously.

Aernath flushed but replied in a light tone, "Cymele incarnate, you might say."

The other man glowered darkly at him. "I wouldn't say that too loudly, spacer. I'm not superstitious but there are those who would believe the goddess herself had a human streak the way things have been going here lately. Do you really intend to have a female working on this project?"

"We will be working together," Aernath asserted with just the barest emphasis on the final word. His tone was mild but his eyes flashed angrily. Jean could have hugged him.

At that moment Kang approached. The third Klingon turned to him accusingly. "You didn't tell us that this human was a female!"

Kang's eyes glinted momentarily with grim amusement. "A human is a human. Her gender is irrelevant to your project so I saw no reason to mention it."

The Klingon exploded, " 'Gath's teeth! You're mad! It won't work. Discipline, morale, efficiency! I won't have a woman mucking up the project!"

"That is unlikely to be your problem with her, Kasoth." Kang's face darkened with a frown that Jean had come to recognize as an analogue to Captain Kirk's stubborn look when a command decision was questioned. "I believe I also neglected to mention that she holds consort-status with me. You will do well to accord her the respect due a member of my *Theld*."

Kasoth's mouth opened, then closed abruptly. He saluted Kang stiffly and stalked off clearly unhappy with the state of affairs. Kang's frown faded into a brief smile as he watched Kasoth's receding back. Jean wondered if this, too, was one of Kang's "reasons". He had had dealings with this planet before. Intended or not, she could see it might make things a little easier for her while she was here. Kang was apparently about to beam up to his ship. Her farewell was brief but sincere: "Clear space and good landings. I shall look forward to your return."

He brushed her chin lightly with a finger tip. "You'll survive." It was said softly but with satisfaction.

Jean felt one of her rare flashes of genuine affection for the man. "Thanks," she said simply. Then as Kang's form disappeared in the characteristic flashing of the Klingon transporter beam, she turned to Aernath. "Come on. Let's go face the D.K.E. again." Then she added, "And thanks, Aernath. If I do survive, it will be as much your doing as his." She gave his hand a quick squeeze. He gave her one of his odd looks in return but said nothing.

They rode in silence as the three car convoy moved past

the I.S.G. checkpoint, out of the spaceport and into the surrounding countryside. The windows were not opaqued so Jean got her first glimpses of Klairos. From the flora and fauna on the tapes, she would have placed Klairos somewhere in the late Tertiary period on the Terran-based geological time scale: late Miocene or early Pliocene. There were some variations, of course. Notable was the persistence of myriad large amphibian species as had been pointed out by Aernath's zoologist friend.

The spaceport and Port Klairos, the capital city, had been built less than three-quarters of a century earlier on the first polderland reclaimed from the sea. Located in the temperate zone of the southern hemisphere, it lay virtually encircled by mountains with only a narrow mouth opening to the sea. It was there that the dike and tide gates had been built which allowed this tidal marsh to be drained. A brief portion of their drive paralleled a section of the dike and she could see the gray sea pounding sullenly against it. The cordillera that formed the ring around Port Klairos valley continued out to sea creating a myriad of small-peaked offshore islands. Jean gasped as she caught sight of them. "Vinh Dong Kinh," she murmured to herself. The scene was virtually identical to one that used to hang in her grandfather's study on Aldebaran Colony. As a recent widower with a small daughter, he had brought few possessions with him when he emigrated from Earth to Aldebaran. One was that picture: a coastal scene from near his birthplace somewhere in Southeast Asia she believed. Like many Asians, he often talked of returning there in his old age. It made her homesick and she was thankful when the road turned away inland.

The land here had been desalted enough to support a variety of vegetation; however, much of the area was devoted to industry and the capital itself. Here and there she saw plantings of evergreens. Although winters were mild on the coast here, it was still early spring so other plants were barely coming out in foliage.

The convoy left the valley and moved into the foothills. The road, obviously new, narrowed to a single lane. The second was still under construction. At the summit of the pass, the remaining lane terminated in front of a massive

131

stone building where Jean learned they would complete their journey to the agricultural station with pack animals.

It was cold on the summit and now she could see snow-covered peaks. She thumbed the thermal control unit on her belt up a couple of notches and pulled her hood forward more snugly over her ears. The building served as a sort of combination hotel and headquarters for the construction crew. After a sparse meal of a sort of vegetable soup and sour Klingon bread in a stand-up canteen, they reassembled outside once again. Jean pulled on her fur-lined gloves as she approached the small group. Kasoth was fuming again.

"No one warned me to bring a back-litter and there's none to be had here. Would serve 'em both proper to put her in an equipment rack but that means leaving some stuff here until tomorrow. 'Gath's teeth! Bloody woman's disrupting things already." He glared at her.

Jean looked questioningly at Aernath. "What's the problem?"

"Kasoth says he doesn't have the proper equipment to transport you to the station."

"Why can't I ride up like everyone else?"

Angrily Kasoth turned to Jean. "Have you ever ridden a *krelk*?"

"No," Jean answered truthfully. She hadn't the faintest idea what a *krelk* was. Then, annoyed with this Klingon's condescension, she added, "But I've ridden worse. If you can ride them, I will." No sooner had she made this rash statement than she remembered the beasts that had pulled the ceremonial carriage on Tahrn. She endured a momentary panic at the thought of having to ride one of those.

When she actually saw the *krelk* a few moments later she laughed, partly from sheer relief. They looked like a cross between a llama and a kangaroo. The average beast's head towered about half a meter above hers with the back at shoulder height; coarse dun-colored hair with black dorsal stripe, black ears and nose; the forelegs were slender and delicate like a goat's. The hind legs were slightly longer and much more heavily muscled. The large tail looked like the formidable weapon it was. The last meter of its length was prehensile, allowing the *krelk* to seize attackers and batter

132

them against any convenient rock. One rode the *krelk,* she discovered, with the prehensile tail wrapped once about the waist and once about the pommel of the saddle. This meant that one had warning of an impending attack as the *krelk* would uncoil its tail unless, Kasoth pointed out, the beast simply forgot and used its rider as a blunt instrument against its assailant.

The rider controlled the *krelk* by foot and knee movements so as to leave hands free for weapons—a system apparently common to Klingon planets but unfamiliar to Jean. Aernath rode alongside, coaching her.

The rough roadbed gave way to a narrow but well-worn trail. For a while they followed a mountain stream edged with a lacy purfle of winter's last ice. Snow still clung to the southern slopes and shaded valleys but faint green showed on the clear northern slopes. The stream dropped away on their left as the trail turned inland to the west. Shortly they passed a trail leading back down toward the sea, giving a glimpse of open lowlands at its foot. "That's the polderland being reclaimed by the agricultural station," Aernath said as they passed. In that universal anticipation of a home stable, the animals quickened their pace, giving powerful leaps that Jean found quite disconcerting. It wasn't until they arrived at the station and she dismounted that she could adequately survey her new surroundings.

Like newly settled Federation worlds, this planet presented a peculiar amalgam of space-age technology and frontier construction. In this gently rolling upland valley it was more apparent than in Port Klairos where the Klingon penchant for massive stone buildings was expressed. Settled before stone quarrying was well underway, this valley presented a different appearance. The oldest buildings were geodesic domes constructed of lightweight materials analogous to duralloy and flex-glas brought by the first settlers. Subsequent structures utilized a plentiful local tree called stonewood, giving a rough-hewn, rustic appearance but lasting for decades without need for further maintenance.

Above the settlement buildings the flashnet guaranteed protection from aerial predators. The perimeter was similarly guarded. Only in the outer fields did one need to be vigilant. Originally a farming village, it had recently been converted to an agricultural experiment station to meet the threat of the blight. Some of the original inhabitants remained; others had been moved out to accommodate the station personnel.

Jean's quarters consisted of a small outbuilding. The single dark room contained a bed, table, bench, and massive stone fireplace. Smoke-blackened beams overhead testified both to the fireplace's long use and faulty draft. Jean distributed her meager belongings on the lone shelf and wooden wall pegs, then tackled the task of building a fire. At least on Tahrn her room had had central heat and lighting. It promised to be a grim summer ahead.

That assessment was promptly underscored by her next encounter with a Klairosian. The fire well established, she set out to locate the mess hall. A chill wind swept down off the peaks, gusting and eddying around the buildings of the compound. Rounding a corner, she spotted a Klingon coming her way. She approached him intending to ask directions. He looked at her with angry astonishment and abruptly sent her sprawling with a powerful blow to her head. Dazed, Jean tried to sit up. The man seized her angrily by the back of her hood. "Insolent scum. What *Theld* owns you that you dare to . . ."

Another voice broke in. "Hold, Kinsman. What's the problem?"

The Klingon paused to glance at the new arrival. "Look for yourself. She approached me like this. Don't interfere, Spacer."

"Hmmm. I see. Allow me." Tirax bent over Jean, inserted a finger under her chin and stripped her hood cleanly off.

The other Klingon growled, "The human!"

"Yes, the human. Unfortunately, she is also of the *Theld* of Kang. You would be ill-advised to rebuke her further—for the moment." He turned to Jean with a malicious grin. "On Klairos, a woman never approaches any man with her head covered. Remember that and keep your place, human!" Turning back to the other Klingon, he clapped him on the shoulder. "Come, Kinsman, let's share a drink before we

134

eat." The two Klingons sauntered off, Tirax swinging her hood mockingly in his hand.

The agonizer, Jean thought vindictively as she watched them leave, was appropriate technology for the Klingon culture. They deserved it. Grimly she got up, dusted herself off, and looked around. She still didn't know where the mess hall was.

When she did find it she joined the line of women and children waiting their turn to eat. Men ate first, then women and children. It was her first close contact with the local inhabitants. The line was laser straight, unmoving and pre-ternaturally quiet. Part of the quiet came from apathy. Only the boys seemed to have any energy or curiosity. How much of the apathy was from malnutrition and how much was culturally determined Jean could not tell, but the ravages of malnutrition were clear to be seen. Even the pregnant women, of whom there were many, looked emaciated. Shocked, she wondered what the infant mortality rate was on this planet this year. Ignoring the curious stares and occasional whispers, Jean moved through the food line and carried her soup and bread to the nearest table. A number of armed guards were posted about the periphery of the room. As she moved to sit down the nearest one snarled at her. "Not there, woman. Over there." He gestured preemptorily. Hastily Jean complied having no wish to provoke another attack. The first table, she now realized, was reserved for the boys. It got extra rations.

The meal proceeded in silence. Jean ate slowly, stealing occasional glances at her tablemates. She shivered. The aura of prison camp was too strong to be ignored. Finished, she followed her tablemates' lead and carried her utensils to the dish line. Then she escaped to her own quarters. She spent a cold night but at least she was left undisturbed.

Breakfast was a kind of gruel and something Jean took to be the Klairosian equivalent of coffee. It was strong and very bitter but definitely a stimulant. Aernath was waiting for her when she emerged from the dining hall. He handed her the hood. "I'm sorry I didn't warn you about that, but I wasn't aware of it myself. Are you all right?"

"I'll survive," Jean said shortly, stuffing the hood in a pocket. "Let's get to work."

Aernath stiffened perceptibly. "Fine. Follow me." He turned on his heel and set off.

Damn! Did it again, Jean thought. She really was glad to see him. Why had she let her general anger spill over at him? Contritely she reached out and took his arm. "Look, I'm sorry, Aernath. Thanks for retrieving my hood. I—"

Now he was curt in return. "That's another thing. Don't touch a man here unless you're given permission first. It's impertinent." Stung, Jean pulled back. In a slightly softer tone he added, "With me, of course, you always have permission. Don't worry about it." Pointedly she ignored him. They passed a group of Klingons going the other way. When they were safely several steps beyond them Aernath quietly exploded, "Blast it, Jean, I don't make the rules here! I'm just trying to keep you out of trouble."

Mollified, she took the proffered elbow. "I know," she said wearily. "Like I said, let's just get to work."

The lab, in contrast to her quarters, was well outfitted and comfortable. By the time Aernath's lunch shift arrived they were nearly set up. Jean finished unpacking by herself. When she returned from her shift she found Aernath elated. "I got an assignation of polderland. We're going down to look at it this afternoon. Come on."

As they approached the group by the *krelk* corral, Jean stared curiously at the contraption atop one *krelk*. "What's that?" she demanded of the Klingon holding the animal.

"The back-litter. What you ride in," he replied.

"I will not," Jean stated flatly. The Klingon looked startled and confused. Aernath busied himself with his own harness, an amused smile on his face. "I will not ride in that . . . that cage!" she declared hotly. "Take it off and get me a saddle." The groom looked even more uncertain. He glanced at Aernath who was suddenly very busy turning his own *krelk* around. Then he turned to Tirax who had just arrived.

"The human—she . . . uh . . . wants a saddle," he explained.

Tirax looked at Jean. She glared back. "I won't ride in that contraption. It's a trap, a . . . a menace."

At that point Kasoth appeared. "Now what's the matter?"

"The human demands a saddle, Commander," said the groom nervously.

"Out of the question . . ."

"Let her have it." Tirax's voice was flat and cold.

Kasoth turned to him furiously. "Are you out of your mind? I suppose you want me to issue her a blaster, too?"

"Obviously not," Tirax responded, unruffled. Then he shrugged. "If she wants to ride unarmed in a saddle, let her. It's her hide."

Kasoth continued to fume. "By the bowels of Durgath, Lieutenant, I won't be responsible for this. I told Kang this woman would be a disruptive influence. It's bad for discipline, morale—"

Tirax overrode him. "You handle the discipline, Commander. I'll look after the woman. As I said, if something unfortunate happens to her, it's her hide. And my problem."

Kasoth turned angrily to the groom. "Get a saddle."

Jean noted Aernath carried a blaster. She hoped he could use it well. Her accidental demise, she was convinced, was just the sort of problem Tirax would welcome.

The trip down was uneventful. Aernath rode beside her constantly coaching her on the foot and knee movements necessary for controlling her mount. By the time they reached the polder she was beginning to get the rhythm of it. It was a beautiful sunny day and quite warm down in the lowlands. If it hadn't been for the presence of Tirax and the other armed guards, Jean would have enjoyed it immensely. Even so, she and Aernath became absorbed in discussion and planning how to lay out their allotted plots. The soil looked good. One area nearest the dike was selected to see how both strains would respond to still salty soil. They also collected soil samples for analysis. It was almost dusk when they set out for the station.

Again Aernath rode beside her watching her movements critically, offering occasional tips. Although it took total concentration, she was managing quite well. Fortunately, she seemed to have a very placid animal. It was not inclined to bridle or sidestep nearly as much as Aernath's or Tirax's *krelk* just in front of her. Her total concentration was broken by a sudden shout. " 'Ware!" It was Tirax. In one smooth motion he rose, turned, and blasted over her head. Almost immediately she heard a second and third shot from beside and behind her even as her *krelk* loosed its tail. Then she was engulfed and carried to the ground by a flopping mass of feathers. Panicked, she struggled under the moving weight of the thing, dimly hearing a confusion of shouts and bleating *krelks*. Then she was pulled free. Tirax was hoisting up an enormous white bird, surveying it critically. Aernath knelt beside her, the amethyst eyes frantic. "Jean! Are you all right?"

She laughed a little shakily as he helped her up. "I seem to be unhurt." She brushed herself off.

"Good shot, Tirax. Look, mine and Aernath's only grazed the tail feathers." Several Klingons were gathered around the snowbird. One black hole was bored neatly through its breast, two through its tail.

Jean remounted and brought her *krelk* alongside Tirax's. She leaned over. "Thanks."

He glanced up at her briefly across his own *krelk*, then swung the bird up to secure it behind his saddle. "Better luck next time." He swung up into his saddle.

Damn you, too! Jean thought and viciously swung her *krelk* back to join Aernath without another word. The adrenaline surge carried her back to camp before she got shaky, but it was several days before she worked up the courage to ride back down to the polder. She took pains to make sure it was always with a party returning well before dusk which was when the greater snow birds began to hunt.

Planting proceeded in the polder and later in the upland plots. The growing season was underway but the food ration didn't improve noticeably. Jean lost weight and though the nights were warmer she still shivered miserably in bed at night. In the three weeks since her arrival, several women and girls and one small boy that she knew of for sure had disappeared from the line. This evening she headed for the mess a little early.

138

Approaching the corner of the building she heard a thin scream followed by an angry voice. "Filthy wretch! I'll teach you to steal food when you're supposed to be serving." Coming on around she saw a Klingon send a girl to the ground with a blow. He drew back his foot to follow with a kick. His back was to Jean. Out of reflex, she launched herself at the back of his other leg. He crumpled suddenly over her back. With an agility that startled her even as she did it, Jean rolled over and up to face the man. His astonishment gave her a momentary advantage.

"Leave her alone!" she raged. "You've got the women on such short rations it's no wonder if she's stealing food."

Recovered now, the man came up with a snarl. "Why you little . . . human!" She ducked sideways and avoided his first lunge. He turned and caught her arm. At the same time she was seized from behind.

"I believe the human interrupted you. My apologies. Please proceed. I'll prevent her further interference." The other Klingon glowered fiercely at Tirax but it was clear the Lieutenant's suggestion had the force of a command. He backed away from Jean and resumed his savage attack on the girl.

Jean watched in helpless fury. "Coward!" she screamed. "You haven't . . ." Tirax clamped a hand over her mouth as the other Klingon turned back to them.

"No, Kinsman, don't let her goad you. Even if it were permitted, I wouldn't advise you to challenge her. She's vicious with a dagger. Better than you have felt her sting." The other Klingon's eyes widened fractionally, then he turned and stalked off. Tirax's fingers clamped painfully into her flesh. "But someday, human, that sting will be pulled," he hissed—". . . someday . . ." He released her with a shove.

By now quite a crowd of women and children had gathered. Jean looked at the form of the girl on the ground. "What about her?" she demanded of Tirax.

He shrugged. "Her Theld will take care of her—if they wish." He went back into the mess hall without further comment.

Jean looked around at the impassive faces. She picked one

young women whom she recognized as one who had sat next to her on a couple of occasions. "You. Do you know this girl?" The woman nodded. "Well, go get someone from her family. Get help."

The woman hesitated, then said. "They don't want her. She's been *Theld-barred.*"

"What! Why?" Jean demanded sharply.

The woman twisted her hands nervously as if frightened to have attention drawn to her. "Too many mouths to feed. She's a girl."

"Well, dammit, if nobody else wants her, I do." Jean snapped. "Here, you." She grabbed the woman by the arm. "And you." She pulled a second girl from the crowd. "Take her to my quarters and wait there with her until I get there. Now move!" Intimidated, the two scrambled to obey her. The mess hall had opened to the waiting line. Jean stalked to the front of the line and no one challenged her. She collected two rations and carried them to her quarters.

The girl who had been beaten lay huddled on the hearth. The other two hovered uncertainly beside her. Jean set the food on the table. "You can go now. You," she indicated one, "go find Aernath in the lab and tell him I'll be late this afternoon." She bolted the door behind them and turned her attention to the girl. Pitifully thin, covered with cuts and welts that would soon be ugly bruises, she moaned in pain when Jean tried to move her. With a wet rag, Jean cleaned her face, arms and hands as best she could. There seemed to be no broken bones but Jean worried about internal injuries. Cradling the girl's head in her lap she urged her to take a little water. The girl retched violently, then started shivering. Alarmed, Jean pulled a blanket off her bed and covered the girl. As she was building up the fire, someone tried the door, then pounded loudly.

Jean went to the door, a stick of wood in hand. "Who is it?"

"Jean, open up. It's me—Aernath."

"Are you alone?"

"Cymele's Cloak! Of course I'm alone. Open up!" She slid back the bolt. Aernath charged into the room, first-aid kit in hand. "Are you all right?"

140

"I'm fine. She's the one who's hurt." Jean gestured to the girl. "Come on. Give me a hand."

"Wait a minute. The woman who came to the lab said you got into a fight with a man because he hit a girl. Is that true?"

"Hit her?! He looked like he was going to kill her. I couldn't just—"

"Jean," he demanded, his voice ominously quiet, "never mind that. Just tell me—what did you do?"

"I . . . I tackled him. Knocked him down." Jean replied, suddenly defensive.

"You saw him hit someone so you . . ." he spluttered unbelievingly, "you . . . just . . . tackled him? Just like that?" She nodded. "By the Lair of Durgath, what did you expect to accomplish by that?"

"I didn't expect to accomplish anything. I was just mad."

"Jean." He took her by the shoulders and shook her gently. "Jean, you can't take on this planet single-handed. If Tirax had not come along you might have been killed. We can't keep you out of trouble if you keep going out of your way to look for it."

She struggled with her anger. She wanted to scream at him just because he was a Klingon, because he accepted it, but she saw the concern in his eyes. She tried. "Aernath, you just don't understand—"

"Maybe I do, maybe I don't, but as I said, I don't make the rules here."

"No," she retorted caustically, "you just follow them. Now give me some help with this kid." He complied stiffly. She had pushed that button again but this time she didn't give a damn.

After Aernath administered a stimulant and a pain-killer from his kit, the girl perked up. Together they patched her up. She looked to be about twelve or thirteen. Jean was seated on the hearth again, cradling the girl in her lap. "What's your name?"

The girl shook her head slightly. "Don't have a name. They call me Aydutywa."

"Unwanted one, huh. Well, I want you. Suppose we call you Tywa from now on. How's that?" The girl looked at her wide-eyed and nodded. Aernath had finished repacking the

141

kit. "Aernath, would you please hand me one of those trays on the table? Let's see if she can eat something now."

He brought both trays and set them on the floor, then stood watching her feed Tywa. "Jean, is that all that you brought for your lunch there?"

Something in his voice made her look up but his face was impassive. "That's the ration," she stated flatly.

"That's all you usually get?"

"I told you they had the women on short rations."

"I know you did but I didn't realize . . ." he broke off and poked the fire watching the smoke curl out and up to the rafters. He turned around and surveyed the room. "These are your quarters?" She nodded, puzzled by his manner. "Durgath take that Tirax!" he muttered, his face suddenly grim. "Jean, stay here with her this afternoon. Don't worry about the lab. I'll take care of things." He picked up the kit and left.

Approximately mid-afternoon, Aernath came bursting in. Jean glanced anxiously at Tywa but she did not wake up. Triumphantly he slapped two colored plastidiscs on the table. "There. Tywa is now officially assigned to you—on standard ration. You're on ration and a half. I'm afraid you're stuck with these quarters but they promised to plaster the chinks in the walls. Pretty soon it should be warm enough that you won't need that blasted fireplace."

"How in space did you arrange all that?"

"I reminded Kasoth that the human digestive system isn't as efficient as ours. I also told him that this was a calculated insult to Kang and that a new rim planet couldn't afford to antagonize the Imperial Fleet let alone the future emperor and . . ." he stopped, seeing the look on her face, then added lamely, "Well, that's all true, after all. And it worked; I succeeded."

"Logical and efficient Klingon tactics. Survive and succeed." Jean sighed. "I think Tywa will be all right. Let's go back to the lab. I need to get back to work before this planet drives me stark raving mad—in both senses of the word."

Things went more smoothly in the ensuing weeks. Most of the Klingons avoided Jean and she avoided them. Frequently Tywa would bring Jean her meals at the lab or her quarters. The girl worshiped her and provided a constant unobtrusive comfort to her in dozens of small ways. At night she curled up beside her as warm and contented as a *jequard* kit.

Weather was favorable and both strains were growing moderately well. The upland soil was thin and the grain was not flourishing there as it had on Tahrn. In the polder, however, it promised to approach the performance on Tahrn except for the patch in brackish soil near the dike. There the "Czerny strain" had apparently contracted some kind of blight; not the *Tseni* virus but some other problem. They had been monitoring it closely.

This morning Jean turned over sleepily and burrowed back under the covers. Comfortably she listened to Tywa puttering at the fireplace. Somewhere the child had acquired a boiling pot. One of her favorite rituals was to fix morning *khizr*, the Klingon equivalent of coffee, for the two of them. In a few moments she would come back with two steaming mugs of it and snuggle happily next to Jean while the two of them nursed their morning drinks and planned the day.

"It's raining," Tywa announced as she handed Jean the cup.

"Rats. Aernath won't be back from the supply trip to Port Klairos until late afternoon and that means I'll have to make the trip to the polder by myself in the rain. Do you think it'll rain all day?"

"No, it will probably stop by noon."

"Well then, I think I'll wait until after lunch to go. I've got to run the next set of tests on that blighted grain today. Can't wait longer and it will take me several hours without Aernath. Why Tywa, you got breakfast already! How did you manage that?"

The girl wrinkled her nose with pleasure. "I've got a friend in the kitchen. If I get there early enough she'll let me sneak ours out before the mess hall opens."

"You're a jewel, Tywa, and so is your friend in the kitchen. Tell her thanks from me." Jean leaned over and kissed the delighted girl on the forehead. "Now I better eat and get to work. See if you can talk your friend into an early lunch and I'll go to the polder after that."

"We'll do it, Jean." Tywa was as good as her word. Shortly before the men's second mess she appeared at the lab with lunch. The rain had stopped.

"Do you know where Tirax is?"

"He and several others went out hunting early this morning. They aren't expected back until mid-afternoon." Among her other skills, Tywa exhibited an omnivorous ability to keep track of people's movements and activities, which was one of the reasons she had survived as long as she had as an outcast.

"Hmm. Well, I guess I'll get one of the guards from the corral. Tywa, keep a sharp eye out for Aernath. If he gets back before I do, ask him to come down and give me a hand."

The Klingon corral guard grumbled at her projected trip. "No one else is scheduled for the polder today."

"Can't be helped. You know Aernath and I have been making trips every other day and today is the day. The sooner we go the sooner we'll be back."

He produced the *krelks* and accompanied her in silence. The road construction crew had reached the polder trail with one lane now she noted. Maybe they would reach the ag-station before the snow flew. The polder was deserted. After a couple of attempts to enlist the guard's aid, Jean gave up in exasperation and resigned herself to doing the work alone. The Klingon retired to the nearby dike muttering sullenly about humans and women in general. Jean ignored him.

A good while later Jean stood up at the far end of the plot to call to him that her work was finished. He was sitting on the dike bank of one of the drainage canals idly tossing pebbles into the water. Rising out of the water onto the dike just behind him was a huge saurian head, nearly a meter in length. Jean stood immobilized for a split second. The head was followed by one and then another ponderous clawed foot. Galvanized, she yelled a warning. The Klingon scrambled up. As he turned to fire he slipped on the wet grass of the dike and his shot glanced off the shoulder of the beast, which was now entirely up on the dike, some four meters of amphibious motion. It spat a shrill hiss of rage and pain, then a sheet of flame.

The flame licked at the Klingon. He screamed and fired wildly, hitting the beast twice more but not vitally. Enraged, it bore down on him with another blast. Jean turned and fled toward the *krelk*. She heard a final strangled scream and then another shrill call from the beast. She glanced back. Moving incredibly fast for such bulk, the enraged amphibian was now coming after her. She glanced ahead. She would never make it to the *krelk*. At the edge of the polder where the cliffs came down to the sea, the tidal wash had undercut the soft stone here and there. One such tidal cave lay just ahead of her. She threw herself down, rolled in, and slid hastily back as far as she could. A scant meter away she could see the beast's snout and forefeet as it stood puzzling where its quarry had gone. Horrified, she watched the tip of the snout begin to swing to and fro, a long lizard-like tongue flicking in and out, seeking her scent. The beast couldn't get in under the overlying ledge but if it sensed her it might fry her in place. Jean reached for the only weapon she had—the dagger in her boot.

The flickering tongue began to probe the crevice. Jean waited and watched. At the precise extreme of one probe she stabbed, pinioning the tongue to the rock. With a scream the beast reared back and released a blast of flame at the rock. As she had hoped, it reared up enough that the flames struck only the ledge above. Now she could hear the panicked bleating of the *krelk*. Apparently it attracted the attention of the amphibian as well. She watched the feet move off in that direction. She heard more bleating and hisses and then finally silence. The fragment of tongue in front of her gave off a nauseating stench.

She waited nearly an hour before she dared slide over to the opening and look out. She saw the amphibian slowly crawling along the opposite side of the valley. It paused, then laboriously began to dig a shallow pit. Jean wondered if it was laying eggs. It seemed a bit late in the summer for that but she knew little about the habits of Klairosian amphibians. It was nearly dusk. Would she be stuck here all night? The stench was still strong. Although she could not sit up, she rolled over and extracted a specimen bag from the pouch at her waist. Gingerly, she edged the fragment into the bag with her dagger and tucked it into her collection pouch. She settled back to wait.

Dusk came and then dark. She dozed fitfully. Suddenly she woke up alert at a sound nearby. Fearing the beast had returned she slid back again. Then, hearing a soft bleat and low voices, she scrambled out of her hiding place. The voices stopped and she was blinded by a bright light being beamed at the cliff.

"Jean!" She recognized Aernath's voice. Putting up her hand to cover her eyes, she stumbled in the direction of the voice.

"Aernath! Thank God! I . . ." A *krelk* tail appeared out of the darkness and picked her up abruptly. She was plunged into darkness again and still could see nothing. Suspended in the air, she heard Tirax's voice.

"What happened to your guard, human?"

The light was back on her. "He's dead, I think. We were attacked by some kind of beast. Tirax, please put me down."

"Where is he? Where were you attacked?"

"I don't know. Over by the dike somewhere . . . it came out of the water . . . Tirax, please!"

Aernath's voice came out of the dark cold and flat. "All right, Tirax, you've made your point. Put her down."

Jean felt herself lowered suddenly, plunged into the dark. She was totally disoriented. The *krelk* released her into someone's arms. "Jean!" The whisper was Aernath's. She clung to him convulsively.

Tirax's voice came out of the dark beside her. "All right. You four go back with Aernath. The rest of us will check out the dike. Hela!" He urged his mount foward.

Aernath was wrapping his cloak around her. Beneath her she felt the *krelk* turn and start uphill. Shaking with fear and exhaustion, she buried her face in his shoulder and began to sob. His arm around her tightened and his other hand cradled the back of her head. She felt his lips at her ear. "Shhh. You're not hurt, are you?" She shook her head. "All right then, get it out of your system before we get back to camp." They rode on in silence. Finally Jean's sobs subsided. Again Aernath murmured in her ear, "By Cymele, you humans cry a lot. Finished?" She nodded against his shoulder. "You were a fool to go down there alone. Why didn't you wait for me?"

"I didn't go alone," she protested weakly. "I took a guard along; besides we'd agreed that those tests should be done today. If I'd waited for you we wouldn't have finished before dusk. As it was we would have, but that thing came up in broad daylight."

"What's done is done. You're safe; that's the main point. But Kasoth is fit to be tied. When that one *krelk* came back riderless and he discovered only two of you had gone down he decked two corral guards on the spot." But Jean was past caring. She simply dozed off on his shoulder.

He awakened her when they reached the corral. "We'll be going to report to Kasoth now. Can you do it coherently?"

"Don't worry," she said firmly, "I'm done weeping."

Kasoth was in the ag-station bar with several other Klingons. Jean glanced about curiously as she had never been in there. Built of stonewood and other local woods, its low-beamed ceilings, massive tables and benches gave the appearance of great age and permanence. Kasoth frowned at the arriving party. "You found the human. Where's the rest of the patrol?"

"Looking for Kinath, Commander. We found his *krelk,* or what was left of it anyway, on the polder. She claims it was a sea beast of some sort."

"Well, human, let's have your story."

"Certainly, Commander." She sank down on the nearest bench. "May I have something hot to drink please?"

Kasoth slammed his hand on the table. "Stand as you were, woman! Your story first, we will see about details later."

Jean shrugged, pulled herself to her feet and proceeded to tell her story. Just as she was completing it Tirax and the rest of the patrol arrived. They reported finding nothing but Kinath's blaster, some blood, and a badly trampled area around the dike. While Tirax was reporting, Aernath unobtrusively set down a mug and a small dish of meat in front of her. She flashed him a grateful look. The meat was excellent, the drink hot and spicy. The discussion turned to speculation on the identity of the amphibian.

"Oh, I almost forgot. I have something that may help with that." Jean fumbled with the collecting pouch on her belt. She found the specimen bag and shook out its contents on the table in front of Kasoth.

"What's that?" he demanded.

"A piece of the beast's tongue."

"Its tongue! 'Gath's Bones, how did you get a piece of its tongue?"

"I told you it chased me into a tidal cave. It couldn't reach me under the ledge—except for its tongue. I was afraid if it sensed me there it would blast me like it did Kinath. I figured I'd try to scare it away so I stabbed it in the tongue with my dagger. It worked. That's when it went after the *krelk.*"

"Dagger? What dagger?"

Jean looked at Kasoth in dismay. His face wore an ominous scowl in response to her inadvertent revelation. Aernath broke in smoothly. "It is customary among Aldebaranians to carry such a weapon. We permitted her to keep it thinking she might need it in the field—a justified assumption as we now see. Besides, it obviously posed no threat to any alert Klingon warrior."

Jean winced inwardly at this barb. Aernath must be really angry with Tirax to bait him openly like that. Emboldened by Kasoth's momentary hesitation, she stepped into Aernath's subterfuge and expanded it into an outrageous tale. "Yes, it's the *schlizls* you see. They're a burrowing animal that's common on Aldebaran. Their bite is toxic to humans, fatal to children. They are agile and attack without warning so we learn to defend ourselves at an early age. No man worth his weapons would take a wife who couldn't match him in dagger throw. She has to protect his offspring."

"So you kill them with your dagger?" one of the Klingons asked.

"It's not quite that simple," Jean assured him solemnly. "They are covered with hard scales, so you have to hit them in the eye. Fortunately, they have very large eyes." She looked around and picked up a five-ring linked puzzle game from the table in front of her. She indicated the middle ring. "About this size."

"Anhh." The Klingon's response was frankly disbelieving.

Jean deftly slipped the middle ring out and walked across the room. She selected a panel of softer wood that would take a dagger point. "This should do." She crossed back to Tirax and offered him the ring. "Lieutenant, would you oblige me?" She smiled sardonically. He shot her a look of pure venom. Grasping her dagger, she took her position in front of Kasoth's table and contemplated Tirax holding the ring across the room. His unblinking gaze met hers steadily, giving no hint that he felt other than the ordinary suspense about her ability to hit the target. She waited. The silence in the room grew. It was the tiniest flicker of a blink by which Tirax finally betrayed his tension. She threw.

Tirax let go of the ring. It dangled from the dagger point. Jean crossed to retrieve her blade from the wall. She met his eyes as she murmured, "Better luck next time."

One of Kasoth's drinking partners inquired, "Tell me, human, did you match Commander Kang in this little dagger game of yours?"

Jean replaced her dagger. She despised these Klingon men of Klairos. Kang was a different matter. One could do worse than persuade them to emulate him. She smiled disarmingly. "He credited me for trying." Then she spread her hands in mock dismay. "I'm afraid if Kang waited to find his match from Aldebaran, he'd be doomed to celibacy." Several of the Klingons chuckled until silenced by a glare from Kasoth. Suddenly, Jean was very tired. "With your permission, Commander, I'll go to my quarters. It's been a long day."

"Dismissed." Kasoth stared morosely at the door as Jean and Aernath exited. "Lieutenant, that human is a menace. Please notify your commander that while we humbly acknowledge our debt to him for the grain, we nonetheless request that woman be removed as soon as possible." He slammed his fist on the tabletop. "Otherwise, I will not be responsible for her safety!" Tirax nodded sympathetically.

As Jean emerged from the bar a small figure detached itself from the shadows and catapulted into her: Tywa. The girl had been listening from the doorstep. Now she clung to Jean covering her face and hands with fervent kisses. "Oh, Jean, I was afraid you'd been killed!"

Jean gathered her up in a warm embrace. "I'm fine, Tywa. We humans are pretty hard to kill off. Come on. Let's go home."

Later as they settled in bed, Tywa tugged shyly at her sleeve. "Jean, please tell me a story before we go to sleep—like always."

"I am not going to tell you about fighting the monster in the polder just before you go to sleep," Jean replied firmly. "No need for both of us to have nightmares." She scooped Tywa into one arm and punched the pillow taut behind her head. "How about the story of how Captain Kirk and the *Enterprise* crew rescued the children from the evil monster on Triacus?"

"No, Jean, tell me about Commander Kang and his ship. Tell me again what it's like to be on an imperial battle cruiser!" The girl's eyes shone.

Jean sighed. "Loyal, true-blue Klingon, aren't you, my dear?" She started once again on Tywa's favorite story. If Kang ever again intended to carry an integrated crew, here was one eager volunteer.

The *krelk* bleated and pranced skittishly on the road. It did not like the highway construction. One lane of the road now stretched beyond the agricultural station to the north. Trips to the polder involved threading one's way through a constant procession of construction equipment and materials. Jean breathed a little easier as she coaxed her *krelk* through the noise and construction. This was only her second trip down since the accident and she hoped it might be her last. Even though she was with a large party, she would be just as happy to get back to the station and never lay eyes on the polder again. Observations were completed and they had begun harvesting the Czerny strain down there today. Of course, the upland plots, having been planted later, were not ready yet. They would stand until snow flew which could be any week now. . . . Her thoughts were interrupted by the sight of an I.S.G. glide-car drawn up to the entrance of the experiment station. Could it be Kang so soon? She glanced back. Aernath and most of the rest of the party were still straggling up the trail to the road. Urging her *krelk* forward she passed the lead Klingon and arrived first at the corral.

"Who came in the I.S.G. car?" she asked as her mount swung her down.

The groom shrugged indifferently, "Someone from I.S.G. H.Q.—Port Klairos."

"Is that all? No one else?" Jean tried not to let her disappointment show. The Klingon shook his head. Impatiently Jean headed for her room. Tywa was as likely as anyone else to know what was going on and she would be more forthcoming.

When she entered the room the first thing she saw was her belongings neatly packed and piled in the center of the room. It took her a moment to locate Tywa. The girl was huddled in a corner by the fireplace. Jean caught a sudden hand movement and then the girl was unmoving again. Alarmed, Jean moved to Tywa's side. She had obviously been crying though her face was impassive now. "Tywa," she asked anxiously, "what's happened to you? What is it?"

"I have your things ready. You will leave soon." The girl's voice was thick and the words came slowly.

"Tywa!" Jean shook her by the shoulders. "What's wrong with you?" She caught a glimpse of something by Tywa's hand and pulled a vial from the ashes on the hearth. Fiercely she grabbed Tywa's head and held the vial before her. "What is this? What have you done?"

"Poison . . . it's . . . faster . . . this . . . way."

"Oh, God! No!" Jean screamed. "Tywa, you can't!" Frantically she forced Tywa's mouth open and rammed her fingers down the girl's throat. This seemed to rouse Tywa who protested faintly. Jean persisted wondering if Klingon physiology was equipped with a gag reflex. Apparently it was. Tywa vomited very satisfactorily. Jean grabbed her mug and forced two cupfuls of lukewarm water from the boiling pot down Tywa's throat, then repeated the maneuver. By this time, no longer lethargic, Tywa attacked her angrily with her fists.

151

"Stop it! Why didn't you just leave me alone?" Then she began to cry.

Jean gathered her into a tight hug. "Shh, child. What a terrible thing to say. Whatever made you do such an idiotic thing in the first place?" She got no answer for long minutes except Tywa's sobs. In those moments Jean wondered what she had done by taking in this waif. Her reactions at the time had been instinctive. Then she had been reassured by Aernath's efforts which had solved the immediate problem. Without explicitly discussing it, she had assumed that he could make some satisfactory arrangement for the girl before they left. "Tywa, Aernath and I will make arrangements for you before we leave. We won't just abandon you."

Her face buried in Jean's shoulder, Tywa shook her head. "You can't. No Theld here will have me. When you leave they're going to send me to the pens."

"Pens? What in space does that mean?"

"The diving pens at Port Klairos. That's where they send . . . extra people. It's a sort of cheap labor pool. Anyone can requisition you from there for day labor or a night's pleasure. All they have to do is feed you. No work—no food. If there's no other work then there's diving for *amarklor*—until a sea beast gets you. Like it did Kinath." By now her voice was bleak but matter of fact.

Jean stared at her aghast to hear such worldly-wise fatalism in an almost child. She pulled the girl up. "Absolute nonsense. They'll do no such thing. Come on—let's get you cleaned up and then we'll go help Aernath in the lab. We can talk it over there."

Aernath was not encouraging. He listened to Jean's story, then sent Tywa on an errand. "Jean, we are being pulled out of here ahead of schedule. I don't know why but whatever it is, it won't be helped by a fuss over this girl. They're not going to kill her. She's a tough girl. She can work and she'll eat. She'll survive."

"Work?!" Jean exploded. "You call prostituting a child work? Or sending her out to face those . . . those sea demons?"

His eyes flashed angrily. "Jean, we can't force a *Theld*

here to take her if they don't want her. Just what in space do you think you can do?"

"Take her with me then," she responded grimly.

Aernath stared at her open-mouthed. "You're crazy! You can't do that."

"Maybe not. But I intend to try." They finished packing in silence. Jean bided her time until Kasoth and the I.S.G. envoy escorted them to the glide-car. Jean gestured Tywa into the car ahead of her. "Get in."

"Hold it! Where do you think you're going? Get out of there." The I.S.G. man grabbed Tywa's arm and roughly pulled her aside.

Tywa looked despairingly at Jean. "Let her go," Jean interposed. "She is assigned to me personally. She goes with me."

The Klingon retained his grip on Tywa and looked questioningly at Kasoth. The commander's face darkened as he started to refute Jean's assertion. Then he apparently thought better of it. "Why not? Better rid of them both sooner than later. By all means, take her. Lieutenant." He gestured to the I.S.G. envoy.

Elated, Jean pushed Tywa into the car. There was still the dilemma of getting her from Port Klairos onto the cruiser but this was the first step. Aernath settled himself opposite Jean shaking his head. Tywa wedged herself on the floor between their knees and wrapped an arm around Jean's leg. Her black eyes stared up at Jean wide and somber. "Don't believe him," she whispered. "It's just a trick."

Jean simply smiled at her. Undoubtedly Kasoth did not expect her to go with Jean; he had merely divested himself of the problem. Tirax arrived and after a brief exchange with Kasoth he and the I.S.G. man got in as well. The trip down to Klairos spaceport went much more quickly than the trip up in the spring. As they drew up before the spaceport warehouse where they had arrived some weeks before, Jean was delighted to see the tall commanding figure of Kang approaching from an adjacent building. She waited impatiently for Tirax and the guardsman to exit; then she emerged and turned to Tywa. Again the guardsman seized her arm. "Hold it there, girl. That's as far as you go. Your ride's not over yet."

"Oh, no you don't." Jean wrenched her free. "She goes with me." Tywa clung desperately to Jean's waist while Jean glared at the I.S.G. man.

"Lieutenant, what seems to be the trouble? What's this child doing here?" Kang stood regarding the scene with faint amusement.

The Klingon saluted. "Commander Kang, the human refused to leave this girl at the experiment station so Commander Kasoth ordered me to bring her along. I'm to deliver her to the pens on my way back to H.Q."

"You'll do no such thing!" Jean declared hotly. Then she turned to Kang. "Kang, please let her come with me—at least to Peneli. I promise you she won't be any trouble."

Kang's face was unreadable. "My ship is a battle cruiser not a passenger liner."

"Kang, I . . ." Aernath's hand on her arm stopped her.

"The child is kin-reft, Commander. No *Theld* will own her," Aernath said quietly.

Kang regarded Jean and the girl speculatively for a moment. When he spoke, it was directly to Tywa. "Can you name one way in which you would be useful to me on my ship?"

She answered him with an ancient Klingon proverb: "The merest feather proves its worth when you need it to trim your arrow. I'm sure there are many ways I could find to be useful, but there is one thing, especially."

"Well?"

"It would make her happy. Would that not be useful to you?"

Kang's eyes twinkled briefly. "What is your name, child?"

Tywa's hand sought Jean's. "She named me Tywa, Commander."

"Tywa. Wouldn't it frighten you to be on a battle cruiser?"

"Of course, but less so than going to the pens."

"Why?"

"There is no higher honor than to serve on an Imperial

154

Fleet ship. And if it comes to that, a noble death is to be preferred to an ignoble one."

Kang nodded grim approval. "Fair enough. You may come as far as our next stop provided you prove useful and no trouble. Then you will be sent planetside again—permanently. Is that understood?" This last question was addressed to Jean.

She nodded. "Agreed, if you vouch for the arrangements." Holding Tywa's hand firmly she followed Kang's already retreating back into the warehouse. But she didn't let herself believe it was true until they were actually beamed aboard.

That evening, Kang summoned Jean to dine with him. She entered his quarters as he was finishing his nightly survey of the ship. Finally he called up the forward view, closed the wall panel and turned toward her. "Come here." He drew her into an embrace and protracted kiss. At length he pulled her head back slightly and chuckled. "I said you'd survive. Tell me, how did you find Klairos, my dear?"

"Terrible," Jean sputtered. "That has got to be one of the hell-holes of the galaxy. I don't care if . . ."

Kang tightened his grip on her hair and shook her head lightly. "What? No talk of negotiation, cooperation, trust? What's happened to your human sentimentality?"

"There's nothing wrong with my human sentiments. They're fine and flourishing, thank you. It's just that those people haven't emerged from barbarity yet." She twisted her head trying unsuccessfully to loosen Kang's hold.

"Such strong words from one whose own race practices the same patrilineal system. Come now." He was openly and amusedly baiting her now.

"There's absolutely no comparison between the two. It has nothing to do with the family system. It's the . . . the . . . that damned Klingon mentality," she finished defiantly.

"I could show you far 'worse' than Klairos. And how, my little human," he asked sotto voce, "would your Federation propose to deal with that?"

Sobered by his change of tone, Jean relinquished her struggle against his hold. "I honestly don't know, Kang, but there must be some solution short of destroying each other.

155

It's unlikely either of us will give up striving for new stars so we will simply have to work it out together. But I must admit," she added ruefully, "that I don't trust a Klairosian as far as I could throw him."

Kang chuckled again. "It would seem the impression was mutual. And I hear you did more throwing than otherwise— accosting and insulting people, harassing them, physically assaulting an officer, engineering a guard's death, even threatening Tirax . . ."

"Now just one minute," Jean protested, "it wasn't like that at all. Take Tirax. I only returned his favor." She recounted the incident of the snowbird, as well as Tirax's treatment of her that later night on the polder. "Not only would he welcome an 'unfortunate' accident to me but he made that abundantly clear to Kasoth and a number of others there. He simply won't accept any gesture of rapprochement from me at all."

Kang nodded. "But of course. You realize I pulled you out of there ahead of schedule. Tirax forwarded Kasoth's recommendation that you be removed as 'a threat to discipline and a menace to morale'. Kasoth said he could no longer guarantee your safety. Tirax concurred and asked to be relieved of assignment to you. I will detach someone else to accompany you to Peneli."

"Well, that alone takes Klairos out of the category of unmitigated disaster," Jean commented drily. "I can almost say I look forward to Peneli in that case."

Kang finally released her. "Let's eat before everything gets colder than a space probe." The food was excellent as was the Tahrnian ale. Kang extended his goblet to be refilled. "If my calculations are correct, this is the time of year when your people would offer a traditional toast." He raised the glass. "To your health, wealth, and a long life."

For a moment Jean was puzzled. Then her eyes widened with delighted surprise. "The lunar new year!" Kang was referring not to an Aldebaranian or general human custom but something much farther back and specific to her Terran-Asian ancestry. She returned the toast with a touch of irony, "And may you also enjoy tranquility and honor as well. But how do you know about that bit of ancient folklore?"

"A good strategist, my dear, always knows his opponent—and his playing pieces—well. I've been doing some reading. That heritage is an important part of your makeup, isn't it?"

"I also carry the European heritage of my father but he was away a lot. My mother and my grandfather raised me. Yes, I suppose you're right," she mused. *"Ngu phuc*—the five happinesses. I remember grandfather teaching me them: *phu, qui, tho, ninh,* and *khang—"*

"Kang?"

She smiled. "No, *khang,* but it is similar, isn't it.? It means health or physical strength. Not inappropriate I'd say, but the two alternate meanings fit you even better: to resist, and to be proud. Does your name have a meaning in your tongue?"

"It's a particular type of granite outcropping in our mountains suitable for a fortification and hence, by derivation, a mountain fastness or fortress." He rotated the stem of his goblet slowly between thumb and forefinger watching the swirl of the dark amber liquid within. *"Jheen* . . .do you know what your name means in our speech?"

"No."

"It's a mischievous and sometimes vicious daemon or spirit who inhabits woods and wild places. She is capricious, unpredictable, and obeys only Cymele herself. 'Tis said that even Durgath can't command one save by Cymele's consent." His glance fastened on her. "Did you really attack the officer who was disciplining your little waif?"

Jean felt the old wariness return. Beneath the casual banter was a shrewd and complex mind at work. One she did not fully understand. Whatever slim chance she had depended as much on his plans and his whim as on his word, she was convinced. "Yes," she answered carefully, "I did. Does that create problems for you?"

"Problems?" He was still watching her, his expression unreadable. "None that I can't handle."

"Actually, I got into several confrontations. Does that make you angry?" she probed tentatively.

He grinned suddenly. "Angry? I'd have been disappointed in you if you hadn't. I said you wouldn't stop easily and you don't. You humans are tenacious but unpredictable adversaries. No, there's no harm done to let a few Klairosians get a taste of what they'd face in confronting the Federation. Individuals, like empires, can get soft and complacent unless they meet new challenges. That can lead to fatal miscalculations. The Empire must stay alert and strong."

"Surely space exploration and colonization of worlds like Klairos present challenges enough to keep anyone from becoming complacent. No need to go looking further for adversaries," Jean argued.

"Quite possibly true," Kang answered sardonically, "unless they happen to be sitting across your space lanes. Or hadn't you noticed?"

"There seems to be precedent. After all, you've reached an understanding with the Romulans."

Kang shot her a suspicious glance. "And what, precisely, do you know of our relations with the Romulans?"

"Nothing," she replied honestly, "except that you obviously have made contact and as far as we can determine are not involved in trying to exterminate each other."

"Suffice it to say that that's a long story and a shaky truce. And not at all analogous to the Federation." He drained his glass and stood up. Jean followed suit and started clearing the table while Kang once again surveyed several key ship locations on his viewscreen. Satisfied, he lay back and lazily watched Jean at work. A faint smile tugged at one corner of his mouth. "I'll say one thing about both the Romulans and the Federation. They make much better use of their people, by using their women more effectively. Take your little Tywa. There's an agile mind and an ardent spirit. A pity to waste it in the diving pens. Terribly inefficient."

"Oh, yes. Twya. I wanted to ask you about her." Jean approached the bed. "What do you propose to do about her?"

"We'll be stopping at Tahrn on our way to Peneli. How about sending her to the ag-station where you were?"

It was news to Jean that Tahrn was their destination but she felt this was no time to haggle. For reasons not entirely clear to her, Kang had been most indulgent in this matter so far. She had no intention of pressing her luck. "The ag-station? Perfect. There's a woman there, Tsuyen, whom I think would take her in. Could you arrange it?"

"I guess I'd better if I don't want to get attacked by her protectress," he replied humorously. With a sudden effort-less movement he swept her down, pinioning her to the bed beside him. He took her dagger and waved it in front of her face. "So, on Aldebaran you would doom me to celibacy, would you? Care to challenge me to a match?"

She made a wry face. "You know you'd win. All my life it's been my fate that when I teach someone something, my students end up outdoing their teacher."

Kang chuckled appreciatively. "Do you know what they nicknamed you after that episode in the bar?"

"No."

" 'Princess Daggertooth.' No, I made no mistake in be-stowing consort status on you. You've proved worthy of the position. It's a pity you're not a Klingon. Still and all, as a human you're a valuable cami."* Laying aside her dagger, he slid his fingers along her jaw and drew his thumb gently over her lips in his characteristic gesture. "It's fitting that you should be my instrument of aid to Peneli. Even Mara should appreciate the irony." Jean suppressed a shiver. The fierce emotion in his eyes at the mention of Mara did not match the smile on his lips. It boded ill for Mara, she was sure. Then it was gone and his eyes mirrored only her face looking up at him. "And since we are not on Aldebaran, there need be no question of celibacy. . . ." He inserted a finger in the catch and slowly unseamed her tunic.

---

* An extremely versatile piece in the Klingon game of tsungu.

Nine

KANG'S MELLOW MOOD lasted until Tahrn. However, when Kang beamed back aboard from Tahrn, his manner was taut and his orders curt. They departed for Peneli almost immediately. Dinner was a silent affair. Jean cleared the table while Kang impatiently checked their progress with the bridge. Then he turned to her. "We'll orbit Peneli tomorrow morning. You and Aernath will remain on board until I summon you." Without further preamble he claimed her roughly and at length. When he was finished, Jean fell asleep too exhausted to puzzle further over what new dilemma might be driving him now.

Aernath also had returned from Tahrn more preoccupied and withdrawn than ever. Jean was able to draw out of him that Tsuyen had agreed to look after Tywa and that all seemed well at the station. Beyond that she could get no details. Finally she hazarded a guess, "Did you hear any new news from Peneli? How are things going?"

Aernath was re-potting some of his collection specimens as part of the general catching up after their absence on Klairos. At her question he made a startled gesture, knocking a pot to the floor. With a muttered oath, he bent to pick up the pieces. As Jean knelt to help him, he asked, "What made you think I had news from Peneli?"

"Well, you seemed so preoccupied, I thought maybe you had heard something new."

"Oh . . . I did hear grim talk though I gather it's not as bad as on Klairos yet. It may be before we catch up with it— unless they find some way to stop the *Tseni* virus. There's no breakthrough with their work there. In retrospect it seems so obvious and stupid. We thought we were being so efficient to develop uniform hybrids of our two main food grains. But it left us like sitting riverbirds when that blight hit. Now they're starting to produce some of the old wild strains for seed at the station but . . ."

Jean frowned as he chattered on. He spoke quickly, nervously, but it was all tangential. Something else was bothering him. She couldn't figure out what it was and his stream of words gave no clues.

By mid-afternoon they had everything ready to go planetside, but no word came from Kang. Aernath, apparently finding the constraint of waiting in the lab too much, went off to Security to see what he could learn. Jean settled down to review tapes of Penelian flora. Peneli was a rich, fertile planet especially by Klingon standards. The main continent was located primarily in the equatorial zone and had a tropical to subtropical climate. She became absorbed in the endless proliferation of new plants that she would meet just on that continent alone.

At the end of one tape Jean suddenly realized it was quite late. Aernath had not returned. He wasn't in his quarters or the science mess. There were several areas of the ship she avoided; one was Security. If he was still there, she wasn't going to go find him. Kang had not returned either so she ate a solitary meal and spent the evening on more tapes. There was still no sign of Kang when she went to bed.

The next morning she found Aernath in the lab. "Well, what's the news?"

"No word yet. Kang, Tirax and the others are still down there."

"What's taking so long? What's the problem?"

"I can't say. All we can do is wait." It was clear that

waiting was even more chafing to Aernath than to her. He drifted nervously from one task to another, then finally left muttering something about helping Zelasz get his specimens transported. Zelasz was the xenozoologist from Peneli. Jean continued her study of the botanical tapes. Shortly after lunch Aernath called her on the intercom. "Come on down to the cargo transporter a minute, will you?"

"Sure. I'll be right down." She was feeling restless, too, and welcomed a break. The cargo transporter room contained a welter of cages and specimen jars and a rather abstracted Zelasz but no Aernath. "Where's Aernath?"

"Huh? Oh, he just went to get something for me. He'll be right back." He turned to the console. "Now watch it with the next batch. They're live specimens."

Jean watched the cages disappear in the flashing transporter beam. At a sound she turned to see Aernath enter. He was wearing his cloak. "Guess what? We're going down now."

"Now? Great! Let's go get the stuff."

"Never mind that. It can come later. Right now it's just us they want. In fact, Zelasz can beam us down from here, can't you?"

"What? Sure, if you don't mind walking a bit."

"No, the exercise will do us good," Aernath responded.

"But what . . . Why do they just—" Jean began.

Aernath was clearly impatient. "Come on." He grasped her arm and urged her onto a transporter pedestal. "I'll explain it all as we walk. Ready, Zelasz."

They materialized in a busy warehouse and Aernath steered her out the door with an air of urgency. As they stepped outside they were met by a rush of warm moist air carrying a profusion of scents and sounds. Ship time was not synchronized with planet time and here it was nearly dusk. Jean stopped and took a deep breath, reveling in the fragrant spicy odor of the flowering bushes beside the building. She turned to Aernath. "It's beautiful!" The breeze caught his cloak blowing it back. He was wearing a sword. She had never seen him wear one before. Startled, Jean glanced at the weapon, then at his face. "Aernath! What's going on?"

"This way," He led her across the street and then into a

narrower one perpendicular to the first. Even as she followed the quick pace he set, Jean was taking in the sights and sounds around them, from the small iridescent jadebirds to the ivy festooning a nearby wall. "The negotiations are taking longer than expected. They are still haggling over the terms."

"Terms? What do you mean?"

"Kang is offering seed grain and your services. The price,"he paused and faced her soberly, "is Mara."

Jean gasped, remembering the look on Kang's face when he last spoke of Mara. She should have guessed it. "Mara! Oh no. There's no telling what Kang will do to her if he gets his hands on her. I can't let that happen. You've got to help me."

He gave her a strange look. "Why do you care what happens to Mara?"

"She's pro-Federation from what you tell me," Jean replied. "I don't want to be responsible for putting her in Kang's power, and I don't want to have to work on Peneli as a result of such a bargain. You once said that her brother wouldn't hesitate to turn her over to Kang if it was expedient so there must be compelling reasons why he hasn't done it if that's Kang's price. Do you have any idea why he hasn't agreed?"

They had turned into a broader avenue with a landscaped median strip. Jean inhaled a fresh heady fragrance from the blossoming trees there. Aernath continued to urge her forward briskly. "Mara's movement has gained a great deal of support. Turning her over to Kang at this point might precipitate open rebellion among her followers. Hard-liners like Tirax would love a chance to jump in on the side of the anti-Federation forces and wipe out the underground."

"Could they do that?"

"Largely depends on the political situation on Tahrn, and on Kang. I suspect he wants to weaken Mara's movement just enough so that he can control it himself as a counterweight to those who want to attack the Federation now. I'm sure he doesn't want an interplanetary war right now but he's juggling a tricky bunch of balls."

Jean stopped precipitously and stared at Aernath in dismay. "And we'll be caught right in the middle of it! We could get stuck here—held hostage in return."

He eyed her curiously. "*You* would be stuck here. Kang's offer does not include me. For some reason, I am to remain on board the ship."

In that instant Jean recalled her confession to Kang and saw the trap he had set for her with that knowledge. She groaned. "As a hostage—to ensure my loyalty and cooperation." Then she added with bitter irony, "But of course, he couldn't do it the other way around."

Aernath glanced at her, askance. "Jean, now that we're here, there's something else." He made as if to move on but Jean caught his arm and pulled his cloak back. She looked at the sword and then at his face.

"Wait, if that's all true . . . who called us down here now and why? Exactly where are we going, Aernath?" As she spoke, a figure rounded the nearby corner and abruptly confronted them.

"You! What are you doing here? Both of you are supposed to be restricted to ship." It was Tirax.

Then both Aernath and Tirax moved with blurring speed. Tirax went for his phaser and Aernath aimed a well-placed kick that sent it flying into the nearby bushes. Both men drew their swords. Jean shrank back against a low stone drywall at the edge of the walk. It was quite dark now and the street globes had come on casting an eerie sodium-orange glow over the scene.

Aernath stood facing Tirax in an *en garde* position. Tirax lunged, his point aimed just below the rib cage. Aernath drifted ever so slightly to his left and caught Tirax's shoulder with the tip before the startled Klingon parried it. Wary now, Tirax pulled back and assessed his opponent. Obviously, he, too, had never seen Aernath fight before. Settling into a more formal stance, Tirax suddenly launched a series of rapid thrusts, parries, and *ripostes*. His superior height and weight forced Aernath back and carried them past Jean.

She saw that Aernath had been hit above the right knee. The two men circled carefully, each seeking an opening. Aernath compensated for Tirax's height and weight by greater agility and speed. She would never have guessed he possessed this skill. Again he shifted lightly, avoiding a thrust from Tirax, and this time inflicted a large gash on the larger Klingon's upper arm. But Tirax recovered and slipped past Aernath's next parry with a *riposte* that reached his ribs. Aernath stumbled but managed to block the next downstroke aimed at him. Then he regained his footing. Alarmed now, Jean looked about for some weapon of her own. She dug her fingers into the dirt behind the drywall and pried free one of the top stones of the wall. She hugged it to her chest and waited for a suitable opening. Tirax connected again, a glancing slice along Aernath's forearm. Aernath countered with a slash that drew blood along Tirax's neck. Both men circled again, more slowly now, their breathing labored. Then Tirax struck Aernath's leg once more. Aernath fell back a couple of paces drawing Tirax abreast of Jean. As he moved for a counter *riposte*, his leg gave way and he fell. As Tirax plunged forward and down, Jean hurled the rock straight at his sword arm. Aernath rolled but the sword caught him in the side nonetheless. He rose to one knee, then faltered. However, Tirax no longer held his sword. His right arm dangled useless by his side. With a roar of pain and rage, Tirax turned and charged Jean.

She dropped into a crouch and met the Klingon's out-thrust arm with a grasp, pirot, and throw that carried him up and over her. As he sailed over she felt a snap and knew in some recess of her mind that his left arm was now broken. Where in space had she learned that? Now, dagger in hand, she waited. The Klingon did not rise. She approached him warily.

Even through the pain the hate was still there, but also the grudging respect. "So, human, in the end you win after all." He spoke with some difficulty. "Very well, finish it. Strike cleanly and I'll salute Durgath in your name when I stand before him." Then there was neither hate nor fear—just a clear gaze meeting hers—waiting.

Jean knelt beside him and shook her head. "Not by my hand, Tirax. I may die regretting this but you'll live to greet Durgath another day." Her hand moved in a flashing blow to his neck. He lost consciousness promptly. *And where in space did I learn that?* Jean wondered as she replaced her dagger. She had never studied any of the so-called arts of self-defense . . . had she? . . . something wrong here . . . She shook her head dazedly. If she could just remember . . . But there was a more immediate problem: Aernath. She stood up and turned to where he had been.

He was gone. Tirax's sword lay on the ground by a small pool of inky wetness. A faint trail of spots, black in the glare of the street globes, led away from the spot into an unlighted passageway between two buildings. She followed them. "Aernath?" she called with soft urgency. "Aernath, where are you?" She was answered only by a soft rustle of movement in the shadow. As she moved toward it she caught a dim glimpse of him leaning against the wall. Simultaneously, she saw emerging from the grayness several other figures who moved purposefully toward her. With the same maneuver that had grounded Tirax, she managed to send one flying before she was overpowered by the weight of numbers. For a brief interval she was reduced to kicking, biting, and scratching. Then a cloth was stuffed in her mouth and some type of hood fastened over her head. She could breathe and hear—nothing else. As her hands were roughly pulled behind her and tied, she heard something that filled her with consternation and despair.

Aernath's voice was faint but clear. "Handle her carefully, Kinsmen. That human is extremely valuable to us right now."

This was followed by urgent mutterings, smothered oaths, and frenetic movement around her. She was hoisted unceremoniously over someone's shoulder, carried a short distance and dumped onto a cold hard surface. She heard a door close. Silence gave way to abrupt movement; she was being taken somewhere in some kind of a vehicle. What in the name of the nine rings of hell was going on here? Who were these Klingons? What was Aernath's connection with them? Obviously he knew them. And Aernath himself—clearly he was more than a simple botanist. Tonight had proved that. How little she knew him. The one certainty she thought she had in this situation suddenly became a chilling unknown. Anger fought panic to a standstill leaving Jean the limp battlefield.

The ride ended and she was extracted to be hauled rudely up steps and along corridors. She was tied in a chair, then footsteps receded and a door closed. In the stillness, she wiggled her hands and feet experimentally. The bonds were tight with no give. She was immobilized. How long she sat like that she had no way of knowing, but it seemed like hours. Finally the door opened and someone approached her. She felt fingers loosen the fastenings at the back of her head. The hood was pulled away and the gag removed. The room was brightly lit. Jean looked down at the floor blinking and squinting as her eyes tried to adjust from the prolonged darkness.

She focused on the boots first: a fine deep blue leather, good workmanship, finely tooled; shapely blue-clad legs, a brief dress—blue with silver accents. A graceful V-neck with pointed collar framed a regal face. The woman regarded her silently with fathomless black eyes. Her appraisal was interrupted by another arrival.

Aernath stood in the doorway, shirtless, with his right arm in a sling and a plastiderm dressing swathing his right rib cage. His face was pale and he favored his right leg as he walked. His eyes met Jean's as he came into the room.

"Jean!" A flush darkened his face as he made his way angrily to her chair. "Blast it, Mara! Why did you let them do this?" He tugged angrily at her bonds with his left hand. "I told you, she has enough trouble trusting us as it is without this. And it wasn't necessary."

The woman watched cooly, making no move to help or hinder his efforts. "She'll have to trust us. She has no choice."

"Well, dammit, you didn't have to make it so difficult for her!" With his dagger he severed the thongs that held her hands and set to work on her feet. This was interrupted as a third person burst into the room, a lithe black-haired girl in a formfitting blue uniform.

"Aernath!" She rushed to embrace him.

"Aeliki!" He rose and hugged her warmly with his left arm.

"I just found out you were here. Thank Cymele you're

167

safe!" She stepped back a pace and surveyed him anxiously. "Are you sure you should be up? They said you were brought in unconscious. What happened?"

"I'll be fine. We ran into a little opposition on the way but . . ." he gestured to Jean with the dagger, "there she is. I got her here."

Aeliki now turned her attention to Jean for the first time. "The human!" She looked at her curiously.

"Yes, the human. Aernath has been chiding me for mistreating her," Mara said drily.

Aernath knelt again to the task of freeing Jean. "Cymele's Cloak, Mara, you can't treat her like this and—" he expostulated.

Mara interrupted, "This is the woman Kang would have used against us, and you admitted yourself you couldn't be sure she would come voluntarily." She turned to Jean. "Stand up." Jean did so returning the woman's gaze as Mara walked around the chair surveying her deliberately. "So. Kang's new consort. He has made you a member of his *Theld*. Would you have come voluntarily?"

Jean rubbed her wrists. "Probably. It would depend on the situation. I don't really understand the terms of my presence here."

"What were Kang's terms? What induced you to cooperate with him?" Mara's voice was sharp but not to the point of hostility.

Jean glanced at Aernath wondering how much and what he had told Mara. She chose her words carefully. "Kang's terms? My freedom if I cooperated and he succeeded. Death by his own hand at the first sign of treachery. But I consented voluntarily to work against the famine when I discovered the true situation. I'm still willing to do that but preferably not at the expense of a pro-Federation cause or you personally, Mara."

"But if I stood in the way of your success, if it were a choice between your freedom and mine, then what, Miss Czerny?"

Jean was spared the necessity of an answer by the interruption of a blue-uniformed man. "Dematrix, you're needed in Operations."

Mara nodded. "Aernath, wait here, I'll be back soon. Follow me, Aeliki." She strode briskly from the room. Aeliki gave Aernath a quick hug and followed her. Aernath watched them go for a long moment before he turned back to Jean.

She looked at him uncertainly. "It would appear that I am in no position to demand anything, but I think you owe me some explanations."

"Jean, I'm sorry. Believe me, I didn't intend . . . Are you hurt in any way?" At the shake of her head, he continued. "None of this would have happened if we hadn't met Tirax. I was sure that once I got you off the ship to a place where I could safely explain everything you'd come freely. But by the time I got into that alley . . ." He raised his hand to brush back the hair from his forehead. It was shaking badly.

She moved to him quickly. "Aernath! You shouldn't even be on your feet. Here, lie down." She guided him to a couch at the side of the room. He sank down wearily but insisted on sitting. She poured a glass of water from the carafe on the table beside the couch and watched anxiously as he drank.

"Thanks, Jean. I'll be all right." Nonetheless, he leaned back and closed his eyes. His face was still very pale. After some moments he opened his eyes again. "Now, where were we?"

She touched the bandage on his side. "How badly did he hit you?"

"Nothing vital. They patched me up pretty thoroughly. I'll be fine in a few days."

"You really astonished me, you know. You never gave any indication you could fight like that," she said with unaccustomed diffidence.

He shrugged his left shoulder. "Just because I choose not to fight doesn't mean I can't if I have to. It's just that usually it's an inefficient way to try to solve the problem." He gave her an appraising look. "You were rather surprising yourself. Did you kill him?"

"Tirax? No." She looked down at her hands. "When it came right down to it, I couldn't. Someday I'll probably regret it."

"Let's hope not."

"Aernath, what's going on? Who . . . or what . . . are you anyway?"

He grinned boyishly. "It should be obvious by now. I am . . . or was . . . Mara's undercover agent to keep an eye on Kang."

A throaty chuckle from the doorway drew their attention. Mara had returned. "And you couldn't ask for a more perfect spy. His loyalty to Kang stands second only to his loyalty to me. He'd pass almost any screening check Kang could put him through."

"True," Aernath protested mildly, "but the same could be said of you, too."

"You and I know that but it wouldn't even occur to him to run the check," Mara sighed. "I'm afraid that even if we succeed it's likely to be a long time before he's convinced."

"Speaking of that, how are things going?"

"With the accelerated timetable it will be tight but I think we have a better than even chance." She turned to Jean. "Well, are you ready to answer my question? If I told you that you could walk through that door free what would you choose to do?"

"I would sit right here until I had a clearer idea of your position. I only know what Aernath has told me, which is vague generalities. If you do favor negotiation with the Federation, then I would like to help you in whatever way I can."

"And what of Kang?"

"I . . . I bear him no enmity, but I wouldn't pass a loyalty check."

"And if you fell back into his hands again? Do you fear that?" Mara watched her intently.

"It's you he wants. I'm merely a pawn in that game. How would you feel if he got you?"

Mara gestured impatiently. "That's my problem. Answer the question."

Jean grimaced. "If you can convince me it's worth it, I guess I'd take that chance. Under the circumstances, I could quite legitimately say I was kidnapped against my will."

Mara looked at her thoughtfully for a long moment, then

nodded abruptly as if she had made a decision. "Very well. We will discuss this further tomorrow. Aernath, do what you like with her so long as you don't breach security. Can you see to the arrangements or shall I call someone?"

"I think I can manage. Where am I assigned?"

"Next to Aeliki, of course. I assumed you'd prefer that."

Aernath smiled. "Thanks. If there's room, I'll put her in with Aeliki then."

"Fine." She gestured toward the door. "Kyrnon can direct you. Get a good night's rest. You both look like you could use it." She picked up the device that had been removed from Jean's head and handed it to Aernath. "At the moment, for her sake as well as ours, the less she knows the better. Good night." She left the room.

Jean backed away from Aernath. "You're not going to put that thing on me again!" she declared belligerently.

He gestured wryly at his bandaged arm. "No, I can't. But I am going to ask you to put it on. Mara's right—what you don't know you can't tell." He held it out to her. "Please. It won't be for long."

Jean took it reluctantly and slipped it on, fighting the urge to retch at the memory of the gag. Aernath took her hand and led her forward. Someone met them outside the door, and Jean felt her other arm grasped firmly but gently. After many twists and turns she came to a stop. "All right. We're here. You can take it off," Aernath said as the other man left.

Gratefully, Jean slipped out of it and looked about. It was a small cubicle just large enough to contain two narrow beds, a desk, and a chair. The door on her right was obviously a closet and the one on her left opened into a small bathroom. Aernath gestured at the bath. "My room's through there. If you need anything come and ask. This room door is unlocked and there is no guard. I want you to feel you are among friends. But for your own sake, don't leave the room unless Aeliki or I come for you. Do you have any questions?"

There were numerous questions but none she was prepared to ask him at the moment. "No, I guess not." She looked at his face. It was drawn and pinched. "Just one thing—you ought to be in bed. Can I . . . do you need any help?"

He flushed slightly. "No. Aeliki will be along shortly. If I need anything I'll ask her. Good night."

"Good night." She watched him go through the bathroom to his quarters with a twinge of jealousy. Who or what was Aeliki to him? He had never mentioned her but then he had never talked much of his personal life. There had always been a reticence there, quite understandable now in light of his espionage role. She had always respected this reserve, having felt that to probe would have been seen as one more humiliating demand on his *bond-status* even if it wasn't meant that way. Now she wished she knew a great deal more about this enigmatic Klingon: most particularly what his feelings were toward her. Questions. But questions that would have to wait.

Resolutely she straightened her shoulders and turned her attention back to the room. Which bed was Aeliki's? The two neat berths gave no clues. The desk was bare except for a reading light in the center and a small opaque cube on the left. Jean picked it up and turned it over idly. It began to glow and clear. One side displayed markings which changed as she watched. Through the other sides she saw a hologram forming. It was a picture of a boy and a girl. With a jolt she realized it was Aernath and Aeliki apparently taken some years earlier. She put it down and it grew opalescent again. She sat down on the right hand bed and pulled off her boots. A murmur of voices came to her from Aernath's room. It must be Aeliki. She stifled an impulse to listen at the door and lay down instead.

After a few moments, Aeliki came in quiet and hesitant. She seemed startled when Jean sat up promptly. "Oh, you're still awake. Aernath said you might be . . ." She seemed at a loss as to how to proceed.

"Is this your bed?" Jean inquired.

"No, I sleep in this one." She indicated the one on the left. "Do hu . . . I mean, is that comfortable for you?"

Jean smiled faintly at the other woman's discomfiture. "Klingons seem to prefer a firmer sleeping surface than humans but I am accustomed to it now. Tell me, does it bother you to have a human in your room?"

Aeliki blushed. "I don't mean to be rude, but I've never met one before. Aernath said just to treat you naturally— that if we want to establish relations with humans, we just have to learn to get along. But it's still strange and scary, isn't it?"

"Oh, I don't think I'm so bad. How would you like to try a whole starship full of aliens?"

"I see what you mean. If Mara did that . . ." she laughed uncertainly, "you must think me rather silly."

That wasn't the comparison Jean intended but she let it go. An awkward silence ensued. Jean yearned momentarily for the solitude of her own quarters on the cruiser or the easy comfort of Tywa's company.

Then Aeliki ventured, "Do you want to go to sleep now or what? Do you need anything?"

"As a matter of fact, cruiser time is out of sync with planet time. Any chance I could get something to eat before we turn in?"

The woman seized on the suggestion with alacrity, disappeared, and returned a few moments later with a small tray of food. The beverage was hot, aromatic, and unfamiliar to Jean. Aeliki explained that it was made from a local fruit. While Jean ate, she went to the closet. "I don't suppose you brought anything with you . . . we'll see about issuing you some things in the morning." She emerged with a short, light shift, then paused uncertainly. "Tonight you could . . . that is, do you . . . uh . . ."

Jean smiled again as she answered, "Thank you, that would do nicely for tonight." She pushed back her tray and crossed to the bathroom. There she paused, baffled. "Aeliki, how do you operate the faucet?"

Aeliki came and pointed to a faint strip above the spigot. "There." When Jean hesitated she said, "Put your finger on it and slide it down until you find the temperature you want; then push. Push it again to turn it off. The shower works the same way." Jean touched the top of the strip. It was quite cold. The bottom was uncomfortably hot.

She emerged shortly, intending to spend some time talking

with Aeliki but abruptly a small reddish light above the door began to blink rhythmically accompanied by a faint chime. "What's that?" Jean asked with some alarm. She still had not fully accepted the fact that the Klingon "Alert" color was amber rather than red.

"It means I'm needed at my post. Don't wait up for me," she called over her shoulder as she left.

As Jean undressed she suddenly felt unnaturally sleepy. She wondered vaguely if Aeliki or someone had drugged her food. She just had time to tumble into bed and then she didn't wonder about anything at all. . . .

Someone was shaking her. "Jean, hey! Wake up! It's morning." Groggily she rolled over and sat up. Her head felt twice its normal size and very fuzzy. Aernath's face shifted into approximate focus in front of her. "You can't be that tired. What's wrong?"

Jean groaned. "Feels like a first class hangover. From the food last night I think. Would Aeliki or someone have drugged it?"

"Drugged your food? Of course not. Why would we want to do that?"

"Search me, but that's what it feels like. Something sure didn't agree with me." She pushed herself erect and staggered to the bathroom. The cold water on her face helped somewhat. She returned to find Aernath holding out a garment to her.

"Here, put this on." Her attire or lack of it seemed to disconcert him. She fumbled with the robe. It felt as if all her movements were being performed through five centimeters of foam rubber. "Come on over and eat. If you don't feel better then we'll have someone see you." As she followed him she noticed that he was fully dressed and appeared perfectly normal except for the sling on his right arm. There was only a trace of a limp. He was certainly making a fast recovery.

Breakfast consisted of *khizr*, a spicy-hot soup, and fruit. The latter tasted familiar, the same as the drink last night. Her head cleared somewhat as they ate. "Has Aeliki been back since last night?"

Aernath shook his head. "I haven't seen her, but she'll probably turn up soon."

"She said before she left last night that she was needed at her post. What does she do?"

Aernath shook his head. "Don't ask. The less you know the better."

"Well, what are we going to do? Can you tell me that? Kang will be taking this planet apart Klingon by Klingon trying to find us and since we don't have any supplies with us we can't do anything about the blight—"

"Wrong. I did bring some samples of both strains along and they're in safe hands already. We're to meet with some colleagues of mine later today to brief them. As for the rest, Mara will discuss that with us over dinner tonight."

"All right. I guess I better get dressed." She pushed back her chair and stood up. It hit even faster this time. She only had time to turn back to him. "Aernath! What are you people trying to do to m—" Then the floor wobbled unsteadily up to meet her forehead.

Jean opened her eyes to a dim light. This time her head was throbbing savagely but retained its normal size. She seemed to be in bed. Her stir of movement brought a response from the opposite berth. Aernath. "The doctor said you would wake up on your own sooner or later but I was beginning to wonder. How do you feel?"

"Terrible. My head hurts."

"He also said you'd probably say that. Here, take this." He held out a pill and a glass of water.

"What's that?"

"I don't know. Something to make your head feel better." She made no move to take the proffered medicine. "Aernath, what happened?"

"Dr. Eknaar checked you out against Peneli pretty thoroughly but he overlooked one thing. Your allergy to lourkain should have tipped him off. There is a related alkaloid that occurs in very high concentrations in the pulp of our *persaba* fruit. It really knocked you for a loop."

Jean looked up at the clear, apparently guileless depths of those amethyst eyes. One part of her wanted—needed—

desperately to believe, to trust this one particular Klingon. Another part of her was virtually screaming caution and suspicion. Although his miscalculations with regard to Kang and Tirax might be chalked up to honest error, it was indisputable that he had dissembled his own role so well she would have staked her life that he was the person he had seemed to be. Could she afford to do so again?

"Will you swear to me by whatever you hold sacred that, this time, you are telling me the truth?"

Aernath flinched as if she had hit him. He set the glass on the desk and turned away, slamming the desk with his hand. "Durgath take them all. I told her you wouldn't trust us, that she had to move carefully." He faced her, his eyes blazing with an intensity she'd never seen before. "I knew it would be a shock when you found out I wasn't what you thought I was, but I hoped you would also be pleased by the discovery. And now this. . . ." He knelt beside the bed. "Once I discovered Kang's plans for Peneli and got my orders to get you down here, I spent most of my waking hours trying to figure out what to do. I just couldn't find any safe way to prepare you ahead of time. Jean, I swear by . . ." he hesitated, then reached out and brushed her eyelashes with a fingertip, ". . . by your tears, I'm telling the truth. Cymele help me, I'm not lying to you in spite of appearances to the contrary."

After a long pause, Jean reached out a hand. "Give me the pill."

Aernath handed her the pill and the water. He slid his left arm behind her shoulders and pulled her to a sitting position. Their eyes met as she set down the glass. Jean poised on the very verge of those depths . . . his right hand moved halfway to her face . . . Then, with a slight shake of his head, Aernath broke the contact and the moment. He seemed to be struggling with some decision. Finally he said, "Mara wants to present this herself after dinner, but I'm going to tell you some of it now. She has something—I don't know what—that she wants to get to your Federation Starfleet now. She wants . . . us to take it."

"Us? Now? How?" Jean was full of questions.

"Shh!" He laid a restraining finger on her lips. "No

questions now. Save them for Mara. I just wanted to warn you. One more thing and that's all I will say. This means your freedom now instead of waiting—if we succeed. But if we are caught . . ." He shrugged expressively.

"But what about the blight, the grain?"

"I said hold the questions."

"Okay, just one more then: what time is it? When do we meet Mara?" That pill must work fast. The headache was better already.

"You've been out most of the day." Aernath leaned across the desk and picked up the cube. "Let's see . . . mm, later than I thought. Mara will probably be ready to see us about as soon as you can get ready." He turned the cube over in his hand looking at the hologram.

"How long have you known her?"

"Mara? Let me see now . . ."

"No, Aeliki."

"My sister? All of her life. We are not raised in test-tubes despite any stories you may have—"

"Sister! Aeliki is your sister?"

"Yes. Didn't she tell you that?"

Jean collapsed back on the bed. "No, that's another thing no one bothered to mention to me yet." Aernath was regarding her with a puzzled look. "I thought she was your fiancée or something. You never mentioned whether or not there was anyone special back home. Is there?" No better time than the present to find out.

"No, does that matter to you?"

"I thought I heard someone talking in here." Aeliki emerged from the bathroom, yawning. "How are you feeling now?"

"Much better, thanks." Jean answered.

Aeliki gave Aernath a quick hug and kiss. "Thanks for the use of your room. What with being up all night and then the excitement here," she waved at Jean, "it sure felt good to get some sleep." As she crossed to the closet she said to Jean, "Oh, yes, I promised you we'd get some things for you today. I hope I got your size right." She pulled a bundle out of the closet, then looked questioningly at Aernath who was still standing by the desk. Finally she added with some

177

asperity, "Aernath, we'll never get you both ready to meet Mara if you just stand there stargazing. Come on—out!"

The setting was as elegant as the meal was simple. They were dining in an alcove off the room where Jean first met Mara. That, she gathered, was the anteroom to Mara's personal quarters. They were seated on some type of resilient matting at floor level with their feet tucked into the recess beneath the low table. Opposite Jean, Mara leaned back against a cushion, glass of wine in hand. She had exchanged her uniform for formal Penelian dress: a bright emerald green bodysuit with long sleeves. Over this she wore a tight bodice of gauzy, light green material that divided at the waist into six panels and floated to ankle length. Aernath wore a similar bodysuit of wine red with a dark brown overtunic of more substantial material. His arm sling was gone and he had worn his sword, though it had been laid aside when they sat down to eat.

They were concluding the meal with fresh fruit, and Aernath was explaining the tableware to her. It was a heavy translucent material with a peach tinge. "It's made from a large shellfish that is extremely common in our oceans. This color is rare. It occurs only when they ingest a particular kind of plankton. This," he indicated the fruit bowl which was a pearly gray, "is the more common color. Here, have some fruit. You've hardly eaten anything. I assure you this is all quite harmless." Jean selected a small fruit, without comment. It was true, she had eaten sparingly. She wished to be alert for whatever conversation might ensue and she was taking no chances.

Mara leaned forward. "Yes, how are you feeling? You appear quite recovered from your encounter with our *per-saba*. Do you think you would be up to traveling soon?"

The conversation throughout dinner had been casual and clearly designed to put her at ease. Alert now, Jean strove for an equally casual response that would give no hint that Aernath had forewarned her. "Travel? You mean to some place where we could safely work on the *quadrotriticale?* Aernath told me he has brought some."

Mara smiled fleetingly as she shook her head. "No, even if our plans here on Peneli succeed, I'm not sure you would be

178

safe anywhere in the Klingon Empire. I had in mind a longer and more difficult journey. As it happens, I need an unimpeachable courier to make an important delivery to your Federation Starfleet. It is fortunate for both of us that you are available and, I understand, quite eager to return."

"I've heard mention of plans several times. May I ask for a briefing and how this uh . . . delivery fits in? How will my travel be arranged if I agree to this? I need a little information." Jean hoped she had hit the right blend of caution and interest.

"Peneli is a rarity in the Klingon Empire: a rich, fertile planet. You've seen a couple of more typical examples. In spite of our low population growth rate, the Empire must expand. The Federation is an obstacle to that expansion. Many Klingons feel therefore that it must be destroyed. Others of us, notably Kang, feel that all-out attack now would so weaken us that even if we did succeed the Empire would be destroyed in the process. What Kang *doesn't* see is that the armed confrontation doesn't have to occur at all; at least not on any major scale. He must be brought to negotiation with the Federation soon—*successful* negotiation. Do you understand me?" Her eyes were like gimlets boring into Jean. Her dress and the setting enhanced her beauty but in no way diminished the sense of commanding presence Jean had felt when she first met her in uniform. "The invitation must come from the Federation—to Kang. And they must make a significant offer when he does meet with them." She pasued.

Jean looked at her. "Go on."

"Peneli, because of its resources is key to the Imperial Fleet. Kang must have Peneli—be able to count on it. And he will, one way or the other. He also wants me. He will succeed in that too, one way or the other. However, if my operation now in progress succeeds, he may not get exactly what he expects."

Jean pushed the plate in front of her carefully to one side. "No unfriendliness intended, but if I do reach Starfleet and report that you expect them to offer a substantial concession, then what do you offer in return?"

"If you make your delivery I will guarantee that Kang will

179

come and negotiate. If I am successful here then Peneli will not only remain firmly in Kang's camp but also firmly committed to continuing negotiation rather than confrontation. I will not see the resources of this planet expended merely to hasten the destruction of the Empire!"

Jean looked at her curiously. "I don't mean to doubt your word. But I've come to know Kang rather well. Just how do you propose to guarantee that he will do something he clearly doesn't want to do, especially if he once gets his hands on you?"

For the first time Jean sensed hesitancy in Mara's bearing. The Klingon woman rang the small table bell and summoned the old woman who had served them. She made a gesture to the woman, who looked visibly startled. "Yes," said Mara, "Now. It is time." She turned back to them. The words came slowly. "What I am about to tell you is known only to two others. It is vitally important that you not reveal this to anyone in the Empire and only to the absolute minimum number of people in Starfleet who must know." Jean glanced at Aernath. He looked as mystified as she felt.

The old woman returned with a young boy of four or five. His face lit up at the sight of Mara; then he hesitated, looking uncertainly at Jean and Aernath. "It's all right," Mara said softly. "Come here." Thus encouraged he came and climbed into her lap. Mara talked to him for a few minutes in a low murmur, apparently about his day's activities. Then she said, "Do you remember the most important rule?" The boy nodded. "Well, tonight, for the first time I want you to tell someone else. The rule is still the rule but right now it is all right. Who are you?"

"I am Aethelnor of Peneli."

"Who is your father?"

The childish singsong was clear and firm. "Kang of Tahrn, emperor-elect, and commander in the Imperial Fleet."

"Who is your uncle?"

"Maelen of Peneli, warrior and regent, defender of the Empire."

Mara smiled fondly, then leaned forward to touch the tip of her nose to his. "Very good, Aethelnor. And who am I?"

Aethelnor giggled suddenly as he twined his arm around her neck. "You're my mother."

She held him close for a moment, then rose. "Now it is time for bed. Come along." She took him out, then returned a moment later and stood regarding her two astonished guests. "Now you know my secret. I want you to take Aethelnor to the Federation. *That* is my guarantee that Kang will come and negotiate in good faith."

Aernath recovered his voice first. "Cymele keep us! Mara, does Kang know about his son?"

Mara shook her head as she reseated herself. "Only my nurse—the woman you saw. She raised me from a child and she alone knew of my pregnancy. As a former Fleet science officer I have a fair knowledge of medicine—as you know." She touched Aernath's side lightly. "She was my only attendant at Aethelnor's birthing. There are a few others who know of the boy's presence here but not his identity. You seem distressed." The last was addressed to Jean.

"How can you give him up—just send off your son as a . . . a hostage to the Federation?"

"Do you have any reason to believe he would be in danger or abused in the custody of your Starfleet?" Mara asked sharply.

"No!" Jean added hastily. "Good gracious, no. It's just that—"

"So I have been assured. It's far more than a question of hostages, Miss Czerny. After all, in a few years he would be leaving me for his uncle's *Theld* anyway." She leaned forward, her voice low but intense. "I want him to spend a few years growing up in human society—to know you from the inside. It will help equip him for his task when he becomes regent of Peneli. Besides, he won't go alone. I'm sending a tutor." She turned to the still startled Aernath. "You."

"Me!" Aernath was clearly astonished. "Why?"

"Because you are far more useful to me, to the cause, there than here. You've briefed our agricultural people. They can work far more inconspicuously without you. In spite of your fascination with humans, there is no question of your loyalty to me or to Kang. Your educational background is sufficiently broad and you have shown an ability to teach. You'd be an excellent tutor."

"But . . ." Aernath began to protest.

"That's an order, Aernath."

"Yes, Dematrix." His reply snapped to match her tone.

She added in a softer tone. "I know it may prove to be an extended exile but not an unduly onerous one I think."

"You've already answered part of my next question. I'm glad to know that Aernath will be along on this trip. When and how do we leave?"

Mara's face reflected approval of Jean's brisk response. "Tonight. Kang, of course, has already started the search for you. It is only a matter of time before he will discover where you have been taken. But he will never expect us to send you off-planet. It would be logical to keep you here. So our greatest chance of success lies in moving quickly." Mara made a move as if to stand up.

"Oh, could I ask you one more thing?" Jean asked.

Mara paused. "What is that?"

"*Aetheln.* What does it mean?"

Mara sat back down. "As in Aethelnor? The suffix means 'bearing'. And *aetheln* is . . . well, it carries some of the meaning of your Terran concept of kismet—one's fate or destiny in life. It also has something of the original Confucian concept of . . . *li* I think it was called—that internal ability to perceive and accept the mandate of heaven, to perform your proper role in the order of things. I guess Aethelnor would translate roughly as Confucius's *chun-tzu*, the prince-son or superior man, wouldn't it? Why do you ask?"

"Nothing important," Jean replied. "It's just that Kang mentioned the word to me once but couldn't explain it. I was struck by the coincidence."

Mara chuckled. "Kang is not as widely read in Terran culture as I." At Jean's questioning look, she continued, "Those days on the *Enterprise* after the truce. Kang wouldn't let me out of our quarters, so I spent a lot of time with computer tapes. Your science officer, Mr. Spock, gave me only limited access to scientific areas so I spent a lot of time on history and culture. Perhaps," she finished almost wistfully as she rose, "it will be different with Aernath."

Jean stood up quickly to match Mara's gesture. "I'm sure we'll work out something."

"Excellent. Survival and success to you both. I hope the next time we meet will be at the negotiating table. Aernath, Kyrnon will have your orders. Good-bye."

Their immediate destination was Tsorn. They had traveled by a small, fast courier ship and the trip went without incident. Jean shivered slightly in her *shurdik* as she stood on the apron of the spaceport and looked out over the red sands of Tsorn. This was a rim planet of the Klingon Empire located in a quadrant tangential to Federation space. The interior of its main continent was dominated by salt flats and great deserts of red sand. A fairly narrow belt around the continental periphery supported a modicum of native vegetation as well as agricultural development with careful management. The capital city, Ichidurtsukaitsorn, or Ichidur as it was often called, was located on the northwest part of the continent not too far inland. The spaceport was sited farther inland on the edge of the desert.

Aethelnor was shivering too. She reached out and wrapped him in a double thickness of her redundant *shurdik*. By custom, women on Tsorn went out only if covered from head to toe by this voluminous garment. It had fine mesh-work in front of the eyes so one could see out—straight ahead. Otherwise, there were no openings. It was winter now so Jean welcomed its warmth as well as the cover but it must be stifling in the summer when the hot dry winds blew off the desert.

"Comfortable now?" she asked Aethelnor.

The boy nodded. "Yes, it's warmer." He was a very reserved child by human standards, at least with Jean. He had spent more time with Aernath than with her on the ship. Aernath took his charge seriously and spent several hours each day in various sorts of lessons with the boy. Now he had left Aethelnor with her while he cleared them through entry formalities. Their documents indicated that she was a

Penelian bringing her son to live with his uncle who was allegedly a wealthy trader in Ichidur. Beyond that, she knew nothing of the plans to get them off Tsorn. If Aernath knew, he gave no indication, saying only that they would be contacted.

The wind blew more insistently now and Jean noticed a few drops of rain on the apron in front of her. She sat down on one of the two pods supposed to be their "luggage" and drew Aethelnor up on her lap. That way she could better shield him from the wind and rain. She wondered how Tsorni women navigated in these garments. She couldn't turn her head to see if Aernath was coming or not. While it's concealment protected her from casual detection, it also made her feel hemmed in and half blind. She jumped nervously at the sound of the voice directly behind her.

"Here. Take these two. Follow me." It was Aernath and a porter. The porter picked up the two dufflepods. With a curt gesture, Aernath set off without a backward glance. The others followed. He was dressed in a gray one-piece suit that seemed to be standard dress for all civilian men on Tsorn. Class and status could probably be distinguished by the subtle differences in markings and decoration but this had not been included in Jean's briefing.

They approached a row of small cubicles. The porter deposited their pods in one and Aernath motioned Jean and Aethelnor to enter also. Following them, he closed the door. The compartment immediately began to subside into the ground. Startled, Jean turned to look at Aernath. His attention was fixed on a wall panel. After a moment's scrutiny of the symbols, he punched several buttons in rapid succession. His explanation to the boy was obviously for her enlightenment as well. "Aethelnor, do you see this panel? It tells you all the places you can go on this subtern. All you have to do is push the buttons for where you want to go." The cubicle halted. "Now we are waiting to be shuttled to a group going in our direction. Pretty soon we will start moving again." The operation proceeded as promised. They were reshuttled at a couple more junctions and finally emerged above ground within Ichidur itself.

A cold rain was falling with a gray dreary steadiness. As

Aernath was removing their pods from the subtern cubicle, a small vehicle pulled up. Its occupant entered another cubicle. As that sank out of sight, Aernath appropriated the street vehicle which was apparently a sort of autotaxi. It operated on the same principle as the subtern: when coordinates were entered on its control panel it set off to the specified location.

As they rode along, Jean took in what she could with her limited view. Ahead, off to one side, she could see the low escarpment that separated this seaward sloping plain from the desert beyond. Though low, it apparently served to set up meteorlogical conditions so that moisture laden clouds coming in from the sea during winter months dumped almost all their moisture here before hitting the desert beyond. Though it seldom got below freezing, winters were very wet in Ichidur. Here, as on Tahrn, Klairos, and Peneli, based on the brief glimpses she had been accorded, urban Klingons seemed to live behind massive stone walls. Little could be seen of the houses except for glimpses of the roof peaks above the walls. None of what little vegetation she saw was familiar. Most striking were the occasional huge trees they passed: great tangles of aerial roots rising some two meters into the air surmounted by an abbreviated trunk that formed almost a platform. Around the periphery, branches reached skyward to the thick gray-green canopy. The shape, Jean decided, was virtually an organic replica of a planetary magnetosphere with its tail stuck in the ground.

The vehicle glided noiselessly to a stop at another nexus. There was very little traffic and the street was deserted. Jean watched in puzzlement as Aernath extracted some type of small device from his belt and applied it to the door of the vehicle they had just exited. He reached in, punched a fresh set of coordinates, then closed the door, removing the device as he did so. He repeated this maneuver with a second vehicle before moving to a third. "Aernath, what are you doing?"

"Taking precautions. We were supposed to be met at the spaceport. The contact didn't show. Don't say anything once we get in now." He motioned her in ahead of him.

Jean perched tensely on the edge of her seat the rest of the brief trip, mentally cursing the limitations of the *shurdick* which left her feeling already half-trapped. Once again they stopped, this time in front of one of the stone-walled compounds. Jean and Aethelnor remained seated as Aernath approached the solid wooden door set in the wall. She could neither see nor hear clearly what he was doing but after some moments the door opened to disclose a large burly Klingon who came and took the dufflepods. They followed him inside and across a rain-slick terrace of red polyhedral tiles to the house beyond.

They learned that, "officially," their contact had met with an unfortunate accident on the way to the spaceport. Unofficially, Aernath was convinced he had died under an I.S.G. agonizer. Unfortunately, he was to have been their liaison with those arranging the next leg of their journey. So now, they were waiting until an alternate contact was made. Jean went to the window for the third time that afternoon. It had been raining steadily for two days. Now it had stopped.

She turned back to the room where Aernath was trying to teach Aethelnor the basic positions used in Klingon swordplay. "The sun is out. Couldn't we all go out in the yard for a bit of air and sun?"

Aernath lowered his fencing wand and looked at her. "Sure, why not—"

"Gotcha!" exclaimed Aethelnor with gleeful satisfaction as his thrust touched Aernath on the hip.

Aernath laughed. "Excellent! Always look for a chance to score when your enemy is paying attention to something else." Then he added more sternly, "But the correct term is 'Mark', *not* gotcha! Remember that. Now let's go outside to finish this practice."

The yard sloped down to a stream in back of the compound. This side was not fenced with stone but rather a delicate metal grillwork and plantings of dwarf trees. Glimmerings of sun-touched water were reflected through the leaves. It was perhaps an hour or so before sunset and even the winter sun was warm. As Aernath continued his drill, Jean wandered contentedly around the yard examining various plants and bushes. As she approached the grillwork her eye was drawn to an odd, brown object in one of the planting beds near the wall. Curious, she reached out and touched it, then recoiled in astonishment. It was furry, warm, and mobile. What she had taken for a tree trunk or dormant plant was an animal. Roused, it uncurled and regarded her with benign curiosity in return.

"Aernath, come here! What in space is this?"

At her call he came to investigate. "Oh, that. I forget what they're called but they're harmless. Aethelnor, if you run into the kitchen and get some bread you can feed it." He turned back to Jean. "They are burrowing creatures native to Tsorn and in settled areas have become pretty good scavengers. Tame, too. Kind of cute, isn't he?" He squatted to stroke the creature's fur as it sniffed Jean curiously.

Reassured, Jean knelt for a closer look at the animal, too. Slightly over a meter long, the sinuous body was covered dorsally with soft mahogany-colored fur. It was six-legged with a fold of furred skin running from forelimbs to hindmost limbs. The sleek head showed no sign of external ears. Two copper-hued eyes regarded her above a slender muzzle. The creature reared up on its back four legs and grasped one of Jean's hands with its front paws as if searching for something.

Entranced, Jean reached out to stroke its head as the moist nose muzzled the palm of her hand. She was engulfed in a cacophony of sounds like a Chinese orchestra that was tuning up. *Solitude!* The sounds died away to a faint chime and tinkle. *You are different. You are* Yumyn. *That is so— yes? You think to disconnect. That is not good, no. You are sought. Come with me.* Jean pulled back with an exclamation. The sounds and sensation ceased.

Aernath looked at her in puzzlement. "Did it nip you?"

"Aernath! It spoke to me!"

He laughed, then stopped when he saw she was serious. "Ridiculous. It didn't make a sound. They seldom do, I understand."

"No, I don't mean talking. I just . . . heard it, inside my head. At first it was like music and then thoughts. Are these animals telepathic?"

"Of course not. They are simple animals that live in burrows near rivers and streams. They give no evidence of social structure or higher intelligence. You're imagining things."

"Aernath, it told me I was different, human, and that I was being looked for. It wants me to go somewhere. Here, you try it."

He made a gesture of impatient disbelief, then faltered in the face of her conviction. Dubiously, he repeated Jean's motions. The animal sat patiently for a moment, then turned back to Jean. He shook his head. "Nothing. You're just . . ." He stopped, noting her rapt attention to the animal again.

The sounds were muted now. *That one cannot connect. His kind is different. Come. You must come now.*

I can't. I cannot go without him and he does not believe you. Where do you want us to go? Why?

The music welled up into the foreground. Jean felt the sense of listening, not her own but that of the animal. *You must come to another one who waits. That one says the strange bird flies when the sun leaves its burrow. Tell this one. Come now.* The sense of urgency was unmistakable, the sense of calling strong even beyond the thought messages she was receiving.

She lifted her hand from the soft furred head. The animal retained its tiny pawed grip on her fingers. "Aernath, it says that Klingons can't connect with them but it clearly wants me to go with it to meet someone. Does this mean anything to you: 'the strange bird flies when the sun leaves it's burrow'?"

Aernath's manner changed instantly. "Incredible! But how could they . . . Never mind, yes, it might. If you think you're 'talking' to that thing—ask it what kind of bird."

Jean turned to the animal, then back to Aernath. "It says it is a strange bird, unfamiliar to it, but a bird of prey of some sort."

Aernath pursed his lips thoughtfully. "It could be . . . all right, wait here a moment." He got up and went into the house. At the same time Aethelnor came out with the bread, and Jean helped him feed the animal. It certainly gave no overt sign of awareness or higher intelligence as it busily consumed the morsels Aethelnor fed it. After the last piece, it nosed his hands hopefully for a moment, then sat back and set to grooming its fur unconcernedly.

Delighted, Aethelnor went back to fetch more bread. Immediately the animal moved to the grillwork gate, then turned to look at Jean. It returned to her again grasping her finger with a forepaw and thrusting its head into her palm like a cat seeking to be petted. Again she felt/heard the urgent *Come!* It had a musical quality and once again she was aware of the undertones, more coherent and harmonic this time . . . quite pleasant really . . .

Aernath was shaking her shoulder gently. "Jean?" He seemed relieved when she looked up. "How are we supposed to go?" She noticed he had his cloak and a *shurdik* draped over his arm.

"That way, along the stream somehow. Apparently it's not too far."

He handed her the *shurdik*. "All right. Put this on and let's go."

"What about Aethelnor?"

"He'll be fine here. The cook has him occupied at the moment." Aernath released the lock on the gate and they stepped through the trees to the river's edge. Like its neighbors, this property had a small quay with a little boat moored to it. It seemed to be intended for fishing or simple outings as it was equipped only with a pole.

Jean knelt in the bow while Aernath cast off. Their guide had disappeared into a burrow hole before they left the yard. Now the animal surfaced silently beside the small craft, its sleek dark head making eddies in water the color of dark red tea. Jean slipped her hand under the edge of the *shurdik* and trailed her fingertips in the water. The wet muzzle touched them. *This way. Against the water.* The music was a tantalizing background. "Head upstream, Aernath."

The water drew its color from the roots of the large *llngen* trees, several of which bordered the stream along this stretch. The sun had sunk nearly to the horizon now and bathed the stream with that surreal, limpid glow that precedes sunset. The trees already held the gloom and stillness of dusk as Aernath poled soundlessly between their roots.

Here and there water dripped from the gray-green leaves. The effect was that of some primeval, temperate rain forest.

Urged forward by periodic encouragement from their aquatic guide, they reached an area more sparsely settled and the *llngen* thinned to reveal a park-like area which had an air of neglect about it. The animal urged them to a decrepit dock on the opposite bank, then disappeared.

Aernath muttered an oath as he secured the painter and helped her out. "Cymele's Cloak! This is a queer business. What are we supposed to do now—take a walk in the park? Careful, there's a missing plank here." He grasped her arm through the enveloping garment.

Infected by his unease, Jean remained close to him and spoke in a virtual whisper though no one was in sight. "I guess so. It said only, 'walk and seek food.' " There was a faint path overgrown with weeds along the edge of the stream. They followed this for some distance encountering only two other persons: a small boy fishing from the bank and a tall spare scholar-robed Romulan seated on a bench, engrossed in a book.

The path twisted and carried them away from the river into a grove. "This is an old botanical garden from the looks of things," Aernath commented. "But it's in woeful shape." On the other side of the grove the path turned back to the river. Here a single immense *llngen* stood overlooking a small lagoon. Atop its platform trunk, skillfully constructed so that it blended into the camouflage of the branches, was an ancient rustic building that served mainly as a restaurant with a few rented rooms for short term visitors. "Perhaps here's the food we are looking for. Come on."

Jean followed Aernath up the narrow, wooden steps as she awkwardly grasped the railing through the folds of the *shurdik* and prayed that she wouldn't trip in the process. They were met at the entrance by the proprietor who greeted Aernath with some regret. "Welcome, Kinsman. Unfortunately, at the moment I have no available, closed dining space. The last one is reserved for a current roomer who usually eats at this hour. If you wish to wait for a while, perhaps one of the other two will be available shortly."

Aernath replied with equally formal courtesy. "No inconvenience at all, Kinsman. I shall wait." The proprietor showed him to a table and Jean followed. She saw him glance around cursorily before he took a seat facing the door. She sat down opposite him as he ordered a drink. Obviously nothing would be ordered for her unless and until they obtained a closed space. She would be expected to sit and wait silently. As far as she could tell, there were only three other occupants in the room: a young man with the air of a scholar, book in one hand and fork in the other; and a pair of old men absorbed in a *tsungu* game in the corner.

The proprietor delivered Aernath's drink and moved to the entrance to greet another arrival. Jean saw Aernath's hand tighten fractionally on the handle of his tankard. The black and scarlet uniform of I.S.G. moved into her field of vision. But the Klingon passed them with the merest of glances and moved to the *tsungu* game. "The usual, Amar, and make it snappy." The proprietor bowed and scurried away.

From Aernath's eyes, Jean read that someone else had come in. Again a figure entered her limited field of vision: the Romulan scholar. He moved smoothly as if by habit to one of the three doors on the opposite side of the room. These were the closed dining spaces, Jean surmised, and he must be the roomer referred to by the proprietor. What, she wondered, would a Romulan scholar be doing here? Aernath had mentioned Romulans on Tahrn, and she had glimpsed a group of them at the spaceport here on Tsorn but had never encountered one at close range. Under other circumstances, it would be an exciting prospect but not here and now. The proprietor returned with the I.S.G. man's order, then disappeared into the door the Romulan had entered. Jean watched the I.S.G. man nervously, thankful for the anonymity afforded by the *shurdik*. The Klingon commenced his meal apparently oblivious to them but following the game at the next table with some interest.

The proprietor appeared at their table with a bottle of ale. "The Romulan scholar sends his compliments and invites you to use his space. He says it won't inconvenience him to delay his meal."

Aernath took the bottle and inspected it critically. "Tell

191

him that I . . . No, I shall respond to his offer myself." He rose with a faint gesture to Jean and crossed the room, bottle in hand. Jean followed dutifully. The proprietor opened the door and stood aside to let them enter.

His back to them, the Romulan was silhouetted against the fine grillwork that constituted the outer wall overlooking the lagoon. The room itself was similar to the one in Mara's quarters with floor matting and a sunken dining recess. Jean followed Aernath's lead and bowed as the Romulan turned to greet them. This had the unhappy effect of dislodging her *shurdik* so she could see nothing for a moment. She heard Aernath say, "It is most gracious of you, sir, to offer us this area. Are you certain it will not be an imposition?"

The Romulan gave a deprecatory wave of his hand. "There is an old saying: 'The gyrfalcon only flies at dawn and dusk . . .' "

". . . 'and the wise hunter does well to discipline himself likewise.' " Aernath finished smoothly. "Yes, I have heard that saying."

"Patience is a virtue to be cultivated by scholars and hunters alike. It is no trouble for me to wait."

Aernath bent to remove his boots. "Perhaps you would honor me with your company and neither of us would be inconvenienced?" Jean abandoned the effort to straighten her *shurdik* and turned her attention to removing her own boots.

The Romulan sounded faintly surprised. "Would that not defeat the purpose of your using a closed area?"

"Like yourself, we are off-world visitors here. Though I respect and observe Tsorni custom while here, it is no affront to me for you to join us if it does not offend you to share table with a female."

"One learns to adopt many customs when one travels," the Romulan responded noncommitally. "I should be happy to join you." He turned and placed his order with the waiting proprietor.

Aernath did likewise, then offhandedly instructed Jean, "After he has brought the meal and left, you may remove your *shurdik* and serve us."

192

Jean said nothing as the situation dictated but she chewed her lip in annoyance. Aernath seemed to be enjoying this bit of role playing a shade too much to suit her. Petulantly she tugged at the sides of the hood portion. How did the natives manage these blasted things so that they weren't perpetually blind or flat on their faces? No wonder one saw so few women in public! Her vision finally restored to the maximum permitted, she saw that Aernath and the Romulan had taken their places at the table. Aernath sat facing her, and the door, with the Romulan opposite him.

". . . my field is philosophy, but my avocation is zoology and botany so this is a fortuitous lodging for me. I have found it a quiet, congenial place where one can pursue one's interests unhindered. You may speak freely and undisturbed here."

"We can speak openly, then?" Aernath inquired.

"This room is indeed private and the proprietor is most . . . discreet."

This must be their contact, Jean thought. He was dressed in a black outfit of velvet texture. The scholar's shawl and cowl which he had brushed back were trimmed in gray. From the back, he looked and sounded remarkably like a Vulcan which was not surprising since the two races sprang from a common ancestry. But, whereas Vulcans had chosen to eschew emotion and such regrettable outgrowths of emotionalism as war, the Romulans had retained more of their passionate and ferocious ancestral traits. They had shown little inclination for contact with the Federation though apparently they had some kind of alliance with the Klingons.

". . . then perhaps you can tell me of your pl . . ." Aernath amended his sentence in mid-syllable as the proprietor reappeared with their meal, ". . . pleasant surprises in observing Tsorni flora and fauna."

"It is indeed a planet full of remarkable surprises. These *llngen* trees, for example, are magnificent; and, though they have not been much studied, your *ngkatha* are fascinating animals. Their communication modes are quite engrossing to observe."

"So I have been told," Aernath observed drily. To the

proprietor he added, "That is most satisfactory, Kinsman. I would be obliged if you would ensure that we not be disturbed."

The proprietor departed with a firm promise to see to it. With a heartfelt sigh of relief, Jean shed her impedimenta and picked up some of the dishes. She set one in front of the Romulan, then went around to set one before Aernath. She had little enough experience to go on but this Romulan looked a great deal like the only Vulcan— She stumbled and fell against the table in her astonishment. Seeing his face clearly in full light there could be no mistake. "Mr. Sp—!" Quickly the Vulcan reached across the table and gently covered her mouth, shaking his head at the same time.

"How careless of me not to have warned you of that rough spot that might trip you. Are you injured?" Still reaching across the small table he guided her to a sitting position keeping his hand on her mouth until she had a grip on her composure again.

"I am quite unharmed, thank you, sir," she managed at last. Aernath was speechless but to the question in his eyes she nodded "yes" that she did indeed know this stranger. Know him? It was practically like seeing the *Enterprise* itself again! For the first time in more than half a year, Jean dared admit to herself a genuine hope of getting back to the Federation. With alacrity she passed the rest of the dishes to Aernath who distributed them on the table.

"It would greatly interest us to hear of your stay on Tsorn and of your projected travels," Aernath said when they were all seated once more.

"And I should like to learn of your travels," Spock responded. He leaned across the table, the fingers of his hands steepled in front of him. "With your permission?"

It took Jean a moment to realize what he was asking. But of course—so logical—a quick and complete report with no possibility of being overheard. Nonetheless, she hesitated. In spite of her complete confidence in him and her unbounded joy at seeing a familiar face from the Federation, it was awesome to contemplate opening to a total mind-meld with a Vulcan. Among other things he would discover that her first impulse on seeing him had been to hug him, an impulse she knew Vulcans would find painfully embarrassing as they did all human emotional displays. Then she thought of all the events of the past few months . . . "Everything?" she asked faintly.

Obviously her hesitation was plain to see. Though she detected no discernible movement there seemed to be some imperceptible withdrawal. "Only whatever facts you deem pertinent."

Immediately she felt apologetic. She was forgetting that this was as demanding and uncomfortable for him as for her, possibly more so. She gestured her assent. "By all means, please." Nonetheless, she felt a twinge of panicked refusal as those strong slender fingers settled to her temples . . .

. . . Ice and Flame. Not far from her girlhood home on Aldebaran there was an area of geothermal springs. There were places one could stand in a stream where the icy runoff from the mountains merged with the steaming outflow from a hot pot. Side by side the currents would flow, twist, swirl, and merge: strange appositions, brisk contrasts, shocking transitions . . . This mental effect was similar. It was also disorienting. To 'see' magnetic fields, for example, as Vulcans did—it was like tasting the color red.

With a start she realized that while she had been enthralled by the wonder and the awe, immersed in the flow and feeling of the experience, that cool logical mind had been flipping switches, closing synapses, perusing memories with rapid methodical thoroughness at a pace that was mindnumbing for human perceptions. She could not have demurred at the examination of any particular item: it proceeded too swiftly. That she was even aware of any single scrutiny was due solely to the fact that, however briefly, it had to involve an interaction—a touching. She could no more control or restrain this Vulcan onslaught than could matter resist the pull of a black hole. Yet the restraint was there. Rather by gestalt than by individual item analysis, she knew that those events and reactions she felt most reluctant to reveal had been touched most lightly. Even as her apprehension waxed and waned the pace slowed; the two currents eddied beside a particular jumble of synapses. She sensed puzzlement, concern, and then acceptance of an answer though she wasn't sure of either the question or the answer. That synaptic node remained a blank gap.

I have endeavored to respect your wishes. I believe I have caused you the minimum discomfort needed to accomplish the task at hand. It was a statement of fact. Her discomfort was plain for him to read and his analysis lay open to her. She realized the statement merely served to allow her time to catch up, to assess her reactions as that Vulcan mind had already done, to confirm it.

She did so. *Yes, thank you.*

There is no need for thanks.

She pushed beyond the analysis to the restraint. There was a tautness there. The current moved and shifted uneasily, then steadied—a disciplined waiting, a conscious act of will to submit to a reciprocal examination conducted in a painstakingly slow and fumbling manner. Poised on the surface of this current, she caught impressions deep within of . . . What? Could one apply human terms to what coursed there? At any rate there flowed energies, impulses, as different from those cold logical currents as those in turn were to her own mental processes. It would not take much to penetrate the surface tension, to probe the depths and touch these impulses, if one were to push . . . Again came the wavering and then the deliberate will to steadiness, to endure the probe if it came. With an intuitive flash she understood the restraint. It did not arise entirely out of consideration for her reluctance. There was a comparable disinclination on the other side. This time it was her turn to touch lightly and withdraw. *Yes, of course,* she responded. *I understand.* The tautness receded. *But one thing puzzles me.* . . . She touched the blank spot.

Yes, he agreed, *we were concerned about you, especially Dr. McCoy—not only because of your injuries on Sherman's planet but also what the Klingons might have done to you. That was one reason I had to check . . . Under the circumstances, I would say you were most fortunate. You have come through virtually unscathed.*

But there is that gap—something I feel as if I ought to remember, almost can—but it eludes me.

I can assure you that it is nothing vital at this point. Dr.

McCoy tells me this is not uncommon following an injury such as you had. I am sure he will go over this with you thoroughly when we return to the Enterprise. The tautness returned. *We will separate again shortly and proceed separately to the rendevous point. It would be advisable to maintain a link. If you agree, I will not break the contact completely when I withdraw. The connection will be barely perceptible in the normal course of events but could be expanded immediately should the occasion require it.*

She assented. *I would welcome it until we get back to the Federation. You know, it's not nearly as difficult the second time.*

The second time?

The nagging puzzlement returned. *You see?* She pointed to the gap. *I don't know why I said that.* Groping for an explanation, she suggested, *Maybe it was the contact through the* ngkatha?

That might indeed account for the impression. Once more the currents moved and twisted, flowed and ebbed as Spock withdrew the meld. At the conclusion there remained a faint cool pulse deep on the subliminal surface of the subconscious.

Safely encapsulated in her own uniqueness again, Jean gazed at the impassive Vulcan face opposite her as Spock withdrew his hands. "Your travels have been indeed most interesting and valuable," he said. Then he turned to Aernath, "And you?"

Aernath paled as he realized the invitation was being extended to him as well. He glanced at Jean, then back to Spock. "A brief exchange of plans might be appropriate," he finally said, giving a hopeful emphasis to *brief*.

It was. Through the link Jean caught a faint echo of the same panicky refusal she had experienced as Spock's fingers reached Aernath. A few seconds later, both Spock and Aernath leaned back, the latter looking shaky but relieved. His only comment was, "Well, that certainly beats my potted plant all hollow."

Their meal proceeded to the accompaniment of casual conversation about the flora and fauna of Tsorn. Jean was astonished at the range of information that Spock had managed to garner in the few days he had been here. At the conclusion of the meal, they made ritual farewells. Jean donned her *shurdik* and followed Aernath back to their boat. It was completely dark but they made their way back without incident.

Jean stood wedged in a corner of the departure area while Aethelnor squirmed restlessly on a nearby bench. She felt tense and restless, too. In a few minutes the signal would come for departure clearances and she would move through the gate with many others waiting here. A few steps, enter the ship, and she would be free! Free of this *shurdik,* free of Tsorn, free of that clotting fear, free of the Klingon Empire, Federation bound! In the meantime she pressed her shoulders gratefully against the cold unyielding stone, knowing that in those final moments, nothing could come at her outside her field of vision.

She gazed enviously at Spock and Aernath. The very picture of an aloof academic, Spock sat casually reading across the room. Aernath stood, one foot on the window ledge, looking out on the bustle and activity of the spaceport beyond, the tip of his sword barely showing beneath the fluted folds of his gray cloak. She wondered what he must be feeling now. Anticipation? Apprehension. She was filled with a sudden eagerness to share that coming adventure with him. It would be so much easier for him in the Federation than it had been for her here. No need for apprehension. She would see to that, and she would have a chance to reciprocate for his . . .

Aethelnor was tugging at her side. She bent to him. "You have to . . . what?" she exclaimed in a low whisper. "Aethelnor, why didn't you go before we left?" She looked around helplessly. This eventuality hadn't been covered in their contingency planning. Aernath would have to handle it. She steered the boy over to the window where Aernath took him in tow. They disappeared around a corner.

A purple glow above the gate announced that it was now open for the next group of departures. Nervously, Jean joined the general flow in that direction. This time it was no problem to give way deferentially as would be expected.

Aernath had their documents so she could not exit until they returned. She drifted to a column near the gate and stopped to wait. At least here she also had her back to something solid. Spock was still seated. She reached inward and down toward that dim cool pulse. Its presence was reassuring. She saw him get up and begin to move unhurriedly toward the queue.

She became aware of a general hue and hubbub from the direction of the main terminal. Jean turned slightly and saw a solid phalanax of I.S.G. guards moving toward this gate. Behind them came a second wave of guards in private livery—obviously that of the Klingon they were preceding. Behind this individual, a corpulent caliginous man, came a following round of guards.

Jean heard a bystander hiss, "Hathak. 'Gath take him. Someday an assassin is going to get him in spite of all his precautions."

The crowd around her milled and eddied before the press of guards clearing the way for this Klingon. Her back already to the column, she could not move so she merely flattened herself against it. Several I.S.G. men brushed her *shurdik* as they passed. The main body of them had already passed abreast of her when one guard halted abruptly. The device he was carrying glowed urgent amber and bleeped stridently. For a fraction of forever he looked at her, his face as startled as hers.

"Seize her!"

The forcible assault of two I.S.G. guards wrenched a brief cry from her lips but it was nothing to the mental scream she sent spinning across the room, *Spock! Help me!*

The link expanded immediately. Even as she struggled blind and hampered in the steely grip of the I.S.G. she saw the scene from across the room. She watched while his mind cooly riffled plans and probabilities with the speed of a cardshark setting up a gull. He included possibilities that never would have occurred to her, but the probabilities of success were uniformly devastating. This time there was no restraint; the full blast of impotent fury hit and merged with her own. It lasted only for an instant to be replaced with glacial calm. She stated the obvious. *It's no use, Spock. Get the others out. No matter what happens to me, we've got to get them safely to the* Enterprise. *And tell Aernath . . .* Again the Vulcan mind anticipated her and touched that node. Then he turned and waded into her naked fear and raw despair, reaching, thrusting, far deeper than she would have imagined was possible. There was a sudden wrench and she tasted the ash grey echo of her own death. *What . . .?*

It isn't much protection but the best I can do at the moment. I will maintain contact as long as possible and send help as soon as feasible. Stall as long as you can. I . . . regret I cannot do more. The link closed down to its former glimmer and she was plunged abruptly back into her own clinging cloth-beswathed hell.

It was an impasse. She stuck by her bare bones story that she was a bona fide off-world traveler but refused to give identifying data, instead threatening them with dire consequences if they continued to detain her. The I.S.G. blustered back that the transceptor identified her as alien but left her standing in her *shurdik*, unwilling, apparently, to take further risk. They had been in this small room for some minutes now and seemed to be simply waiting. She heard a door open and a new voice spoke.

"Well, *Tormin,* what seems to be the problem?"

"The unit assigned to escort Hathak picked her up, sir. Transceptor readings show Alien but . . ."

"But, what?"

"She insists she is an off-worlder of rank and refuses to give any identity corroboration."

"And you let that stop you—from a woman? 'Gath's Bones, you're little more than a woman yourself. Strip her and settle it. Little enough harm if you're wrong." Matching deed to word, the newcomer seized Jean's shurdik and ripped it off sending her crashing into the wall in the process.

She turned and stared into a menacingly familiar face. "Tirax!" Her knees gave way and she collapsed in a heap.

He seemed as phaserstruck as she for a moment. Then, recovering himself, he turned to his subordinate. "That would seem to settle it beyond doubt now, wouldn't it? Take her to interrogation."

Ten

AERNATH EMERGED INTO the corridor with Aethelnor to be greeted by tumult and confusion. There was enough pushing and shoving that he picked up the boy. It wouldn't do to lose him or have him hurt at this juncture. Now where in Peneli had Jean and that Vulcan gone to? The gate was open. He began to move in that direction, wondering what all the commotion was about. Suddenly he felt a touch on his shoulder. Aethelnor slumped over tiredly as Aernath glanced around. It was the Vulcan.

"This way. Quickly, please." They edged their way fairly rapidly toward the gate. Many people had been distracted from the queue by whatever had happened. But Jean was not waiting for them at the gate. Vaguely alarmed, Aernath turned to go back. Again the gentle touch on his neck. This time there was no warning. The Vulcan mind met his with a slamming penetration that halted him in his boots. *Excuse me. Explanations later.*

What in the lair of Durgath are you do— His anger and resistance were brushed aside as easily as meteors by a deflector shield. He found himself approaching the gate completely without any volition of his own. The words he heard with his ears also reverberated peculiarly in his head.

"Kindly expedite this gentleman's processing. The child has not been well and is quite tired as you can see."

Aernath felt his hand fumble in the pouch, pass over one set of documents and hand over the other two. Where was Jean? He fought to turn his head. That mental vise-grip held his eyes fixed on the pass official. His head nodded in acknowledgment as his hand received and deposited the documents back in their pouch. A quick transit to the ship—a small craft, unfamiliar design but old, space battered, more than a handful of different registry marks on her side. Aethelnor was slipped from his grasp. Climbing now, slowly, fighting every movement . . . a pudgy beringed hand reaching for his . . . inside. The Vulcan coming up behind him. Whir and click of the spacelock. Release.

Aernath whirled angrily. The Vulcan moved smoothly to lay the limp form of the boy on an auxiliary jump cot. "What do you think you're doing? Where's Jean?" He grabbed the Vulcan's elbow roughly. Spock snapped the restrainer belts shut and straightened to lay a gentle hand on his shoulder, close to the neck . . .

"Yes, I must explain . . . ." Aernath winked out.

He awoke to a faint hum of machinery and a more immediate chitter of something non-mechnical. He was lying tightly restrained on his back while some maenadic space-sprite executed a victory dance on his chest. It was also painfully pulling his mustache. He opened his eyes to chaos.

He was fastened into an emergency jump cot that had been folded down from the bulkhead. Another one was still secured above him. A white-furred refugee from a kanish-smoke dream with long slender digits and an even longer tail ceased it's capers to regard him curiously. He hissed warn-ingly as it reached for his moustache again. The beast scampered away. After a few moments of fumbling with unfamiliar catches he released the restrainer belts and sat up. The room was redolent of stale food, unwashed clothing, several types of animal, and some more exotic scents he could not place even by category. One wall of this space was entirely occupied with small drawers labeled in several different tongues and symbologies, including Klingon. Bits and fragments of cloth, possibly clothing, were scattered—negligently on the floor.

Aernath ran an exploratory hand over his neck, shoulder, chest, waist'. . . . his sword was gone. Swiftly he checked the flat receptacle behind his belt—empty. So was the loop in his boot. Someone had been very thorough. He eased himself to his feet and made a threatening gesture to the little animal that was creeping up to him. Then he whirled at a sound in the doorway.

An astoundingly large rotund human filled it. Water-thin blue eyes shifted rapidly in that face; then the human smiled expansively and advanced upon him, arms outstretched. "Ah, my friend, you are awake. I see you have already met Agrippina. Sweet little creature, isn't she? *Arcturean chworkt*, that one—quite rare. And charming company for long lonely trips I assure you."

Aernath was engulfed in a pungent embrace. This human certainly smelled differently than Jean or the Vulcan whom Jean had said was half-human. Right now he reeked of fear just past, a heavy clogging almost intoxicating scent not at all like the piquant tang of Jean's. Interesting.

The human continued to talk. "Well, we're away. Gave them the slip we did. Federation space, dead ahead. Welcome to my humble home among the stars. Cyrano Jones is the name: prospector, trader, and occasional transport-for-hire is the occupation." He clapped Aernath about the shoulders and effused, "Make yourself comfortable, at home. What is mine is yours for our brief trip together. Can I offer you a spot of something?"

Totally bemused, Aernath let himself be propelled to the opposite side of the room by this animated avalanche of goodwill. The display of hospitality was interrupted by a cool voice from the entry way. "You were coming, I believe, for a cup of coffee, Mr. Jones, which you intend to consume at your controls. I think you will find my course coordinates satisfactory."

Momentarily disconcerted, Cyrano Jones mumbled, "Yes, of course, Mr. Spock." He dipped a pudgy finger into a welter of grimy objects in what apparently served as this ship's galley and extracted a moderately unsoiled cup.

Turning to Aernath, he smiled ingratiatingly, "Coffee, Mr. uh . . . ?"

"Aernath. No, thank you."

With an edgy glance at the Vulcan, Jones quickly heated a cup of coffee and departed for the bridge under the glacial scrutiny of Mr. Spock. The Vulcan entered the room, cleared a seat and sat down. He indicated the jump cot. "Sit down, please."

Aernath remained standing. "You forced me to come aboard, knocked out both me and the boy, and my weapons are gone. I didn't see Jean come aboard. Who are you, mister, and what's your game?"

"I apologize for the force; however, it was the most efficient means of getting us aboard. Considering your emotional state of mind it seemed prudent to put your weapons in safe-keeping. I regret that Specialist Czerny did not make it aboard. She was apprehended by the I.S.G. at the boarding gate. It was imperative that we move quickly before we were taken also."

"The I.S.G.? Jean!" Aernath exploded toward the door. "I can't leave her there. I've got to go . . ."

The Vulcan caught him at the door. "Believe me, if there were any way we could have effected her release, we would have done so."

He struggled futilely in Spock's grip. "You don't understand. I'm pledged to—"

"Klingons, like humans, I have observed, succumb to the irrational just when logic is most needed. I understand your feelings but our best chance of helping Miss Czerny is by completing our mission and sending less conspicuous help from another quarter."

Aernath regarded the Vulcan suspiciously: smooth black hair, upswept eyebrows, pointed ears, impassive features, clean untrammeled scent—no trace of fear, anger, aggression or hostility and . . . no anguish. He replied carefully. "For the moment then, it would appear that I have no choice but to proceed."

"That is correct."

"May I see the boy?" This was Federation territory now. For the first time he was out of his own element.

204

"Of course. He is not yet awake. I think it would be best for you to be with him when he does." Spock released him and then paused in the door. "Your previous experience of humans is limited to Specialist Czerny?"

"Yes."

"A piece of advice then about the captain of this vessel. Mr. Jones is, fortunately, not typical of humans. Keep that in mind. Oh, and don't let him sell you anything." On that puzzling note he left.

Aernath followed him, his mind a welter of conflicting emotions. The Vulcan had reminded him of his primary duty which was to deliver Aethelnor safely for Mara. But quite apart from any consideration of how her capture might jeopardize the success of their mission was the fact that he was *bond-pledged* to protect her as long as she was in the Klingon Empire. Some would argue it was a fortunate stroke of Durgath to release him this way but it rankled his sense of honor. As for his other feelings toward her, best not to dwell on that. One most emphatically did not covet a fleet commander's consort, even with encouragement. That way lay only pain, humiliation, and disaster. Strange, he mused, to find oneself welcoming *bond-status* because it permitted liberties that otherwise would be unthinkable. Best not to dwell on that either—a false hope. Even if the commander might somehow spare her, she was unlikely to survive long enough for Kang to get a hold of her . . . In the meantime, here he was being plunged at warp speed into the Federation without benefit of weapons or a trusted guide, and the responsibility to protect one small boy, a sobering prospect indeed.

Aethelnor lay just where Spock had put him when they first came aboard. His slow even breathing indicated a deep sleep but mild stimulation produced no arousal response. Aernath turned to Spock. "What did you do to him—us?"

"The Vulcan nerve pinch. If sufficient force is applied to the precise neurological junction for a brief interval, it renders most humanoid species unconscious for varying periods of time without any permanent damage. I estimate that the boy will regain consciousness in seventeen to twenty-three minutes."

Aernath did not realize that this statement indicated a greater than usual uncertainty for the Vulcan. Accepting the statement, he looked about curiously. The human, Jones, sat at the ship's console while the *chworkt* sat on its haunches beside him, its tail wrapped several times around his ankle. It busied itself by going through the lowermost set of pockets on his voluminous jacket, occasionally consuming tidbits it filched.

The human heaved his bulk from the chair, apparently satisfied with the settings. "Mr. Spock, I'd be obliged if you'd keep an eye on the controls. I'm going to give the engine room a once-over now that we are well under way. No, stay, my darlin'. Engine room is off limits to you, remember?" The last was addressed to his pet with an affectionate pat.

Whatever his unredeeming qualities, Jones was a crack pilot and meticulous about the maintenance of his craft's vital functions. Were this not so, the galaxy would have been rid of one Interstellar trader and general nuisance (as Kirk once labeled him) long ago. Numerous individuals in four arms of the galaxy had vied for the honor—unsuccessfully, to date. Like an eccentric comet, he wandered the galaxy peddling his wares and leaving chaos in his wake.

All of this Aernath was to learn later. For the moment his mind was on other things. Satisfied that Aethelnor was in no distress, he slipped into the auxiliary chair next to Spock. "How soon do we reach our destination? And how soon can help be sent to Czerny?"

"Traveling at top speed, which is habitual with Mr. Jones, we should arrive at Space Station K-seven in two-point-seven standard days. From there we should be able to contact suitable persons to send help to her. The *Enterprise* will pick us up at K-seven."

"I have a suggestion to make."

"Yes?" Aernath noted curiously that the Vulcan seemed unperturbed by the fact that the little white beast was now seated at his knee busily plucking lint from his trousers.

"If Czerny is still alive by the time you reach your agents, which is dubious, her best hope might be for Commander

Kang to learn of her whereabouts. Otherwise you'll never spring her loose from I.S.G. alive."

"At this point what advantage would she have with Kang compared to the I.S.G.?"

"If Mara succeeds in her plans, she may be able to have some influence with the commander."

"Logical. We shall pass that suggestion along for consideration."

"Did you see exactly what happened at the gate? How did they discover her?"

The Vulcan half-turned to face him. Suddenly Spock gave a gasp and for a second his face was contorted with agony. It passed as quickly as it came and his face was impassive again. "It was an unfortunate coincidence, I believe. Some high-ranking official chose that moment to be escorted past our gate and one of his guards' scanners apparently registered her as non-Klingon. They seized her immediately. There was no way I could intervene successfully."

"There must be something I could have done if I'd been there." Aernath brought his fist down on the console.

"No, Czerny and I agreed there was no feasible plan to . . ."

"Agreed? She spoke to you?"

"No." Spock spoke more slowly now as if reluctant. "We had maintained a mind-link since the meeting in the botanical gardens. She communicated to me through that. She asked me to get you two out and—"

"You mean you've been in mental contact all this time? Are you in contact now?"

"No."

"When? How long? I mean, did you lose contact when we left Tsorn?"

"No."

Aernath was severely frustrated by the Vulcan's reticence. He fairly seethed. "Well, if not then, when. When did you lose contact with her?"

Spock glanced at the control panel. "Approximately one point three-five minutes ago."

Aernath sat immobilized by icy premonition for a moment before he asked the obvious question. "Why?"

"I believe they used the agonizer."

Aernath rose and moved unsteadily over to Aethelnor. He did not want anyone to see his face for a few moments. When he finally looked back the Vulcan was bent over the console with his back to him. Without looking in Aernath's direction, he spoke again. "She asked me to give you two messages. The first was to do everything in your power to get Aethelnor to Starfleet regardless of any consequences to her. The second was an answer to your question."

"My question?"

"She said she never answered the question you asked her on Peneli. The answer is, 'Yes, it is important. It matters a great deal to me.' "

Aethelnor chose that moment to wake up and promptly began to cry. Aernath was grateful for the excuse to pick him up and console him. At least one of them could cry and be comforted. He and Jean had both known the risks, and duty was duty, but, for the moment, that was no balm.

Just then Jones came ambling back munching on some unfamiliar item. "Motor's purring like a baby with a fresh diaper change," he announced with cheerful disregard for the scrambled metaphor. He beamed at Aethelnor. "Ah, the young man is awake. How do you do, chappie? What is your name?" He bent over until his face was level with Aethelnor's and enveloped the boy's hand in one of his.

Aethelnor, his composure barely restored, stared round-eyed at the trader, then whispered to Aernath, "What is that, *Korin?*"*

"This is Mr. Jones, a human, who is captain of this ship we're on."

Suddenly shy, Aethelnor pulled back and buried his head in Aernath's neck. Then he whispered in Aernath's ear. "But he doesn't smell like *Thelsa†* Jean."

"Of course not. People are different. Now turn around

---

* Korin. A Klingon term of respect for elder males of the maternal line, roughly analogous to the human term "uncle."

† Thelsa. An elder female of the maternal line, e.g. older female cousin, aunt-by-marriage, or grandmother.

and say hello properly." But Aethelnor simply shook his head and buried it even more firmly.

Undeterred, Cyrano Jones tacked slightly. "Now there's a good fellow. Here, would you like some *ndalj?* It's really very nice stuff." He offered a piece of his snack. Aernath sniffed appreciatively. The aroma really was quite enticing. Tempted, Aethelnor peeked dubiously at the looming human.

Spock spoke sharply, "Are you certain that is suitable, Mr. Jones?"

"Ah, now, Mr. Spock. Surely you'll not begrudge the little fellow a small sweet just because it might spoil his supper?"

"I was asking, Mr. Jones, if you had checked its compatibility with Klingon physiology. I was not referring to the human proclivity for indulging their juvenile offspring in foolish and unnutritional dietary propensities."

"Oh. Um, yes, I see what you mean. I guess I better check that. An honest mistake though, we humans are fond of giving kids candy."

"As I have just observed," Spock rejoined expressionlessly.

A quick check showed that this Arcturean delicacy was indeed toxic to Klingon physiology, even potentially fatal to the young of the species. Cyrano Jones hastened to mollify Aethelnor with a suitable Klingon sweet but Aernath was left with a gnawing uncertainty.

This human seemed a model of friendliness and good will but he recalled the numerous stories told of humans. This was one of their most dangerous traits. They would appear deceptively friendly but they used this as a camouflage for their devious and cunning machinations. It is true that certain Penelian xenopsychologists argued that this was a fundamental misperception of human nature and Aernath had been prepared to accept this. But that, after all, was academic theory. Those with combat-contact experience told very different stories, if they survived. His observations of Jean tended to support the hypothesis of Mara's theoreticians but Jean was a human outside her natural habitat. Now this human in his own setting had very nearly killed

Aethelnor. Obviously the duty Mara had assigned him was a heavy one indeed. He would have to proceed most cautiously and guard against letting his fascination with this species lull him into a false sense of trust.

He returned to Spock's cryptic warning. Certainly there might be factions among humans as there were among Klingons. Was Spock trying to warn him that this human was one who would try to sabotage any negotiations with the Empire? Certainly this Jones would bear careful watching.

Cyrano announced he would "rustle the vittles" if Spock would stay at the controls. This, Aernath gathered, meant Jones would fix something to eat. He followed the trader into his living quarters and observed his meal preparation scrupulously but could detect nothing alarming. It was all standard Klingon fare. Aernath noted that Spock ate only fruits and vegetables just as Jean had reported. Jones directed, with substantial success, considerable efforts at charming Aethelnor during the meal. After the meal they adjourned to the control room to rejoin Spock. Jones became even more expansive. "Now then, chappie, how would you like to have me tell you a bedtime story before you go off to sleep?" Still round-eyed but fascinated, the boy nodded. "Well now, up we come. Have a seat here on Uncle Cyrano's knee." He scooped the boy up and placed him on his lap. "Let's see, what would I have here for such a handsome little boy?" He patted the pockets of his voluminous jacket. "Ahh. Why don't you try this one?" He indicated a pouch.

Watching from the auxiliary seat, Aernath felt as if he were sitting on activated agonizers. What was this human's next move likely to be? He glanced surreptitiously at Spock. The Vulcan seemed unconcerned. But then he had evinced no emotion over Jean's fate either. Aethelnor was poking in the indicated pocket and giggled when the human responded with feigned ticklishness. Finally, he brought out a smooth flat object. Unable to contain his concern, Aernath crossed to look at the toy. It was a flat container filled with some substance that responded to temperature and pressure changes by producing a coruscating kaleidoscope of colors from orange to kalish. It seemed harmless enough.

Cyrano rumbled on. "Tell me, Aethelnor, do you like true

adventure stories? You do? Well, I've scoured this end of the galaxy and had more than my share. Suppose I tell you one . . . Once upon a time I found myself on a rather nasty planet—natives weren't too friendly. Sales were pretty slow, too. I was about to give it up as a poor choice when I happened on the nicest little creature. A *glommer* it was called. Stood about this high and had a fee-rocious appetite. Poor little fellow really needed a good home and a steady diet, so I took him to my bosom." He matched deed to word and swept Aethelnor into a hug. "It just so happened I knew a place where he could feast to his heart's content. Excellent commercial possibiilties, too. So off we set. Now alas, some of the inhabitants, as nasty a set of Kli—" he stammered in mid-phrase at a sudden glance and raised eyebrow from Spock, "er . . . set of Kli . . . ver rascals as you'd never want to meet, resented my kindness to this poor little creature and began to chase me with their big spaceship."

"How big?" Aethelnor demanded.

"Why, oh . . . as big as a Klingon battle cruiser. Do you know how big those are?" Aethelnor nodded. "Well, so here was uncle Cyrano being chased across the galaxy by this huge ship and they were shooting at me . . ." He went on to describe incredible pyrotechnics and battle maneuvers culminating in a brilliant pincer movement accomplished with the help of his dear and beloved life-long friend, Captain Kirk of the *Enterprise*, by which means they utterly routed the dastardly villains.

Spock greeted the conclusion of the story with both eyebrows raised. "That is undoubtedly the most unabashed flight of fancy it has been my mischance to listen to in a good many years."

Cyrano grinned modestly. "One of my more minor adventures, really, but I admit it was a lot of fancy flying."

"I have no doubt whatsoever that this was one of your lesser contretemps," Spock replied energetically.

The remaining two nights and days aboard Jones's craft passed without incident unless one wished to quibble over such minor things as twenty-seven sales pitches for items ranging from Spican flame gems to the white-furred *chworkt*, or the escape of Juliette.

The second night out, Aernath went into the personal quarters to check on Aethelnor who was sleeping on the upper jump cot. As he approached the cot he accidentally struck a soft, yielding mass with his foot. Instantly he was assailed by a maddening screech and a sensation analogous to that produced when a nail is scraped across a school child's slate. With an exclamation of loathing and revulsion, he gave a reflexive kick that sent the object tumbling into the far corner of the room. Though the sensation abated somewhat, the screeching did not. Both Jones and Spock appeared in the entryway. "How in the name of Durgath did this get aboard?" he demanded.

Jones crossed hastily to the object of Aernath's ire and picked it up, uttering comforting noises as he did so. "There now, poor Juliette . . ." The creature ceased screeching and began to trill softly under his ministrations.

"Mr. Jones, you know *tribbles* don't like Klingons and Klingons don't like *tribbles*. That, is a *tribble*. Our agreement specified no *tribbles* aboard this trip. I, too, would like to know what it is doing here."

The look Jones gave Spock was wide-eyed, injured innocence. "Mr. Spock, do you think I would abrogate our agreement? I have no stock *tribbles* on this trip, but they did say I could bring along personal effects. Juliette is practically a member of my family." He looked down at the *tribble* humming contentedly on his arm and said reproachfully, "I couldn't leave her behind, now could I?"

"Are you certain that is the only one?" Spock demanded with unwonted vehemence. "May I remind you that payment of your fee depends in part upon your meeting the stipulation of our contract that this trip not be disturbed by any *tribble* incidents. I suggest you ensure that."

"Of course, Mr. Spock, of course." Then he added plaintively, "I did have her caged. It must have been Agrippina—they're great friends you know." Jones replaced the *tribble* in its cage and took pains to keep the cage in his sight for the rest of the journey but Aernath slept uneasily nonetheless.

Spock was in the pilot's seat when they established subspace contact with K-7. After initial exchange pertaining to identification and docking clearance, he turned to Jones and asked, "Mr. Jones, what did you do with your *tribble* stock before you left on this trip?"

"Deep hypothermia storage on K-Seven, Mr. Spock. Less expensive than boarding them."

"Did you label your container as to contents?"

"Why, ah, I don't believe I did. It's optional, you know."

"In this instance, you'd have been well-advised to exercise that option. It seems that that particular hypothermia unit became temporarily inoperative and so it was dumped. Unfortunately, the *tribbles* seem to have survived. Station Manager Lurry is most insistent on meeting with you as soon as we dock."

Jones muttered something under his breath about mishandling of valuable merchandise but nonetheless his face assumed a worried expression as the final docking maneuvers were carried out. As the space lock cycled open they emerged to face a harried looking white-haired man in an orange uniform, an ominously grim Starfleet captain, and several dozen *tribbles* of varying sizes. Kirk took in Spock and the Klingon with a quick glance but his interest was in the trader.

"Cyrano Jones! You miserable, fleabitten excuse for a Federation citizen. You're a free-floating cosmic recipe for disaster. I just wish I could figure a way to keep you off my menu. This time you won't leave until every last *tribble* is accounted for."

"Captain Kirk, my friend, your attitude is most bewildering. I really must protest. It is not *my* fault if you have er . . . an abundance of *tribbles* because someone foolishly dumped them loose. As I have remarked before, you really should get more competent help. I, on the other hand, have just undertaken a patriotic and perilous mission for the Federation virtually singlehanded and, I might modestly add, completed it successfully. Really, my friends, I think an apology is due me for your bungling ineptitude which has er . . . scattered my valuable cargo."

Kirk turned a delicate shade of purple and Mr. Lurry bid fair to match him. Taking a deep breath, Kirk proceeded firmly. "Mr. Jones, I am aware of the service you have rendered. For that reason, and that reason alone, I am prepared to recommend to Mr. Lurry that he extend to you the hospitality of this station until every *tribble* is accounted for *and removed*. If and when that is accomplished, your ship will be released to you again. If not, I find there is still the matter of citations for violations of three Federation mandates and several dozen local laws still pending . . . by the way, how did you wriggle out of that the last time I turned you over to the authorities?''

''I volunteered for hazardous duty like any good patriotic Federation citizen would in the time of need,'' Cyrano offered blandly. ''In return, they suspended sentencing.''

As Mr. Lurry escorted Cyrano Jones from the room with the spirited assistance of two security guards, Captain Kirk turned his attention to the remaining passengers. ''Welcome back, Mr. Spock.'' For the first time he registered Aethelnor's presence. The boy had been standing behind Aernath. Kirk gave Spock a questioning look. ''This is the, uh . . . expected delivery—all of it?''

''Yes, Captain.''

''I see.'' But his expression indicated otherwise.

Aernath was surprised that Aethelnor remained calm in the face of the plenitude of *tribbles*. He was controlling his own reactions with difficulty. A *tribble* that had crept behind them now began to shrill insistently. Aethelnor glanced back uneasily and clutched Aernath's leg tightly with his free hand. Aernath bent to pick him up. He addressed Captain Kirk. ''If possible, sir, could we arrange to have these *tribbles* removed?''

Kirk nodded. ''Better yet, let's go over to the *Enterprise*. There aren't any *tribbles* there, I hope.'' He gestured to the two remaining security detail, and the party made its way to the transporter.

As the materialization process finished, Kirk stepped down briskly to face chief engineer Scott. ''Thank you, Scotty. No sign of *tribbles* here I take it?''

''No, sir!'' the engineer replied in his faint Highland burr. Then he caught sight of Aethelnor. ''By the holy Stone of Scotland! 'Tis a wee Klingon bairn. What's he doing here?''

''I expect Mr. Spock will explain that to us shortly. Get

hold of Dr. McCoy and both of you meet us in the conference room."

"Aye, sir."

With a gesture to the security guards, Captain Kirk headed for the door. A preemptory prod from one of them induced Aernath to follow him, still carrying the boy. As they walked, he tried to assimilate the myriad new sights, sounds, and smells of the microcosmic human society that was a Federation starship. There were numbers of blue-, gold-, and black-uniformed humans in the corridor. Many looked at him curiously as they passed. He picked up occasional scents of fear, several of anger or hostility. One of the guards behind him was particularly hostile. Aernath moved very carefully. Most of the crew carried no weapons. Mara had reported this but he hadn't really believed it. Perhaps they carried them concealed in some way . . . Mr. Spock was addressing the captain.

"How long have the *tribbles* been at large in K-Seven, Captain?"

"We discovered them yesterday. As near as we can reconstruct, they were dumped four standards days ago and got into the ventilator conduits. McCoy has been over there supervising the spraying of neoethylene aerosol into the ventilating system for the last seventeen hours but it's a slow process."

They entered a turbo-lift and Kirk directed it to the conference room. Then he turned his attention to Aernath. "My apologies for not introducing myself. Captain James Kirk, U.S.S. Enterprise. Welcome aboard. Oh, you may put him down now if you like. No danger from *tribbles* here." He extended a hand toward Aernath.

Aernath hesitated in an agony of indecision. The threat he feared now was not from *tribbles*. He had been attempting unobtrusively to body-shield Aethelnor from the hostile guard behind them. He sensed his own fear scent climbing well above detection level. He looked warily at the extended hand. What did that gesture signify? This man's anger was fading rapidly: no hostility evident, merely curiosity. Then he remembered: oh, yes, the hand-clasping ritual. Awkwardly he freed one hand and extended it. "Agricultural Specialist Aernath, sir."

"Please to meet you. And your little friend?"

He could not restrain a sidewise glance at the threatening guard. "Aethelnor, from our planet Peneli."

Kirk assessed his state accurately. He gestured to the guards. "At ease, gentlemen." To Aernath's immense relief they put away their weapons. The turbolift door opened. He put Aethelnor down and taking him by the hand followed Spock and Kirk into the conference room. The security detail remained outside.

Kirk waved at the table. "Sit down please." Rubbing the back of his neck with his hand, he crossed to a small inset at the side of the room. "Coffee, Mr. Aernath?"

Aernath directed an inquiring glance at Mr. Spock. The Vulcan gave a faint nod. "It is similiar to your *khizr* and as harmless to Klingons as it is to humans which is to say it is a moderate stimulant that also has the long term effects of—"

"Mr. Spock, I was offering him some refreshment, not a lecture on physiology," the Captain interrupted with gentle amusement. "How about cocoa for the boy?"

"That is equally acceptable, Captain," Mr. Spock replied.

As Kirk was still looking at him, Aernath replied, "Yes, thank you." Spock, he noticed, took neither. He wondered if it was a breach of protocol for an inferior to accept service from a captain in this way. If so, Kirk gave no indication. Just as he set their cups in front of them the doors opened and two more men joined them. One was Mr. Scott, the sturdy dark-haired chief engineer whom he had seen in the transporter room. The other was a slender intense figure in a blue and black uniform. Right now he wore a harried look and was in need of a shave.

"Well, Bones, how goes the *tribble* treatment?"

The doctor groaned. "Jones! Blast that ring-tailed renegade from whatever swamp that spawned him. I'd like to put him in deep freeze, permanently. It's the only way to make this galaxy safe for sanity. We've stopped their multiplication before it reached the danger point, but Jim, those critters are everywhere!"

"I know, Bones. I'd like to throw the book at Jones

myself. Unfortunately, we can't this time. Just so long as they don't get on the ship.''

"Dinna worry, Captain. Security in the transporter room couldn't be tighter if we were expecting an invasion of Klingons," Scott replied with nice disregard for Aernath's presence.

"Well, speaking of Klingons, at least this time Jones seems to have brought along only two and one of them a rather small one at that," Kirk observed as Dr. McCoy set down a cup of coffee in front of Scott, then rounded the table to slip into a seat next to Aethelnor. "Agricultural Specialist Aernath and Aethelnor from Peneli. This is Montgomery Scott, our chief engineer, and Leonard McCoy, chief medical officer." Scott nodded brusquely at the introduction, neither friendly nor hostile. McCoy leaned over Aethelnor and extended a hand.

"Nice to meet you, Aernath."

Aernath took the proffered hand. "Thank you. Pleased to meet you, sir."

Gravely, McCoy then offered his hand to Aethelnor. "And how do you do, young man?"

Aethelnor looked at him wide-eyed over his cup of cocoa. "Do what?"

McCoy smiled gently. "What I mean is I'd like to be friendly. Do you want to be friendly to me?"

Aethelnor looked at Aernath who nodded permission. So he returned McCoy's gesture. "Sure. I'll be your friend. I like your *koko.*"

Kirk brought them down to business. "Well, Mr. Spock, we're all here now. Suppose you and Specialist Aernath fill us in on the situation. I thought Czerny was to come with you also."

Spock quickly and concisely outlined the course of his mission since he had left the *Enterprise* some three weeks earlier, including the contact on Tsorn, Jean's capture in the spaceport, and their escape. Then he gave a nod across the table. "I'll let Aernath tell you himself about Aethelnor and Mara's plans."

Aernath started to speak, then hesitated. "What I have to say is known to only one or two persons in the Empire. Mara instructed me to inform as few people as possible in the Federation. Secrecy is of the utmost importance."

Kirk responded quietly, "These men are my trusted senior officers. I have very few secrets from any of them. You may rely on their discretion."

"But . . ." Aernath floundered.

Spock came to his rescue. "Federation starships are not routinely wired for silent surveillance. It is customary to inform anyone if they are being electronically monitored. Your words will not go beyond this room."

It took Aernath an astonished moment to grasp the implications of that statement. Then he plunged into a brief explanation of Aethelnor's identity and Mara's strategy.

Scott gave an appreciative whistle at the revelation. "Kang's son! Och, you've got to hand it to the lady. That's as neat a caber toss as ye could ask for."

The object of their discussion, having finally finished his cocoa, was sliding sleepily out of his chair. McCoy gently gathered the boy onto his lap where he drowsed off comfortably.

"Possibly, Scotty. Obviously Mara thinks so. But tell me, Aernath," Kirk's eyes fastened on the Klingon's face. "Kang has never laid eyes on his son from what you say. Might he not just write him off as an unfortunate casualty? And even if he does come, what sort of weight can we give to his word? Mara's asking the Federation to make significant gestures of negotiation with Kang. Even assuming he's willing, can he deliver? How does he stand in the Empire?"

Aernath stared at the human across the table from him for a long moment, wondering where to begin. What did these humans know of more civilized emotions? With their barbarous family structure, how could they appreciate the discipline that balanced the deep parental instincts evoked by their firstborn against the demands of societal duty, relinquishing him forever from their *Theld* in just a few brief years? How could they understand the importance of the sibling relationship, or the care with which a man helped his parents select his sister's mate as well as his own?

Even his association with Jean had not yielded much insight into how humans balanced their breeding and rearing instincts with the demands of organized society. They obviously had both but . . . He decided to start with the political answers. Political power balances seemed to be something humans understood. "In the normal course of events, Commander Kang will succeed his uncle as emperor of Tahrn, the most ancient and therefore highest position in the Council of Rulers. His son, Aethelnor, is next in line to succeed Mara's brother, Maelen, as regent of Peneli. This puts Kang in an extremely powerful position . . ." He went on earnestly drawing the complex picture of political power balances that moved the Klingon Empire. Beside him, McCoy's head nodded down toward the small one on his chest.

Finally, Kirk held up a hand. "Thank you, Aernath. I think that's enough to give us the picture, at least for tonight. He reached over and pressed an intercome button. A lovely brown-skinned face appeared on the table viewscreen. "Lieutenant Uhura, you're working late tonight."

She smiled affectionately. "No later than yourself, Captain. What can I do for you?"

"Secure appropriate quarters for our guests and send . . . um . . . Ensign Tamura up to conference room please. Then I'm going to call it a day. I suggest you do too and let your relief earn his pay."

"Yes, sir. Goodnight, Captain." The screen went blank and Kirk stood up signaling the close of the meeting.

McCoy rose still cradling the sleeping Klingon boy in his arms. He shook his head as Aernath made an offer to relieve him. "That's all right, I don't mind carrying him. Interesting, isn't it? It seems to be a universal rule that the young of a species, especially when they're sleeping, exert a powerful appeal. I guess that's how we survive." Aernath regarded the doctor thoughtfully. Maybe there was something about human instincts after all. Different certainly, but something he must explore. After all, it was their differences as much as their similarities that had fascinated him in the first place. There seemed to be so much variation among them though, maybe that was why they were so unpredictable.

The door opened and a young woman entered. Her somber uniform marked her as a member of *Enterprise* Security. "Ensign Tamura, this is Agricultural Specialist Aernath and his charge, Aethelnor. They will be our guests for a while. I'm detaching you from regular duty and assigning you full time to them. It's a matter of top priority that the boy be protected from any harm. Requisition any additional help you need. Don't hesitate to call on me or Mr. Spock if you have any problems. Questions, Ensign?"

"No, sir." She turned demurely to Aernath. "Follow me please."

Aernath looked at her with profound respect. Petite, shiny black hair, eyes to match, golden skin, basic scent reminiscent of the spicy Penelian *kalimbok* bush, she vaguely resembled Jean. A deceptively fragile impression he knew. He had seen Jean in action and besides, any female that was a member of Security . . . Captain Kirk may have intended to lend a casual air to his detention but he was not deceived. Very clever, these humans.

Speaking of which . . . he turned to Captain Kirk. "Excuse me, sir."

"Yes?"

"When we boarded Mr. Jones's craft, Mr. Spock took my weapons for . . . uh . . . safekeeping. I'd like to ask they be transferred aboard for me."

Kirk nodded. "They'll be brought aboard but let me make one thing absolutely clear from the outset. On a Federation ship no one carries weapons of any kind except Security when they're on duty. No one. But we'll hold them for you."

"Of course, sir." Aernath didn't believe for a minute that the whole crew was really unarmed but it did make his status very clear. He thought longingly of his dagger. He was slow to use it and it wasn't of much use against a phaser or tactics such as Jean had displayed, but nonetheless the press of cold metal against his calf was comforting somehow. With a resigned shrug, he followed Tamura and McCoy down the corridor to the turbolift.

They emerged in another corridor and the woman directed them to a door. Aernath looked around, startled, as the doctor laid the boy on one of the beds. Immense by Klingon standards, the room contained two large beds, two desks with computer video consoles, numerous bookshelves and some items he did not immediately recognize.

Doctor McCoy yawned as he shook Aernath's hand again. "Good night. I'll plan to see you both sometime tomorrow for your physicals. Sleep well; I know I will."

The woman closed the door behind him and turned back to Aernath. "My name is Keiko Tamura. You may call me Keiko if you wish. Let me show you how things work. I hope this will be satisfactory. It's the only double we have available at the moment and we assumed the boy would be more comfortable if he wasn't separated from you." She showed him how to control the lights, use the bathroom fixtures, and work the intercom. "My own quarters are just down the hall so don't hesitate to call if you have any problems. Also, there will be a sentry on duty at night or any other time one of you is in the room. I'll come by for you in the morning before breakfast. Any questions?"

Aernath shook his head.

"Oh, one other thing. You'll find standard issue outfits for you in the closet. I'm afraid we don't have anything for Aethelnor tonight, but we'll see what we can do tomorrow. Good night."

Aernath stood where she had left him in the middle of the room. If these were detention quarters what must regular crew quarters be like? And why have double rooms in detention? The door opened and Tamura popped back in. "Two more things I forgot." She beckoned him to the door. "This in Ensign Sakarov who's on sentry duty tonight. And I also forgot to show you how to open the door." She demonstrated the mechanism to him.

Aernath went back inside and carefully closed the door, shaking his head. They certainly were going to a lot of trouble to make the whole thing look innocuous. The bed was another surprise. It was outrageously soft. It took him a long time to go to sleep.

Eleven

JEAN AWOKE SCREAMING, the agony in her voice matched by that of her body. When they did let her sleep, the nightmares merely served to replay the torture they administered at other times, except Spock's protection didn't work when she dreamed. She knew that if somehow she survived, those nightmares would be with her for years.

They had abandoned the agonizer when it became apparent that Spock had made her bluff a reality. Application of the agonizer instantly caused her heart to stop. Progressively lowering the strength had no influence. Finally, the doctor had remonstrated that he could not cardiovert her indefinitely—sooner or later her heart wouldn't start again.

When they resorted to cruder methods, Jean had played what she thought was her last card: she asked to be sent to Kang. She harbored few illusions as to his probable disposition of her but it might gain her a respite. Tirax, who had been present, merely laughed cruelly. "Don't worry, human, the final disposition will he his, but in the meantime, Kang is otherwise occupied." He pursued her torment with clinical detachment however, making no reference to past animosities, as if that incandescent hate had burned itself out somewhere. But Jean was allowed no interval of coherence to contemplate this anomaly.

It was only some unmeasured time later that she discovered Spock's other trigger mechanism: any attempt to divulge information about Aethelnor also caused cardiac arrest. After she resorted to this several times the medic refused to take further responsibility for keeping her going. So they left her mainly to her nightmares.

Now she levered grating bone against raw flesh to rise and face whoever was coming, preferring her own carefully incremental self-administered agony to the brutal bath of pain that would rack her if someone else pulled her up. They must have done something to her eyes . . . She saw three Klingons and two of them were Tirax. She stared stuporously at the double Tirax while the I.S.G. doctor went through his grotesque parody of a healer's function. "There are two of you," she said at length with schoolchild simplicity. Somehow that bald elemental statement carried some immense significance but she couldn't remember what it was . . .

The second Tirax smiled with evil satisfaction. "You're very observant today. My brother tells me that he has never disabused you of your assumption and so you've never been introduced." As he turned to the first Tirax, Jean noted he moved his left arm rather awkwardly and there was a fresh scar on his neck that she had not noted before. That also carried a significance that escaped her at the moment . . . "My elder, but twin, brother, Kahlex, I.S.G. commandant for the Ichidur spaceport complex. To whom I am indebted for his exertions in my behalf."

Jean closed her eyes and the tears began without sound or effect. Each drop that bled free from her was replaced by an imaged Tirax marching at her from all points of the Klingon Empire—an unceasing cosmic joke. Somewhere she heard the faint echo of ironic laughter. The medic undid her carefully calculated maneuvers with one brusque stroke, laying her back on the bench. Her scream of response was almost perfunctory by now.

"Check her over thoroughly, Doctor. It would be most unfortunate if you overlooked anything."

Jean was dimly aware that the practitioner was being more than usually meticulous in his exam. Finally he finished with, "No broken bones that need to be set, no irreversible internal damage. She can travel whenever you wish."

"Now that is a pity," Tirax said softly. "How regrettable that we can't stay to enjoy your hospitality a bit longer, but Kang must not be kept waiting. Perhaps another time . . . Well, see to it. Come brother, a final drink before I leave."

The trip back to Peneli brought exquisite torture of a third kind. Tirax stayed with her constantly, taunting, gloating—thirty hours a day. Though he never harmed her, neither did he grant her any respite, nor any pain medication. "Don't harm her or let anyone else. Those were my orders. Period. And that is precisely all you'll get from me." He was simply watching her as the snake watches a caged mouse when it is not yet feeding time.

Having thus to cope with both Tirax and the painful recovery process on her own, Jean turned inward. She clung grimly to two facts: no one here had learned of Aethelnor; secondly, Spock and the others had made it clear of planetary orbit and were at least headed for Federation space. She had received that much from the "link" before it faded below her ability to detect it. Whether any link at all remained she could not say. Occasionally she had a fleeting impression of a brief cool pulse but it always passed quickly.

Thinking of Spock, she went back to that encounter seeking one particular item: the Vulcan discipline of blocking pain and promoting healing. She went over and over her impressions, the insights she had gained. It was not enough. She had insufficient understanding to make it work, but the exercise itself proved useful: it did at least distract her from her agony.

They beamed directly aboard Kang's cruiser and Tirax walked her to sick bay. Eknaar did a quick scan and promptly put her in a berth. "Gath's teeth! Someone sure did a professional job on you!" He cast an appraising eye at the door where Tirax had just exited. "Tirax?" he inquired laconically.

Jean shook her head. "No, his double."

"What?"

"His twin brother, Kahlex."

"I see. And along comes Tirax and rescues you in the nick of time?"

"You might say that."

"You know, it's the strangest thing," he said as he twirled dials and selected medications. "Kang's been going over this planet with a fine-tuned phaser—nothing. No hints. He even thought you might've been taken to Tahrn, to throw him off, so he sent out a net there, too. And that's where the message came. Scuttlebut is it was some double agent. Try Tsorn, he said. Then Tirax up and says he's just been in touch with his brother." He shook his head. "Tough luck for you, but it was a good run you made. Hold still now, this'll just sting a bit."

"Another professional job?" Jean rejoined drily.

"Of course," he said, then looked at her sharply. "What? Oh, I see what you mean . . . no, nothing like that. I'm just going to give you a good thirty hours sleep. That's all." It didn't sting much. Jean was half inclined to believe him. He slid the blanket down and looked at her chest. "You must have arrested at least a dozen times. What did they use on you anyway?"

"The agonizer."

Eknaar whistled. "And Kang was sure you were bluffing."

Whatever he had given her was beginning to work. She could feel it lapping around the edges. On an impulse she reached out and touched his wrist. "Dr. Eknaar, I arrested without the agonizer too, and I know how to do it again. If I do will you do me a favor? Don't bring me back. Let me go."

He paused in the act of putting away his instruments and looked at her for a long moment, then said gruffly, "Go to sleep. We'll talk about it later."

The smell came back first—of sick bay, and then she was looking up again at the black webbing. Eknaar had been as good as his word: painless, dreamless sleep. Eknaar also let her dress and eat before he called the guard but he wouldn't say a thing. Jean wondered if she'd eaten her last meal.

She knew this cruiser and its occupants well enough now to know as she was escorted along its corridors that something was disturbing the routine. Something besides her, although she could not determine what it was. Also, Eknaar must have slipped her something before she woke up. The block of ice in her stomach wasn't nearly as big or cold as it ought to be. She was taken not to detention or Security as she had expected, but to Kang's quarters. The council room was empty. Evidently her fate was not to be a public affair. The guard knocked on the door to Kang's room, then motioned her through with his phaser.

"Excellent. Dismissed." The voice was not Kang's.

"Mara!" Jean forgot her own plight in a moment of genuine dismay over Mara's. "Oh, no! So he got you, too!"

The room was rather dimly lit. Mara, dressed in her blue and silver uniform, was sitting on a chair near the bed. She seemed quite at ease as she beckoned Jean to her. "On the contrary. The coup was successful. I'm here on my own terms."

"The coup?"

"Yes, my forces now control the military and civilian administration alike. Peneli will move as I direct."

"And your brother?"

"Is still regent, of course. But tell me, what happened with you?"

Jean glanced around. "You want me to talk here?"

Mara laughed throatily. "My dear, this is the one place on an imperial cruiser where you can talk freely." Her voice snapped taut. "What happened?"

"The contact didn't show when we arrived on Tsorn. He had an 'accident' on the way to the port so we had to wait for a second contact to be set up. We managed that and all got to the port all right, then I got picked up. A fluke, I think. But the others got away, at least out of planetary orbit and headed for Federation space—that much I know. I have good reason to hope that your son is with Starfleet by now; he was in good hands."

Mara's smile was pure triumph. "Thank you, my dear. That is most reassuring. You will no doubt be interested in this message I received yesterday shortly before I came aboard." She handed Jean a paper.

SHIPMENT RECEIVED INTACT   AWAIT FURTHER
    INSTRUCTIONS   SUGGEST IMMEDIATE
              MEETING   STAFLK

Jean grasped Mara's hand impulsively as she handed back the message. "Then they're safe! We actually did it!"

Mara nodded. "And last night Kang received a tramsmission from Starfleet strongly suggesting that he meet an envoy to discuss Sherman's planet and 'other urgent matters.' " She raised her voice slightly, "Well? Now you've heard. Is that enough to convince you?"

Jean turned. Kang stood in the doorway that led through the bathroom to Mara's quarters. His hands gripped the jamb until his knuckles were white. Mara got up, opened the closet door and brought out a small machine. She extracted a plastic disc, then with the merest of glances held it out to him. "There it is. No drugs, no coercion, and it will show that she's telling the unrehearsed truth."

Kang let go of the doorjamb with an effort and moved into the room. He took the disc from Mara's fingers, glanced at it, then tossed it on his bed. He closed the closet door, then turned to face them like a wild *jequard* pursued and driven finally to stand at bay.

"Only a mortal fool would think to play Durgath to Cymele and her *jheens*." He made a gesture of concession with one hand. "I will meet with Kirk." Even in defeat he was proud and it was a painful thing to see.

Had it been her move, Jean would have gone to him. As it was, she watched Mara and in that moment of response read the measure of that woman's steel. Mara's hands were clasped behind her back. They opened, once, in that same impulse that moved Jean, then were stilled—waiting. Mara breathed a single word. "Finally."

"Mara!" It was a groan. Then Kang gave a short bitter laugh. "Durgath knows, I thought when I got you back I would be safe—the one person in the Empire who could be held hostage against me. I swore never again . . . You could command the legions of space itself and I would *laugh* if I held you here." He cupped a single fist in front of her. "You walk in and hand me my victory for the taking; then when I reach to grasp it you snatch it away with the one other bond . . . Sweet Cymele! Your revenge is thorough. Mara! Why?"

"Because it must be done soon. You are the only one in the Empire with the strength and the vision to do it. And you refused, so I had no choice." At last Mara allowed her hands to move, first to the ritual gesture of submission before Kang's belt, then to his face. "Milord."

Jean glided noiselessly through to Mara's room and shut the door. She curled up on the couch next to Mara's bed and went to sleep. No one, she decided, was likely to disturb her tonight.

She was left essentially undisturbed not only that night but for several days. There was a guard at the door and the door to Kang's room was locked. Her meals were brought to her. She saw Mara infrequently. On one of the first of those occasions, she asked, uncertainly, if she was expected to remain in Mara's quarters. The Klingon woman looked at her with genuine surprise. "But, of course, my dear, where else would you stay?" Jean left it at that, thankful for time and for a haven to recover from her ordeal on Tsorn. She contented herself with library tapes and solitude.

Her chief moments of unease came when Mara was present. Although the Klingon woman gave no indication of it, Jean felt, at the least, that her presence must be an inconvenience to Mara and possibly much more: a constant rankling reminder that not only had Kang taken another consort but had intended to use her against Mara. Since she was here—relatively safe—solely on the sufferance of Mara, Jean reasoned, she did not wish to antagonize her in any way. To do so would be to throw herself back into the grip of Kang, or worse, Tirax. What might happen then, she had no desire to find out.

Tonight she was seated at the small desk watching a tape and finishing her supper when Mara came in from Kang's room. Mara deposited some documents on her bed, took her robe, and disappeared back into the shower. Jean was somewhat surprised when she reappeared a few moments later. Hastily, Jean snapped off the console and took her tray to the door. Then she retreated to the couch, the position she usually occupied when Mara was in the room. Although ostensibly occupied with the personal journal in her lap, Jean found herself watching Mara as the Klingon woman shed her robe and began to apply the body oil Klingons prized so highly. Mara had a superb body and she gave it the same meticulous attention she gave to other things she deemed important.

Mara turned to her with the container. "My back, if you please." Startled at this first-time request, Jean put down her journal and complied. Mara stretched like a stroked cat. "Thanks." She slipped into her gown and robe and transferred her materials from bed to desk. "Oh, Kang expects you tonight. You had best go soon."

"Me?" squeaked Jean, her throat suddenly dry. "Why?"

"Why not?" Mara seemed unconcerned, her back to Jean as she arranged her things on the desk.

Jean stood uncertainly in the center of the room still holding the oil. "Uh . . . I mean . . . is that what you want?"

"Now why should it matter . . ." Mara stopped in mid-sentence and turned in her chair to look at Jean, whereupon her inflection changed subtly, ". . . what *I* want?" When Jean made no answer she went on, "It's what Kang wants. Why do you think you're here?" She continued to look at Jean with some puzzlement.

"Well, I . . ." Jean floundered, "I thought you had . . . I mean . . ."

Mara rose quickly and crossed to face Jean. She cupped Jean's face in her hands and tipped it up to meet her gaze. "Are you trying to tell me you thought you were here at my behest?" she asked gently. Jean nodded. Mara's hands tightened on her face for a moment almost as an embrace; then she gave a brief mirthless laugh as she released her. "My dear child, you credit me with more power than I possess. Whatever leverage I have must be devoted entirely to the success of this mission: meeting the Federation for negotiation. I would not *dare* defy him in any other thing. You are here because you are Kang's consort and he has use for you, not because of any thing I have or can do."

Jean looked down at the oil container in her hands. "You know I didn't seek this. The last thing I want is your hostility."

"Hostility?" Mara was genuinely puzzled; then with a sudden intake of breath she pulled Jean's face up again. "Ah, I forgot, it's no longer the custom among humans is it? You have the habit of single pairing. Cymele preserve us! Jean, I don't blame you that Kang has taken Second-Consort. Were he planetside instead of in the Imperial Fleet he probably would have done so long ago. In one of such exalted rank it would not be remarkable. Why should I be angry with you? After all, I am First-Consort with all that that implies and," she added with some emphasis, "don't you ever forget that. But all things considered I couldn't be more pleased with his choice. You have no powerful connections in the Empire to worry me, and you are a human, a condition I find useful both to Kang and me."

Not exactly a comforting speech but on the other hand not as bad as Jean had feared when Mara had first begun. Wordlessly, she twisted the closure of the oil container as if by doing so she could somehow screw up her composure.

Mara watched her closely for a moment. "Do you really find it that difficult?" Jean looked up at her again, wondering if the anguish and uncertainty she felt showed in her eyes. Apparently some of it did. "He doesn't expect you to love him, you know. Certainly not immediately. Even I didn't at first. That comes later. What he does expect is . . . *aetheln*. And," she added fiercely, "he deserves it. That, surely, is his right. You've seen enough by now to recognize what he is; what he can mean for the Empire! For the Federation even. Don't betray that—no matter how you feel personally."

"I am not . . . unattracted to him. It's just that it's like . . ." Jean struggled for an adequate metaphor. She was reminded of a time she had stood by Scott in the *Enterprise* engine room enrapt at the spectacle of the matter-antimatter warp drive pulsing just a meter or so away from them. To her comment on the hypnotic fascination that display evoked, the chief engineer had replied, *Aye, lass, 'tis a thing of beauty to work with—as long as you have the protection of the magnetic field betwixt you.*

She continued, ". . . it's like trying to work with a warp drive that has no magnetic field to shield you."

"I know exactly what you mean." Mara smiled as she extricated the oil from Jean's hands then added quietly, "You'd better not keep him waiting any longer."

Thus reft of illusions, Jean went to face Kang. He was sitting on the bed, one knee propped up as a working surface with a profusion of documents similar to Mara's scattered about him. He glanced up briefly as she entered then continued working. "Strip."

"What?"

"I said strip yourself."

"No." At this he raised his head with a glare that caused her to retreat to, "Why?"

He laid down the stylus he had been using. "I gave you an order," he answered in a tone that brooked no further temporizing. Jean moved to comply. Satisfied, he resumed the calculation he had been working on. After some moments, he laid aside his hand computer and came off the bed with that singular fluid grace of his. He proceeded to examine her with detached and clinical thoroughness. Some of the spots he probed were still painful enough to make her wince. "Hmm. Eknaar wasn't exaggerating," he muttered. He was down on one knee looking at hers which was still somewhat swollen. He glanced up at her. "Did you break?"

She borrowed a phrase from Mara. "You credit me with more stamina than I possess if you think I can hold out indefinitely against 'some of the Empire's finest'. I told them plenty but not about Aernath and his 'package'."

"Good." Kang sighed as he stood up. "If Kahlex had been efficient enough to catch me, all of you, including Aernath . . . if I ever get my hands on that traitorous tool of . . ." he checked himself then resumed, *"If* Kahlex had succeeded, it wouldn't have mattered what you told him and I could have overlooked a lot of things. As things stand, it is fortunate he bungled it almost totally: Only you, Mara, and I—in the Empire—know the nature of your mission. I'm perfectly prepared to take on either the Empire or the Federation but if she's going to force me to take this insane gamble now, I'd vastly prefer not to have to face them both at once."

"You would revenge yourself on Aernath rather than Mara, then?" Jean tried to keep her voice steady and casual.

He knew why she asked but answered her honestly anyway. "I need Mara . . ." His eyes unexpectedly flashed with the old pain. Jean held his gaze until he turned away, adding reluctantly, "and I . . . love her." He gave a short joyless laugh. "Does that surprise you, human? That a Klingon can love?" He glared at her defiantly. "It's a weakness, I know. I've tried to overcome it." He rubbed a clenched fist across his chest in an unconscious reflection of his mental efforts. "Durgath knows, I've tried. But I have not succeeded and it may prove to be my fatal flaw. Ah, yes, Cymele will have Her revenge, because I dared give to a mortal what belongs to Her alone." For a moment he stood absorbed in his own thoughts.

"I don't consider it a weakness at all. In fact, I think I'd like you a whole lot better if you would indulge that tendency more often," Jean said quietly.

He focused back on her abruptly. "Never mind. Now tell me about your interrogation on Tsorn. I want to know who and when—exactly."

Clothed only in his preoccupation, Jean struggled painfully to dredge up details from that ordeal while Kang probed mercilessly for precise documentation. Finally, he sat silently figuring. "Then that means the initiative came from Kahlex. His inquiry to Tirax came after it commenced and Tirax merely responded." From his seat on the bed he glanced up at her inquiringly. "Well, what do you want me to do with him?"

"Whom?"

"Kahlex—and his unit."

"You're asking me?" she replied with some surprise.

"I didn't say I'd take your advice, but you may offer an opinion."

"Boil them in oil!" Jean exclaimed venomously.

"That sounds interesting. How is it done?"

"I didn't mean that literally!" Jean retreated hastily at the serious gleam in his eye. "Do you really want my opinion?"

"I wouldn't have asked for it if I didn't," he replied acerbically.

Sobered, Jean paused to reflect. Finally she said firmly, "Bust them. Take away their rank in such a way that they will never be able to do that again, and never be able to rise to any position of influence."

Kang looked at her thoughtfully. "I see. And Tirax?"

"For which particular offenses?"

"I had in mind just the present episode: for responding to Kahlex's inquiry personally, *then* informing me of his Intelligence coup. Thus he neatly makes me indebted to him for locating and retrieving you, stays within his orders, and gets a small measure of revenge to boot."

Small. Jean thought back to Tirax's gloating face on Tsorn and to his hypocritical solicitude on the returning shuttle as he had 'helped her get on her feet' and put her through endless unnecessary walking and other activity merely to enjoy her agony, always scrupulously within the letter of his orders. He would find a way to get her no matter what the situation. Yet she had had the opportunity to kill him and found herself unwilling to do so. Should she now ask someone else to do it for her? She shook her head. "Ship him away somewhere, where his loyalty will be helpful to you and his animosity towards humans will be harmless, if that's possible."

Kang was standing in front of her now, close enough to bring the faint scent of oil and sweat. He lifted her chin with a finger. "Your plea to spare Aernath I can understand. Possibly even Kahlex. After all, he was doing his duty. But Tirax? You've made an implacable enemy there. Yet you didn't kill him on Peneli, and you had the chance. Eknaar got that out of him. Now you pass up another opportunity to be rid of him?" He was obviously perplexed. "Why? What is it about you humans? You clearly possess the courage to tackle situations even when the odds against you are over-whelming but . . . you seem to lack the stomach for the

233

messy infighting needed to finish it. How then do you clinch your victories?"

Jean leaned against him, the rough fabric of his uniform rasping against her skin. She shook her head. "I'm not sure I can explain it to you. One of our most honored human prophets once told us to love our enemies. In this case, I don't pretend I know how to do that. But one of the fundamental convictions I do hold is that any intelligent being can adapt, can grow in understanding to meet new challenges—even Tirax, though I grant you, in his case, I believe the odds of it are incalculably small. However, if I kill him, two more Klingons will simply take his place, their resolve redoubled to revenge his death. What does that gain me? Someone far more recently has said, 'Those who fight must stop themselves.' I can stop myself. The most I can do for anyone else is to help them find a situation where they can stop themselves."

Kang supported her weight for a moment longer, his hand resting on her shoulder. "Can you personally name one instance where you've seen that theory work?" he asked curiously.

She looked up at him. "I don't know. Once, maybe. You tell me."

Disengaging himself, he turned and swept the clutter from his bed. He turned back and this time his touch was distinctly unclinical. "I can see there is still much for me to learn about you humans, but at the moment my interest is not in fighting or stopping." He deposited her gently on the bed and shortly joined her. As his hands moved lightly over her skin, he gave a faint chuckle. "In the case of Tirax perhaps your suggestion has some merit after all. He is a fine line officer except for this one understandable obsession and I should hate to lose him . . ." He grinned appreciatively. "Besides, it appeals to me—'the human has interceded in your behalf, arguing that I need not be concerned in stopping your bumbling efforts. Therefore, I shall be lenient with you this time.'—then let him stew in that *tribble*-brew for a while."

Jean grimaced, "You certainly don't believe in making life easy for anyone, do you?"

"He's not intended to like it," Kang rejoined grimly, "but he'll survive it."

"It's me I was thinking of," Jean answered wryly.

He chuckled again as he moved over her. "You haven't let Tirax stop you yet. Besides, he can't possibly hate you any more than he does now. I have no doubt you, too, will survive." His lips met hers and spoke of other things.

Twelve

SULU HAD AGREED to share his assigned section in the botany lab with Aernath and now he was showing him around. Aernath was astounded at the size and scope of the *Enterprise*'s botany section. It was nearly as well outfitted as the Imperial Experiment Station on Tahrn. These humans took their science very seriously. Having completed his orientation, Sulu was now rummaging around in the supply bin. "Look's like I'm out of nitrogen supplement. Oh well, you can pick some up in central supply. I'd go with you but I'm due on the bridge now. If they give you any hassle just tell them it's for me." Hurriedly the helmsman gave him the directions to central supply, then dashed off for bridge duty. As Aernath watched the slim dark-haired human leave, he reflected on how much had happened in the two or three weeks he had been aboard.

McCoy had certainly been right about Aethelnor's appeal. Ensign Tamura had no lack of volunteers to help her look after him. After sticking with him every moment for the first week, Aernath had been convinced that while some humans regarded him with suspicion, no one evinced any hostility toward the boy. It took a while longer for the petite security guard to convince him that her assignment was to protect Aethelnor rather than keep Aernath under surveillance and that he was in fact free to move around in the non-restricted areas of the ship at will. Now he was content to relinquish Aethelnor to Keiko and her friends several hours a day. The boy was getting ample exposure to humans!—no problem meeting that expectation of Mara's.

Aernath also rigorously maintained several hours a day of lessons. In conjunction with this he had, out of curiosity, checked the *Enterprise* computer file on Klingons. He could not get any military information more recent than the battle of Donatu V which occurred nearly thirty years ago. Recent military information, Klingon or otherwise, was one of the areas Mr. Spock had blocked from his use. Other information on Klingons was available to him. He found it amazingly deficient and shockingly inaccurate. Some of the best of it, when he checked reference sources, was recent material added by Spock himself. Clearly the computer would be no aid in his teaching. When Kang and Mara did turn up, he would have to get some tapes from them.

He could do other things. That was how he met Sulu. Early in the first week, the helmsman had stopped by the gym when Aernath was drilling Aethelnor. At the conclusion of practice, Sulu had invited him to fence a bit. Now it had become a daily habit.

Aernath left the lab and took a turbolift in the direction of central supply. It still seemed a little strange to wander freely on a Federation ship unescorted. He never doubted for a moment that he was under surveillance, but they were very subtle about it. And that was fine with him because he had no intention of doing anything that might jeopardize his mission. Sometimes he walked a full circumference of the saucer section just for the exercise and fun of it; but one could get lost, too. In that case, however, there was always the turbolift to get you back. The doors opened and he stepped out looking about to get his bearings. Probably off this way—it looked like Supply. After wandering a couple of minutes, he decided that he wasn't going to find it with Sulu's directions alone. Time to ask directions. A crewman had entered a door just up ahead of him. He'd try there. It was certainly some sort of supply area . . . "Excuse me, could you tell me where—"

The crewman turned, box in hand, and gave him a wild startled look. "Klingons!" he yelled, hurling the box at Aernath. He slammed a button on the wall with his fist and then threw himself at the startled Klingon. Klaxons sounded and by the time Aernath fought himself to the top of his assailant he found himself facing the business end of six lethal looking phasers.

"Wait a minute, he attacked me," Aernath protested.

"You bet he did, Mister. What in blazes did you think he'd do—shake your hand?" One security guard pulled him roughly to his feet. The smell of hostility hung heavily around him.

"I was lost. I wanted directions to Central Supply."

"In a restricted area? A likely story. Come on you—move."

Aernath found himself rapidly escorted to Security. Even on a Federation ship he had no trouble recognizing it, and it bore little resemblance to his quarters.

"Sit there, Klingon."

He sat trying to puzzle out what had happened. The guard had said something about a restricted area. Had Sulu deliberately sent him into a restricted area? No one had warned him in the corridors. He had seen no warnings posted. Was this an elaborate trap to get him out of the way? He knew many people in Security regarded him with suspicion. If anything happened to him, what would become of Aethelnor? His anxiety grew. A stern looking gray-haired man of medium height entered. His expression grew grim when he saw Aernath.

"All right, Johnson. What is it?"

"We picked him up in the dilithium storage tank room, Chief. He just walked right in and tackled the yeoman there."

"No I didn't," Aernath protested firmly. "I was lost. I went in to ask directions." Inwardly his heart flip-flopped. Dilithium storage. An inescapable trap. If it wasn't a trap why in the name of space hadn't they posted it?

"Into a restricted area? You expect us to believe a cock-eyed story like that?" Johnson retorted.

"It wasn't posted. I didn't know it was a restricted area!" Aernath maintained.

"Why you filthy Klingon liar! It was as plain as the nose on your face." The guard nearest him suddenly struck him across the mouth.

"Easy, Sanders, we'll handle this by the book." This came from Security Chief Giotto.

But Aernath tasted his own blood in his mouth and felt the trigger release of fury that smell produces rising in him. He fought desperately to control that reflex: *No, not here . . . it's suicidal . . . remember duty . . . Aethelnor . . .* He failed. It took six men to pry them apart: two for Sanders and four for him.

Now, shackled to the chair, breathing heavily, Aernath struggled to dissipate the orange haze in front of his eyes and regain control of his emotions. Dimly, in the background, he heard Giotto talking.

"Captain Kirk? Sorry to bother you, sir, but we have a little problem. Could you come down for a few minutes? A couple of my men just picked up your Klingon in the dilithium storage area."

The Captain appeared promptly, accompanied by Mr. Spock. Under their observation, Security Chief Giotto himself repeated the questioning. Aernath stuck to his story.

"How can you say you didn't know you were in a restricted area? It was posted in big black letters. Can't you read?"

"I didn't see any sign, sir."

Giotto threw up his hands. Kirk looked at a crewman seated to one side. "Readings, Ensign?" The man pushed a button for computer playback.

"Erratic readings. Subject exhibits marked anxiety and stress reactions. Sixty-five percent probability story is truth as subject sees it."

"Well, Giotto, where does that leave us?" Kirk demanded with exasperation.

"Excuse me, Captain," said Spock, "I have an idea. Perhaps I can clear this up."

Kirk turned to his first officer. "Of course, Mr. Spock. Please go ahead."

The Vulcan approached Aernath and stood in front of him, hands clasped in his usual manner behind his back. "I know you better than any of the crew and I don't believe you knowingly entered that restricted area."

Aernath relaxed a trifle. Having Spock on your side was a tremendous asset. "Thank you, Mr. Spock."

"You know, of course, what dilithium is?"

"Of course. Dilithium crystals are an essential component of the warp drive."

"Is their storage area a restricted section of a Klingon cruiser?"

"Absolutely. Very few people are authorized to enter it."

"What would happen to a human, say someone like Jean Czerny, if she were found in such an area?"

"She'd have been shot on sight," Aernath replied grimly. He wondered what Spock was getting at. This certainly didn't seem to be helping his case any.

"Would you expect the same to be true of a Federation ship?"

"You'd be fools not to. I don't take humans for fools."

"Of course not. Would you expect the dilithium storage to be guarded?"

"Absolutely."

"Thank you. Now, would you mind describing my uniform, please?"

Aernath stared at the Vulcan wondering if he'd heard correctly. "Describe your uniform?" Spock nodded. Completely baffled, Aernath replied, "Ankle top black boots, black trousers, blue shirt with two gold stripes on the sleeves and science section insignia on the left breast, black collar."

"Correct. Now please describe Captain Kirk's uniform."

"Same boots and trousers, dark yellow shirt, commander's stripes on the sleeves, command section insignia, black collar."

"And Lieutenant Commander Giotto's?"

"That's easy. All black with support services insignia and two gold stripes on the sleeves."

"What?" This came from the man called Sanders.

From the looks on their faces, he'd said something wrong; but he didn't know what. Spock was speaking again.

"What color is the chair you are sitting in?"

"Well, sort of a pale, um, I'd say yellow-green."

Giotto looked very dubious. "It may be a bit dingy, but it's not far enough off white to be called green."

Spock turned to Kirk. "With your permission, Captain, I'd like to have Dr. McCoy examine him in sick bay. I think we can demonstrate that Aernath is telling the truth. His intrusion was inadvertent."

"By all means. If you don't mind I think I'll get back to the bridge. Let me know when you and Bones and Giotto get it all sorted out."

Flanked by two security men, Aernath followed Spock to sick bay. McCoy, at the bedside of an acute post-op patient, greeted the entourage with a belligerent cock of his eyebrow. "Now what in the world is this all about?"

"If you don't mind, Doctor, I'd like to use you visual testing apparatus on Aernath."

McCoy gave a quick wave of his hand. "Sure, sure, Spock—go ahead. You know how to run the machine. I'll be with you in a few minutes, as soon as I'm finished here."

Spock directed Aernath to an apparatus on a small table in one corner of the sick bay. A small boxlike portion of the machine fitted snugly over the top of his face excluding all exterior light. "Now, Aernath, I'm going to start running spectral wavelengths. I want you to report to me what you see."

For some minutes there was no sound except the quiet one of his own voice reporting the colors as he saw them. Then Dr. McCoy came and leaned over Spock's shoulder. "Well, what are you . . . Jehosophat, Spock! What are you doing? Do you want to give him a retinal burn?" Aernath recoiled from the box at the vehemence in McCoy's voice.

Spock was unperturbed as usual. "Not at all, Doctor. Observe what we have so far."

The doctor bent over Spock's sheet. "You started at ten-thousand Angstroms and he came in here?"

"That's correct."

"Did the colors all match standard?"

"Yes."

"And you were still going?"

"Yes." Spock was very patient.

"Hmmm. Mind if I check it? At least let's turn down the gain a bit." McCoy slid into the seat Spock had vacated for him. "Now, Aernath, if you don't mind let's just run through this again."

Dutifully Aernath reported as soon as the deep, orange glow appeared on the screen. He continued on down the spectrum.

"What do you see now?"

"Blue-violet."

"Fine, we'll keep going." McCoy encouraged. "What now?"

"Violet."

"And now?"

"Violet-*amarklor*."

"What's that?"

"It's a very deep violet," Aernath said.

"All right. Now?"

"Amarklor." For some reason the room seemed strangely quiet now.

"Now?"

"*Amarklor-kalish*."

"I see." The doctor sounded rather excited. "And now?"

"Pure *kalish*."

"How about now?"

"Black, there's nothing visible beyond *kalish*, Doctor."

"Nothing visible beyond *kalish*, he says. Spock, he cut out at thirty-two hundred Angstroms!" McCoy looked at the security guards. "What'd he do anyway?"

"Walked into the dilithium storage area to ask directions." Spock turned to the watching security detail. "Ensign, go find Ensign Tamura and the boy. Take them down to the storage area and ask the boy what color the door is. Also ask him if he sees anything on the door."

"Yes, sir, Mr. Spock."

Dr. McCoy was gazing at Aernath with a speculative look. "To borrow your phrase, Mr. Spock, fascinating. I'd like to take a closer look at this. There's a piece of equipment in zoology I think will be just the ticket. Come on."

In zoology Aernath reacted with some alarm as they wheeled out a rather vicious looking machine and proceeded to immobilize his head in it. "What are you going to do, Doctor?"

"I'm going to put a couple kinds of drops in your eyes, to dilate your pupils and paralyze ocular muscle movement temporarily. Then I'm going to run retinal absorption spectra on your eyes under a couple different conditions."

"Will it hurt?"

"The drops sting a little. There's no danger to your eyes. Hold still now."

The drops did sting. Then they left him for a few minutes while they retreated to a computer console at the far end of the lab and carried on a murmuring conversation. It was dark in the lab but Aernath could tell his vision was getting blurred and his eyes wouldn't move. In spite of Dr. McCoy's reassurance, he noted his fear scent rising steadily. What if the doctor was wrong or miscalculated? At this moment Spock's rescue seemed almost worse than whatever fate had awaited him in security.

Finally the two science officers came back. "He's darkadapted by now. Let's try and see what we get with low intensity light." That was McCoy.

"Start with fifty-two hundred Angstroms." That was Spock.

It went on and on. Aernath had no idea how long. However, McCoy was right about the fact that it didn't hurt. Gradually he relaxed. Obviously Klingon eyes didn't function exactly like human or Vulcan eyes and something they were pursuing had them really absorbed. Even Spock sounded enthusiastic. Maybe this hadn't been a trap after all. Finally McCoy snapped off the instrument light and released him. "Here, put these on. It's going to take a while for your eyes to recover from the drops." He handed Aernath a pair of dark glasses. "We'll help you back to sick bay; then I'll keep you there until it's worn off."

When they got back to sick bay, Ensign Tamura, Aethelnor, Giotto, and Kirk were waiting for them. "The kid doesn't see it either," Giotto informed them. "Says the whole door is black."

"Exactly, just as it appeared to Aernath," Spock replied.

"What color is it to you?" Aernath ventured to ask.

"Deep red with bold, black letters saying KEEP OUT, RESTRICTED AREA, AUTHORIZED PERSONNEL ONLY," Spock informed him.

"Are you trying to tell me that Klingons can't tell the difference between black and red?" Giotto demanded.

"Precisely. We have just demonstrated that conclusively," Spock answered.

"I never heard of such a thing. And how come he called a white chair, green?" Giotto wanted to know. "Is he some kind of color-blind or something?"

"I think you better explain it to us all," Kirk encouraged.

"First, let me get Aernath in a bed. Here, up you go." McCoy gave him a hand. This bed was just as soft as the one in his quarters.

"You are familiar with the primary spectral colors," Spock was saying.

"Of course," Kirk replied, "red, green, and blue."

"Wait a minute," Giotto objected, "I thought the three primary colors were red, yellow, and blue."

"That refers to pigments. Spock and the captain are referring to light wavelengths," McCoy picked up. "But do you know why those three wavelengths are considered primary?"

"Oh, sure. Because by mixing them together you can get any color of the rainbow and if you put them all together you get white," Giotto answered.

"To the normal human eye, yes. And do you know why?"

Giotto shook his head. Kirk interposed, "But if a person is color-blind, then they can't distinguish blue and green. Yet Aernath can recognize blue, can't he?"

"You're referring to a deuteranope, a green blind person," McCoy explained. "On the other hand, if Aernath were a protanope, a red blind person, in the usual human sense, he would be able to distinguish blue and green but all reds, yellows, and oranges would appear green to him."

"But he sees my shirt as yellow," Kirk pointed out.

"Exactly," said Spock, "which brings us back to the question of why red, green, and blue are called the primary spectral colors."

Kirk grinned. "O.K. Spock, you tell us. Why are they the primary colors?"

"Because they correspond to the wavelengths of maximal absorption of the three visual pigments of the human eye: erythrolabe, chlorolabe, and rhodopsin. All sensations of color are mediated by the varying stimulation of one or more of these pigments in the human retina. Klingons don't have erythrolabe. At least Aernath doesn't," Spock explained.

"Well, that doesn't explain how he can see yellow then," Kirk pursued.

"Exactly," McCoy pounced. "And that's what is so remarkable. Aernath can't see red, but he can see orange. His visual light range runs from about sixty-four hundred Angstroms clear down into the ultraviolet range to about thirty-two hundred Angstroms."

"He can see ultraviolet?" Kirk questioned.

"You bet your boots he can," McCoy responded enthusiastically.

"What does it look like?"

"*Amarklor* and *kalish,*" McCoy assured him solemnly.

"What?" Kirk asked.

"Klingons have names for two major colors in the ultraviolet range."

"Oh. Well, how do they do it? See, I mean," Kirk persisted.

"That is what is so fascinating." Spock picked up the thread of explanation. "According to the retinal absorption spectra and the spectral sensitivity curves we have just done on him, Aernath possesses four retinal pigments: chlorolabe and rhodopsin, or their analogs, plus one with maximal absorption in the orange range and one in the ultraviolet range. He has a double Purkinje shift with maximum scotopic vision occurring in both the yellow and the blue-violet ranges."

"Oh." Kirk looked helplessly at McCoy. "Bones, in plain English, what does that mean?"

"It means he sees green and blue by the same mechanism

we do but has two pigments we don't have: one that lets him see from orange to green and one that lets him see from blue to *kalish*. At night or in dim light he sees best with either yellow or blue light whereas we humans do best with blue light."

"So he was telling the truth when he said he got into dilithium storage by accident?" Giotto wanted to know.

Spock nodded. "Yes. Unfortunately for him the black and red on that door are of the same intensity so there was no contrast. To his eyes it appears uniformly black."

"Well, in that case, I think I'll get back to work." Giotto left.

"I still don't understand the chair." Kirk was a stickler for nailing down loose details.

"Something painted white appears white to us because it absorbs none of the wavelengths in our visible spectrum. They are all reflected back to us," Spock explained.

"I see." Kirk went on, "And for a Klingon to see white, the object must also reflect back ultraviolet rays as well. Our chair didn't."

"That's right," McCoy put in. "With the deep violet end of his spectrum subtracted by absorption he saw a sort of yellow-green. To a Klingon we are color blind, in a sense, so we see white when he wouldn't. It's like a human who is color blind to green. If you mix red and blue light for him it will be white but we would see it as purple."

Kirk threw up his hands. "Well, if you and Spock agree on it, it must be true. I'll take your word for it. It's been a long time since I saw you two work on a project together without arguing about it. Spock, what made you suspect it in the first place?"

"Something I noticed through mind-touch with him on Tsorn. When I met him he was wearing gray, but I saw that to his eyes it appeared to have color. I had intended to explore that with him once we came aboard but hadn't the opportunity until now."

"Dr. McCoy?" Aernath saw a fuzzy figure approach the periphery of his field of vision in response to his call.

"Yes, Aernath?"

"What does red look like to you anyway?"

246

"Well now, Aernath, how would you explain the difference between *amarklor* and *kalish* to someone who can't see beyond purple?"

Aernath paused for a moment trying to grasp that idea. The two were really quite different . . . "I see what you mean. They are as different from each other and from purple as orange and yellow and green." He went on regretfully, "It's a pity you can't appreciate them. But I suppose you would say the same about red."

"It's a warm exciting color," the doctor admitted. "I'd hate to do without it. But I guess it's what you're used to. Mr. Spock here says he finds a lot of aesthetic satisfaction in the patterns of magnetic force that he sees. I think it would be disconcerting to always see those wiggly little lines everywhere I went."

"On the contrary, Doctor . . ." What might have been a classic Spock-McCoy interchange was interrupted by the intercom.

"Captain Kirk, Sulu here. We've just picked up Klingon cruisers on our sensors." There was a heavy pause. "Five of them, sir." Sulu sounded awed.

"Red Alert, Sulu. We're on our way." Kirk and Spock left on the run. Tamura left to take Aethelnor to a safe spot and sick bay personnel began swift preparation for possible combat casualties.

In the excitement, Sulu forgot to close the connection. Thus sick bay continued to monitor the bridge. Aernath listened intently. A full hand of cruisers! The Imperial Fleet rarely deployed even a formation of three cruisers. Five was unprecedented unless . . . What had happened within the Empire the past few weeks? Had the 'Confront and Annihilate' faction won an upper hand somehow? Aernath cursed silently at his temporary blindness, not realizing that sick bay was getting only audio, not video. He heard Spock and Kirk arrive on the bridge.

"Status, Sulu?"

"Full battle readiness, Captain. Deflector shields up."

"Chekov?"

"The five cruisers are coming in from Klingon space on a very oblique course to ours, Captain. Calculations show interception just this side of Sherman's planet. There has been no change in their course since first sighting."

"Thank you. All right, Mr. Sulu, let's see them—top mag on the viewer."

The listeners in sick bay heard only silence for a long moment, then Captain Kirk's voice. "Any identification, Mr. Spock?"

"The lead cruiser is the *Klolode Two*, commander of last report, Kang of Tahrn. Next two are the *Kahless*, last known Commander was Ekthorn; and the *Devisor*, Commander Koloth's ship. The other two are not listed in our computer banks."

Kirk gave a low whistle. "So that's Kang, is it? Lieutenant Uhura, I want you to transmit a full report to Starfleet Command, bearings, calculated courses, identification, the works. On an open channel—use Code Two—and also alert the U.S.S. *Hood* and U.S.S. *Lexington* as if they were standing by. Indicate no reply expected."

"Yes, sir," Uhura replied.

Ekthorn's with him! Aernath thought exultantly. That's the first payoff from Klairos already. Ekthorn carried a lot of weight in the Fleet, and he had a younger brother high in the Klairosian Council. Koloth was to be expected; his sector after all, but an uncertainty in the long haul. One of the others had to be Kasob. His uncle was highly placed in the Peneli court. The other: several possibilities. The bridge conversation continued.

"Well, Mr. Spock, it looks like either Commander Kang is very serious about negotiating or this sector of space is about to be treated to the biggest fireworks display since the Battle of Donatu Five. Care to give us the odds before we place our bets?"

"I fail to see any value in placing a wager on an outcome if one is not around to collect, Captain. However, I do have another item of information which you might find interesting. Specialist Czerny is definitely aboard one of those cruisers."

"Interesting. I would say that adds some weight to the odds for negotiating, wouldn't you, Spock?"

"A logical conclusion."

Jean! Aernath sat up with a brief exclamation which brought McCoy to his side. "What is it, Aernath? Got a problem?"

She's alive! Jean made it! sang jubilantly through his mind. All he said rather stiffly was, "I'm surprised but pleased to hear that your Miss Czerny survived." Then to cover his feelings he went on, "It's important that Captain Kirk understand that those five cruisers are not just a show of force to impress the Federation. It also gives you a measure of Kang's current influence in the Fleet. Ekthorn's presence is especially significant." He clenched his fist helplessly. "I wish I could see. Maybe I could tell you who the others are."

"I'll see that Captain Kirk gets the message." The doctor touched his shoulder lightly. "We are all very pleased to hear that Czerny made it. She is very special, isn't she?" If Aernath could have seen the doctor's face, he would have realized that McCoy had not been at all misled by his diversionary stratagem. He probably wouldn't have realized that it didn't matter either.

"Transmission to Starfleet completed, Captain," Uhura's well-modulated voice reported.

"Fine. Open a channel to Commander Kang."

"Yes, sir."

"Captain Kirk." Chekov sounded excited. "The Klingon cruisers are breaking formation!"

From the conversation on the bridge it became apparent that the cruisers were peeling off one by one from Kang's lead cruiser and assuming stationary positions well within undisputed Klingon space but in easy striking distance of Sherman's planet.

"Lieutenant Uhura, any acknowledgement of our signal from Kang?"

"No sir . . . wait, I'm getting something now."

"Put it on audio. Sulu, keep wide-angle projection of those five cruisers on front screen. I want to keep track of them." Kirk punched an arm console button. *"Klolode Two.* This is Captain Kirk of the U.S.S. *Enterprise.* Acknowledge please."

There was a crackle of static, then the cool crisp voice of

Kang. "Commander Kang of *Klolode Two* speaking. It is our understanding that the Federation wishes to rectify some previous errors. As representative of the emperor, I am willing to listen to your proposals. We come in peace."

"In a pig's eye! More like several belligerent pieces if you ask me," McCoy muttered under his breath. But Aernath did not pick up much scent of hostility. These humans could be so misleading. Which sense did they rely on when such conflicting signals were given out? He strained to hear Kirk's reply.

"I'm glad to hear that, Commander. It's not immediately obvious to the casual observer."

"Changing the bait is not the same as removing the trap. Only by vigilance does one survive to hunt another day, Captain Kirk. You suggested Sherman's planet as a 'neutral' meeting place. How do you propose to guarantee that?"

"It's the one planet in the galaxy where we each have a settlement. You have your base of operations. We have ours. We can use the new conference hall at our agricultural station or alternate with your settlement as you prefer, Commander," Kirk replied evenly.

Kang's dry chuckle came through clearly. "So, you weren't able to wipe out my colony after all. Interesting."

"We didn't try," came Kirk's terse reply. "Our party did try to communicate with them but we got nowhere. You will have to make your own arrangements with them."

"Of course," Kang responded noncommittally. "We will take up standard orbit about the planet. I suggest you parallel us, Captain. Notify your subordinates on the planet to stand by to receive my envoy who will handle arrangements. This time, no tricks, Captain Kirk, or I assure you you will live just long enough to regret it."

"No tricks, Commander Kang. Kirk, out." The exchange terminated with the abrupt snap of a switch.

"Why that arrogant, overbearing son-of-a-Saurian-sea-sow!" Scott exploded. "Just who does he think he is, talking to a Starfleet captain like that!"

"An emissary of the Empire with his back against a particularly nasty wall, I'd say, Mr. Scott. At least he didn't lead with his photon torpedoes. If we want him to negotiate,

250

we need to give him a little maneuvering room. I think we're big enough to do that." But Kirk's voice held rather more sympathy than reproof for the engineer.

"Aye, that we are, Cap'n," Scotty grumbled, "but I don't mind saying it 'ud be a pleasure to take him down a peg or two." The Scotsman's anger was slow to kindle but long to smolder once ignited. He had never quite forgiven Kang for the rape of his engineering room at the hands of Kang's Klingons some years earlier.

"I'm sure it would, Mr. Scott, but that's not what we're here for at the moment. Mr. Sulu, take us down·to Yellow Alert and maintain status until further notice."

McCoy snapped off the intercom and crossed to Aernath's bed once more. "Well, how are the eyes coming?" He pulled off the dark glasses and turned Aernath's face toward him.

Aernath looked up at the blurred image in front of him. "I still can't move my eyes or see anything clearly. How much longer will this last?"

"Oh, the worst will be gone in a few hours. The light may bother you for a couple days." McCoy replaced the glasses. "Now that we seem to be past the risk of immediate fireworks, I think I'll just deliver your message to the Captain myself." With that, McCoy exited leaving Aernath alone to sort out his own reactions.

Thirteen

JEAN'S HEART RACED and her eyes darted impatiently ahead as the six passenger glide-car approached the Federation station. The landscape was familiar to her in spite of the changes from the earthquake. She was seated next to the window with Mara and Kang on her right. Opposite them sat Lieutenant Klen from the Klingon post and Lieutenant Klyndur, tactics officer just transferred from Commander Ekthorn's cruiser. The third seat was occupied by an I.S.G. man carrying a heavy duty weapon. The driver and his partner were similarly armed. Today was the first day of negotiations and the first face-to-face meeting of Kang and Kirk since the time aboard the *Enterprise* following the Beta XIIA incident some years earlier.

Jean glanced sideways at her seatmates each clad in dress uniforms of their respective Imperial colors: Kang in silver and white, Mara in blue and argent. Jean knew them both well enough now to know that those outwardly self-assured poses concealed considerable apprehension. Kang revealed his by the faint scowl that drew his slanted eyebrows toward each other and Mara's was betrayed by the tight set of her lips.

Jean glanced down at her own hands lying tightly clasped

252

against the somber background of a simple, unadorned Klingon cruiser uniform. No one would have any difficulty reading her nervous tension, but it was wrought of anticipation not apprehension.

Some of the fields here were planted and growing. They had rebuilt the station closer to the river and away from the foothills. There was still some rubble to be cleared away up near the hills where her lab had been. The car slowed. Down here it was all neat and trim with new buildings. In front of a nearby building was a reception committee. She picked out Captain Kirk, First Officer Spock and Lieutenant Uhura in full dress uniform. The others mostly wore the standard red and black of Security. A sole Klingon approached the glide-car, saluted, the opened the door. "Commander."

Kang emerged first followed by Mara and the two lieutenants. Then the I.S.G. man gestured Jean out ahead of him. The Klingon advance envoy was explaining the protocol to Kang. "Their unarmed security forces will check our delegation for weapons and we will do the same with their representatives. Each of us will supply two armed guards for joint patrols outside the building. Our other two guards will remain with the car. The remaining Federation Security forces will withdraw to set up a hundred meter perimeter."

Kang confirmed the arrangements with a grim nod. "Very well, *Tormin,* carry on. Through vigilance comes victory." He watched while his men approached the Federation trio and satisfied themselves that Kirk, Spock, and Uhura were unarmed. They returned followed by a man and woman from *Enterprise* Security. Jean recognized Ensign Tamura who had been her roommate during her brief tour on the *Enterprise*. As the Federation man approached him, Kang deliberately removed his blaster and sword, handing them to the *tormin*. Although he appeared stoically indifferent to the process, Jean could read his fury at this indignity by the vein that throbbed in his temple.

The ensign paused at his boot and looked up at Kang somewhat uncertainly. "This weapon, sir. Will you remove it please?"

Kang flushed and for a moment Jean thought he would hit the man. It was purely a ceremonial dagger. A belt could be used as a weapon but one didn't ask an ambassador to remove his belt before sitting down at a negotiating table. Kang's voice dripped with sarcasm as he handed the dagger to his security attache. "Do you also wish my wife to remove her hairpins for fear she will stab your captain with one?"

Now it was the security guard's turn to crimson but he answered evenly, "No, Commander, that won't be necessary."

Mara followed Kang's suit and relinquished her dagger to Ensign Tamura without a word. The security man moved on to Klyndur while Tamura approached Jean. She smiled a brief greeting. As her hands moved lightly over Jean's uniform she murmured, "How did you come by that, Jean?"

Jean was startled by the question, feeling suddenly as if she didn't have the right answer. It wasn't her choice to be coming back to Federation soil in a Klingon uniform. "I . . . one makes do with what one can get."

Keiko glanced at her intently for a moment, then continued her search. "How are you?" She was moving down Jean's legs towards her boots.

"I guess as well as—"

Kang turned to glare at her. "You will not speak to anyone unless I command it."

Keido's hands were at her boots now. Jean looked back at Kang. "Yes, Milord," she said very meekly. It had the desired effect. She felt the sudden sympathetic squeeze of Keiko's hand, then the ensign's fingers passed lightly over the dagger in her boot without pause or comment. Jean fought the urge to heave a sigh of relief. When the uniform had been issued to her someone had overlooked the dagger and for the first time since her capture on Tsorn she now had one again. She had not wanted to give it up. Was it a measure of her acclimation to Klingon thinking that it hadn't occurred to her that Federation Security would confiscate it, she wondered? For the moment, at least, her secret was safe.

Tamura and her partner escorted the Klingon delegation across the open space to meet the three Enterprise officers waiting by the door of the conference hall.

Kirk stepped forward and extended his hand. "Greetings,

Commander Kang. It's a pleasure and an honor to welcome you and your delegation to our station."

Hands clasped behind his back, Kang responded with a formal bow. "Captain Kirk. I accept your greetings and welcome. Kindly accompany me and explain your conference room arrangement to me."

Kirk recovered smoothly and fell in step beside Kang. Jean bit her lip, wondering if either man realized he had just insulted the other. Spock and Mara went in next, followed by Uhura and Klyndur. Jean and Klen brought up the rear and the hall doors closed behind them.

The conference room was furnished with austere simplicity. Inside the entrance were two small stands with various drinks and light refreshments. The center of the room was occupied by two tables facing each other, each equipped with a communication console. At the far end of the room were two mirrors flanked by two doors. There was a chair by each door and four behind each table. The Klingon delegation took the table to the right, the Federation the one on the left.

"The communication console may be tied into your ship's communication system if you wish, Commander Kang." Uhura demonstrated the operation of it. Klyndur checked it minutely before approving the linkup. As they settled into their places, Kirk glanced at Jean. "It's good to see you again, Czerny. Please feel free to have a seat." He indicated the seats by the doors.

"You will stand here," Kang snapped, indicating a spot just behind his right shoulder.

Kirk's eyes flashed but his voice remained quiet. "The chair can be moved if you wish, Commander."

"Unnecessary, Captain. Shall we proceed?" Kang's eyes dared him to provoke a confrontation over the control of the woman.

"Of course," Kirk acceded smoothly. "We have many important items to discuss. I suggest we begin—"

"We will begin," Kang interrupted firmly, "by establishing the agenda. You have received our written one. The Empire, of course, earnestly desires a peaceful relationship with your Federation, but unfortunately there are a number of regrettable acts of aggression and hostility that have been directed against us. Naturally, reparations must be made before there exists any basis for peaceful relationships. There is continued Federation interference in Klingon Empire star system one-zero-four-three-seven which I believe you refer to as the Tellun system, and ongoing harrassment of our representatives and their protectorates on Ke nine-two-three-six which you call Neural. There is also the matter of wrongful death at the hands of Federation agents of our representative on the planet you call Capella Four. There is the grave matter of ecological sabotage of one of our planets by an agent of the Federation, one Cyrano Jones, and a related blatant sabotage of one of our cruisers. Also there is the abduction and detention of a number of our subjects including, I believe, two allegedly held this moment on your ship, Captain Kirk."

Kirk's jaw tightened fractionally at Kang's recital but his voice betrayed no annoyance. "I accept those all as valid items for discussion here; however, since we are on Sherman's planet, I suggest we take that up first."

Kang made a move to protest. Mara laid her fingers lightly on his wrist as she leaned forward and spoke for the first time. "One moment, Captain Kirk. It is alleged that you are holding two of our subjects currently. Do you affirm or deny that?"

Kirk nodded. "We do have two Klingons with us at the moment, but I wouldn't say we are detaining them. They are under the protection of the Federation."

Mara nodded with a faint smile. "However you wish to phrase it, Captain Kirk. You can see for yourself that your Miss Czerny is alive and well. What evidence do you offer that your charges are well-treated?"

Kirk glanced at Uhura who rose and went to one door at the inner end of the room. She opened it, and Dr. McCoy entered with Aernath. Jean's elation at seeing him once more was tempered by the fact that he was wearing dark glasses and seemed to walk uncertainly even with McCoy holding his elbow. Lieutenant Klyndur went over and quickly satisfied himself that neither was armed.

"Aernath, Commander Kang and Mara have asked about

the treatment of you and your colleague. Your report would be appreciated." Kirk said when the Klingon lieutenant was seated once more.

"I'm fine. I ran into a little trouble with my eyes but with medical help it's clearing up now. I've been well treated."

"And your companion?" Mara's voice held a slight edge.

"He's absolutely fine. We have encountered no problems there," Aernath replied.

Kirk broke in gently. "He is still aboard my ship but we could make arrangements for one or two of you to meet him later and personally confirm that report if you wish." Kang nodded tightly but made no reply. Kirk continued as McCoy gestured Aernath into the chair behind him, then joined the other *Enterprise* officers at the table. "If we can move on now to the issue of Sherman's planet; I'm curious, Commander, why you have consistently refused to acknowledge Organian transmission signals?"

Jean saw Kang's fingers tighten almost imperceptibly on the recording stylus he held and the stubborn scowl on his face deepened. She knew from snatches of conversation that Kang felt his position vis-à-vis Sherman's planet was one of the weaker points in the Klingon case. It did not surprise her that Kang would have avoided any communication with the Organians but she wondered why Kirk chose this issue to begin with. It certainly was not calculated to reassure Kang.

"We have not violated their treaty in establishing our colony here. If they wish to annihilate us nonetheless, then let them come and do it," Kang replied scowling. "We are prepared for that. I see no reason to argue with them about it."

Kirk smiled. "That's not exactly the gist of their message. They have agreed with your arguments and suggested it would be appropriate to allow a Klingon scientific post to be established here along with ours. Mr. Spock?" The Vulcan rose and carried a document across to the Klingon's table.

Jean saw Kang's right foot move in startled response to Kirk's revelation and knew the Klingon commander had been taken by surprise. His two lieutenants were not so adept at controlling their astonishment over the news. From what Jean had seen and heard during her brief time in the

Klingon outpost, she knew that this had been regarded as a suicide mission with scant chance for survival. Its only purpose had been as a feint for the *Enterprise*. Beyond that, it was expendable.

Kang perused the document in front of him, then passed it to Mara and Klyndur. His face carefully expressionless, he demanded of Kirk, "And what is the Federation's response to this decision?"

Elbows on the table, Kirk clasped his hands in front of him and briefly touched one thumb to his chin before answering. "There are those who are disappointed, arguing extenuating circumstances in the problems we have encountered here," he admitted. "But I am prepared to explore it in discussions with you. I believe we can reach an agreement."

Kang waited some moments until his delegation had time to read the document. Then he addressed Kirk again. "You have a proposal in mind then?" At Kirk's nod he went on, "Very well, we will listen. Proceed."

Kirk turned to Spock who outlined the Federation's proposal. In essence it specified the types and numbers of personnel permitted, limited weapons to sidearms only, delineated boundaries, specified joint patrols, and laid out mechanisms for joint projects and resolution of disagreements. At the conclusion of his presentation, Spock handed the Klingons copies of the protocols.

Kang acknowledged receipt. "We will consider this and take it up with you later. Now let's take up the matter of this criminal, Cyrano Jones. We demand reparations for damages and insist that this scoundrel be turned over to us for appropriate punishment."

The response of the Federation delegation was puzzling. Uhura sighed, McCoy spluttered, and even Spock looked faintly sympathetic. Kirk groaned. "Please believe me, Kang," he said fervently, "it would be almost a pleasure to hand that man over to you but he is a Federation citizen and at the moment he is uh . . . already serving a Federation sentence for offenses committed here. I'm afraid he is unavailable at the moment. As for reparations, may I remind you that it was sabotage of the *quadrotriticale* by a Klingon agent that led to some of our difficulties on this planet. I think we are about even on that score. However," he continued, ignoring Kang's baleful glare, "as a gesture of good will, I believe Dr. McCoy is willing to share a recent discovery of his with you. Bones?"

With an expression that would have done a Vulcan credit, Dr. McCoy proceeded. "Yes, I understand you have had trouble with *tribbles* aboard certain of your ships as well as on planets and we thought our defensive measures developed as a result of similar problems might augment your genetic research with *glommers*." He went on to outline the synthesis and use of neoethylene and its effects on *tribble* metabolism.

Mara leaned forward at the conclusion of McCoy's speech and responded. "Thank you, Dr. McCoy. That sounds very promising. We will certainly follow up on that line of research. But tell me, I thought you humans loved *tribbles*?"

McCoy grimaced. "Taken individually, Ma'am, we do find them rather pleasant, but as our Captain has remarked, too much of anything, even love, is not necessarily a good thing. We prefer our *tribbles* in controllable doses."

At Kang's suggestion the discussion moved on to the question of the Tellun star system with its two inhabited planets: Troyius and Elas. Jean did not know much about this system but she gathered that the *Enterprise* had once been there. From his comments, she gathered that Kirk's sympathies lay primarily with the Troyians and he seemed to feel it would serve some sort of poetic justice if the Klingons and the Elasians got together. There was considerable discourse back and forth concerning resources, trade agreements, travel restrictions, etc., until Lieutenant Uhura suggested that they break for lunch.

Captain Kirk invited the Klingon delegation to join them but Kang declined and took his group into the small inner room set aside for them. It was comfortably furnished with a couple of sofas, overstuffed chairs, and a well-stocked buffet of both Klingon and human dishes. Kang and Mara seemed familiar with all of them, probably from their time on the *Enterprise*, but Jean noticed Klen and Klyndur suspiciously avoided the unfamiliar items. The meal was a desultory affair with little conversation.

Finally, Kang remarked conversationally, "I think we will all go out for a walk before the afternoon session convenes." It was clear from the look on his face that this was not a suggestion. Jean realized that the Klingons assumed the room was wired and that they intended to find a place where they could talk freely.

"Shall I stay here or go with you?" she inquired.

Kang glanced at her briefly. "You'll go to the car," he decided.

As they left the building, Kang directed the Klingon half of the pair posted there to take her to the glide-car. Then the four Klingons set off for a nearby copse of trees. Lieutenant Johnson, the Federation Security guard, accompanied Jean and her escort to the car. A blast of heat greeted them as the door was opened. "Hey, you can't put her in there!" Johnson protested, "It's like an oven."

"Commander's orders, human. Don't interfere," the Klingon escort growled, gesturing at Jean with his weapon.

Jean looked at the two Klingons assigned to the car and then at the patrol. "It must be pretty hot for them too, Lieutenant, out here with no shade. Could you arrange for the car to be moved somewhere cooler?"

He gave her a strange look. "Well, I'll see what I can do. Come on, you." He beckoned to his Klingon partner and they set off. It was terribly hot inside and Jean persuaded the guards to leave the door open. They both lounged beside the car in what shade there was.

It was not Johnson but Tamura who returned shortly with the news that they could move their car to the shade of a solitary tree somewhat closer to the conference hall. She smiled disarmingly at the driver. "Do you mind if I ride over with you? I've never been insisde one of those things."

The driver, a weatherbeaten veteran of numerous battles and now a member of the outpost contingent, glowered at her. "Not on my life. I can't drive and keep a bead on you, too. You just walk on ahead and show us where to go."

"Aw, *tormin,* she's just a slip of a thing and not armed either. What harm can she do?" the other guard protested. "Here, human, jump in back with her. I can cover them both," he assured his comrade. "But no talking to each other," he added severely.

Keiko smiled demurely as she climbed in beside Jean and Jean allowed herself a brief flash of a smile in return. She knew that given a half-second head start, Keiko could disarm and disable them both if she chose. That, plus her deceptively petite appearance, made her extremely valuable in security work such as this. The Klingon watched them carefully as the car moved to the indicated tree. He eyed the container slung over Tamura's shoulder. "What's that gadget?"

"Oh, I thought you might like something cold to drink. It really is hot out here, isn't it?" she answered.

"Hotter than a mad Vulcan," the man acknowledged wiping his forehead. "Whups. Hold it right there, human." He steaded his weapon on Tamura as she made a move to unsling her canteen. "No funny moves. Wait 'til you're out of the car."

Tamura shrugged and waited. Once parked in the shade, the guards let both women out of the car and Tamura repeated her offer of cold lemonade. The driver would have no part of it, but the other guard, after observing no untoward effects on Czerny or Tamura, consented to try some and grudgingly pronounced it good. "I thought you'd like it," Tamura said, "because our two Klingon guests have developed quite a taste for it." She chatted on amiably for some minutes with the two guards about Aernath and his companion aboard the *Enterprise*, casually referring to their freedom of movement and interactions with the crew. Thus, obliquely, she let Jean know how things were with Aernath, and Jean absorbed the information avidly. Finally, Tamura glanced back at the conference building. "I guesss I better be getting back. See you later."

"Friendly little thing, isn't she?" the guard remarked as she made her way across the lawn.

"Don't let that fool you, Kinsman," the driver responded as he took Jean by the elbow. He touched her lips lightly with a knuckle. "They still have sharp teeth."

"But that doesn't mean we're going to use them," Jean

protested mildly as he bundled her back into the car. That, she thought, had been the whole point of Tamura's little exercise.

She was roused from a brief nap by the return of the Klingon delegation. She accompanied them to the conference room and once more took up her position standing just behind Kang and Mara. Aernath was back also, and she noticed with some relief that he had now removed his dark glasses. She caught his eye from time to time but mostly concentrated on the exchanges in front of her. They resumed their discussions of the Tellun system. Kang and his party seemed a trifle more relaxed now. Proposals and counter-proposals, arguments, and rebuttals flew across the room.

Finally, Mr. Spock observed, "Captain Kirk, we seem to be at an impasse on several items here. May I suggest each delegation consider these proposals overnight and we take this topic up again tomorrow?"

"Excellent suggestion, Mr. Spock. Commander, do you agree?"

"It's reasonable, Captain. Perhaps we could now take up a preliminary discussion of your Sherman's planet proposal before we adjourn," Kang replied.

The two delegations quickly agreed in principal to the concept of two scientific settlements and to certain types of personnel. Then the discussion turned to security and weapons. Both sides wanted elaborate verification of the other's arrangements and the Klingons were protesting the proposed restrictions on heavy armaments.

Jean shifted her position slightly and wondered idly if she could fake a convincing enough faint to persuade Kang to let her sit down. Surely he'd made his point by now and it really was ridiculous when Aernath was sitting there and another chair was available. Klyndur had just fnished a particularly impassioned argument on some obscure point. Her mind wandered inward, downward . . . yes, the link was still there now that they were in proximity again . . .

Kirk responded impatiently, "I realize all that, Lieutenant, but under your proposed status you do have considerable latitude."

. . . lieutenant . . . status . . . latitude . . .

Jean blinked, suddenly very dizzy. "Oh!" she exclaimed. Two things happened simultaneously. The silent node suddenly synapsed into life, and the link surged—first as if to break off—then quickly expanding to block and control. *She remembered!* It all came back: the mission, the briefing, the training, the code words. Dimly she saw the startled faces of Kang and Mara turn toward her. Across the room, Kirk looked at her with sudden puzzlement while Spock sat immobile with a look of intense concentration on his face. Kang rose from his chair, his face dark with alarm and suspicion. Jean struggled to communicate while that relentless mind bore down on hers. "Spock, let go of me! Get out of my mind, you . . . sir." Belatedly she realized one did not address a superior officer that way even in this kind of privacy.

The pressure shifted and she realized that part of it was not Spock but the physical stranglehold Kang had on her. She also realized he was holding her own dagger aimed at her belly. Suddenly she knew it had not been an oversight. He had known she had it; in fact, had calculated on human sympathy operating toward her to allow him a ready weapon at hand should he need it. She had let him neatly maneuver her into a trap again.

Everyone was on their feet now except Spock and Uhura. Kirk bent over Spock, and Jean heard the whisper in her head. "Unfortunately, Captain, you inadvertently used the trigger mnemonic. She has recovered her memory entirely. I'm holding a mind-block on her now until she recovers her equilibrium but coming at this moment it has created a difficult situation."

Damn Vulcan understatement! Jean thought furiously as the dagger bit deeply into her skin. Her anger was as much at herself as at the mental control Spock had imposed on her. If she could just have controlled her surprise . . .

"More treachery Kirk?" Kang hissed above her head. "What sort of tricks are you and that Vulcan up to? What are you trying to do with this woman?" Jean wondered how much she had said out loud. She sagged against Kang seeking relief from the double pressure on her throat and belly.

Spock! she pleaded internally, *We've got to tell him the truth. Everything. It's our only chance. Please, ask the Captain to let me tell him.*

Kirk held up his hands. "I assure you, Kang, this was *not* planned and it's no trick. It was an accident. Please, everyone sit down. Just give me a minute and I'll explain everything." Kang and his two lieutenants remained standing. Everyone else sat down. Once again Jean heard Spock's whispered explanation to Kirk and Kirk's response. "What do you recommend, Spock?"

"I'm not sanguine about her chances, Captain, but I do agree it has the best chance of success of the options available to us."

Jean saw Kirk look speculatively at her and at Kang for a moment. "All right, Spock. Kang, if you will release Czerny we will let her speak for herself. I think she can explain it as well as anyone."

The link closed down again to a glimmer. For a long moment it seemed as if Kang would not release her; then slowly that double pressure also yielded. She turned to face him. *Shit!* she thought as she looked up at his face. Not a shred of anything but suspicion and mistrust. Months of patient work—reasoning, yielding, arguing—wiped out in a few minutes. Was there any way any of it could be recovered? She took a deep breath.

"Ever since the injury in my lab here there's been a blank spot in my memory. Things I knew I ought to remember but couldn't. For some reason, just now, it all came back to me. You're not going to like what you hear and you probably won't want to believe me but I swear it's the truth. Just a little over a year ago, I volunteered for a mission into Klingon territory; Starfleet Intelligence had learned of the blight. Obviously this was a situation to be exploited." Kang's face grew darker still but she persisted. "Then they learned that a raid on Sherman's planet was also likely in the offing. Except we thought it would be Koloth, not you. Clearly, with this information a number of options were open to Starfleet."

"Obviously," Kang said acridly.

"They chose the plan I volunteered for. When the raid

264

came, I was supposed to 'defect' and work on fighting the blight—no, really work on it," she averred to Kang's disbelieving look, "on Peneli. I was supposed to link up with Mara's movement there and look for an opportunity to influence Maelen and possibly you, through Maelen and Mara, to consider negotiation and cooperation with the Federation."

"Just waiting for the weak spot," Kang snarled bitterly, "the soft underbelly, then—"

"Kang! Listen to me!" Her eyes pleaded along with her voice. "What you feared was true. Starfleet *did* know about the blight but what they chose to do with that knowledge was to send help." She grimaced ruefully. "The only problem was, when I woke up on your ship I didn't remember I was supposed to cooperate." Her voice softened. "All we wanted in return was your willingness to do just what you've been doing here today. Nothing more."

Kang stood stolidly saying nothing, radiating hostility and suspicion like a cornered animal.

Finally Jean broke eye contact with him for a moment and glanced at the dagger which now lay on the table just under his fingertips. She hesitated a moment, then sighed as she slowly picked up the dagger. "I guess, after all, it is what you would call another one of 'Kirk's devious plots'. You can do what you like with me . . . but, dammit Kang . . ." she lifted her chin as she held out her palm to him, the dagger balanced on it point towards her ". . . Match me!"

For an interminable moment he looked at her, his face an unreadable enigma. Then very slowly, he reached out and rotated the blade ninety degrees on her palm. "Take this and go sit down. The stakes are high but I'm still in the game." With a decisive movement he turned and sat down. "Well, Captain Kirk, now that we've cleared up that little mystery, if you're willing to guarantee that your first officer won't indulge in any more of those surprise maneuvers, I think we can proceed."

It was hard to say which side of the room was most astonished at his response. Kang seemed to enjoy their discomfiture equally. He really was a gambler, Jean decided as she sat down weak-kneed with relief. The higher the stakes and the greater the challenge the more he enjoyed the game as long as the risk and stakes were matched on the other side.

That evening when Kang beamed aboard his ship, he took Jean and Mara directly to his quarters. "Wait in your room," he ordered Mara. "I'll talk to you later." Then he turned to Jean who was standing quietly in the middle of his room. "Well," he demanded grimly, "do you take me as a man of my word?"

To that, Jean decided, there was no safe reply so she said nothing.

"I asked you a question."

"To which there is no satisfactory reply," she answered.

"Let me be the judge of that." He seized her hair and wrenched her head back painfully. "Answer me. Do you take me to be a man of my word?"

"Ouch . . . Dammit . . . Yes! . . . when it suits your sense of honor!"

He released her and struck her with a glancing backhand blow that sent her flying onto the bed. She lay where she fell. Kang began to pace agitatedly to and fro across the room muttering to himself. Then he paused and looked at the crumpled figure on the bed, head down, loose ebony hair falling over her face. "Don't cower. It's unbecoming," he told her curtly.

"I'm not cowering, you damn fool. I'm trying to keep from fighting back," Jean answered, her voice thick with anger. With the restoration of her memory had come full awareness of those skills and reflexes which had puzzled her so on Peneli. She had not sought that particular set of tools but Kirk had refused to let her go into the Empire without them, and Keiko had been painstakingly thorough in her instruction. Now she struggled for control.

Planting a knee on the bed, he seized her with a despairing laugh and shook her limp, unresisting form. "Fight? No, that would be too simple and straightforward, wouldn't it? You wouldn't make it so easy for me. I'll answer my own question. Yes, I'll keep my word. But you are right. There is a question for which there is no satisfactory answer. How do

I keep my word? Kill you or set you free? You have cloaked my defeat in victory. Oh, I will take that mantle. I must. But it will become the rack on which I will be drawn and skewered at your pleasure. From the seeds of my success will grow the destruction of the Empire. Against this it cannot stand." He let go of her and knelt above her staring morosely into space.

Jean looked at him completely baffled. Gingerly she ventured, "Kang, I don't understand . . ."

His face was contorted from his agony. "Empty. The one thing Kirk took from me that I most want is not in his power to return."

Touched by his obvious torment, Jean reached out a tentative hand to brush his cheek. "The Federation doesn't hold hostages. Captain Kirk *can* and *will* give your son back to you—very soon I expect."

The bitter fierceness of the look he turned on her made her flinch. "Like he returned Mara?" he demanded.

Suddenly Jean understood. She smiled as she placed her hands on his hips and gave a gentle shove. "Kang, you are a damn fool. Of course Captain Kirk couldn't return Mara to you. He never *had* her to return." Then she probed shrewdly. "You haven't asked Mara to tender Vow since she came back aboard have you?"

Kang smiled grimly. "I may be five kinds of fool but I am not an imbecile. Of course not. She couldn't do it."

"You mean you can't believe she could," Jean countered. "Mara is completely loyal to the Empire and to you personally though she knows you don't believe it. She predicted that when I first met her."

"I suppose next you're going to tell me you are loyal to me, too?" he said sarcastically.

"It has never been a secret where my loyalties lay," Jean answered quietly, lifting her hands from his hips. "You knew that from the beginning."

"Yes," he said drily, "that has certainly been clear and unwavering from the outset." Jean was startled to see the old pain mirrored momentarily in his eyes again. "I begin to see," he breathed, "why your captain is so sparing of tactical sacrifices. Is that part of the price he pays to possess what can't be bought? How does he do it? What power does he possess that in a few short hours he can demolish a lifetime of loyalty yet what he engenders cannot be touched?"

Jean shook her head. "You miss the point, Kang. And you won't see it until you learn to use the same strength in yourself. It is there, you know."

He shook his head stubbornly. "You sound like Mara." He buried an enmeshing fist in her hair and leaned down over her face. "High stakes, this game of yours, little human. Trust for trust, my death against yours. But there are some fates to which death, no matter how lingeringly bestowed, is preferable, aren't there? Your Captain Kirk has raised the ante: my bondage to yours. Do you then expect greater mercy from me?"

"But you've already admitted Kirk can't give you what you want. He can't possibly win," Jean protested.

"Precisely. Nor can I," Kang returned implacably. "We're matched. Now let's see how your captain plays for your life."

Fourteen

JEAN LEANED BACK in her seat, eyes closed, as the glide-car moved leisurely toward the agriculture station once more. After nearly two weeks the negotiations were drawing to a close. On the surface it had gone extremely well. Only a few minor points remained to be worked out. The measure of Kang's public success could be read in the demeanors of Klen and Klyndur. Their attitudes had changed over the days from suspicion and hostility to a bemused admiration for Kang's achievements and a grudging respect for the tough but flexible approaches of the Federation team, although Klen privately maintained that it had all been gained purely as a result of the five Klingon cruisers Kang had bracketing the planet. By now it was clear to all that the *Enterprise* was indeed the only Federation ship in the area, though this garnered Kirk a grim accolade from the two lieutenants for his courage.

One of the minor points that had not been settled was the disposition of Jean, Aernath, and his "companion." Kirk had presented the Federation proposal that all three be left on Sherman's planet to head up joint work on the "Czerny strain." Kang had refused to commit himself. Jean wondered if even Mara knew of the depth of his internal struggle and how her fate hung in the balance. However, Kang had reminded Kirk of his promise to permit a visit to Aethelnor and that was the purpose of their trip today.

No negotiations were scheduled. Jean, Kang, and Mara were alone in the car. They moved on past the newer part of the station to an attractive one-story flagstone house that had been part of the original colony settlement. This was the place Kirk had proposed for housing the two Klingon "guests," and he had suggested Kang and Mara hold their visit here.

Federation Security stopped the car some fifty meters from the house. All weapons left behind in the car, the three walked slowly to the house. It had always been one of Jean's favorites and she was glad it had survived the earthquake. The rather extensive garden surrounding it contained numerous imported species. Large Terran bougainvillea flanked the broad stone steps leading up to the main door. The spicy aroma of a nearby Aldebaran *lesquit* bush brought memories of home.

Kirk had guaranteed that their meeting would be private. No one came to greet them. Kang opened the door and they went in to a cool, dim, empty room. Aernath appeared through an open doorway from an adjacent room and approached them with a subdued salute. "Commander."

"By Kahless! You dare to salute me after what you have done? You traitorous, lying scum!" Kang's voice shook with fury.

Aernath paused in mid-stride, then stood his ground resolutely. "Commander, I am not disloyal. I do not now and never have worked for anything but your survival and success."

"Liar!" Kang moved toward him, fist clenched. "You have defiled your honor as a Klingon warrior, desecrated your vow!"

Jean stepped between them. "Stop it!" she said fiercely. "Stop it!" She gestured at Mara. "The three of us share equal responsibility for what was done. If you choose to spare us then don't take it out on him. It's unworthy of you. Now shake hands—or whatever it is Klingons do—and let what is past be past!" Kang brushed her aside angrily, his glare still fixed on Aernath.

A hostile silence took over the room. Aernath made the first move. "I swear by Durgath and by His Throne which shall be yours: I have not defiled my vow." Then slowly, deliberately, he knelt before Kang in the classic Klingon posture of submission: knees wide apart, hands on heels, head bowed.

Jean waited in agony for Kang's response. By this gesture Aernath had literally offered Kang permission to kill him if he so chose. A single swift blow and Aernath would lie writhing helpless at Kang's feet to be dispatched at his leisure. The cool dimness of the room seemed to deepen to match the cold brooding anger on Kang's face. Seconds ticked by. Kang looked at Aernath, then at Mara and finally at Jean. Then his right boot moved, slowly, to the outside of Aernath's right knee.

"It is true that your actions have brought me here, but it is also true we have met with some success in this endeavor." The admission came grudgingly. "I accept your affirmation of the vow . . ." His right hand dropped to Aernath's right shoulder. ". . .Kinsman."

Jean blinked back sudden tears of relief. Kang looked at her as she cleared her vision with a quick furtive brush of her hand. She recalled his question of some days earlier: *Can you personally name one instance where you've seen that theory work?* "You have just answered one of your questions," she told him softly. "Yes, I have seen it work. Once." She thought she caught an answering gleam in his eye.

"I thought we were to meet another here today," Kang said to Aernath.

The young Klingon rose to his feet. "Yes, Commander. He's here." He crossed to a door leading toward the back of the house. He opened it and called softly, then stood aside. Aethelnor came into the room and took in the three waiting figures. His face lit up at the sight of Mara but his attention quickly fastened on Kang. Kang's gaze was equally riveted on the boy. Seeing the two of them together in the room, there could be no doubt of the boy's parentage.

271

Aernath took the boy by the hand and led him forward. "Aethelnor, Commander Kang. Kang, Aethelnor."

Kang dropped to one knee in front of the boy, his eyes hungrily taking in each line and curve of the boy's face. One hand moved impulsively halfway to the boy's shoulder, then dropped back in hesitation. "Do you know who I am?" The question was barely audible to Jean.

"Yes, sir. You are my father, Kang of Tahrn, emperor-elect . . . and the best damn commander in the whole Klingon fleet!" These last words came out in a rush of childish delight.

Kang shot a quick glance at Mara. "I see," he said, "And who told you that?"

"*Korin* did, sir." Aethelnor indicated Aernath.

"Mmm . . ." Kang gave Aernath a thoughtful look. "And what did she say to that?" he asked, indicating Jean.

"She said I should listen to *Korin* Aernath because he knows more about us Klingons than she does."

"I see." This time the hand completed it's quest and gently touched Aethelnor's shoulder. "That's true but she also seems to understand us pretty well." Kang's hand moved lightly over the boy, touching, caressing with a kind of famished wonderment. He indicated Mara with a nod. "What did she tell you?"

"To remember the most important rule: never to tell anyone except you who I am. To obey *Korin* and *Thelsa*. To do nothing that would dishonor my father's name."

"My name?" Kang questioned.

The boy nodded but his attention was on something else. He stepped closer to Kang's knee looking at the Commander curiously. "Where are your weapons? Why don't you have them with you?"

Kang slipped an arm around the boy's back. His fingers crept up to Aethelnor's shoulder. "They're in our car. It makes humans very nervous for us to carry them here so we left them behind."

"Are they going to fight you?"

"No, I don't think so. At least not today. Does that worry you?"

"No, sir," the boy responded confidently. "You'd win."

"And how do you know that?"

"Mother said so. She says you'll always win."

Kang gave Mara another quick glance. "Mmm, yes. Tell me, you've been on the humans' ship. What do you think about them?"

Aethelnor placed a tentative hand on the collar of Kang's uniform. "They smell different than us," he observed with childish candor, "and they don't fight as well mostly. 'Cept Sulu. They have nice *koko*. K'iko is fun. She knows lots of tricks." He fingered the silver braid of his father's dress uniform.

"Sulu?"

"Yes, he fights *Korin*. Sometimes he wins."

To Kang's inquiring glance Aernath explained, "Duelling partner."

Suddenly Aethelnor slipped his arms around Kang's neck. "Can I go with you now—on your ship?"

For a brief moment Kang's arm tightened convulsively around his son. Then he released the boy. "You haven't greeted your mother yet. Do so now. She can talk to you about that."

Aethelnor displayed far less reserve with Mara. His greeting was accompanied by an enthusiastic hug. Then he whispered something in her ear. She smiled fondly. "Yes, I would like to see that. Do you want to show me now?" She looked at the other three. "If you'll excuse us, we will be in the back garden."

Kang nodded and watched them exit. He went to the window and watched them as they went around the side of the house. For some moments he stood looking out the window, one arm resting on the upper sash, a dark silhouette framed against the light and riot of colors in the garden beyond. He turned back to the others with a sardonic smile. "While she deals with her decision, I shall proceed with mine." He beckoned to Jean. "Come here." When she did, he put a finger under her chin tilting her face up to his. "Name your fate. Success or failure?"

"That's for you to say."

His hand tigthened on her chin. "I asked you a question." She replied evenly, "I've already named my price."

He shook his head and gave a small sigh. "You will do it your own way won't you?" His eyes narrowed as he inquired softly, "You still stand by that request—nothing more, nothing less?"

She nodded.

"Very well." He pointed to the glass breakfront across the room. "Bring me a goblet." Aernath crossed to the cupboard and brought one back. Grasping its stem between thumb and forefingers, Kang snapped it neatly in two. "It is broken." He placed one fragment in one of Jean's hands. "It is broken." Then the remaining piece in her other hand. "It is broken. Neither bond nor consort be, you are free."

"As simple as that?" Jean said quizzically.

"Yes." Then he added somewhat hesitantly, "You retain the claim to *Theld-right* if you choose it. I would not leave you kin-reft in the Empire."

"You mean I can claim the protection of your household as a sort of relative, like a sister?" Jean asked, unsure of exactly what he meant.

Kang's eyes widened momentarily in startled reaction. Then he looked at her thoughtfully. "Something like that . . . a sister . . . yes, perhaps . . ."

A gasp from the doorway behind her caused Jean to turn. Mara and Aethelnor had returned from the garden. Mara was staring at them incredulous. "Sister! Milord, your audacity never ceases to amaze me. Even I never would have thought . . ."

Kang cut her off with a gesture. "If she were a Klingon, would you find her unworthy?"

Mara looked at Jean for a long careful moment. "No."

"Then," Kang persisted obdurately, "as I said . . . perhaps . . ."

"I'm afraid I don't understand . . ." Jean said with a puzzled look at first one, then the other.

It was Aernath who answered her question. "Kang's sister died at an early age—before she bore a son."

Suddenly Jean saw the enormity of what she had suggested. "I . . . I'm sorry. I didn't know that. I certainly had no intention to be so presumptuous." She bowed her head briefly. "I would be honored to be counted in the Theld of

Kang, a distant relative. I shall try to be worthy of that honor." She met Kang's eyes. *"Hathak Kang, kla i'il kurin aetheln."**

An answering flash of fierce pride in those eyes was Kang's triumphant acknowledgement that with her freedom he had earned what he had most desired but never obtained from her in bondage. "As I have said before: 'tis a pity you're not a Klingon, *Thelerrin*.† Even so, who knows . . . perhaps . . ." The thoughtful look returned to his face. It changed a moment later to one of tenderness as he walked over and took Aethelnor's hand. "Now, my son, suppose you and your mother show me this house and garden that interest you so much."

Aernath and Jean stood side by side at the window and watched as the three disappeared into the garden. Suddenly she became acutely aware of his nearness, silent, taut, waiting at her side. Jean looked at his hands resting on the sill in front of her, then at the goblet fragments in her hand. She set them down on the small stand beside her. The finger she stretched out to touch his was trembling. ". . . for as long as I'm stuck in your Klingon Empire . . . I'm back on Federation soil, Aernath. I'm free . . . you're free. No more bonds." The hands gave no clues but she didn't dare look at those eyes . . .

He pulled his hand out from under her touch. "I'm afraid it's not as simple as that, Jean. Spock gave me your message." Jean's heart lurched. She had forgotten that frantic message given when she was certain death was imminent and that she would never see Aernath again. But if that sentiment were not returned . . . better he never knew. His arms folded her in a gentle embrace and she felt his lips at her ear. "Do you suppose two ex-spies could somehow chart a course for Empire and Federation to follow?"

She reached for his face and at long last let herself plunge into those amethyst depths. "It does present an interesting problem in navigation," she murmured.

---

* Roughly: I salute you Kang with the *aetheln* which is your due.

† Thelerrin. A general term for a younger female of a household.

Epilogue

SPOCK, KIRK, AND MCCOY stood in the transporter room of Space Station K-7 and watched as Kang, Mara, and Klyndur were beamed back aboard the *Klolode II*. They had just concluded a formal banquet climaxing two days of protocols and ceremonies following the successful negotiations on Sherman's planet. At the technician's "all-clear" signal, they stepped onto the pedestals, in turn, to be beamed aboard the *Enterprise*.

Kirk heaved a sigh of relief as he stepped down in the *Enterprise* transporter room, running a finger around the neck of his dress uniform. He called the bridge on the wall intercom. "Scotty, Kirk here. That diplomatic mission's over. How's the ship?"

"No problem here, sir," came the Scotsman's reply. "Uhura said to tell you there's a small celebration in Deck Five rec room if you gentlemen 'ud care to join them."

"Thanks, Scotty. A nightcap might be just the ticket before we turn in. Kirk, out." He snapped off the intercom and turned to his officers. "Spock? Bones? Care to join me?"

"Just what the doctor ordered," McCoy replied as they headed for the turbolift. "It's good to be back aboard.

K-Seven looked as clean as a whistle, but I kept having the feeling I could still smell neoethylene everywhere I went."

"As usual, doctor, your feelings are totally unreliable," Spock rejoined. "Neoethylene is virtually ordorless and certainly not detectable to the human senses this long after use. Perhaps your illogical fondness for those creatures has induced an ambivalence about your role in eradicating the outbreak that manifests itself as an olfactory hallucination."

"Oh, you're probably right, Spock," McCoy responded affably. "It's certainly totally illogical and emotional to let oneself get engrossed in a warm, furry little creature when all it does is make a pleasant sound, wouldn't you say, Captain?" McCoy gave a knowing smile to Kirk who merely pantomimed his agreement.

Spock raised an eyebrow at McCoy's uncharacteristic agreeableness and rationality. But he saw no reason to disagree with the doctor's statement. "I believe I have pointed out in the past that I find no practical use for such a creature."

"Yes," McCoy went on as they approached the rec room, "you said, I believe, that you found them of no more practical use than an ermine violin."

Their entrance was greeted by a chorus of welcome from *Enterprise* officers already present. In the confusion, McCoy signaled unobtrusively to Uhura who disappeared for a moment. As the hubbub subsided McCoy remarked nonchalantly, "Oh, by the way, Mr. Spock, before he left K-Seven, Cyrano Jones entrusted me with a farewell present for you." He grinned broadly as Spock's face took on a look almost akin to alarm.

"Surely, doctor," Spock said with some force, *"Not another tribble?"*

"Of course not." He raised his voice slightly, "Uhura, Maevlynin." The two women entered each bearing a mahogany furred, six-legged Tsorni *ngkatha*. McCoy had gone to considerable efforts to arrange this surprise gift since learning of Spock's fascination with these creatures. The look on the Vulcan's face was ample reward but, as it turned out, McCoy also got the last word. "Instead, Mr. Spock, a *pair* of ermine violins!"

STAR TREK® NOVELS

Join Captain Kirk, Mr. Spock and the crew of the *Enterprise* in totally original adventures. Written by an array of major science fiction authors, these journeys through the galaxies are sparklingly fresh and exciting sagas.

____	477196	THE ABODE OF LIFE by Lee Correy	$3.50
____	836323	BLACK FIRE by Sonni Cooper	$3.50
____	493000	THE ENTROPY EFFECT by Vonda N. McIntyre	$2.95
____	47720X	THE KLINGON GAMBIT by Robert E. Vardeman	$3.50
____	492993	THE PROMETHEUS DESIGN by Sondra Marshak & Myrna Culbreath	$2.95
____	60550X	YESTERDAY'S SON by A. C. Crispin	$3.95
____	605518	MUTINY ON THE ENTERPRISE by R. E. Vardeman	$3.95
____	465430	THE TRELLISANE CONFRONTATION by David Dvorkin	$3.50
____	473905	CORONA by Greg Bear	$3.50
____	473883	THE FINAL REFLECTION by John M. Ford	$3.50
____	495003	STAR TREK III: THE SEARCH FOR SPOCK by Vonda N. McIntyre	$3.50
____	605496	WEB OF THE ROMULANS by Murdock	$3.95
____	492985	TRIANGLE by Marshak & Culbreath	$3.50
____	554468	MY ENEMY, MY ALLY by Diane Duane	$3.95
____	500546	VULCAN ACADEMY MURDERS by Jean Lorrah	$3.95
____	547305	UHURA'S SONG by Janet Kagan	$3.95

 BOOKS BY MAIL
320 Steelcase Road E., Markham, Ontario L3R 2M1

Please send me the books I have checked above. I am enclosing a total of $_____ (Please add 75 cents for postage and handling.) My cheque or money order is enclosed. (No cash or C.O.D.'s please.)

Name_____

Address_____ Apt._____

City_____

Prov._____ Postal Code _____

Prices subject to change without notice   (C304)

FREE!!
BOOKS BY MAIL
CATALOGUE

BOOKS BY MAIL will share with you our current bestselling books as well as hard to find specialty titles in areas that will match your interests. You will be updated on what's new from Pocket Books at no cost to you. Just fill in the coupon below and discover the convenience of having books delivered to your home. Please add $1.00 to cover the cost of postage and handling.

- -

BOOKS BY MAIL

320 Steelcase Road E.,
Markham, Ontario L3R 2M1

Please send Books By Mail catalogue to:

Name_____
(please print)

Address_____

City_____

Prov._____ Postal Code _____
(BBM2)